Legends and Romances of

Brittany

Lewis Spence

Illustrated by
W. Otway Cannell

DOVER PUBLICATIONS, INC.
Mineola, New York

Published in Canada by General Publishing Company, Ltd., 30 Lesmill Road, Don Mills, Toronto, Ontario.

Published in the United Kingdom by Constable and Company, Ltd., 3 The Lanchesters, 162–164 Fulham Palace Road, London W6 9ER.

Bibliographical Note

This Dover edition, first published in 1997, is a republication of the work originally published by Frederick A. Stokes Company, New York, n.d. Several of the plates have been repositioned, and eight illustrations that appeared in color in the original edition are reprinted here in black and white. In addition, the original color frontispiece depicting Graelent and the Fairy-Woman has been moved to the front cover, so that this edition begins on page 3.

Library of Congress Cataloging-in-Publication Data

Spence, Lewis, 1874–1955.
Legends and romances of Brittany / Lewis Spence ; illustrated by W. Otway Cannell.
p. cm.
Includes index.
ISBN 0-486-29660-1 (pbk.)
1. Legends—France—Brittany. 2. Folklore—France—Brittany. 3. Brittany (France)—Antiquities. I. Title.
DC611.B85S6 1997
398.2'0944'1—dc21 96-54004
CIP

Manufactured in the United States of America
Dover Publications, Inc., 31 East 2nd Street, Mineola, N.Y. 11501

PREFACE

ALTHOUGH the folk-tales and legends of Brittany have received ample attention from native scholars and collectors, they have not as yet been presented in a popular manner to English-speaking readers. The probable reasons for what would appear to be an otherwise incomprehensible omission on the part of those British writers who make a popular use of legendary material are that many Breton folk-tales strikingly resemble those of other countries, that from a variety of considerations some of them are unsuitable for presentation in an English dress, and that most of the folk-tales proper certainly possess a strong family likeness to one another.

But it is not the folk-tale alone which goes to make up the romantic literary output of a people ; their ballads, the heroic tales which they have woven around passages in their national history, their legends (employing the term in its proper sense), along with the more literary attempts of their romance-weavers, their beliefs regarding the supernatural, the tales which cluster around their ancient homes and castles—all of these, although capable of separate classification, are akin to folk-lore, and I have not, therefore, hesitated to use what in my discretion I consider the best out of immense stores of material as being much more suited to supply British readers with a comprehensive view of Breton story. Thus, I have included chapters on the lore which cleaves to the ancient stone monuments of the country, along with some account of the monuments themselves. The Arthurian matter especially connected with Brittany I have relegated to a separate chapter, and I have considered it only fitting to include such of the *lais* of that rare and human songstress Marie de France as deal with the Breton land. The legends of those sainted men to whom Brittany owes so much will be found in a separate chapter, in collecting the matter for which I have obtained the kindest assistance from Miss Helen Macleod Scott, who has the preservation of the Celtic spirit so much at heart. I have also included chapters on the interesting theme of the black art in Brittany, as well as on the several species of fays and demons which haunt its moors and forests ; nor will the heroic tales of its great warriors and champions be found wanting. To assist the reader to obtain the atmosphere of Brittany and in order that he may read these tales without feeling that he is perusing matter relating to a race of which he is otherwise ignorant, I have afforded him a slight sketch of the Breton environment and historical development, and in an attempt to lighten his passage through the volume I have here and there told a tale in verse, sometimes translated, sometimes original.

As regards the folk-tales proper, by which I mean stories collected from the peasantry, I have made a selection from the works of Gaidoz, Sébillot, and Luzel. In no sense are these translations; they are rather adaptations. The profound inequality between Breton folk-tales is, of course, very marked in a collection of any magnitude, but as this volume is not intended to be exhaustive I have had no difficulty in selecting material of real interest. Most of these tales were collected by Breton folk-lorists in the eighties of the last century, and the native shrewdness and common sense which characterize much of the editors' comments upon the stories so carefully gathered from peasants and fishermen make them deeply interesting.

It is with a sense of shortcoming that I offer the reader this volume on a great subject, but should it succeed in stimulating interest in Breton story, and in directing students to a field in which their research is certain to be richly rewarded, I shall not regret the labour and time which I have devoted to my task.

L. S.

NOMENOË

CONTENTS

CHAPTER		PAGE
I	THE LAND, THE PEOPLE AND THEIR STORY	13
II	MENHIRS AND DOLMENS	37
III	THE FAIRIES OF BRITTANY	54
IV	SPRITES AND DEMONS OF BRITTANY	96
V	WORLD-TALES IN BRITTANY	106
VI	BRETON FOLK-TALES	156
VII	POPULAR LEGENDS OF BRITTANY	173
VIII	HERO-TALES OF BRITTANY	211
IX	THE BLACK ART AND ITS MINISTERS	241
X	ARTHURIAN ROMANCE IN BRITTANY	254
XI	THE BRETON LAYS OF MARIE DE FRANCE	283
XII	THE SAINTS OF BRITTANY	332
XIII	COSTUMES AND CUSTOMS OF BRITTANY	372
	GLOSSARY AND INDEX	392

THE DEATH OF MARGUERITE IN THE CASTLE OF TROGOFF

ILLUSTRATIONS

	PAGE
Graelent and the Fairy-Woman *Front Cover*	
Nomenoë	8
The Death of Marguerite in the Castle of Trogoff	10
Raising a Menhir	44
The Seigneur of Nann and the Korrigan	45
Merlin and Vivien	66
The Fairies of Broceliande find the Little Bruno	67
Fairies in a Breton 'Houle'	80
The Poor Boy and the Three Fairy Damsels	81
The Demon-Dog	102
N'Oun Doare and the Princess Golden Bell	103
The Bride of Satan	144
Gwennolaïk and Nola	145
The Devil in the Form of a Leopard appears before the Alchemist	178
The Escape of King Gradlon from the Flooded City of Ys	179
A Peasant Insurrection	196
Morvan returns to his Ruined Home	197
The Finding of Silvestik	232
Heloïse as Sorceress	233
King Arthur and Merlin at the Lake	256
Tristrem and Ysonde	257
King Arthur and the Giant of Mont-Saint-Michel	276
The Were-Wolf	277
Gugemar comes upon the Magic Ship	294

Legends & Romances of Brittany

	PAGE
Gugemar's Assault on the Castle of Meriadus	295
Eliduc carries Guillardun to the Forest Chapel	312
Convoyon and his Monks carry off the Relics of St Apothemius	313
St Tivisiau, the Shepherd Saint	338
St Yves instructing Shepherd-boys in the Use of the Rosary	339
Queen Queban stoned to Death	368
Modern Brittany	369
The Souls of the Dead	384

CHAPTER I: THE LAND, THE PEOPLE AND THEIR STORY

THE romantic region which we are about to traverse in search of the treasures of legend was in ancient times known as Armorica, a Latinized form of the Celtic name, Armor ('On the Sea'). The Brittany of to-day corresponds to the departments of Finistère, Côtes-du-Nord, Morbihan, Ille-et-Vilaine, and Loire-Inférieure. A popular division of the country is that which partitions it into Upper, or Eastern, and Lower, or Western, Brittany, and these tracts together have an area of some 13,130 square miles.

Such parts of Brittany as are near to the sea-coast present marked differences to the inland regions, where raised plateaux are covered with dreary and unproductive moorland. These plateaux, again, rise into small ranges of hills, not of any great height, but, from their wild and rugged appearance, giving the impression of an altitude much loftier than they possess. The coast-line is ragged, indented, and inhospitable, lined with deep reefs and broken by the estuaries of brawling rivers. In the southern portion the district known as 'the Emerald Coast' presents an almost subtropical appearance; the air is mild and the whole region pleasant and fruitful. But with this exception Brittany is a country of bleak shores and grey seas, barren moorland and dreary horizons, such a land as legend loves, such a region, cut off and isolated from the highways of humanity, as the discarded genii of ancient faiths might seek as a last stronghold.

Regarding the origin of the race which peoples this

secluded peninsula there are no wide differences of opinion. If we take the word 'Celt' as describing any branch of the many divergent races which came under the influence of one particular type of culture, the true originators of which were absorbed among the folk they governed and instructed before the historic era, then the Bretons are 'Celts' indeed, speaking the tongue known as 'Celtic' for want of a more specific name, exhibiting marked signs of the possession of 'Celtic' customs, and having those racial characteristics which the science of anthropology until recently laid down as certain indications of 'Celtic' relationship—the short, round skull, swarthy complexion, and blue or grey eyes. It is to be borne in mind, however, that the title 'Celtic' is shared by the Bretons with the fair or rufous Highlander of Scotland, the dark Welshman, and the long-headed Irishman. But the Bretons exhibit such special characteristics as would warrant the new anthropology in labelling them the descendants of that 'Alpine' race which existed in Central Europe in Neolithic times, and which, perhaps, possessed distant Mongoloid affinities. This people spread into nearly all parts of Europe, and later in some regions acquired Celtic speech and custom from a Celtic aristocracy.

It is remarkable how completely this Celtic leaven —the true history of which is lost in the depths of prehistoric darkness — succeeded in impressing not only its language but its culture and spirit upon the various peoples with whom it came into contact. To impose a special type of civilization upon another race must always prove a task of almost superhuman proportions. To compel the use of an alien tongue by a conquered folk necessitates racial tact as well as strength of purpose. But to secure the adoption of the racial *spirit* by the conquered, and adherence to it for centuries, so that men of widely divergent origins shall all have the same point of view, the same mode of thought, manner of address, aye, even the same *facies* or general racial appearance, as have Bretons, some Frenchmen, Cornishmen, Welshmen, and Highlanders—that surely would argue an indwelling racial strength such as not even the Roman or any other world-empire might pretend to.

But this Celtic civilization was not one and undivided. In late prehistoric times it evolved from one mother tongue two dialects which afterward displayed all the differences of separate languages springing from a common stock. These are the Goidelic, the tongue spoken by the Celts of Scotland, Ireland, and the Isle of Man, and the Brythonic, the language of the Welsh, the Cornish, and the people of Brittany.

The Breton Tongue

The Brezonek, the Brythonic tongue of Brittany, is undoubtedly the language of those Celtic immigrants who fled from Britain the Greater to Britain the Less to escape the rule of the Saxon invaders, and who gave the name of the country which they had left to that Armorica in which they settled. In the earliest stages of development it is difficult to distinguish Breton from Welsh. From the ninth to the eleventh centuries the Breton language is described as 'Old Breton.' 'Middle Breton' flourished from the eleventh to the seventeenth centuries, since when 'Modern Breton' has been in use. These stages indicate changes in the language more or less profound, due chiefly to admixture with

French. Various distinct dialects are indicated by writers on the subject, but the most marked difference in Breton speech seems to be that between the dialect of Vannes and that of the rest of Brittany. Such differences do not appear to be older than the sixteenth century.[1]

The Ancient Armoricans

The written history of Brittany opens with the account of Julius Cæsar. At that period (57 B.C.) Armorica was inhabited by five principal tribes: the Namnetes, the Veneti, the Osismii, the Curiosolitæ, and the Redones. These offered a desperate resistance to Roman encroachment, but were subdued, and in some cases their people were sold wholesale into slavery. In 56 B.C. the Veneti threw off the yoke and retained two of Cæsar's officers as hostages. Cæsar advanced upon Brittany in person, but found that he could make no headway while he was opposed by the powerful fleet of flat-bottomed boats, like floating castles, which the Veneti were so skilful in manœuvring. Ships were hastily constructed upon the waters of the Loire, and a desperate naval engagement ensued, probably in the Gulf of Morbihan, which resulted in the decisive defeat of the Veneti, the Romans resorting to the stratagem of cutting down the enemy's rigging with sickles bound upon long poles. The members of the Senate of the conquered people were put to death as a punishment for their defection, and thousands of the tribesmen went to swell the slave-markets of Europe.

[1] Consult E. Ernault, *Petite Grammaire bretonne* (Saint-Brieuc, 1897); L. Le Clerc, *Grammaire bretonne* (Saint-Brieuc, 1908); J. P. Treasure, *An Introduction to Breton Grammar* (Carmarthen, 1903). For the dialect of Vannes see A. Guillevic and P. Le Goff, *Grammaire bretonne du Dialect de Vannes* (Vannes, 1902).

Between A.D. 450 and 500, when the Roman power and population were dwindling, many vessels brought fugitives from Britain to Armorica. These people, fleeing from the conquering barbarians, Saxons, Picts, and Scots, sought as asylum a land where a kindred race had not yet been disturbed by invasion. Says Thierry, in his *Norman Conquest*: "With the consent of the ancient inhabitants, who acknowledged them as brethren of the same origin, the new settlers distributed themselves over the whole northern coast, as far as the little river Coesoron, and southward as far as the territory of the city of the Veneti, now called Vannes. In this extent of country they founded a sort of separate state, comprising all the small places near the coast, but not including within its limits the great towns of Vannes, Nantes, and Rennes. The increase of the population of this western corner of the country, and the great number of people of the Celtic race and language thus assembled within a narrow space, preserved it from the irruption of the Roman tongue, which, under forms more or less corrupted, was gradually becoming prevalent in every other part of Gaul. The name of *Brittany* was attached to these coasts, and the names of the various indigenous tribes disappeared; while the island which had borne this name for so many ages now lost it, and, taking the name of its conquerors, began to be called the land of the Saxons and Angles, or, in one word, *England*."

Samson

One of these British immigrants was the holy Samson, who laboured to convert pagan Brittany to Christianity. He hailed from Pembrokeshire, and the legend relates that his parents, being childless, constructed a menhir[1] of pure silver and gave it to the poor in the hope that a son might be born to them. Their desire was fulfilled, and Samson, the son in question, became a great missionary of the Church. Accompanied by forty monks, he crossed the Channel and landed on the shores of the Bay of Saint-Brieuc, a savage and deserted district.

As the keel of his galley grated on the beach the Saint beheld a man on the shore seated at the door of a miserable hut, who endeavoured to attract his attention by signs. Samson approached the shore-dweller, who took him by the hand and, leading him into the wretched dwelling, showed him his wife and daughter, stricken with sickness. Samson relieved their pain, and the husband and father, who, despite his humble appearance, was chief of the neighbouring territory, gave him a grant of land hard by. Here, close to the celebrated menhir of Dol, he and his monks built their cells. Soon a chapel rose near the ancient seat of pagan worship—in later days the site of a great cathedral.

Telio, a British monk, with the assistance of St Samson, planted near Dol an orchard three miles in length, and to him is attributed the introduction of the apple-tree into Brittany. Wherever the monks went they cultivated the soil; all had in their mouths the words of the Apostle: "If any would not work, neither should he eat." The people admired the industry of

[1] Lit. 'long stone,' a megalithic monument. See Chapter II, "Menhirs and Dolmens." Students of folk-lore will recognize the symbolic significance of the offering. We seem to have here some connexion with pillar-worship, as found in ancient Crete, and the adoration of the Irminsul among the ancient Saxons.

the new-comers, and from admiration they passed to imitation. The peasants joined the monks in tilling the ground, and even the brigands from the hills and forests became agriculturists. "The Cross and the plough, labour and prayer," was the motto of these early missionaries.

Wax for Wine

The monks of Dol were renowned bee-farmers, as we learn from an anecdote told by Count Montalembert in his *Moines d'Occident*. One day when St Samson of Dol, and St Germain, Bishop of Paris, were conversing on the respective merits of their monasteries, St Samson said that his monks were such good and careful preservers of their bees that, besides the honey which the bees yielded in abundance, they furnished more wax than was used in the churches for candles during the year, but that the climate not being suitable for the growth of vines, there was great scarcity of wine. Upon hearing this St Germain replied: "We, on the contrary, produce more wine than we can consume, but we have to buy wax; so, if you will furnish us with wax, we will give you a tenth of our wine." Samson accepted this offer, and the mutual arrangement was continued during the lives of the two saints.

Two British kingdoms were formed in Armorica—Domnonia and Cornubia. The first embraced the Côtes-du-Nord and Finistère north of the river Élorn, Cornubia, or Cornouaille, as it is now known, being situated below that river, as far south as the river Ellé. At first these states paid a nominal homage to their native kings in Britain, but on the final fall of the British power they proclaimed a complete independence.

The Vision of Jud-Hael

A striking story relating to the migration period is told concerning a Cambrian chieftain of Brittany, one Jud-Hael, and the famous British bard Taliesin. Shortly after the arrival of Taliesin in Brittany Jud-Hael had a remarkable vision. He dreamt that he saw a high mountain, on the summit of which was placed a lofty column fixed deeply in the earth, with a base of ivory, and branches which reached to the heavens. The lower part was iron, brilliantly polished, and to it were attached rings of the same metal, from which were suspended cuirasses, casques, lances, javelins, bucklers, trumpets, and many other warlike trophies. The upper portion was of gold, and upon it hung candelabra, censers, stoles, chalices, and ecclesiastical symbols of every description. As the Prince stood admiring the spectacle the heavens opened and a maiden of marvellous beauty descended and approached him.

"I salute you, O Jud-Hael," she said, "and I confide to your keeping for a season this column and all that it supports"; and with these words she vanished.

On the following day Jud-Hael made public his dream, but, like Nebuchadnezzar of old, he could find no one to interpret it, so he turned to the bard Taliesin as to another Daniel. Taliesin, says the legend, then an exile from his native land of Britain, dwelt on the seashore. To him came the messenger of Jud-Hael and said: "O thou who so truly dost interpret all things ambiguous, hear and make clear the strange vision which my lord hath seen." He then recounted Jud-Hael's dream to the venerable bard.

For a time the sage sat pondering deeply, and then

replied: "Thy master reigneth well and wisely, O messenger, but he has a son who will reign still more happily even than himself, and who will become one of the greatest men in the Breton land. The sons of his loins will be the fathers of powerful counts and pious Churchmen, but he himself, the greatest man of that race, shall be first a valiant warrior and later a mighty champion of heaven. The earlier part of his life shall be given to the world; the latter portion shall be devoted to God."

The prophecy of Taliesin was duly fulfilled. For Judik-Hael, the son of Jud-Hael, realized the bard's prediction, and entered the cloister after a glorious reign.

Taliesin

Taliesin ('Shining Forehead') was in the highest repute in the middle of the twelfth century, and he was then and afterward, unless we except Merlin, the bardic hero of the greatest number of romantic legends. He is said to have been the son of Henwg the bard, or St Henwg, of Caerleon-upon-Usk, and to have been educated in the school of Cattwg, at Llanvithin, in Glamorgan, where the historian Gildas was his fellow-pupil. Seized when a youth by Irish pirates, he is said, probably by rational interpretation of a later fable of his history, to have escaped by using a wooden buckler for a boat. Thus he came into the fishing weir of Elphin, one of the sons of Urien. Urien made him Elphin's instructor, and gave him an estate of land. But, once introduced into the Court of that great warrior-chief, Taliesin became his foremost bard, followed him in his wars, and sang his victories. He celebrates triumphs over Ida, the Anglian King of Bernicia (*d.* 559) at Argoed about the year 547, at Gwenn-Estrad between that year and 559, at Menao about the year 559. After the death of Urien, Taliesin was the bard of his son Owain, by whose hand Ida fell. After the death of all Urien's sons Taliesin retired to mourn the downfall of his race in Wales, dying, it is said, at Bangor Teivi, in Cardiganshire. He was buried under a cairn near Aberystwyth.

Hervé the Blind

There is nothing improbable in the statement that Taliesin dwelt in Brittany in the sixth century. Many other British bards found a refuge on the shores of Britain the Less. Among these was Kyvarnion, a Christian, who married a Breton Druidess and who had a son, Hervé. Hervé was blind from birth, and was led from place to place by a wolf which he had converted (!) and pressed into the service of Mother Church. One day, when a lad, Hervé had been left in charge of his uncle's farm, when a ploughman passed him in full flight, crying out that a savage wolf had appeared and had killed the ass with which he had been ploughing. The man entreated Hervé to fly, as the wolf was hard upon his heels; but the blind youth, undaunted, ordered the terrified labourer to seize the animal and harness it to the plough with the harness of the dead ass. From that time the wolf dwelt among the sheep and goats on the farm, and subsisted upon hay and grass.

Nomenoë

Swarms of Irish from Ossory and Wexford began to arrive about the close of the fifth century, settling along the west and north coasts. The immigrants from

Nomenoë

Britain the Greater formed by degrees the counties of Vannes, Cornouaille, Léon, and Domnonée, constituted a powerful aristocracy, and initiated a long and arduous struggle against the Frankish monarchs, who exercised a nominal suzerainty over Brittany. Louis the Pious placed a native chief, Nomenoë, at the head of the province, and a long period of peace ensued. But in A.D. 845 Nomenoë revolted against Charles the Bald, defeated him, and forced him to recognize the independence of Brittany, and to forgo the annual tribute which he had exacted. A ballad by Villemarqué describes the incident. Like Macpherson, who in his enthusiasm for the fragments of Ossianic lore 'reconstructed' them only too well, Villemarqué unfortunately tampered very freely with such matter as he collected, and it may even be that the poem on Nomenoë, for which he claims authority, is altogether spurious, as some critics consider. But as it affords a spirited picture of the old Breton chief the story is at least worth relating.

The poem describes how an aged chieftain waits on the hills of Retz for his son, who has gone over to Rennes to pay the Breton tribute to the Franks. Many chariots drawn by horses has he taken with him, but although a considerable time has elapsed there is no indication of his return. The chieftain climbs to an eminence in the hope of discerning his son in the far distance, but no sign of his appearance is to be seen on the long white road or on the bleak moors which fringe it.

The anxious father espies a merchant wending slowly along the highway and hails him.

"Ha, good merchant, you who travel the land from end to end, have you seen aught of my son Karo, who has gone to conduct the tribute chariots to Rennes?"

"Alas! chieftain, if your son has gone with the tribute it is in vain you wait for him, for the Franks found it not enough, and have weighed his head against it in the balance."

The father gazes wildly at the speaker, sways, and falls heavily with a doleful cry.

"Karo, my son! My lost Karo!"

The scene changes to the fortress of Nomenoë, and we see its master returning from the chase, accompanied by his great hounds and laden with trophies. His bow is in his hand, and he carries the carcass of a boar upon his shoulder. The red blood drops from the dead beast's mouth and stains his hand. The aged chief, well-nigh demented, awaits his coming, and Nomenoë greets him courteously.

"Hail, honest mountaineer!" he cries. "What is your news? What would you with Nomenoë?"

"I come for justice, Lord Nomenoë," replies the aged man. "Is there a God in heaven and a chief in Brittany? There is a God above us, I know, and I believe there is a just Duke in the Breton land. Mighty ruler, make war upon the Frank, defend our country, and give us vengeance—vengeance for Karo my son, Karo, slain, decapitated by the Frankish barbarians, his beauteous head made into a balance-weight for their brutal sport."

The old man weeps, and the tears flow down his grizzled beard.

Then Nomenoë rises in anger and swears a great oath.

"By the head of this boar, and by the arrow which slew him," cries he, "I will not wash this blood from off my hand until I free the country from mine enemies."

Nomenoë has gone to the sea-shore and gathered

pebbles, for these are the tribute he intends to offer the bald King.[1] Arrived at the gates of Rennes, he asks that they shall be opened to him so that he may pay the tribute of silver. He is asked to descend, to enter the castle, and to leave his chariot in the courtyard. He is requested to wash his hands to the sound of a horn before eating (an ancient custom), but he replies that he prefers to deliver the tribute-money there and then. The sacks are weighed, and the third is found light by several pounds.

"Ha, what is this?" cries the Frankish castellan. "This sack is under weight, Sir Nomenoë."

Out leaps Nomenoë's sword from the scabbard, and the Frank's head is smitten from his shoulders. Then, seizing it by its gory locks, the Breton chief with a laugh of triumph casts it into the balance. His warriors throng the courtyard, the town is taken; young Karo is avenged!

Alain Barbe-torte

The end of the ninth century and the beginning of the tenth were remarkable for the invasions of the Northmen. On several occasions they were driven back—by Salomon (*d.* 874), by Alain, Count of Vannes (*d.* 907)—but it was Alain Barbe-torte, 'Alain of the Twisted Beard,' or 'Alain the Fox' (*d.* 952), who gained the decisive victory over them, and concerning him an ancient ballad has much to say. It was taken down by Villemarqué from the lips of a peasant, an old soldier of the Chouan leader Georges Cadoudal.

In his youth Alain was a mighty hunter of the bear and the boar in the forests of his native Brittany, and

[1] Charles the Bald.

the courage gained in this manly sport stood him in good stead when he came to employ it against the enemies of his country, the hated Northmen. Rallying the Bretons who lurked in the forests or hid in the mountain fastnesses, he led them against the enemy, whom he surprised near Dol in the middle of the night, making a great carnage among them. After this battle the Scandinavian invaders were finally expelled from the Breton land and Alain was crowned King or Arch-chief in 937.

A free translation of this ballad might run as follows :

Lurks the Fox within the wood,
His teeth and claws are red with blood.

Within his leafy, dark retreat
He chews the cud of vengeance sweet.

Oh, trenchant his avenging sword !
It falls not on the rock or sward,

But on the mail of Saxon foe :
Swift as the lightning falls the blow.

I've seen the Bretons wield the flail,
Scattering the bearded chaff like hail :

But iron is the flail they wield
Against the churlish Saxon's shield.

I heard the call of victory
From Michael's Mount to Élorn fly,

And Alain's glory flies as fast
From Gildas' church to every coast.

Ah, may his splendour never die,
May it live on eternally !

But woe that I may nevermore
Declaim this lay on Armor's shore,

For the base Saxon hand has torn
My tongue from out my mouth forlorn.

But if my lips no longer frame
The glories of our Alain's name,

My heart shall ever sing his praise,
Who won the fight and wears the bays![1]

The Saxons of this lay are, of course, the Norsemen, who, speaking a Teutonic tongue, would seem to the Celtic-speaking Bretons to be allied to the Teuton Franks.

Bretons and Normans

During the latter half of the tenth and most of the eleventh century the Counts of Rennes gained an almost complete ascendancy in Brittany, which began to be broken up into counties and seigneuries in the French manner. In 992 Geoffrey, son of Conan, Count of Rennes, adopted the title of Duke of Brittany. He married a Norman lady of noble family, by whom he had two sons, Alain and Eudo, the younger of whom demanded a share of the duchy as his inheritance. His brother made over to him the counties of Penthièvre and Tréguier, part of the old kingdom of Domnonia in the north. It was a fatal transference, for he and his line became remorseless enemies of the ducal house, with whom they carried on a series of disastrous conflicts for centuries. Conan II, son of Alain, came under the regency of Eudo, his uncle, in infancy, but later turned his sword against him and his abettor, William of Normandy, the Conqueror.

[1] For the Breton original and the French translation from which the above is adapted see Villemarqué, *Barzaz-Breiz*, p. 112.

Notwithstanding the national enmity of the Normans and Bretons, there existed between the Dukes of Normandy and the Dukes of Brittany ties of affinity that rendered the relations between the two states somewhat complicated. At the time when Duke Robert, the father of William of Normandy, set out upon his pilgrimage, he had no nearer relative than Alain, Duke of Brittany, the father of Conan II, descended in the female line from Rollo, the great Norse leader, and to him he committed on his departure the care of his duchy and the guardianship of his son. Duke Alain declared the paternity of his ward doubtful, and favoured that party which desired to set him aside from the succession; but after the defeat of his faction at Val-ès-Dunes he died, apparently of poison, doubtless administered by the contrivance of the friends of William. His son, Conan II, succeeded, and reigned at the period when William was making his preparations for the conquest of England. He was a prince of ability, dreaded by his neighbours, and animated by a fierce desire to injure the Duke of Normandy, whom he regarded as a usurper and the murderer of his father Alain. Seeing William engaged in a hazardous enterprise, Conan thought it a favourable moment to declare war against him, and dispatched one of his chamberlains to him with the following message: "I hear that you are ready to pass the sea to make conquest of the kingdom of England. Now, Duke Robert, whose son you feign to consider yourself, on his departure for Jerusalem left all his inheritance to Duke Alain, my father, who was his cousin; but you and your abettors have poisoned my father, you have appropriated to yourself the domain of Normandy, and have kept possession of it until this day, contrary to all right, since you are not the legitimate heir. Restore to me, therefore, the duchy of Normandy, which belongs to me, or I shall levy war upon you, and shall wage it to extremity with all my forces."

The Poisoned Hunting-Horn

The Norman historians state that William was much startled by so hostile a message; for even a feeble diversion might render futile his ambitious hopes of conquest. But without hesitation he resolved to remove the Breton Duke. Immediately upon his return to Conan, the envoy, gained over, doubtless, by a bribe of gold, rubbed poison into the inside of the horn which his master sounded when hunting, and, to make his evil measures doubly sure, he poisoned in like manner the Duke's gloves and his horse's bridle. Conan died a few days after his envoy's return, and his successor, Eudo, took especial care not to imitate his relative in giving offence to William with regard to the validity of his right; on the contrary, he formed an alliance with him, a thing unheard of betwixt Breton and Norman, and sent his two sons to William's camp to serve against the English. These two youths, Brian and Alain, repaired to the rendezvous of the Norman forces, accompanied by a body of Breton knights, who styled them Mac-tierns.[1] Certain other wealthy Bretons, who were not of the pure Celtic race, and who bore French names, as Robert de Vitry, Bertrand de Dinan, and Raoul de Gael, resorted likewise to the Court of the Duke of Normandy with offers of service.

[1] 'Sons of the Chief.' MacTier is a fairly common name in Scotland to-day.

Later Brittany became a bone of contention between France and Normandy. Hoel, the native Duke, claimed the protection of France against the Norman duchy. A long period of peace followed under Alain Fergant and Conan III, but on the death of the latter a fierce war of succession was waged (1148–56). Conan IV secured the ducal crown by Norman-English aid, and gave his daughter Constance in marriage to Geoffrey Plantagenet, son of Henry II of England. Geoffrey was crowned Duke of Brittany in 1171, but after his death his son Arthur met with a dreadful fate at the hands of his uncle, John of England. Constance, his mother, the real heiress to the duchy, married again, her choice falling upon Guy de Thouars, and their daughter was wed to Pierre de Dreux, who became Duke, and who defeated John Lackland, the slayer of his wife's half-brother, under the walls of Nantes in 1214.

French Influence

The country now began to flourish apace because of the many innovations introduced into it by the wisdom of its French rulers. A new way of life was adopted by the governing classes, among whom French manners and fashions became the rule. But the people at large retained their ancient customs, language, and dress; nor have they ever abandoned them, at least in Lower Brittany. On the death of John III (1341) the peace of the duchy was once more broken by a war of succession. John had no love for his half-brother, John of Montfort, and bequeathed the ducal coronet to his niece, Joan of Penthièvre, wife of Charles of Blois, nephew of Philip VI of France. This precipitated a conflict between the rival parties which led to years of bitter strife.

Bertrand Du Guesclin

The War of the Two Joans

Just as two women, Fredegonda and Brunhilda, swayed the fortunes of Neustria and Austrasia in Merovingian times, and Mary and Elizabeth those of England and Scotland at a later day, so did two heroines arise to uphold the banners of either party in the civil strife which now convulsed the Breton land. England took the side of Montfort and the French that of Charles. Almost at the outset (1342) John of Montfort was taken prisoner, but his heroic wife, Joan of Flanders, grasped the leadership of affairs, and carried on a relentless war against her husband's enemies. After five years of fighting, in 1347, and two years subsequent to the death of her lord, whose health had given way after his imprisonment, she captured her arch-foe, Charles of Blois himself, at the battle of La Roche-Derrien, on the Jaudy. In this encounter she had the assistance of a certain Sir Thomas Dagworth and an English force. Three times was Charles rescued, and thrice was he retaken, until, bleeding from eighteen wounds, he was compelled to surrender. He was sent to London, where he was confined in the Tower for nine years. Meanwhile his wife, Joan, imitating her rival and namesake, in turn threw her energies into the strife. But another victory for the Montfort party was gained at Mauron in 1352. On the release of Charles of Blois in 1356 he renewed hostilities with the help of the famous Bertrand Du Guesclin.

Bertrand Du Guesclin

Bertrand Du Guesclin (*c.* 1320–80), Constable of France, divides with Bayard the Fearless the crown of medieval

French chivalry as a mighty leader of men, a great soldier, and a blameless knight. He was born of an ancient family who were in somewhat straitened circumstances, and in childhood was an object of aversion to his parents because of his ugliness.

One night his mother dreamt that she was in possession of a casket containing portraits of herself and her lord, on one side of which were set nine precious stones of great beauty encircling a rough, unpolished pebble. In her dream she carried the casket to a lapidary, and asked him to take out the rough stone as unworthy of such goodly company; but he advised her to allow it to remain, and afterward it shone forth more brilliantly than the lustrous gems. The later superiority of Bertrand over her nine other children fulfilled the mother's dream.

At the tournament which was held at Rennes in 1338 to celebrate the marriage of Charles of Blois with Joan of Penthièvre, young Bertrand, at that time only some eighteen years old, unhorsed the most famous competitors. During the war between Blois and Montfort he gathered round him a band of adventurers and fought on the side of Charles V, doing much despite to the forces of Montfort and his ally of England.

Du Guesclin's name lives in Breton legend as Gwezklen, perhaps the original form, and approximating to that on his tomb at Saint-Denis, where he lies at the feet of Charles V of France. In this inscription it is spelt "Missire Bertram du Gueaquien," perhaps a French rendering of the Breton pronunciation. Not a few legendary ballads which recount the exploits of this manly and romantic figure remain in the Breton language, and I have made a free translation of the following, as it is perhaps the most interesting of the number:

THE WARD OF DU GUESCLIN

TROGOFF'S strong tower in English hands
Has been this many a year,
Rising above its subject-lands
And held in hate and fear.
That rosy gleam upon the sward
Is not the sun's last kiss;
It is the blood of an English lord
Who ruled the land amiss.

"O sweetest daughter of my heart,
My little Marguerite,
Come, carry me the midday milk
To those who bind the wheat."
"O gentle mother, spare me this!
The castle I must pass
Where wicked Roger takes a kiss
From every country lass."

"Oh! fie, my daughter, fie on thee!
The Seigneur would not glance
On such a chit of low degree
When all the dames in France
Are for his choosing." "Mother mine,
I bow unto your word.
Mine eyes will ne'er behold you more.
God keep you in His guard."

Young Roger stood upon the tower
Of Trogoff's grey château;
Beneath his bent brows did he lower
Upon the scene below.
"Come hither quickly, little page,
Come hither to my knee.
Canst spy a maid of tender age?
Ha! she must pay my fee."

Fair Marguerite trips swiftly by
Beneath the castle shade,
When villain Roger, drawing nigh,
Steals softly on the maid.
He seizes on the milking-pail
She bears upon her head;
The snow-white flood she must bewail,
For all the milk is shed.

"Ah, cry not, pretty sister mine,
There's plenty and to spare
Of milk and eke of good red wine
Within my castle fair.
Ah, feast with me, or pluck a rose
Within my pleasant garth,
Or stroll beside yon brook which flows
In brawling, sylvan mirth."

"Nor feast nor flowers nor evening air
I wish; I do entreat,
Fair Seigneur, let me now repair
To those who bind the wheat."
"Nay, damsel, fill thy milking-pail:
The dairy stands but here.
Ah, foolish sweeting, wherefore quail,
For thou hast naught to fear?"

The castle gates behind her close,
And all is fair within;
Above her head the apple glows,
The symbol of our sin.
"O Seigneur, lend thy dagger keen,
That I may cut this fruit."
He smiles and with a courteous mien
He draws the bright blade out.

She takes it, and in earnest prayer
Her childish accents rise:
"O mother, Virgin, ever fair,
Pray, pray, for her who dies

For honour !" Then the blade is drenched
With blood most innocent.
Vile Roger, now, thine ardour quenched,
Say, art thou then content?

"Ha, I will wash my dagger keen
In the clear-running brook.
No human eye hath ever seen,
No human eye shall look
Upon this gore." He takes the blade
From out that gentle heart,
And hurries to the river's shade.
False Roger, why dost start?

Beside the bank Du Guesclin stands,
Clad in his sombre mail.
"Ha, Roger, why so red thy hands,
And why art thou so pale?"
"A beast I've slain." "Thou liest, hound!
But I a beast will slay."
The woodland's leafy ways resound
To echoings of fray.

Roger is slain. Trogoff's château
Is level with the rock.
Who can withstand Du Guesclin's blow,
What towers can brave his shock?
The combat is his only joy,
The tournament his play.
Woe unto those who would destroy
The peace of Brittany!

In the decisive battle of Auray (1364) Charles was killed and Du Guesclin taken prisoner. John of Montfort, son of the John who had died, became Duke of Brittany. But he had to face Oliver de Clisson, round whom the adherents of Blois rallied. From a war the strife degenerated into a vendetta. Oliver de Clisson seized the person of John V and imprisoned him. But in the end John was liberated and the line of Blois was finally crushed.

Anne of Brittany

The next event of importance in Breton history is the enforced marriage of Anne of Brittany, Duchess of that country in her own right, to Charles VIII of France, son of Louis XI, which event took place in 1491. Anne, whose father, Duke Francis II, had but recently died, had no option but to espouse Charles, and on his death she married Louis XII, his successor. Francis I, who succeeded Louis XII on the throne of France, and who married Claude, daughter of Louis XII and Anne, annexed the duchy in 1532, providing for its privileges. But beneath the cramping hand of French power the privileges of the province were greatly reduced. From this time the history of Brittany is merged in that of France, of which country it becomes one of the component parts in a political if not a racial sense.

We shall not in this place deal with the people of modern Brittany, their manners and customs, reserving the subject for a later chapter, but shall ask the reader to accompany us while we traverse the enchanted ground of Breton story.

CHAPTER II : MENHIRS AND DOLMENS

IN the mind of the general reader Brittany is unalterably associated with the prehistoric stone monuments which are so closely identified with its folk-lore and national life. In other parts of the world similar monuments are encountered, in Great Britain and Ireland, Scandinavia, the Crimea, Algeria, and India, but nowhere are they found in such abundance as in Brittany, nor are these rivalled in other lands, either as regards their character or the space they occupy.

To speculate as to the race which built the primitive stone monuments of Brittany is almost as futile as it would be to theorize upon the date of their erection.[1] A generation ago it was usual to refer all European megalithic monuments to a 'Celtic' origin, but European ethnological problems have become too complicated of late years to permit such a theory to pass unchallenged, especially now that the term 'Celt' is itself matter for fierce controversy. In the immediate neighbourhood of certain of these monuments objects of the Iron Age are recovered from the soil, while near others the finds are of Bronze Age character, so that it is probably correct to surmise that their construction continued throughout a prolonged period.

What Menhirs and Dolmens are

Regarding the nomenclature of the several species of megalithic monuments met with in Brittany some

[1] That it was Neolithic seems undoubted, and in all probability Alpine—*i.e.* the same race as presently inhabits Brittany. See Dottin, *Anciens Peuples de l'Europe* (Paris, 1916).

definitions are necessary. A menhir is a rude monolith set up on end, a great single stone, the base of which is buried deep in the soil. A dolmen is a large, table-shaped stone, supported by three, four, or even five other stones, the bases of which are sunk in the earth. In Britain the term 'cromlech' is synonymous with that of 'dolmen,' but in France and on the Continent generally it is exclusively applied to that class of monument for which British scientists have no other name than 'stone circles.' The derivation of the words from Celtic and their precise meaning in that tongue may assist the reader to arrive at their exact significance. Thus 'menhir' seems to be derived from the Welsh or Brythonic *maen*, 'a stone,' and *hir*, 'long,' and 'dolmen' from Breton *taol*, 'table,' and *men*, 'a stone.'[1] 'Cromlech' is also of Welsh or Brythonic origin, and is derived from *crom*, 'bending' or 'bowed' (hence 'laid across'), and *llech*, 'a flat stone.' The *allée couverte* is a dolmen on a large scale.

The Nature of the Monuments

The nature of these monuments and the purpose for which they were erected were questions which powerfully exercised the minds of the antiquaries of a century ago, who fiercely contended for their use as altars, open-air temples, and places of rendezvous for the discussion of tribal affairs. The cooler archæologists of a later day have discarded the majority of such theories as untenable in the light of hard facts. The dolmens, they say, are highly unsuitable for the purpose of altars, and as it has been proved that this class of monument

[1] But *tolmen* in Cornish meant 'pole of stone.'

was invariably covered in prehistoric times by an earthen tumulus its ritualistic use is thereby rendered improbable. Moreover, if we chance upon any rude carving or incised work on dolmens we observe that it is invariably executed on the *lower* surface of the table stone, the upper surface being nearly always rough, unhewn, often naturally rounded, and as unlike the surface of an altar as possible.

Recent research has established the much more reasonable theory that these monuments are sepulchral in character, and that they mark the last resting-places of persons of tribal importance, chiefs, priests, or celebrated warriors. Occasionally legend assists us to prove the mortuary character of menhir and dolmen. But, without insisting any further for the present upon the purpose of these monuments, let us glance at the more widely known of Brittany's prehistoric structures, not so much in the manner of the archæologist as in that of the observant traveller who is satisfied to view them as interesting relics of human handiwork bequeathed from a darker age, rather than as objects to satisfy the archæological taste for discussion.

For this purpose we shall select the best known groups of Breton prehistoric structures, and shall begin our excursion at the north-eastern extremity of Brittany, following the coast-line, on which most of the principal prehistoric centres are situated, and, as occasion offers, journeying into the interior in search of famous or interesting examples.

Dol

Dol is situated in the north of the department of Ille-et-Vilaine, not far from the sea-coast. Near it, in a field called the Champ Dolent (' Field of Woe'), stands a gigantic menhir, about thirty feet high and said to measure fifteen more underground. It is composed of grey granite, and is surmounted by a cross. The early Christian missionaries, finding it impossible to wean the people from frequenting pagan neighbourhoods, surmounted the standing stones with the symbol of their faith, and this in time brought about the result desired.[1]

The Legend of Dol

A strange legend is connected with this rude menhir. On a day in the dark, uncharted past of Brittany a fierce battle was fought in the Champ Dolent. Blood ran in streams, sufficient, says the tale, to turn a mill-wheel in the neighbourhood of the battle-field. When the combat was at its height two brothers met and grappled in fratricidal strife. But ere they could harm one another the great granite shaft which now looms above the field rose up between them and separated them.

There appears to be some historical basis for the tale. Here, or in the neighbourhood, A.D. 560, met Clotaire, King of the Franks, and his son, the rebel Chramne. The rebellious son was signally defeated. He had placed his wife and two little daughters in a dwelling hard by, and as he made his way thence to convey them from the field he was captured. He was instantly strangled, by order of his brutal father, in the sight of his wife and little ones, who were then burned alive in the house where they had taken refuge. The Champ Dolent does not belie its name, and even thirteen

[1] Ostensibly, at least; but see the remarks upon modern pagan survivals in Chapter IX, p. 246.

centuries and a half have failed to obliterate the memory of a savage and unnatural crime, which, its remoteness notwithstanding, fills the soul with loathing against its perpetrators and with deep pity for the hapless and innocent victims.

A Subterranean Dolmen Chapel

At Plouaret, in the department of Côtes-du-Nord, is a curious subterranean chapel incorporating a dolmen. The dolmen was formerly partially embedded in a tumulus, and the chapel, erected in 1702, was so constructed that the great table-stone of the dolmen has become the chapel roof, and the supporting stones form two of its sides. The crypt is reached by a flight of steps, and here may be seen an altar to the Seven Sleepers, represented by seven dolls of varying size. The Bretons have a legend that this structure dates from the creation of the world, and they have embodied this belief in a ballad, in which it is piously affirmed that the shrine was built by the hand of the Almighty at the time when the world was in process of formation.

Camaret

Camaret, on the coast of Finistère, is the site of no less than forty-one standing stones of quartz, which outline a rectangular space 600 yards in length at its base. Many stones have been removed, so that the remaining sides are incomplete. None of these monoliths is of any considerable size, however, and the site is not considered to be of much importance, save as regards its isolated character. At Penmarch, in the southern extremity of Finistère, there is an 'alignment' of some two hundred small stones, and a dolmen of some importance is situated at Trégunc, but it is at Carnac, on the coast of Morbihan, that we arrive at the most important archæological district in Brittany.

Carnac

The Carnac district teems with prehistoric monuments, the most celebrated of which are those of Plouharnel, Concarneau, Concurrus, Locmariaquer, Kermario, Kerlescant, Erdeven, and Sainte-Barbe. All these places are situated within a few miles of one another, and a good centre from which excursions can be made to each is the little town of Auray, with its quaint medieval market-house and shrine of St Roch. Archæologists, both Breton and foreign, appear to be agreed that the groups of stones at Ménéac, Kermario, and Kerlescant are portions of one original and continuous series of alignments which extended for nearly two miles in one direction from south-west to north-east. The monolithic avenue commences quite near the village of Ménéac, stretching away in eleven rows, and here the large stones are situated, these at first rising to a height of from 10 to 13 feet, and becoming gradually smaller, until they attain only 3 or 4 feet. In all there are 116 menhirs at Ménéac. For more than three hundred yards there is a gap in the series, which passed, we come to the Kermario avenue, which consists of ten rows of monoliths of much the same size as those of Ménéac, and 1120 in number.

Passing on to Kerlescant, with its thirteen rows of menhirs made up of 570 individual stones, we come to the end of the avenue and gaze backward upon the plain covered with these indestructible symbols of a forgotten past.

A Vision

Carnac! There is something vast, Egyptian, in the name! There is, indeed, a Karnak in Egypt, celebrated for its Avenue of Sphinxes and its pillared temple raised to the goddess Mut by King Amenophis III. Here, in the Breton Carnac, are no evidences of architectural skill. These sombre stones, unworked, rude as they came from cliff or seashore, are not embellished by man's handiwork like the rich temples of the Nile. But there is about this stone-littered moor a mystery, an atmosphere no less intense than that surrounding the most solemn ruins of antiquity. Deeper even than the depths of Egypt must we sound if we are to discover the secret of Carnac. What mean these stones? What means faith? What signifies belief? What is the answer to the Riddle of Man? In the words of Cayot Délandre, a Breton poet:

> Tout cela eut un sens, et traduisit
> Une pensée; mais clé de ce mystère,
> Où est elle? et qui pourrait dire aujourd'hui
> Si jamais elle se retrouvera? [1]

A Vision

Over this wild, heathy track, covered with the blue flowers of the dwarf gentian, steals a subtle change. Nor air nor heath has altered. The lichen-covered grey stones are the same. Suddenly there arises the burden of a low, fierce chant. A swarm of skin-clad figures appears, clustering around a gigantic object

[1] Which might be rendered:

> All here is symbol; these grey stones translate
> A thought ineffable, but where the key?
> Say, shall it be recovered soon or late,
> To ope the temple of this mystery?

which they are painfully dragging toward a deep pit situated at the end of one of the enormous alleys of monoliths. On rudely shaped rollers rests a huge stone some twenty feet in length, and this they drag across the rough moor by ropes of hide, lightening their labours by the chant, which relates the exploits of the warrior-chief who has lately been entombed in this vast pantheon of Carnac. The menhir shall serve for his headstone. It has been vowed to him by the warriors of his tribe, his henchmen, who have fought and hunted beside him, and who revere his memory. This stone shall render his fame immortal.

And now the task of placing the huge monolith in position begins. Ropes are attached to one extremity, and while a line of brawny savages strains to raise this, others guide that end of the monolith destined for enclosure in the earth toward the pit which has been dug for its reception. Higher and higher rises the stone, until at last it sinks slowly into its earthy bed. It is held in an upright position while the soil is packed around it and it is made secure. Then the barbarians stand back a space and gaze at it from beneath their low brows, well pleased with their handiwork. He whom they honoured in life rests not unrecognized in death.

The Legend of Carnac

The legend of Carnac which explains these avenues of monoliths bears a resemblance to the Cornish story of 'the Hurlers,' who were turned into stone for playing at hurling on the Lord's Day, or to that other English example from Cumberland of 'Long Meg' and her daughters. St Cornely, we are told, pursued by an

RAISING A MENHIR

THE SEIGNEUR OF NANN AND THE KORRIGAN

army of pagans, fled toward the sea. Finding no boat at hand, and on the point of being taken, he transformed his pursuers into stones, the present monoliths The Saint had made his flight to the coast in a bullock-cart, and perhaps for this reason he is now regarded as the patron of cattle. Should a bullock fall sick, his owner purchases an image of St Cornely and hangs it up in the stable until the animal recovers. The church at Carnac contains a series of fresco paintings which outline events in the life of the Saint, and in the churchyard there is a representation of the holy man between two bullocks. The head of St Cornely is said to be preserved within the edifice as a relic. On the 13th of September is held at Carnac the festival of the 'Benediction of the Beasts,' which is celebrated in honour of St Cornely. The cattle of the district are brought to the vicinity of the church and blessed by the priests—should sufficient monetary encouragement be forthcoming.

Mont-Saint-Michel

In the neighbourhood is Mont-Saint-Michel,[1] a great tumulus with a sepulchral dolmen, first excavated in 1862, when late Stone Age implements, jade celts, and burnt bones were unearthed. Later M. Zacharie Le Rouzic, the well-known Breton archæologist, tunnelled into the tumulus, and discovered a mortuary chamber, in which were the incinerated remains of two oxen. To this tumulus each pilgrim added a stone or small quantity of earth, as has been the custom in Celtic countries from time immemorial, and so the funerary mound in the course of countless generations grew into

[1] Not to be confused, of course, with the well-known island mount of the same name.

quite a respectable hill, on which a chapel was built, dedicated to St Michael, from the doorway of which a splendid prospect of the great stone alignments can be had, with, for background, the Morbihan and the long, dreary peninsula of Quiberon, bleak, treeless, and deserted.

Rocenaud

Near Carnac is the great dolmen of Rocenaud, the 'cup-and-ring' markings on which are thought by the surrounding peasantry to have been made by the knees and elbows of St Roch, who fell upon this stone when he landed from Ireland. When the natives desire a wind they knock upon the depressions with their knuckles, murmuring spells the while, just as in Scotland in the seventeenth century a tempest was raised by dipping a rag in water and beating it on a stone thrice in the name of Satan.

Cup-and-Ring Markings

What do these cup-and-ring markings so commonly discovered upon the monuments of Brittany portend? The question is one well worth examining at some length, as it appears to be almost at the foundations of Neolithic religion. Recent discoveries in New Caledonia have proved the existence in these far-off islands, as in Brittany, Scotland, and Ireland, of these strange symbols, coupled with the concentric and spiral designs which are usually associated with the genius of Celtic art. In the neighbourhood of Glasgow, and in the south-west of Scotland generally, stones inscribed with designs closely resembling those on the New Caledonian rocks have been found in abundance, as at Auchentorlie and Cockno, Shewalton Sands, and in the Milton of Colquhoun district, where the famous 'cup-and-ring altar' was discovered. At Shewalton Sands in particular, in 1904, a number of stones were found bearing crosses like those discovered in Portugal by Father José Brenha and Father Rodriguez. These symbols have a strong resemblance to certain markings on the Breton rocks, and are thought to possess an alphabetic or magical significance. In Scotland spirals are commonly found on stones marked with ogham inscriptions, and it is remarkable that they should occur in New Caledonia in connexion with a dot 'alphabet.' The New Caledonian crosses, however, approximate more to the later crosses of Celtic art, while the spirals resemble those met with in the earlier examples of Celtic work. But the closest parallel to the New Caledonian stone-markings to be found in Scotland is supplied by the examples at Cockno, in Dumbartonshire, where the wheel symbol is associated with the cup-and-ring markings.

The cup-and-ring stones used to be considered the peculiar product of a race of 'Brythonic' or British origin, and it is likely that the stones so carved were utilized in the ritual of rain-worship or rain-making by sympathetic magic. The grooves in the stone were probably filled with water to typify a country partially covered with rain-water.[1]

From these analogies, then, we can glean the purpose of the cup-and-ring markings upon the dolmens of Brittany, and may conclude, if our considerations are

[1] A Scottish sixteenth-century magical verse was chanted over such a stone:

"I knock this rag wpone this stone,
And ask the divell for rain thereon."

well founded, that they were magical in purpose and origin. Do the cup-shaped depressions represent water, or are they receptacles for rain, and do the spiral symbols typify the whirling winds?

The Gallery of Gavr'inis

Nowhere are these mysterious markings so well exemplified as in the wonderful tumulus of Gavr'inis. This ancient place of sepulture, the name of which means 'Goat Island,' lies in the Morbihan, or 'Little Sea,' an inland sea which gives its name to a department in the south of Brittany. The tumulus is 25 feet high, and covers a fine gallery 40 feet long, the stones of which bear the markings alluded to. Whorls and circles abound in the ornamentation, serpent-like figures, and the representation of an axe, similar to those to be seen in some of the Grottes aux Fées, or on the Dol des Marchands. The sculptures appear to have been executed with metal tools. The passage ends in a square sepulchral chamber, the supports of which are eight menhirs of grained granite, a stone not found on the island. Such of the menhirs as are carved were obviously so treated before they were placed *in situ*, as the design passes round the edges.

The Ile aux Moines

The Ile aux Moines ('Monks' Island') is also situated in the Morbihan, and has many prehistoric monuments, the most extensive of which are the circle of stones at Kergonan and the dolmen of Penhapp. On the Ile d'Arz, too, are megalithic monuments, perhaps the best example of which is the cromlech or circle at Penraz.

The folk-beliefs attached to the megalithic monuments

of Brittany are numerous, but nearly all of them bear a strong resemblance to each other. Many of the monuments are called Grottes aux Fées or Roches aux Fées, in the belief that the fairies either built them or used them as dwelling-places, and variants of these names are to be found in the Maison des Follets ('House of the Goblins') at Cancoet, in Morbihan, and the Château des Paulpiquets, in Questembert, in the same district. Ty en Corygannt ('The House of the Korrigans') is situated in the same department, while near Penmarch, in Finistère, at the other end of the province, we find Ty C'harriquet ('The House of the Gorics' or 'Nains'). Other mythical personages are also credited with their erection, most frequently either the devil or Gargantua being held responsible for their miraculous creation. The phenomenon, well known to students of folk-lore, that an unlettered people speedily forgets the origin of monuments that its predecessors may have raised in times past is well exemplified in Brittany, whose peasant-folk are usually surprised, if not amused, at the question "Who built the dolmens?" Close familiarity with and contiguity to uncommon objects not infrequently dulls the sense of wonder they should otherwise naturally excite. But lest we feel tempted to sneer at these poor folk for their incurious attitude toward the visible antiquities of their land, let us ask ourselves how many of us take that interest in the antiquities of our own country or our own especial locality that they demand.[1]

[1] The writer's experience is that unlettered British folk often possess much better information concerning the antiquities of a district than its 'educated' inhabitants. If this information is not scientific it is full and displays deep personal interest.

Fairy Builders

For the most part, then, the megaliths, in the opinion of the Breton peasant, are not the handiwork of man. He would rather refer their origin to spirits, giants, or fiends. If he makes any exception to this supernatural attribution, it is in favour of the saints he reverences so profoundly. The fairies, he says, harnessed their oxen to the mighty stones, selected a site, and dragged them thither to form a dwelling, or perhaps a cradle for the infant fays they were so fond of exchanging for human children. Thus the Roches aux Fées near Saint-Didier, in Ille-et-Vilaine, were raised by fairy hands, the elves collecting "all the big stones in the country" and carrying them thither in their aprons. These architectural sprites then mounted on each other's shoulders in order that they might reach high enough to place the mighty monoliths securely in position. This practice they also followed in building the dolmen near the wood of Rocher, on the road from Dinan to Dol, say the people of that country-side. But the actual purpose of the megaliths has not been neglected by tradition, for a venerable farmer at Rouvray stated that the fairies were wont to honour after their death those who had made good use of their lives and built the dolmens to contain their ashes. The presence of such a shrine in a country-side was a guarantee of abundance and prosperity therein, as a subtle and indefinable charm spread from the saintly remnants and communicated itself to everything in the neighbourhood.[1] The fairy builders, says tradition, went about their work in no haphazard manner. Those

[1] *Collectionneur breton*, t. iii, p. 55.

among them who possessed a talent for design drew the plans of the proposed structure, the less gifted acting as carriers, labourers, and masons. Apron-carrying was not their only method of porterage, for some bore the stones on their heads, or one under each arm, as when they raised the Roche aux Fées in Retiers, or the dolmen in La Lande Marie.[1] The space of a night was usually sufficient in which to raise a dolmen. But though 'run up' with more than Transatlantic dispatch, in view of the time these structures have endured for, any charge of jerry-building against their elfin architects must fall to the ground. Daylight, too, frequently surprised the fairy builders, so that they could not finish their task, as many a 'roofless' dolmen shows.

There are many Celtic parallels to this belief. For example, it is said that the Picts, or perhaps the fairies, built the original church of Corstorphine, near Edinburgh, and stood in a row handing the stones on, one to another, from Ravelston Quarry, on the adjacent hill of Corstorphine. Such is the local folk-tale; and it has its congeners in Celtic and even in Hindu myth. Thus in the Highland tale of Kennedy and the *claistig*, or fairy, whom he captured, and whom he compelled to build him a house in one night, we read that she set her people to work speedily:

> And they brought flags and stones
> From the shores of Cliamig waterfall,
> Reaching them from hand to hand.[2]

Again, the Round Tower of Ardmore, in Ireland, was

[1] See *Comptes rendus de la Société des Antiquaries de France*, pp. 95 ff. (1836).

[2] J. G. Campbell, *Superstitions of the Scottish Highlands.*

built with stones brought from Slieve Grian, a mountain some four or five miles distant, "without horse or wheel," the blocks being passed from hand to hand from the quarry to the site of the building. The same tradition applied to the Round Tower of Abernethy, in Perthshire, only it is in this case demonstrated that the stone of which the tower is composed was actually taken from the traditional quarry, even the very spot being geologically identified.[1] In like manner, too, was Rama's bridge built by the monkey host in Hindu myth, as recounted in the *Mahābhārata* and the *Rāmāyana*.

Tales, as apart from beliefs, are not often encountered in connexion with the monuments. Indeed, Sébillot, in the course of his researches, found only some dozen of these all told.[2] They are very brief, and appear for the most part to deal with fairies who have been shut up by the power of magic in a dolmen. Tales of spirits enclosed in trees, and even in pillars, are not uncommon, and lately I have heard a peculiarly fearsome ghost story which comes from Belgium, in which it is related how certain spirits had become enclosed in a pillar in an ancient abbey, for the saintly occupants of which they made it particularly uncomfortable. Mr George Henderson, in one of the most masterly and suggestive studies of Celtic survivals ever published, states that stones in the Highlands of Scotland were formerly believed to have souls, and that those too large to be moved "were held to be in intimate connexion with spirits." Pillared stones are not employed in building dwellings in the Highlands, ill luck, it is believed, being

[1] Small, *Antiquities of Fife*.

[2] *Traditions de la Haute-Bretagne*, t. i, p. 26.

sure to follow their use in this manner, while to 'meddle' with stones which tradition connects with Druidism is to court fatality.[1]

Stones that Travel

M. Salomon Reinach tells us of the Breton belief that certain sacred stones go once a year or once a century to 'wash' themselves in the sea or in a river, returning to their ancient seats after their ablutions.[2] The stones in the dolmen of Essé are thought to change their places continually, like those of Callernish and Lewis, and, like the Roman Penates, to have the gift of coming and going if removed from their habitual site.

The megalithic monuments of Brittany are undoubtedly the most remarkable relics of that epoch of prehistoric activity which is now regarded as the immediate forerunner of civilization. Can it be that they were miraculously preserved by isolation from the remote beginnings of that epoch, or is it more probable that they were constructed at a relatively late period? These are questions of profound difficulty, and it is likely that both theories contain a certain amount of truth. Whatever may have been the origin of her megaliths, Brittany must ever be regarded as a great prehistoric museum, a unique link with a past of hoary antiquity.

[1] Henderson, *Survivals in Belief among the Celts* (1911).

[2] *Cultes, Mythes, et Religiones*, t. iii, pp. 365–433.

CHAPTER III: THE FAIRIES OF BRITTANY

WHATEVER the origin of the race which conceived the demonology of Brittany—and there are indications that it was not wholly Celtic—that weird province of Faëry bears unmistakable evidence of having been deeply impressed by the Celtic imagination, if it was not totally peopled by it, for its various inhabitants act in the Celtic spirit, are moved by Celtic springs of thought and fancy, and possess not a little of that irritability which has forced anthropologists to include the Celtic race among those peoples described as 'sanguine-bilious.' As a rule they are by no means friendly or even humane, these fays of Brittany, and if we find beneficent elves within the green forests of the duchy we may feel certain that they are French immigrants, and therefore more polished than the choleric native sprites.

Broceliande

Of all the many localities celebrated in the fairy lore of Brittany none is so famous as Broceliande. Broceliande! "The sound is like a bell," a far, faëry chime in a twilit forest. In the name Broceliande there seems to be gathered all the tender charm, the rich and haunting mystery, the remote magic of Brittany and Breton lore. It is, indeed, the title to the rarest book in the library of poetic and traditional romance.

"I went to seek out marvels," said old Wace. "The forest I saw, the land I saw. I sought marvels, but I found none. A fool I came back, a fool I went; a fool

I went, a fool I came back; foolishness I sought; a fool I hold myself."[1]

Our age, even less sceptical than his, sees no folly in questing for the beautiful, and if we expect no marvels, nor any sleight of faëry, however desirous we are, we do not hold it time lost to plunge into the enchanted forest and in its magic half-gloom grope for, and perchance grasp, dryad draperies, or be trapped in the filmy webs of fancy which are spun in these shadows for unwary mortals.

Standing in dream-girt Broceliande of a hundred legends, its shadows mirrored by dim meres that may never reflect the stars, one feels the lure of Brittany more keenly even than when walking by its fierce and jagged coasts menaced by savage grey seas, or when wandering on its vast moors where the monuments of its pagan past stand in gigantic disarray. For in the forest is the heart of Arthurian story, the shrine of that wonder which has drawn thousands to this land of legend, who, like old Wace, trusted to have found, if not elfin marvels, at least matter of phantasy conjured up by the legendary associations of Broceliande.

But we must beware of each step in these twilit recesses, for the fays of Brittany are not as those of other lands. Harsh things are spoken of them. They are malignant, say the forest folk. The note of Brittany is scarce a joyous one. It is bitter-sweet as a sad chord struck on an ancient harp.

The fays of Brittany are not the friends of man. They are not 'the good people,' 'the wee folk'; they have no endearing names, the gift of a grateful peasantry. Cold and hostile, they hold aloof from human converse, and,

[1] *Roman de Rou*, v. 6415 ff.

should they encounter man, vent their displeasure at the interruption in the most vindictive manner.

Whether the fairies of Brittany be the late representatives of the gods of an elder day or merely animistic spirits who have haunted these glades since man first sheltered in them, certain it is that in no other region in Europe has Mother Church laid such a heavy ban upon all the things of faëry as in this strange and isolated peninsula. A more tolerant ecclesiastical rule might have weaned them to a timid friendship, but all overtures have been discouraged, and to-day they are enemies, active, malignant, swift to inflict evil upon the pious peasant because he is pious and on the energetic because of his industry.

The Korrigan

Among those forest-beings of whom legend speaks such malice none is more relentless than the Korrigan, who has power to enmesh the heart of the most constant swain and doom him to perish miserably for love of her. Beware of the fountains and of the wells of this forest of Broceliande, for there she is most commonly to be encountered, and you may know her by her bright hair—"like golden wire," as Spenser says of his lady's—her red, flashing eyes, and her laughing lips. But if you would dare her wiles you must come alone to her fountain by night, for she shuns even the half-gloom that is day in shadowy Broceliande. The peasants when they speak of her will assure you that she and her kind are pagan princesses of Brittany who would have none of Christianity when the holy Apostles brought it to Armorica, and who must dwell here under a ban, outcast and abhorred.

The Seigneur of Nann

The Seigneur of Nann[1]

The Seigneur of Nann was high of heart, for that day his bride of a year had presented him with two beautiful children, a boy and a girl, both white as May-blossom. In his joy the happy father asked his wife her heart's desire, and she, pining for that which idle fancy urged upon her, begged him to bring her a dish of woodcock from the lake in the dale, or of venison from the greenwood. The Seigneur of Nann seized his lance and, vaulting on his jet-black steed, sought the borders of the forest, where he halted to survey the ground for track of roe or slot of the red deer. Of a sudden a white doe rose in front of him, and was lost in the forest like a silver shadow.

At sight of this fair quarry the Seigneur followed into the greenwood. Ever his prey rustled among the leaves ahead, and in the hot chase he recked not of the forest depths into which he had plunged. But coming upon a narrow glade where the interlacing leaves above let in the sun to dapple the moss-ways below, he saw a strange lady sitting by the broken border of a well, braiding her fair hair and binding it with golden pins.

The Seigneur louted low, begged that he might drink, and bending down set his lips to the water; but she, turning strange eyes upon him—eyes not blue like those of his bride, nor grey, nor brown, nor black, like those of other women, but red in their depths as the heart's blood of a dove—spoke to him discourteously.

"Who are you who dare to trouble the waters of my

[1] Consult original ballad in Vicomte de la Villemarqué's *Chants populaires de la Bretagne.*

fountain?" she asked. "Do you not know that your conduct merits death? This well is enchanted, and by drinking of it you are fated to die, unless you fulfil a certain condition."

"And what is that?" asked the Seigneur.

"You must marry me within the hour," replied the lady.

"Demoiselle," replied the Seigneur, "it may not be as you desire, for I am already espoused to a fair bride who has borne me this very day a son and a daughter. Nor shall I die until it pleases the good God. Nevertheless, I wot well who you are. Rather would I die on the instant than wed with a Korrigan."

Leaping upon his horse, he turned and rode from the woodland as a man possessed. As he drew homeward he was overshadowed by a sense of coming ill. At the gate of his château stood his mother, anxious to greet him with good news of his bride. But with averted eyes he addresses her in the refrain so familiar to the folk-poetry of all lands:

> "My good mother, if you love me, make my bed. I am sick unto death. Say not a word to my bride. For within three days I shall be laid in the grave. A Korrigan has done me evil."

Three days later the young spouse asks of her mother-in-law:

"Tell me, mother, why do the bells sound? Wherefore do the priests chant so low?"

"'Tis nothing, daughter," replies the elder woman. "A poor stranger who lodged here died this night."

"Ah, where is gone the Seigneur of Nann? Mother, oh, where is he?"

"He has gone to the town, my child. In a little he will come to see you."

"Ah, mother, let us speak of happy things. Must I wear my red or my blue robe at my churching?"

"Neither, daughter. The mode is changed. You must wear black."

Unconscious in its art, the stream of verse carries us to the church, whence the young wife has gone to offer up thanks for the gift of children. She sees that the ancestral tomb has been opened, and a great dread is at her heart. She asks her mother-in-law who has died, and the old woman at last confesses that the Seigneur of Nann has just been buried.

That same night the young mother was interred beside her husband-lover. And the peasant folk say that from that tomb arose two saplings, the branches of which intertwined more closely as they grew.

A Goddess of Eld

In the depths of Lake Tegid in our own Wales dwelt Keridwen, a fertility goddess who possessed a magic cauldron—the sure symbol of a deity of abundance.[1] Like Demeter, she was strangely associated with the harmless necessary sow, badge of many earth-mothers, and itself typical of fertility. Like Keridwen, the Korrigan is associated with water, with the element which makes for vegetable growth. Christian belief would, of course, transform this discredited goddess into an evil being whose one function was the destruction of souls. May we see a relation of the Korrigan and Keridwen in Tridwan, or St Triduana, of Restalrig,

[1] MacCulloch, *The Religion of the Ancient Celts*, p. 116 (Edinburgh, 1911).

near Edinburgh, who presided over a certain well there, and at whose well-shrine offerings were made by sightless pilgrims for many centuries?

Many are the traditions which tell of human infants abducted by the Korrigan, who at times left an ugly changeling in place of the babe she had stolen. But it was more as an enchantress that she was dreaded. By a stroke of her magic wand she could transform the leafy fastnesses in which she dwelt into the semblance of a lordly hall, which the luckless traveller whom she lured thither would regard as a paradise after the dark thickets in which he had been wandering. This seeming castle or palace she furnished with everything that could delight the eye, and as the doomed wretch sat ravished by her beauty and that of her nine attendant maidens a fatal passion for her entered his heart, so that whatever he cherished most on earth—honour, wife, demoiselle, or affianced bride—became as naught to him, and he cast himself at the feet of this forest Circe in a frenzy of ardour. But with the first ray of daylight the charm was dissolved and the Korrigan became a hideous hag, as repulsive as before she had been lovely; the walls of her palace and the magnificence which had furnished it became once more tree and thicket, its carpets moss, its tapestries leaves, its silver cups wild roses, and its dazzling mirrors pools of stagnant water.

The Unbroken Vow [1]

Sir Roland of Brittany rides through gloomy Broceliande a league ahead of his troop, unattended by squire or by page. The red cross upon his shoulder is witness that

[1] See *Ballads and Metrical Tales, illustrating the Fairy Mythology of Europe* (anonymous, London, 1857) for a metrical version of this tale.

he is vowed to service in Palestine, and as he passes through the leafy avenues on his way to the rendezvous he fears that he will be late, most tardy of all the knights of Brittany who have sworn to drive the paynim from the Holy Land. Fearful of such disgrace, he spurs his jaded charger on through the haunted forest, and with anxious eye watches the sun sink and the gay white moon sail high above the tree-tops, pouring light through their branches upon the mossy ways below.

A high vow has Roland taken ere setting out upon the crusade—a vow that he will eschew the company of fair ladies, in which none had delighted more than he. No more must he mingle in the dance, no more must he press a maiden's lips with his. He has become a soldier of the Cross. He may not touch a lady's hand save with his mailed glove, he must not sit by her side. Also must he fast from dusk till dawn upon that night of his setting forth. "Small risk," he laughs a little sadly, as he spurs his charger onward, "small risk that I be mansworn ere morning light."

But the setting of the moon tells him that he must rest in the forest until dawn, as without her beams he can no longer pursue his way. So he dismounts from his steed, tethers it to a tree, and looks about for a bed of moss on which to repose. As he does so his wandering gaze fixes upon a beam of light piercing the gloom of the forest. Well aware of the traditions of his country, he thinks at first that it is only the glimmer of a will-o'-the-wisp or a light carried by a wandering elf. But no, on moving nearer the gleam he is surprised to behold a row of windows brilliantly lit as if for a festival.

"Now, by my vow," says Roland, "methought I knew well every château in this land of Brittany, nor wist

I that seigneur or count held court in this forest of Broceliande."

Resolved to view the château at still closer quarters, he draws near it. A great court fronts him where neither groom nor porter keeps guard, and within he can see a fair hall. This he enters, and immediately his ears are ravished by music which wanders through the chamber like a sighing zephyr. The murmur of rich viols and the call of flutes soft as distant bird-song speak to his very soul. Yet through the ecstasy comes, like a serpent gliding among flowers, the discord of evil thoughts. Grasping his rosary, he is about to retire when the doors at the end of the hall fly open, and he beholds a rapturous vision. Upon a couch of velvet sits a lady of such dazzling beauty that all other women compared with her would seem as kitchen-wenches. A mantle of rich golden hair falls about her, her eyes shine with the brightness of stars, her smile seems heavenly. Round her are grouped nine maidens only less beautiful than herself.

As the moon moving among attendant stars, so the lady comes toward Roland, accompanied by her maidens. She welcomes him, and would remove his gauntlet, but he tells her of the vow he has made to wear it in lady's bower, and she is silent. Next she asks him to seat himself beside her on the couch, but he will not. In some confusion she orders a repast to be brought. A table is spread with fragrant viands, but as the knight will partake of none of them, in chagrin the lady takes a lute, which she touches with exquisite skill. He listens unmoved, till, casting away her instrument, she dances to him, circling round and round about him, flitting about his chair like a butterfly, until at length she sinks down near him and lays her head upon his mailed bosom. Upward she turns her face to him, all passion-flushed, her eyes brimming with love. Sir Roland falters. Fascinated by her unearthly beauty, he is about to stoop down to press his lips to hers. But as he bends his head she shrinks from him, for she sees the tender flush of morning above the eastern tree-tops. The living stars faint and fail, and the music of awakening life which accompanies the rising of the young sun falls upon the ear. Slowly the château undergoes transformation. The glittering roof merges into the blue vault of heaven, the tapestried walls become the ivied screens of great forest trees, the princely furnishings are transformed into mossy banks and mounds, and the rugs and carpets beneath Roland's mailed feet are now merged in the forest ways.

But the lady? Sir Roland, glancing down, beholds a hag hideous as sin, whose malicious and distorted countenance betrays baffled hate and rage. At the sound of a bugle she hurries away with a discordant shriek. Into the glade ride Roland's men, to see their lord clasping his rosary and kneeling in thanksgiving for his deliverance from the evils which beset him. He had been saved from breaking his vow!

The nine attendant maidens of the Korrigan bring to mind a passage in Pomponius Mela[1]: "Sena [the Ile de Sein, not far from Brest], in the British Sea, opposite the Ofismician coast, is remarkable for an oracle of the Gallic god. Its priestesses, holy in perpetual virginity, are said to be nine in number. They are called Gallicenæ, and are thought to be endowed with singular powers. By their charms they are able to raise the

[1] Lib. III, cap. vi.

winds and seas, to turn themselves into what animals they will, to cure wounds and diseases incurable by others, to know and predict the future. But this they do only for navigators, who go thither purposely to consult them."

Like the sylphs and salamanders so humorously described by the Abbé de Villars in *Le Comte de Gabalis*,[1] the Korrigans desired union with humanity in order that they might thus gain immortality. Such, at least, is the current peasant belief in Brittany. "For this end they violate all the laws of modesty." This belief is common to all lands, and is typical of the fay, the Lorelei, countless well and water sprites, and that enchantress who rode off with Thomas the Rhymer:

For if you dare to kiss my lips
Sure of your bodie I shall be.

Unlike the colder Sir Roland, 'True Thomas' dared, and was wafted to a realm wondrously described by the old balladeer in the vivid phrase that marks the poetry of vision.

Merlin and Vivien

It was in this same verdant Broceliande that Vivien, another fairy, that crafty dame of the enchanted lake, the instructress of Lancelot, bound wise Merlin so that he might no more go to Camelot with oracular lips to counsel British Arthur.

But what say the folk of Broceliande themselves of

[1] Paris, 1670. Strange that this book should have been seized upon by students of the occult as a 'text-book' furnishing longed-for details of the 'lost knowledge' concerning elementary spirits, when it is, in effect, a very whole-hearted satire upon belief in such beings!

this? Let us hear their version of a tale which has been so battered by modern criticism, and which has been related in at least half a score of versions, prose and poetic. Let us have the Broceliande account of what happened in Broceliande.[1] Surely its folk, in the very forest in which he wandered with Vivien, must know more of Merlin's enchantment than we of that greater Britain which he left to find a paradise in Britain the Less, for, according to Breton story, Merlin was not imprisoned by magic art, but achieved bliss through his love for the fairy forest nymph.

Disguised as a young student, Merlin was wandering one bright May morning through the leafy glades of Broceliande, when, like the Seigneur of Nann, he came to a beautiful fountain in the heart of the forest which tempted him to rest. As he sat there in reverie, Vivien, daughter of the lord of the manor of Broceliande, came to the water's edge. Her father had gained the affection of a fay of the valley, who had promised on behalf of their daughter that she should be loved by the wisest man in the world, who should grant all her wishes, but would never be able to compel her to consent to his.

Vivien reclined upon the other side of the fountain, and the eyes of the sage and maiden met. At length Merlin rose to depart, and gave the damsel courteous good-day. But she, curious and not content with a mere salutation, wished him all happiness and honour. Her voice was beautiful, her eyes expressive, and Merlin, moved beyond anything in his experience, asked her name. She told him she was a daughter of a gentleman of that country, and in turn asked him who he might be. "A scholar returning to his master," was the reply.

[1] Villemarqué, *Myrdhinn, ou l'Enchanteur Merlin* (1861).

"Your master? And what may he teach you, young sir?"

"He instructs me in the magic art, fair dame," replied Merlin, amused. "By aid of his teaching I can raise a castle ere a man could count a score, and garrison it with warriors of might. I can make a river flow past the spot on which you recline, I can raise spirits from the great deeps of ether in which this world rolls, and can peer far into the future—aye, to the extreme of human days."

"Would that I shared your wisdom!" cried Vivien, her voice thrilling with the desire of hidden things which she had inherited from her fairy mother. "Teach me these secrets, I entreat of you, noble scholar, and accept in return for your instruction my most tender friendship."

Merlin, willing to please her, arose, and traced certain mystical characters upon the greensward. Straightway the glade in which they sat was filled with knights, ladies, maidens, and esquires, who danced and disported themselves right joyously. A stately castle rose on the verge of the forest, and in the garden the spirits whom Merlin the enchanter had raised up in the semblance of knights and ladies held carnival. Vivien, delighted, asked of Merlin in what manner he had achieved this feat of faëry, and he told her that he would in time instruct her as to the manner of accomplishing it. He then dismissed the spirit attendants and dissipated the castle into thin air, but retained the garden at the request of Vivien, naming it 'Joyous Garden.'

Then he made a tryst with Vivien to meet her in a year on the Vigil of St John.

Now Merlin had to be present at the espousal of Arthur,

MERLIN AND VIVIEN

THE FAIRIES OF BROCELIANDE FIND THE LITTLE BRUNO

his King, with Guinevere, at which he was to assist the archbishop, Dubric, as priest. The festivities over, he recalled his promise to Vivien, and on the appointed day he once more assumed the guise of a travelling scholar and set out to meet the maiden in the forest of Broceliande. She awaited him patiently in Joyous Garden, where they partook of a dainty repast. But the viands and the wines were wasted upon Merlin, for Vivien was beside him and she alone filled his thoughts. She was fair of colour, and fresh with the freshness of all in the forest, and her hazel eyes made such fire within his soul that he conceived a madness of love for her that all his wisdom, deep as it was, could not control.

But Vivien was calm as a lake circled by trees, where no breath of the passion of tempest can come. Again and again she urged him to impart to her the secrets she so greatly longed to be acquainted with. And chiefly did she desire to know three things; these at all hazards must she have power over. How, she asked, could water be made to flow in a dry place? In what manner could any form be assumed at will? And, lastly, how could one be made to fall asleep at the pleasure of another?

"Wherefore ask you this last question, demoiselle?" said Merlin, suspicious even in his great passion for her.

"So that I may cast the spell of sleep over my father and my mother when I come to you, Merlin," she replied, with a beguiling glance, "for did they know that I loved you they would slay me."

Merlin hesitated, and so was lost. He imparted to her that hidden knowledge which she desired. Then they dwelt together for eight days in the Joyous Garden, during which time the sage, to Vivien's delight and amaze, related to her the marvellous circumstances of his birth.

Next day Merlin departed, but came again to Broceliande when the eglantine was flowering at the edge of the forest. Again he wore the scholar's garments. His aspect was youthful, his fair hair hung in ringlets on his shoulders, and he appeared so handsome that a tender flower of love sprang up in Vivien's heart, and she felt that she must keep him ever near her. But she knew full well that he whom she loved was in reality well stricken in years, and she was sorrowful. But she did not despair.

"Beloved," she whispered, "will you grant me but one other boon? There is one secret more that I desire to learn."

Now Merlin knew well ere she spoke what was in her mind, and he sighed and shook his head.

"Wherefore do you sigh?" she asked innocently.

"I sigh because my fate is strong upon me," replied the sage. "For it was foreseen in the long ago that a lady should lead me captive and that I should become her prisoner for all time. Neither have I the power to deny you what you ask of me."

Vivien embraced him rapturously.

"Ah, Merlin, beloved, is it not that you should always be with me?" she asked passionately. "For your sake have I not given up father and mother, and are not all my thoughts and desires toward you?"

Merlin, carried away by her amorous eloquence, could only answer: "It is yours to ask what you will."

Vivien then revealed to him her wish. She longed to learn from his lips an enchantment which would keep him ever near her, which would so bind him to her in the chains of love that nothing in the world could part him from her. Hearkening to her plea, he taught her such enchantment as would render him love's prisoner for ever.

Evening was shrouding the forest in soft shadows when Merlin sank to rest. Vivien, waiting until his deep and regular breathing told her that he was asleep, walked nine times around him, waving her cloak over his head, and muttering the mysterious words he had taught her. When the sage awoke he found himself in the Joyous Garden with Vivien by his side.

"You are mine for ever," she murmured. "You can never leave me now."

"My delight will be ever to stay with you," he replied, enraptured. "And oh, beloved, never leave me, I pray you, for I am bespelled so as to love you throughout eternity!"

"Never shall I leave you," she replied; and in such manner the wise Merlin withdrew from the world of men to remain ever in the Joyous Garden with Vivien. Love had triumphed over wisdom.

The Arthurian version of the story does not, of course, represent Vivien as does the old Breton legend. In Geoffrey of Monmouth's book and in the *Morte d'Arthur* she is drawn as the scheming enchantress who wishes to lure Merlin to his ruin for the joy of being able to boast of her conquest. In some romances she is alluded to as Nimue, and in others is described as the daughter of Dyonas, who perhaps is the same as Dylan, a Brythonic (British) sea-god. As the Lady of the Lake she is the foster-mother of Lancelot, and we should have no difficulty in classing her as a water deity or spirit very much like the Korrigan.

Merlin

But Merlin is a very different character, and it is probable that the story of his love for Vivien was composed at a comparatively late date for the purpose of rounding off his fate in Arthurian legend. A recent hypothesis concerning him is to the effect that "if he belongs to the pagan period [of Celtic lore] at all, he was probably an ideal magician or god of magicians."[1] Canon MacCulloch smiles at the late Sir John Rhys's belief that Merlin was "a Celtic Zeus," but his later suggestion seems equally debatable. We must remember that we draw our conception of Merlin as Arthurian archimagus chiefly from late Norman-French sources and Celtic tradition. Ancient Brythonic traditions concerning beings of much the same type as Merlin appear to have existed, however, and the character of Lailoken in the life of St Kentigern recalls his life-story. So far research on the subject seems to show that the legend of Merlin is a thing of complex growth, composed of traditions of independent and widely differing origin, most of which were told about Celtic bards and soothsayers. Merlin is, in fact, the typical Druid or wise man of Celtic tradition, and there is not the slightest reason for believing that he was ever paid divine honours. As a soothsayer of legend, he would assuredly belong to the pagan period, however much he is indebted to Geoffrey of Monmouth for his late popularity in pure romance.

The Fountain of Baranton

In the country of Broceliande lies the magic fountain of

[1] MacCulloch, *The Religion of the Ancient Celts*, p. 122.

Baranton, sequestered among hills and surrounded by deep woods. Says a thirteenth-century writer of this fountain:

"Oh, amazing wonder of the Fountain of Brecelien! If a drop be taken and poured on a certain rock beside the spring, immediately the water changes into vapour, forms itself into great clouds filled with hail; the air becomes thick with shadows, and resonant with the muttering of thunder. Those who have come through curiosity to behold the prodigy wish that they had never done so, so filled are their hearts with terror, and so does fear paralyse their limbs. Incredible as the marvel may seem, yet the proofs of its reality are too abundant to be doubted."

Huon de Méry was more fortunate than Wace. He sprinkled the magic stone which lay behind the fountain with water from the golden basin that hung from the oak that shaded it, and beheld many marvels. And so may he who has the seeing eye to-day.

BROCELIANDE

AH, how remote, forlorn
Sounded the sad, sweet horn
In forest gloom enchanted!
I saw the shadows of kings go riding by,
But cerements mingled and paled with their panoply,
And the moss-ways deadened the steps of steeds that never
panted.

Ah, what had phantasy
In that sad sound to say,
Sad as a spirit's wailing?
A call from over the seas of shadowland,
A call the soul of the soul might understand,
But never, ah, never the mind, the steeps of soul assailing.

Bruno of La Montagne

The old fragmentary romance of Bruno of La Montagne is eloquent of the faëry spirit which informs all Breton lore. Butor, Baron of La Montagne, had married a young lady when he was himself of mature years, and had a son, whom he resolved to take to a fountain where the fairies came to repose themselves. The Baron, describing this magic well to the child's mother, says (we roughly translate):

> "Some believe 'tis in Champagne,
> And others by the Rock Grifaigne;
> Perchance it is in Alemaigne,
> Or Bersillant de la Montagne;
> Some even think that 'tis in Spain,
> Or where sleeps Artus of Bretaigne."

The Seigneur gave his infant son into the keeping of Bruyant, a trusty friend of his, and they set out for the fairy fountain with a troop of vassals. They left the infant in the forest of Broceliande. Here the fairies soon found him.

"Ha, sisters," said one whose skin was as white as the robe of gossamer she wore, and whose golden crown betokened her the queen of the others, "come hither and see a new-born infant. How, I wonder, does he come to be here? I am sure I did not behold him in this spot yesterday. Well, at all events, he must be baptized and suitably endowed, as is our custom when we discover a mortal child. Now what will you give him?"

"I will give him," said one, "beauty and grace."

"I endow him," said a second, "with generosity."

"And I," said a third, "with such valour that he will

overthrow all his enemies at tourney and on the battlefield."

The Queen listened to these promises. "Surely you have little sense," she said. "For my part, I wish that in his youth he may love one who will be utterly insensible to him, and although he will be as you desire, noble, generous, beautiful, and valorous, he will yet, for his good, suffer keenly from the anguish of love."

"O Queen," said one of the fairies, "what a cruel fate you have ordained for this unfortunate child! But I myself shall watch over him and nurse him until he comes to such an age as he may love, when I myself will try to engage his affections."

"For all that," said the Queen, "I will not alter my design. You shall not nurse this infant."

The fairies then disappeared. Shortly afterward Bruyant returned, and carried the child back to the castle of La Montagne, where presently a fairy presented herself as nurse.

Unfortunately the manuscript from which this tale is taken breaks off at this point, and we do not know how the Fairy Queen succeeded with her plans for the amorous education of the little Bruno. But the fragment, although tantalizing in the extreme, gives us some insight into the nature of the fairies who inhabit the green fastnesses of Broceliande.

Fairies in Folk-lore

Nearly all fairy-folk have in time grown to mortal height. Whether fairies be the decayed poor relations of more successful deities, gods whose cult has been forgotten and neglected (as the Irish *Sidhe*, or fairy-folk), or diminutive animistic spirits, originating in the belief that every object, small or great, possessed a personality, it is noticeable that Celtic fairies are of human height, while those of the Teutonic peoples are usually dwarfish. Titania may come originally from the loins of Titans or she may be Diana come down in the world, and Oberon may hail from a very different and more dwarfish source, but in Shakespeare's England they have grown sufficiently to permit them to tread the boards of the Globe Theatre with normal humans. Scores of fairies mate with mortal men, and men, as a rule, do not care for dwarf-wives. Among Celts, at least, the fay, whatever her original stature, in later times had certainly achieved the height of mortal womanhood.

In Upper Brittany, where French is the language in general use, the usual French ideas concerning fairies prevail. They are called *fées* or *fetes* (Latin *fata*), and sometimes *fions*, which reminds us of the *fions* of Scottish and Irish folk-lore.[1] There are old people still alive who claim to have seen the fairies, and who describe them variously, but the general belief seems to be that they disappeared from the land several generations ago. One old man described them as having teeth as long as one's hand, and as wearing garments of sea-weed or leaves. They were human in aspect, said another ancient whom Sébillot questioned; their clothes were seamless, and it was impossible to say by merely looking at them whether they were male or female. Their garments were of the most brilliant colours imaginable, but if one approached them too closely these gaudy hues disappeared. They wore a kind of bonnet shaped like a crown, which appeared to be part of their person.

[1] Or subterranean dwellers. See D. MacRitchie's *Fians, Fairies, and Picts* (1893).

The people of the coast say that the fairies are an accursed race who are condemned to walk the earth for a certain space. Some even think them rebellious angels who have been sent to earth for a time to expiate their offences against heaven. For the most part they inhabit the dolmens and the grottos and caverns on the coast.[1] On the shores of the Channel are numerous grottos or caverns which the Bretons call *houles*, and these are supposed to harbour a distinct class of fairy. Some of these caverns are from twenty to thirty feet high, and so extensive that it is unwise to explore them too far. Others seem only large enough to hold a single person, but if one enters he will find himself in a spacious natural chamber. The inhabitants of these depths, like all their kind, prefer to sally forth by night rather than by day. In the day-time they are not seen because they smear themselves with a magic ointment which renders them invisible; but at night they are visible to everybody.

The Lost Daughter

There was once upon a time a labourer of Saint-Cast named Marc Bourdais, but, according to the usage of the country, he had a nickname and was called Maraud. One day he was returning home when he heard the sound of a horn beneath his feet, and asked a companion who chanced to be with him if he had heard it also.

"Of course I did," replied the fellow; "it is a fairy horn."

"Umph," said Maraud. "Ask the fairies, then, to bring us a slice of bread."

His companion knelt down and shouted out the request, but nothing happened and they resumed their way.

[1] See the chapter on "Menhirs and Dolmens."

They had not gone far, however, when they beheld a slice of beautiful white bread lying on a snowy napkin by the roadside. Maraud picked it up and found that it was well buttered and as toothsome as a cake, and when they had divided and eaten it they felt their hunger completely satisfied. But he who has fed well is often thirsty, so Maraud, lowering his head, and speaking to the little folk beneath, cried: "Hullo, there! Bring us something to drink, if you please."

He had hardly spoken when they beheld a pot of cider and a glass reposing on the ground in front of them. Maraud filled the glass, and, raising it to his lips, quaffed of the fairy cider. It was clear and of a rich colour, and he declared that it was by far the best that he had ever tasted. His friend drank likewise, and when they returned to the village that night they had a good story to tell of how they had eaten and drunk at the expense of the fairies. But their friends and neighbours shook their heads and regarded them sadly.

"Alas! poor fellows," they said, "if you have eaten fairy food and drunk fairy liquor you are as good as dead men."

Nothing happened to them within the next few days, however, and it was with light hearts that one morning they returned to work in the neighbourhood of the spot where they had met with such a strange adventure. When they arrived at the place they smelt the odour of cakes which had been baked with black corn, and a fierce hunger at once took possession of them.

"Ha!" said Maraud, "the fairies are baking to-day. Suppose we ask them for a cake or two." "No, no!" replied his friend. "Ask them if you wish, but I will have none of them."

"Pah!" cried Maraud, "what are you afraid of?" And he cried: "Below there! Bring me a cake, will you?" Two fine cakes at once appeared. Maraud seized upon one, but when he had cut it he perceived that it was made of hairs, and he threw it down in disgust.

"You wicked old sorcerer!" he cried. "Do you mean to mock me?"

But as he spoke the cakes disappeared.

Now there lived in the village a widow with seven children, and a hard task she had to find bread for them all. She heard tell of Maraud's adventure with the fairies, and pondered on the chance of receiving a like hospitality from them, that the seven little mouths she had to provide for might be filled. So she made up her mind to go to a fairy grotto she knew of and ask for bread. "Surely," she thought, "what the good people give to others who do not require it they will give to me, whose need is so great." When she had come to the entrance of the grotto she knocked on the side of it as one knocks on a door, and there at once appeared a little old dame with a great bunch of keys hanging at her side. She appeared to be covered with limpets, and mould and moss clung to her as to a rock. To the widow she seemed at least a thousand years old.

"What do you desire, my good woman?" she asked.

"Alas! madame," said the widow, "might I have a little bread for my seven children? Give me some, I beseech you, and I will remember you in my prayers."

"I am not the mistress here," replied the old woman. "I am only the porteress, and it is at least a hundred years since I have been out. But return to-morrow and I will promise to speak for you."

Next day at the same time the widow returned to the cave, and found the old porteress waiting for her.

"I have spoken for you," said she, "and here is a loaf of bread for you, and those who send it wish to speak to you."

"Bring me to them," said the widow, "that I may thank them."

"Not to-day," replied the porteress. "Return to-morrow at the same hour and I will do so."

The widow returned to the village and told her neighbours of her success. Every one came to see the fairy loaf, and many begged a piece.

Next day the poor woman returned to the grotto in the hope that she would once more benefit from the little folks' bounty. The porteress was there as usual.

"Well, my good woman," said she, "did you find my bread to your taste? Here is the lady who has befriended you," and she indicated a beautiful lady, who came smilingly from the darkness of the cavern.

"Ah, madame," said the widow, "I thank you with all my heart for your charity."

"The loaf will last a long time," said the fairy, "and you will find that you and your family will not readily finish it."

"Alas!" said the widow, "last night all my neighbours insisted on having a piece, so that it is now entirely eaten."

"Well," replied the fay, "I will give you another loaf. So long as you or your children partake of it it will not grow smaller and will always remain fresh, but if you should give the least morsel to a stranger the loaf will disappear. But as I have helped you, so must you help me. I have four cows, and I wish to send them out to pasture. Promise me that one of your daughters will guard them for me."

The widow promised, and next morning sent one of her daughters out to look for the cows, which were to be pastured in a field where there was but little herbage. A neighbour saw her there, and asked what she was doing in that deserted place.

"Oh, I am watching the fairy cows," replied she. The woman looked at her and smiled, for there were no cows there and she thought the girl had become half-witted.

With the evening the fairy of the grotto came herself to fetch the cows, and she said to the little cowherd: "How would you like to be godmother to my child?"

"It would be a pleasure, madame," replied the girl.

"Well, say nothing to any one, not even to your mother," replied the fairy, "for if you do I shall never bring you anything more to eat."

A few days afterward a fairy came to tell the girl to prepare to come to the cavern on the morrow, as on that day the infant was to be named. Next day, according to the fairy's instructions, she presented herself at the mouth of the grotto, and in due course was made godmother to the little fairy. For two days she remained there, and when she left her godchild was already grown up. She had, as a matter of fact, unconsciously remained with the 'good people' for ten years, and her mother had long mourned her as dead. Meanwhile the fairies had requested the poor widow to send another of her daughters to watch their cows.

When at last the absent one returned to the village she went straight home, and her mother on beholding her gave a great cry. The girl could not understand her agitation, believing as she did that she had been absent for two days only.

"Two days!" echoed the mother. "You have been away ten years! Look how you have grown!"

After she had overcome her surprise the girl resumed her household duties as if nothing particular had happened, and knitted a pair of stockings for her godchild. When they were finished she carried them to the fairy grotto, where, as she thought, she spent the afternoon. But in reality she had been away from home this time for five years. As she was leaving, her godchild gave her a purse, saying: "This purse is full of gold. Whenever you take a piece out another one will come in its place, but if any one else uses it it will lose all its virtue."

When the girl returned to the village at last it was to find her mother dead, her brothers gone abroad, and her sisters married, so that she was the only one left at home. As she was pretty and a good housewife she did not want for lovers, and in due time she chose one for a husband. She did not tell her spouse about the purse she had had from the fairies, and if she wanted to give him a piece of gold she withdrew it from the magic purse in secret. She never went back to the fairy cavern, as she had no mind to return from it and find her husband an old man.

The Fisherman and the Fairies

A fisherman of Saint-Jacut-de-la-Mer, walking home to his cottage from his boat one evening along the wet sands, came, unawares, upon a number of fairies in a *houle*. They were talking and laughing gaily, and the fisherman observed that while they made merry they

FAIRIES IN A BRETON 'HOULE'

THE POOR BOY AND THE THREE FAIRY DAMSELS

rubbed their bodies with a kind of ointment or pomade. All at once, to the old salt's surprise, they turned into ordinary women. Concealing himself behind a rock, the fisherman watched them until the now completely transformed immortals quitted their haunt and waddled away in the guise of old market-women.

The fisherman waited until they were well out of sight, and then entered the cavern, where the first object that met his gaze was the pot of ointment which had effected the marvellous change he had witnessed. Taking some of the pomade on his forefinger, he smeared it around his left eye. He afterward found that he could penetrate the various disguises assumed by the fairies wherever he met them, and that these were for the most part adopted for the purposes of trickery. Thus he was able to see a fairy in the assumed shape of a beggar-woman going from door to door demanding alms, seeking an opportunity to steal or work mischief, and all the while casting spells upon those who were charitable enough to assist her. Again, he could distinguish real fish caught in his net at sea from merwomen disguised as fish, who were desirous of entangling the nets or otherwise distressing and annoying the fishermen.

But nowhere was the disguised fairy race so much in evidence as at the fair of Ploubalay, where he recognized several of the elusive folk in the semblance of raree-showmen, fortune-tellers, and the like, who had taken these shapes in order to deceive. He was quietly smiling at their pranks, when some of the fairies who composed a troupe of performers in front of one of the booths regarded him very earnestly. He felt certain that they had penetrated his secret, but ere he could make off one of them threw a stick at him with such violence that it struck and burst the offending left eye.

Fairies in all lands have a constitutional distaste for being recognized, but those of Brittany appear to visit their vengeance upon the members with which they are actually beheld. "See what thieves the fairies are!" cried a woman, on beholding one abstract apples from a country-woman's pocket. The predatory elf at once turned round and tore out the eye that had marked his act.

A Cornish woman who chanced to find herself the guardian of an elf-child was given certain water with which to wash its face. The liquid had the property of illuminating the infant's face with a supernatural brightness, and the woman ventured to try it upon herself, and in doing so splashed a little into one eye. This gave her the fairy sight. One day in the market-place she saw a fairy man stealing, and gave the alarm, when the enraged sprite cried:

> "Water for elf, not water for self.
> You've lost your eye, your child, and yourself."

She was immediately stricken blind in the right eye, her fairy foster-child vanished, and she and her husband sank into poverty and want.

Another Breton tale recounts how a mortal woman was given a polished stone in the form of an egg wherewith to rub a fairy child's eyes. She applied it to her own right eye, and became possessed of magic sight so far as elves were concerned. Still another case, alluded to in the *Revue Celtique*,[1] arose through 'the sacred bond' formed between a fairy man and a mortal woman where both stood as god-parents to a child. The association

[1] Vol. i, p. 231.

enabled the woman to see magically. The fairy maiden Rockflower bestows a similar gift on her lover in a Breton tale from Saint-Cast, and speaks of "clearing his eyes like her own."[1]

Changelings

The Breton fairies, like others of their race, are fond of kidnapping mortal children and leaving in their places wizened elves who cause the greatest trouble to the distressed parents. The usual method of ridding a family of such a changeling is to surprise it in some manner so that it will betray its true character. Thus, on suspicion resting upon a certain Breton infant who showed every sign of changeling nature, milk was boiled on the fire in egg-shells, whereupon the impish youngster cried: "I shall soon be a hundred years old, but I never saw so many shells boiling! I was born in Pif and Paf, in the country where cats are made, but I never saw anything like it!" Thus self-revealed, the elf was expelled from the house. In most Northern tales where the changeling betrays itself it at once takes flight and a train of elves appears, bringing back the true infant. Again, if the wizened occupant of the cradle can be made to laugh that is accepted as proof of its fairy nature. "Something ridiculous," says Simrock, "must be done to cause him to laugh, for laughter brings deliverance."[2] The same stratagem appears to be used as the cure in English and Scots changeling tales.

The King of the Fishes

The Breton fays were prone, too, to take the shape of

[1] *Contes populaires de la Haute-Bretagne* (Paris, 1880).

[2] *Handbuch der deutschen Mythologie.*

animals, birds, and even of fish. As we have seen, the sea-fairies of Saint-Jacut-de-la-Mer were in the habit of taking the shape of fish for the purpose of annoying fishermen and damaging their gear. Another Breton tale from Saint-Cast illustrates their penchant for the fish shape. A fisherman of that town one day was lucky enough to catch the King of the Fishes disguised as a small golden fish. The fish begged hard to be released, and promised, if he were set free, to sacrifice as many of his subjects as would daily fill the fisherman's nets. On this understanding the finny monarch was given his liberty, and fulfilled his promise to the letter. Moreover, when the fisherman's boat was capsized in a gale the Fish King appeared, and, holding a flask to the drowning man's lips, made him drink a magic fluid which ensured his ability to exist under water. He conveyed the fisherman to his capital, a place of dazzling splendour, paved with gold and gems. The rude caster of nets instantly filled his pockets with the spoil of this marvellous causeway. Though probably rather disturbed by the incident, the Fish King, with true royal politeness, informed him that whenever he desired to return the way was open to him. The fisherman expressed his sorrow at having to leave such a delightful environment, but added that unless he returned to earth his wife and family would regard him as lost. The Fish King called a large tunny-fish, and as Arion mounted the dolphin in the old Argolian tale, so the fisherman approached the tunny, which

> Hollowed his back and shaped it as a selle.[1]

[1] Saddle.

The fisherman at once

> Seized the strange sea-steed by his bristling fin
> And vaulted on his shoulders; the fleet fish
> Swift sought the shallows and the friendly shore.[1]

Before dismissing the fisherman, however, the Fish King presented him with an inexhaustible purse—probably as a hint that it would be unnecessary for him on a future visit to disturb his paving arrangements.

Fairy Origins

Two questions which early obtrude themselves in the consideration of Breton fairy-lore are: Are all the fays of Brittany malevolent? And, if so, whence proceeds this belief that fairy-folk are necessarily malign? Example treads upon example to prove that the Breton fairy is seldom beneficent, that he or she is prone to ill-nature and spitefulness, not to say fiendish malice on occasion. There appears to be a deep-rooted conviction that the elfish race devotes itself to the annoyance of mankind, practising a species of peculiarly irritating trickery, wanton and destructive. Only very rarely is a spirit of friendliness evinced, and then a motive is usually obvious. The 'friendly' fairy invariably has an axe to grind.

Two reasons may be advanced to account for this condition of things. First, the fairy-folk—in which are included house and field spirits—may be the traditional remnant of a race of real people, perhaps a prehistoric race, driven into the remote parts of the country by strange immigrant conquerors. Perhaps these primitive folk were elfish, dwarfish, or otherwise peculiar in

[1] See the author's *Le Roi d'Ys and other Poems* (London, 1910).

appearance to the superior new-comers, who would in pride of race scorn the small, swarthy aborigines, and refuse all communion with them. We may be sure that the aborigines, on their part, would feel for their tall, handsome conquerors all the hatred of which a subject race is capable, never approaching them unless under compulsion or necessity, and revenging themselves upon them by every means of annoyance in their power. We may feel certain, too, that the magic of these conquered and discredited folk would be made full use of to plague the usurpers of the soil, and trickery, as irritating as any elf-pranks, would be brought to increase the discomfort of the new-comers.

There are, however, several good objections to this view of the origin of the fairy idea. First and foremost, the smaller prehistoric aboriginal peoples of Europe themselves possessed tales of little people, of spirits of field and forest, flood and fell. It is unlikely that man was ever without these.

> Yea, I sang, as now I sing, when the Prehistoric Spring
> Made the piled Biscayan ice-pack split and shove,
> And the troll, and gnome, and dwerg, and the gods of cliff and berg
> Were about me and beneath me and above.[1]

The idea of animism, the belief that everything had a personality of its own, certainly belonged to the later prehistoric period, for among the articles which fill the graves of aboriginal peoples, for use on the last journey, we find weapons to enable the deceased to drive off the evil spirits which would surround his own after death. Spirits, to early man, are always relatively smaller than himself. He beholds the "picture

[1] Kipling, "Primum Tempus."

of a little man" in his comrade's eyes, and concludes it to be his 'soul.' Some primitive peoples, indeed, believe that several parts of the body have each their own resident soul. Again, the spirit of the corn or the spirit of the flower, the savage would argue, must in the nature of things be small. We can thus see how the belief in 'the little folk' may have arisen, and how they remained little until a later day.

A much more scientific theory of the origin of the belief in fairies is that which sees in them the deities of a discredited religion, the gods of an aboriginal people, rather than the people themselves. Such were the Irish *Daoine Sidhe*, and the Welsh *y Mamau* ('the Mothers')—undoubtedly gods of the Celts. Again, although in many countries, especially in England, the fairies are regarded as small of stature, in Celtic countries the fay proper, as distinct from the brownie and such goblins, is of average mortal height, and this would seem to be the case in Brittany. Whether the gorics and courils of Brittany, who seem sufficiently small, are fairies or otherwise is a moot point. They seem to be more of the field spirit type, and are perhaps classed more correctly with the gnome race; we thus deal with them in our chapter on sprites and demons. It would seem, too, as if there might be ground for the belief that the normal-sized fairy race of Celtic countries had become confounded with the Teutonic idea of elves (Teut. *Elfen*) in Germany and England, from which, perhaps, they borrowed their diminutive size.

But these are only considerations, not conclusions. Strange as it may seem, folk-lore has by no means solved the fairy problem, and much remains to be accomplished ere we can write 'Finis' to the study of fairy origins.

The Margots

Another Breton name for the fairies is *les Margots la fée*, a title which is chiefly employed in several districts of the Côtes-du-Nord, principally in the *arrondissements* of Saint-Brieuc and Loudéac, to describe those fairies who have their abode in large rocks and on the wild and extensive moorlands which are so typical of the country. These, unlike the *fées houles*, are able to render themselves invisible at pleasure. Like human beings, they are subject to maladies, and are occasionally glad to accept mortal succour. They return kindness for kindness, but are vindictive enemies to those who attempt to harm them.

But fairy vindictiveness is not lavished upon those unwitting mortals who do them harm alone. If one chances to succeed in a task set by the immortals of the forest, one is in danger of death, as the following story shows.

The Boy who Served the Fairies

A poor little fellow was one day gathering faggots in the forest when a gay, handsomely dressed gentleman passed him, and, noticing the lad's ragged and forlorn condition, said to him: "What are you doing there, my boy?"

"I am looking for wood, sir," replied the boy. "If I did not do so we should have no fire at home."

"You are very poor at home, then?" asked the gentleman.

"So poor," said the lad, "that sometimes we only eat once a day, and often go supperless to bed."

"That is a sad tale," said the gentleman. "If you

will promise to meet me here within a month I will give you some money, which will help your parents and feed and clothe your small brothers and sisters."

Prompt to the day and the hour, the boy kept the tryst in the forest glade, at the very spot where he had met the gentleman. But though he looked anxiously on every side he could see no signs of his friend. In his anxiety he pushed farther into the forest, and came to the borders of a pond, where three damsels were preparing to bathe. One was dressed in white, another in grey, and the third in blue. The boy pulled off his cap, gave them good-day, and asked politely if they had not seen a gentleman in the neighbourhood. The maiden who was dressed in white told him where the gentleman was to be found, and pointed out a road by which he might arrive at his castle.

"He will ask you," said she, "to become his servant, and if you accept he will wish you to eat. The first time that he presents the food to you, say: 'It is I who should serve you.' If he asks you a second time make the same reply; but if he should press you a third time refuse brusquely and thrust away the plate which he offers you."

The boy was not long in finding the castle, and was at once shown into the gentleman's presence. As the maiden dressed in white had foretold, he requested the youth to enter his service, and when his offer was accepted placed before him a plate of viands. The lad bowed politely, but refused the food. A second time it was offered, but he persisted in his refusal, and when it was proffered to him a third time he thrust it away from him so roughly that it fell to the ground and the plate was broken.

"Ah," said the gentleman, "you are just the kind of servant I require. You are now my lackey, and if you are able to do three things that I command you I will give you one of my daughters for your wife and you shall be my son-in-law."

The next day he gave the boy a hatchet of lead, a saw of paper, and a wheelbarrow made of oak-leaves, bidding him fell, bind up, and measure all the wood in the forest within a radius of seven leagues. The new servant at once commenced his task, but the hatchet of lead broke at the first blow, the saw of paper buckled at the first stroke, and the wheelbarrow of oak-leaves was broken by the weight of the first little branch he placed on it. The lad in despair sat down, and could do nothing but gaze at the useless implements. At midday the damsel dressed in white whom he had seen at the pond came to bring him something to eat.

"Alas!" she cried, "why do you sit thus idle? If my father should come and find that you have done nothing he would kill you."

"I can do nothing with such wretched tools," grumbled the lad.

"Do you see this wand?" said the damsel, producing a little rod. "Take it in your hand and walk round the forest, and the work will take care of itself. At the same time say these words: 'Let the wood fall, tie itself into bundles, and be measured.'"

The boy did as the damsel advised him, and matters proceeded so satisfactorily that by a little after midday the work was completed. In the evening the gentleman said to him:

"Have you accomplished your task?"

"Yes, sir. Do you wish to see it? The wood is cut and tied into bundles of the proper weight and measurement."

"It is well," said the gentleman. "To-morrow I will set you the second task."

On the following morning he took the lad to a knoll some distance from the castle, and said to him:

"You see this rising ground? By this evening you must have made it a garden well planted with fruit-trees and having a fish-pond in the middle, where ducks and other water-fowl may swim. Here are your tools."

The tools were a pick of glass and a spade of earthenware. The boy commenced the work, but at the first stroke his fragile pick and spade broke into a thousand fragments. For the second time he sat down helplessly. Time passed slowly, and as before at midday the damsel in white brought him his dinner.

"So I find you once more with your arms folded," she said.

"I cannot work with a pick of glass and an earthenware spade," complained the youth.

"Here is another wand," said the damsel. "Take it and walk round this knoll, saying: 'Let the place be planted and become a beautiful garden with fruit-trees, in the middle of which is a fish-pond with ducks swimming upon it.'"

The boy took the wand, did as he was bid, and the work was speedily accomplished. A beautiful garden arose as if by enchantment, well furnished with fruit-trees of all descriptions and ornamented with a small sheet of water.

Once more his master was quite satisfied with the result,

and on the third morning set him his third task. He took him beneath one of the towers of the castle.

"Behold this tower," he said. "It is of polished marble. You must climb it, and at the top you will find a turtle-dove, which you must bring to me."

The gentleman, who was of opinion that the damsel in white had helped his servant in the first two tasks, sent her to the town to buy provisions. When she received this order the maiden retired to her chamber and burst into tears. Her sisters asked her what was the matter, and she told them that she wished to remain at the castle, so they promised to go to the town in her stead. At midday she found the lad sitting at the foot of the tower bewailing the fact that he could not climb its smooth and glassy sides.

"I have come to help you once more," said the damsel. "You must get a cauldron, then cut me into morsels and throw in all my bones, without missing a single one. It is the only way to succeed."

"Never!" exclaimed the youth. "I would sooner die than harm such a beautiful lady as you."

"Yet you must do as I say," she replied.

For a long time the youth refused, but at last he gave way to the maiden's entreaties, cut her into little pieces, and placed the bones in a large cauldron, forgetting, however, the little toe of her left foot. Then he rose as if by magic to the top of the tower, found the turtle-dove, and came down again.[1] Having completed his task, he took a wand which lay beside the cauldron, and when he touched the bones they came together again and the

[1] In folk-tales of this nature a ladder is usually made of the bones, but this circumstance seems to have been omitted in the present instance.

damsel stepped out of the great pot none the worse for her experience.

When the young fellow carried the dove to his master the gentleman said:

"It is well. I shall carry out my promise and give you one of my daughters for your wife, but all three shall be veiled and you must pick the one you desire without seeing her face."

The three damsels were then brought into his presence, but the lad easily recognized the one who had assisted him, because she lacked the small toe of the left foot. So he chose her without hesitation, and they were married.

But the gentleman was not content with the marriage. On the day of the bridal he placed the bed of the young folks over a vault, and hung it from the roof by four cords. When they had gone to bed he came to the door of the chamber and said:

"Son-in-law, are you asleep?"

"No, not yet," replied the youth.

Some time afterward he repeated his question, and met with a similar answer.

"The next time he comes," said the bride, "pretend that you are sleeping."

Shortly after that his father-in-law asked once more if he were asleep, and receiving no answer retired, evidently well satisfied.

When he had gone the bride made her husband rise at once. "Go instantly to the stables," said she, "and take there the horse which is called Little Wind, mount him, and fly."

The young fellow hastened to comply with her request, and he had scarcely left the chamber when the master of the castle returned and asked if his daughter were asleep. She answered "No," and, bidding her arise and come with him, he cut the cords, so that the bed fell into the vault beneath. The bride now heard the trampling of hoofs in the garden outside, and rushed out to find her husband in the act of mounting.

"Stay!" she cried. "You have taken Great Wind instead of Little Wind, as I advised you, but there is no help for it," and she mounted behind him. Great Wind did not belie his name, and dashed into the night like a tempest.

"Do you see anything?" asked the girl.

"No, nothing," said her husband.

"Look again," she said. "Do you see anything now?"

"Yes," he replied, "I see a great flame of fire."

The bride took her wand, struck it three times, and said: "I change thee, Great Wind, into a garden, myself into a pear-tree, and my husband into a gardener."

The transformation had hardly been effected when the master of the castle and his wife came up with them.

"Ha, my good man," cried he to the seeming gardener, "has any one on horseback passed this way?"

"Three pears for a sou," said the gardener.

"That is not an answer to my question," fumed the old wizard, for such he was. "I asked if you had seen any one on horseback in this direction."

"Four for a sou, then, if you will," said the gardener.

"Idiot!" foamed the enchanter, and dashed on in pursuit. The young wife then changed herself, her horse, and her husband into their natural forms, and, mounting once more, they rode onward.

"Do you see anything now?" asked she.

"Yes, I see a great flame of fire," he replied.

Once more she took her wand. "I change this steed into a church," she said, "myself into an altar, and my husband into a priest."

Very soon the wizard and his wife came to the doors of the church and asked the priest if a youth and a lady had passed that way on horseback.

"Dominus vobiscum," said the priest, and nothing more could the wizard get from him.

Pursued once more, the young wife changed the horse into a river, herself into a boat, and her husband into a boatman. When the wizard came up with them he asked to be ferried across the river. The boatman at once made room for them, but in the middle of the stream the boat capsized and the enchanter and his wife were drowned.

The young lady and her husband returned to the castle, seized the treasure of its fairy lord, and, says tradition, lived happily ever afterward, as all young spouses do in fairy-tale.

CHAPTER IV: SPRITES AND DEMONS OF BRITTANY

THE idea of the evil spirit, malicious and revengeful, is common to all primitive peoples, and Brittany has its full share of demonology. Wherever, in fact, a primitive and illiterate peasantry is found the demon is its inevitable accompaniment. But we shall not find these Breton devils so very different from the fiends of other lands.

The Nain

The nain is a figure fearsomely Celtic in its hideousness, resembling the gargoyles which peer down upon the traveller from the carven 'top-hamper' of so many Breton churches. Black and menacing of countenance, these demon-folk are armed with feline claws, and their feet end in hoofs like those of a satyr. Their dark elf-locks, small, gleaming eyes, red as carbuncles, and harsh, cracked voices are all dilated upon with fear by those who have met them upon lonely heaths or unfrequented roads. They haunt the ancient dolmens built by a vanished race, and at night, by the pale star-light, they dance around these ruined tombs to the music of a primitive refrain:

> "Monday, Tuesday, Wednesday,
> Thursday and Friday."

Saturday and Sunday they dare not mention as being days sacred from fairy influence. We all remember that in the old tale of Tom Thumb the elves among whom the hero fell sang such a refrain. But wherefore? It would indeed be difficult to say. Deities, credited and discredited, have often a connexion with the calendar, and we may have here some calendric reference, or again the chant may be merely a nonsense rhyme. Bad luck attached itself to the human who chanced to behold the midnight revels of the nains, and if he entered the charmed circle and danced along with them his death was certain to ensue before the year was out. Wednesday was the nains' high-day, or rather night, and their great *nuit festale* was the first Wednesday in May. That they should have possessed a fixed festival at such a period, full of religious significance for most primitive peoples, would seem to show that they must at one time have been held in considerable esteem.

But although the nains while away their time in such simple fashion as dancing to the repetition of the names of the days of the week, they have a less innocent side to their characters, for they are forgers of false money, which they fabricate in the recesses of caverns. We all recall stories of fairy gold and its perishable nature. A simple youth sells something on market day to a fairy, and later on turning over in his pocket the money he has received he finds that it has been transformed into beans. The housewife receives gold from a fairy for services rendered, and carefully places it in a drawer. A day when she requires it arrives, but, alas! when she opens the cabinet to take it out she finds nothing but a small heap of withered leaves. It is such money that the nains manufacture in their subterranean mints—coin which bears the fairy impress of glamourie for a space, but on later examination proves to be merely dross.

The nains are also regarded as the originators of a cabalistic alphabet, the letters of which are engraved on several of the megalithic monuments of Morbihan, and especially those of Gavr'inis. He who is able to decipher this magic script, says tradition, will be able to tell where hidden treasure is to be found in any part of the country. Lest any needy folk be of a mind to fare to Brittany to try their luck in this respect it is only right to warn them that in all probability they will find the treasure formula in ogham characters or serpentine markings, and that as the first has long ago been deciphered and the second is pure symbolism they will waste their time and money in any event.

Sorcery hangs about the nain like a garment. Here he is a prophet and a diviner as well as an enchanter, and as much of his magic power is employed for ill, small wonder that the Breton peasant shudders and frowns when the name of the fearsome tribe is spoken and gives the dolmens they are supposed to haunt the widest of wide berths *au clair de la lune.*

Crions, Courils, and Gorics

Brittany has a species of dwarfs or gnomes peculiar to itself which in various parts of the country are known as crions, courils, or gorics. It will at once be seen how greatly the last word resembles Korrigan, and as all of them perhaps proceed from a root meaning 'spirit' the nominal resemblance is not surprising. Like the nains, these smaller beings inhabit abandoned Druidical monuments or dwell beneath the foundations of ancient castles. Carnac is sometimes alluded to in Breton as 'Ty C'harriquet,' 'the House of the Gorics,' the country-folk in this district holding the belief that its megalithic monuments were reared by these manikins, whom they describe as between two and three feet high, but exceedingly strong, just as the Scottish peasantry speak of the Picts of folk-lore—'wee fouk but unco' strang.' Every night the gorics dance in circles round the stones of Carnac, and should a mortal interrupt their frolic he is forced to join in the dance, until, breathless and exhausted, he falls prone to the earth amid peals of mocking laughter. Like the nains, the gorics are the guardians of hidden treasure, for the tale goes that beneath one of the menhirs of Carnac lies a golden hoard, and that all the other stones have been set up the better to conceal it, and so mystify those who would discover its resting-place. A calculation, the key to which is to be found in the Tower of London, will alone indicate the spot where the treasure lies. And here it may be of interest to state that the ancient national fortalice of England occurs frequently in Breton and in Celtic romance.[1] Some of the immigrant Britons into Armorica probably came from the settlement which was later to grow into London, and may have carried tales of its ancient British fortress into their new home. The courils are peculiar to the ruins of Tresmalouen. Like the gorics, they are fond of dancing, and they are quite as malignantly inclined toward the unhappy stranger who may stumble into their ring. The castle of Morlaix, too, is haunted by gorics not more than a foot high, who dwell beneath it in holes in the ground. They possess treasures as great as those of the gnomes of Norway or Germany, and these they will sometimes bestow on lucky mortals, who are permitted, however, to take but one handful. If a person should attempt to seize more the whole of the money vanishes, and the offender's ears are soundly boxed by invisible hands.

[1] See Nutt, *Celtic and Mediæval Romance.*

The night-washers (*eur tunnerez noz*) are evil spirits who appear at night on the banks of streams and call on the passers-by to assist them to wash the linen of the dead. If they are refused, they seize upon the person who denies them, drag him into the water, and break his arms. These beings are obviously the same as the Bean Nighe, 'the Washing Woman' of the Scottish Highlands, who is seen in lonely places beside a pool or stream, washing the linen of those who will shortly die. In Skye she is said to be short of stature. If any one catches her she tells all that will befall him in after life. In Perthshire she is represented as "small and round and dressed in pretty green."

The Teurst

In the district of Morlaix the peasants are terribly afraid of beings they call teursts. These are large, black, and fearsome, like the Highland ourisk, who haunted desert moors and glens. The *teursta poulict* appears in the likeness of some domestic animal. In the district of Vannes is encountered a colossal spirit called Teus or Bugelnoz, who appears clothed in white between midnight and two in the morning. His office is to rescue victims from the devil, and should he spread his mouth over them they are secure from the Father of Evil. The Dusii of Gaul are mentioned by St Augustine, who regarded them as *incubi*, and by Isidore of Seville, and in the name we may perhaps discover the origin of our expression 'the deuce!'

The Nicole

The Nicole is a spirit of modern creation who torments the honest fishermen of the Bay of Saint-Brieuc and

Saint-Malo. Just as they are about to draw in their nets this mischievous spirit leaps around them, freeing the fish, or he will loosen a boat's anchor so that it will drift on to a sand-bank. He may divide the cable which holds the anchor to the vessel and cause endless trouble. This spirit received its name from an officer who commanded a battalion of fishermen conscripts, and who from his intense severity and general reputation as a martinet obtained a bad reputation among the seafaring population.

The Mourioche

The Mourioche is a malicious demon of bestial nature, able, it would seem, to transform himself into any animal shape he chooses. In general appearance he is like a year-old foal. He is especially dangerous to children, and Breton babies are often chided when noisy or mischievous with the words: "Be good, now, the Mourioche is coming!" Of one who appears to have received a shock, also, it is said: "He has seen the Mourioche." Unlucky is the person who gets in his way; but doubly so the unfortunate who attempts to mount him in the belief that he is an ordinary steed, for after a fiery gallop he will be precipitated into an abyss and break his neck.

The Ankou

Perhaps there is no spirit of evil which is so much dreaded by the Breton peasantry as the Ankou, who travels the duchy in a cart, picking up souls. In the dead of night a creaking axle-tree can be heard passing down the silent lanes. It halts at a door; the summons has been given, a soul quits the doomed house, and the wagon of the Ankou passes on. The Ankou herself—for the dread death-spirit of Brittany is probably female—is usually represented as a skeleton. M. Anatole le Braz has elaborated a study of the whole question in his book on the legend of death in Brittany,[1] and it is probable that the Ankou is a survival of the death-goddess of the prehistoric dolmen-builders of Brittany. MacCulloch[2] considers the Ankou to be a reminiscence of the Celtic god of death, who watches over all things beyond the grave and carries off the dead to his kingdom, but greatly influenced by medieval ideas of 'Death the skeleton.' In some Breton churches a little model or statuette of the Ankou is to be seen, and this is nothing more nor less than a cleverly fashioned skeleton. The peasant origin of the belief can be found in the substitution of a cart or wagon for the more ambitious coach and four of other lands.

The Youdic

Dark and gloomy are many of the Breton legends, of evil things, gloomy as the depths of the forests in which doubtless many of them were conceived. Most folk-tales are tinged with melancholy, and it is rarely in Breton story that we discover a vein of the joyous.

Among the peaks of the Montagnes d'Arrée lies a vast and dismal peat bog known as the Yeun, which has long been regarded by the Breton folk as the portal to the infernal regions. This Stygian locality has brought forth many legends. It is, indeed, a remarkable territory. In summer it seems a vast moor carpeted by glowing purple heather, which one can traverse up to a

[1] *La Legende de la Mort.*

[2] *Religion of the Ancient Celts*, p. 345.

THE DEMON-DOG

N'OUN DOARE AND THE PRINCESS GOLDEN BELL

certain point, but woe betide him who would advance farther, for, surrounded by what seems solid ground, lies a treacherous quagmire declared by the people of the neighbourhood to be unfathomable. This part of the bog, whose victims have been many, is known as the Youdic. As one leans over it its waters may sometimes be seen to simmer and boil, and the peasants of the country-side devoutly believe that when this occurs infernal forces are working beneath, madly revelling, and that it is only the near presence of St Michael, whose mount is hard by, which restrains them from doing active harm to those who may have to cross the Yeun.

Countless stories are afloat concerning this weird maelstrom of mud and bubbling water. At one time it was the custom to hurl animals suspected of being evil spirits into its black depths. Malevolent fiends, it was thought, were wont to materialize in the form of great black dogs, and unfortunate animals of this type, if they evinced such peculiarities as were likely to place them under suspicion, were taken forthwith to the Youdic by a member of the enlightened priesthood of the district, and were cast into its seething depths with all the ceremonies suitable to such an occasion.

A story typical of those told about the place is that of one Job Ann Drez, who seems to have acted as sexton and assisted the parish priest in his dealings with the supernatural. Along with the priest, Job repaired one evening after sunset to the gloomy waters of the Youdic, dragging behind him a large black dog of the species most likely to excite distrust in the priestly mind. The priest showed considerable anxiety lest the animal should break loose.

"If he should get away," he said nervously, "both of us are lost."

"I will wager he does not," replied Job, tying the cord by which the brute was led securely to his wrist.

"Forward, then," said the priest, and he walked boldly in front, until they came to the foot of the mountain on the summit of which lies the Youdic.

The priest turned warningly to Job. "You must be circumspect in this place," he said very gravely. "Whatever you may hear, be sure not to turn your head. Your life in this world and your salvation in the next depend absolutely on this. You understand me?"

"Yes, sir, I understand."

A vast desolation surrounded them. So dark was the night that it seemed to envelop them like a velvet curtain. Beneath their feet they heard the hissing and moaning of the bog, awaiting its prey like a restless and voracious wild beast. Through the dense blackness they could see the iridescent waters writhing and gleaming below.

"Surely," said Job half to himself, "this must be the gateway to hell!"

At that word the dog uttered a frightful howl—such a howl as froze Job's blood in his veins. It tugged and strained at the cord which held it with the strength of a demon, striving to turn on Job and rend him.

"Hold on!" cried the priest in mortal terror, keeping at a safe distance, however. "Hold on, I entreat you, or else we are undone!"

Job held on to the demon-dog with all his strength. Indeed, it was necessary to exert every thew and sinew if the animal were to be prevented from tearing him to pieces. Its howls were sufficient to strike terror to the stoutest heart. "Iou! Iou!" it yelled again and again. But Job held on desperately, although the cord cut his hands and blood ran from the scarified palms. Inch by inch he dragged the brute toward the Youdic. The creature in a last desperate effort turned and was about to spring on him open-mouthed, when all at once the priest, darting forward, threw his cloak over its head. It uttered a shriek which sounded through the night like the cry of a lost soul.

"Quick!" cried the priest. "Lie flat on the earth and put your face on the ground!"

Scarcely had the two men done so than a frightful tumult ensued. First there was the sound of a body leaping into the morass, then such an uproar as could only proceed from the mouth of the infernal regions. Shrieks, cries, hissings, explosions followed in quick succession for upward of half an hour; then gradually they died away and a horrible stillness took their place. The two men rose trembling and unnerved, and slowly took their way through the darkness, groping and stumbling until they had left the awful vicinity of the Yeun behind them.

CHAPTER V: WORLD-TALES IN BRITTANY

I HAVE entitled this chapter 'World-Tales' to indicate that the stories it contains are in plot or *motif* if not in substance common to the whole world—that, in short, although they are found in Brittany, they are no more Breton than Italian, Russian, American, or Australian. But although the story which tells of the search for the golden-haired princess on the magic horse is the possession of no one particular race, the tales recounted here have the Breton colouring and the Breton spirit, and in perusing them we encounter numerous little allusions to Breton customs or manners and obtain not a few sidelights upon the Breton character, its shrewdness and its goodwill, while we may note as well the narrowness of view and meanness so characteristic of peoples who have been isolated for a long period from contact with other races.

The first two of these tales are striking ones built upon two world-*motifs*—those of the magic horse and the search for the golden-haired princess, who is, of course, the sun, two themes which have been amalgamated in not a few deathless stories.

The Youth who did not Know

One day the Marquis of Coat-Squiriou was returning from Morlaix, when he beheld lying on the road a little fellow of four or five years of age. He leapt from his horse, picked the child up, and asked him what he did there.

"I do not know," replied the little boy.

"Who is your father?" asked the Marquis.

"I do not know," said the child for the second time.

"And your mother?" asked the kindly nobleman.

"I do not know."

"Where are you now, my child?"

"I do not know."

"Then what is your name?"

"I do not know."

The Marquis told his serving-man to place the child on the crupper of his horse, as he had taken a fancy to him and would adopt him. He called him N'Oun Doare, which signifies in Breton, 'I do not know.' He educated him, and when his schooling was finished took him to Morlaix, where they put up at the best inn in the town. The Marquis could not help admiring his adopted son, who had now grown into a tall, handsome youth, and so pleased was he with him that he desired to signify his approval by making him a little present, which he resolved should take the form of a sword. So they went out into the town and visited the armourers' shops in search of a suitable weapon. They saw swords of all kinds, but N'Oun Doare would have none of them, until at last they passed the booth of a seller of scrap-metal, where hung a rusty old rapier which seemed fit for nothing.

"Ha!" cried N'Oun Doare, "that is the sword for me. Please buy it, I beg of you."

"Why, don't you see what a condition it is in?" said the Marquis. "It is not a fit weapon for a gentleman."

"Nevertheless it is the only sword I wish for," said N'Oun Doare.

"Well, well, you are a strange fellow," said the Marquis, but he bought the sword nevertheless, and they returned to Coat-Squiriou. The next day N'Oun Doare examined his sword and discovered that the blade had the words "I am invincible" engraved upon it.

Some time afterward the Marquis said to him: "It is time that you had a horse. Come with me to Morlaix and we will purchase one." They accordingly set out for Morlaix. In the market-place they saw many fine animals, but with none of them was N'Oun Doare content. On returning to the inn, however, he espied what looked like a broken-down mare standing by the roadside, and to this sorry beast he immediately drew the attention of the Marquis.

"That is the horse for me!" he cried. "I beg of you, purchase it for me."

"What!" cried the Marquis, "that broken-down beast? Why, only look at it, my son." But N'Oun Doare persisted, and at last, despite his own better judgment, the Marquis bought the animal. The man who sold it was a cunning-looking fellow from Cornouaille, who, as he put the bridle into N'Oun Doare's hand, whispered: "You see the knots on the halter of this animal?"

"Yes," replied N'Oun Doare; "what of them?"

"Only this, that each time you loosen one the mare will immediately carry you five hundred leagues from where you are."

The Marquis and his ward returned once more to the château, N'Oun Doare riding his new purchase, when it entered into his head to untie one of the knots on the halter. He did so, and immediately descended in the middle of Paris—which we must take the story-teller's word for it is five hundred leagues from Brittany! Several months afterward the Marquis had occasion to go to Paris, and one of the first people he met there was N'Oun Doare, who told him of his adventure.

The Marquis was going to visit the King, and took his *protégé* along with him to the palace, where he was well received.

Some nights afterward the youth was walking with his old mare outside the walls of Paris, and noticed something which glittered very brightly at the foot of an ancient stone cross which stood where four roads met. He approached it and beheld a crown of gold, set with the most brilliant precious stones. He at once picked it up, when the old mare, turning its head, said to him: "Take care; you will repent this."

Greatly surprised, N'Oun Doare thought that he had better replace the crown, but a longing to possess it overcame him, and although the mare warned him once more he finally resolved to take it, and, putting it under his mantle, rode away.

Now the King had confided to his care part of the royal stables, and when N'Oun Doare entered them their darkness was immediately lit up by the radiance of the crown which he carried. So well had the Breton lad attended to the horses under his charge that the other squires had become jealous, and, observing the strange light in N'Oun Doare's part of the stable, they mentioned it to the King, who in turn spoke of it to the Marquis of Coat-Squiriou. The Marquis asked N'Oun Doare the meaning of the light, and the youth replied that it came from the ancient sword they had bought at Morlaix, which was an enchanted weapon and shone at intervals with strange brilliance. But one night his enemies resolved to examine into the matter more closely, and, looking through the keyhole of the stable, they saw that the wondrous light which had so puzzled them shone from a magnificent crown of gold. They ran at once to tell the King, and next night N'Oun Doare's stable was opened with a master-key and the crown removed to the King's quarters. It was then seen that an inscription was engraved upon the diadem, but in such strange characters that no one could read it. The magicians of the capital were called into consultation, but none of them could decipher the writing. At last a little boy of seven years of age was found who said that it was the crown of the Princess Golden Bell. The King then called upon N'Oun Doare to approach, and said to him: "You should not have hidden this thing from me, but as you are guilty of having done so I doom you to find the Princess Golden Bell, whom I desire shall become my wife. If you fail I shall put you to death."

N'Oun Doare left the royal presence in a very perturbed state of mind. He went to seek his old mare with tears in his eyes.

"I know," said the mare, "the cause of your sorrow. You should have left the golden crown alone, as I told you. But do not repine; go to the King and ask him for money for your journey."

The lad received the money from the King, and set out on his journey. Arriving at the sea-shore, one of the first objects he beheld was a little fish cast up by the waves on the beach and almost at its last gasp.

"Throw that fish back into the water," said the mare. N'Oun Doare did so, and the fish, lifting its head from the water, said:

"You have saved my life, N'Oun Doare. I am the King of the Fishes, and if ever you require my help call my name by the sea-shore and I will come." With these words the Fish-King vanished beneath the water.

A little later they came upon a bird struggling vainly to escape from a net in which it was caught.

"Cut the net and set that poor bird free," said the wise mare.

Upon N'Oun Doare doing so the bird paused before it flew away and said:

"I am the King of the Birds, N'Oun Doare. I will never forget the service you have rendered me, and if ever you are in trouble and need my aid you have only to call me and I shall fly swiftly to help you."

As they went on their way N'Oun Doare's wonderful mare crossed mountains, forests, vast seas, and streams with a swiftness and ease that was amazing. Soon they beheld the walls of the Château of the Golden Bell rising before them, and as they drew near they could hear a most confused and terrible noise coming from it, which shook N'Oun Doare's courage and made him rather fearful of entering it. Near the door a being of the most curious aspect was hung to a tree by a chain, and this peculiar individual had as many horns on his body as there are days in the year.

"Cut that unfortunate man down," said the mare. "Will you not give him his freedom?"

"I am too much afraid to approach him," said N'Oun Doare, alarmed at the man's appearance.

"Do not fear," said the sagacious animal; "he will not harm you in any manner."

N'Oun Doare did so, and the stranger thanked him most gratefully, bidding him, as the others whom he had rescued had done, if he ever required help to call upon Grifescorne, King of the Demons, for that was his name, and he would be with him immediately.

"Enter the château boldly and without fear," said the

mare, "and I will await you in the wood yonder. After the Princess Golden Bell has welcomed you she will show you all the curiosities and marvels of her dwelling. Tell her you have a horse without an equal, which can dance most beautifully the dances of every land. Say that your steed will perform them for her diversion if she will come and behold it in the forest."

Everything fell out as the mare had said, and the Princess was delighted and amused by the mare's dancing.

"If you were to mount her," said N'Oun Doare, "I vow she would dance even more wonderfully than before!"

The Princess after a moment's hesitation did so. In an instant the adventurous youth was by her side, and the horse sped through the air, so that in a short space they found themselves flying over the sea.

"You have tricked me!" cried the infuriated damsel. "But do not imagine that you are at the end of your troubles; and," she added viciously, "you will have cause to lament more than once ere I wed the old King of France."

They arrived promptly at Paris, where N'Oun Doare presented the lovely Princess to the monarch, saying:

"Sire, I have brought to you the Princess Golden Bell, whom you desire to make your wife."

The King was dazed by the wondrous beauty of the Princess, and was eager for the marriage to take place immediately, but this the royal maiden would not hear of, and declared petulantly that she would not be wed until she had a ring which she had left behind her at her château, in a cabinet of which she had lost the key.

Summoning N'Oun Doare, the King charged him with

the task of finding the ring. The unfortunate youth returned to his wise mare, feeling much cast down.

"Why," said the mare, "foolish one! do you not remember the King of the Birds whom you rescued? Call upon him, and mayhap he will aid you as he promised to do."

With a return of hope N'Oun Doare did as he was bid, and immediately the royal bird was with him, and asked him in what way he could help him. Upon N'Oun Doare explaining his difficulty, the Bird-King summoned all his subjects, calling each one by name. They came, but none of them appeared to be small enough to enter the cabinet by way of the keyhole, which was the only means of entrance. The wren was decided to be the only bird with any chance of success, and he set out for the château.

Eventually, with much difficulty and the loss of the greater part of his feathers, the bird procured the ring, and flew back with it to Paris. N'Oun Doare hastened to present the ring to the Princess.

"Now, fair one," said the impatient King, "why delay our wedding longer?"

"Nay," said she, pouting discontentedly, "there is one thing that I wish, and without it I will do nothing."

"What do you desire? You have only to speak and it shall be brought.

"Well, transport my château with all it contains opposite to yours."

"What!" cried the King, aghast. "Impossible!"

"Well, then, it is just as impossible that I should marry you, for without my château I shall not consent."

For a second time the King gave N'Oun Doare what seemed an insurmountable task.

"Now indeed I am as good as lost!" lamented the youth as they came to the château and he saw its massive walls towering above him.

"Call Grifescorne, King of the Demons, to your assistance," suggested the wise mare.

With the aid of the Demon-King and his subjects N'Oun Doare's task was again accomplished, and he and his mare followed the demon army to Paris, where they arrived as soon as it did.

In the morning the people of Paris were struck dumb to see a wonderful palace, its golden towers flashing in the sun, rising opposite to the royal residence.

"We shall be married at last, shall we not?" asked the King.

"Yes," replied the Princess, "but how shall I enter my château and show you its wonders without a key, for I dropped it in the sea when N'Oun Doare and his horse carried me over it."

Once more was the youth charged with the task, and through the aid of the Fish-King was able to procure the key, which was cut from a single diamond. None of the fishes had seen it, but at last the oldest fish, who had not appeared when his name was pronounced, came forward and produced it from his mouth.

With a glad heart the successful N'Oun Doare returned to Paris, and as the Princess had now no more excuses to make the day of the wedding was fixed and the ceremony was celebrated with much splendour. To the astonishment of all, when the King and his betrothed entered the church N'Oun Doare followed behind with his mare. At the conclusion of the ceremony the mare's skin suddenly fell to the ground, disclosing a maiden of the most wonderful beauty.

Smiling upon the bewildered N'Oun Doare, the damsel gave him her hand and said: "Come with me to Tartary, for the king of that land is my father, and there we shall be wed amid great rejoicing."

Leaving the amazed King and wedding guests, the pair quitted the church together. More might have been told of them, but Tartary is a far land and no news of them has of late years reached Brittany.

The Princess of Tronkolaine

There was once an old charcoal-burner who had twenty-six grandchildren. For twenty-five of them he had no great difficulty in procuring godparents, but for the twenty-sixth—that, alas! was a different story. God-mothers, indeed, were to be found in plenty, but he could not find anyone to act as godfather.

As he wandered disconsolately along the high road, dwelling on his bad luck, he saw a fine carriage coming toward him, its occupant no less a personage than the King himself. The old man made an obeisance so low that the King was amused, and threw him a handful of silver.

"My good man," he said, "here are alms for you."

"Your Majesty," replied the charcoal-burner, "I do not desire alms. I am unhappy because I cannot find a godfather for my twenty-sixth grandchild."

The King considered the matter.

"I myself will be godfather to the child," he said at length. "Tell me when it is to be baptized and I will meet you at the church."

The old man was delighted beyond measure, and in due time he and his relatives brought the child to be baptized. When they reached the church, sure enough, there was the King waiting to take part in the ceremony, and in his honour the child was named Charles. Before taking leave the King gave to the charcoal-burner the half of a coin which he had broken in two. This Charles on reaching his eighteenth birthday was to convey to the Court at Paris, as a token whereby his godfather should know him. His Majesty also left a thousand crowns, which were to be utilized in the education and general upbringing of the child.

Time passed and Charles attained his eighteenth birthday. Taking the King's token, he set out for the royal abode. As he went he encountered an old man, who warned him on no account to drink from a certain well which he would pass on his way. The lad promised to regard the warning, but ere he reached the well he had forgotten it.

A man sat by the side of the well.

"You are hot and tired," he said, feigning courtesy, "will you not stop to drink?"

The water was cool and inviting. Charles bent his head and drank thirstily. And while he drank the stranger robbed him of his token; but this he did not know till afterward.

Gaily Charles resumed his way, while the thief went to Paris by a quicker route and got there before him.

Boldly the thief demanded audience of the King, and produced the token so wickedly come by. The sovereign ordered the other half of the coin to be brought out, and lo! they fitted exactly. And because the thief had a plausible face the good King did not doubt that he was indeed his godson. He therefore had him treated with all honour and respect, and bestowed gifts upon him lavishly.

Meanwhile Charles had arrived in Paris, and, finding that he had been deprived of his only means of proving his identity to the King, he accepted the situation philosophically and set about earning his living. He succeeded in obtaining a post as herdsman on the royal estates.

One day the robber was greatly disconcerted to find the real Charles at the very gates of the palace. He determined to be rid of him once for all, so he straightway approached the King.

"Your Majesty, there is a man among your retainers who has said that he will demand of the sun why it is so red at sunrise."

"He is indeed a foolish fellow," said the King. "Our decree is that he shall carry out his rash boast to-morrow ere sunset, or, if it be but idle folly, lose his head on the following morning."

The thief was delighted with the success of his plot. Poor Charles was summoned before the King and bidden to ask the sun why he was so red at sunrise. In vain he denied having uttered the speech. Had not the King the word of his godson?

Next morning Charles set out on his journey. Ere he had gone very far he met an old man who asked him his errand, and afterward gave him a wooden horse on which to ride to the sun. Charles thought this but a sorry joke. However, no sooner had he mounted his wooden steed than it rose into the air and flew with him to where the sun's castle towered on the peak of a lofty mountain.

To the sun, a resplendent warrior, Charles addressed his query.

"In the morning," said the sun, "I pass the castle of the

Princess of Tronkolaine, and she is so lovely that I must needs look my best."

Charles, mounted on his wooden horse, flew with this answer to Paris. The King was satisfied, but the thief gnashed his teeth in secret rage, and plotted yet further against the youth.

"Your Majesty," he said, "this herdsman who tends your herds has said that he will lead hither the Princess of Tronkolaine to be your bride."

"If he has said so," replied the King, "he shall lead her hither or forfeit his life."

"Alas!" thought Charles, when he learned of the plot, "I must bid farewell to my life—there is no hope for me!"

All the same he set out boldly enough, and by and by encountered the old man who had helped him on his previous mission. To him Charles confided his troubles, begging for advice and assistance.

The old man pondered.

"Return to the Court," he said, "and ask the King to give you three ships, one laden with oatmeal, another with bacon, and the third with salt meat. Then sail on till you come to an island covered with ants. To their monarch, the Ant-King, make a present of the cargo of oatmeal. He will direct you to a second island, whereon dwell fierce lions. Fear them not. Present your cargo of bacon to their King and he will become your friend. Yet a third island you will touch, inhabited only by sparrow-hawks. Give to their King your cargo of salt meat and he will show you the abode of the Princess."

Charles thanked the sage for his advice, which he promptly proceeded to follow. The King granted him the three ships, and he sailed away in search of the Princess.

When he came to the first island, which was swarming with ants, he gave up his cargo of grain, and so won the friendship of the little creatures. At the second island he unloaded the bacon, which he presented to the King of the Lions; while at the third he gave up the salt beef to the King of the Sparrow-hawks, who directed him how to come at the object of his quest. Each monarch bade Charles summon him instantly if he had need of assistance.

Setting sail from the island of the sparrow-hawks, the youth arrived at length at the abode of the Princess.

She was seated under an orange-tree, and as Charles gazed upon her he thought her the most beautiful woman in the world, as indeed she was.

The Princess, looking up, beheld a comely youth, beneath whose ardent gaze her eyes fell. Smiling graciously, she invited him into her castle, and he, nothing loath, followed her into the great hall, where tempting viands were spread before him.

When he had supped he made known his errand to the Princess, and begged her to accompany him to Paris. She agreed only on condition that he would perform three tasks set him, and when Charles was curious to know what was required of him she led him into another room where was a large heap of every kind of seed—corn, barley, clover, flax—all mixed up anyhow.

"This is the first task," said the Princess: "you must put each kind of seed into a different heap, so that no single seed shall be out of its place. This you must accomplish ere to-morrow at sunrise." With that she left the room.

Charles was in despair, until he bethought him of his friend the King of the Ants, whom he begged to help him. Scarcely had he uttered the words when ants began to fill the room, coming from he knew not where. In less time than it takes to tell they had arranged the seeds into separate heaps, so that no single seed was out of its place.

When the Princess arrived in the morning she was astonished to find the hero fast asleep and the work accomplished. All day she entertained him hospitably in her castle, and at nightfall she showed him the second task. An avenue of great oaks led down from the castle. Giving him a wooden axe and a wooden saw, the Princess bade him cut down all the trees ere morning.

When she had left him Charles called upon the King of the Lions. Instantly a number of lions bounded upon the scene, and with teeth and claws soon performed the task.

In the morning the Princess, finding Charles asleep and all the trees cut down, was more astonished than ever.

The third task was the most difficult of all. A high mountain had to be levelled to the plain in a single night. Without the help of the sparrow-hawks, Charles would certainly have failed, but these faithful creatures worked with a will, and soon had the great mountain carried away piece by piece and dropped into the sea.

When the Princess came for the third time and found the hero asleep by the finished task she fell in love with him straightway, and kissed him softly on the brow.

There was now nothing further to hinder his return, and he begged the Princess to accompany him to Paris. In due time they arrived in that city, to be welcomed with great warmth by the people. The beauty of the lady won all hearts. But great was the general astonishment when she declared that she would marry, not the King, but the youth who had brought her to Paris! Charles thereupon declared himself the true godson of the King, and the monarch, far from being angry, gave the couple his blessing and great estates; and when in course of time he died they reigned in his stead.

As for the thief, he was ordered to execution forthwith, and was roasted to death in a large oven.

The Princess Starbright

This is another tale which introduces the search for the sun-princess in a peculiar setting.

In the long ago there lived near the Lake of Léguer a jolly miller who found recreation after his work in shooting the wild swans and ducks which frequented that stretch of water. One December day, when it was freezing hard and the earth was covered with snow, he observed a solitary duck near the edge of the lake. He shot at it, and went forward to pick it up, when he saw to his amazement that it had changed into a beautiful princess. He was ready to drop into the snow with fright, but the lady came graciously forward to him, saying:

"Fear not, my brave fellow, for know that I have been enchanted these many years under the form of a wild duck, because of the enmity of three malicious demons. You can restore me permanently to my human shape if you choose to show only a litle perseverance and courage."

"Why, what do you desire me to do, madam?"

stammered the miller, abashed by the lady's beauty and condescension.

"What only a brave man could accomplish, my friend," she replied; "all that you have to do is to pass three consecutive nights in the old manor which you can see over there."

The miller shuddered, for he had heard the most terrible stories in connexion with the ruined manor, which had an evil name in the district.

"Alas! madam," he said, "whom might I not encounter there! Even the devil himself——"

"My good friend," said the Princess, sadly, "if you do as I ask you will have to encounter not one but a dozen devils, who will torment you in every possible way. But fear nothing, for I can provide you with a magic ointment which will preserve you entirely from all the injuries they would attempt to inflict upon you. Even if you were dead I could resuscitate you. I assure you that if you will do as I ask you will never regret it. Beneath the hearthstone in the hall of the manor are three casks of gold and three of silver, and all these will belong to you and to me if you assist me; so put your courage to the proof, I pray you."

The miller squared his shoulders. "Lady," he said, "I will obey you, even if I have to face a hundred devils instead of twelve."

The Princess smiled encouragingly and disappeared. On the following night the miller set out for the old manor, carrying a bundle of faggots to make a fire, and some cider and tobacco to refresh him during his vigil. When he arrived in the dismal old place he sat himself down by the hearth, where he had built a good fire, and lit his pipe. But he had scarcely done so when he heard a most tremendous commotion in the chimney. Somewhat scared, he hid himself under an old bed which stood opposite the hearth, and, gazing anxiously from his place of concealment, beheld eleven grisly fiends descend from the flue. They seemed astonished to find a fire on the hearth, and did not appear to be in the best of tempers.

"Where is Boiteux?" cried one. "Oh," growled another, who appeared to be the chief of the band, "he is always late."

"Ah, behold him," said a third, as Boiteux arrived by the same road as his companions.

"Well, comrades," cried Boiteux, "have you heard the news?" The others shrugged their shoulders and shook their heads sulkily.

"Well," said Boiteux, "I am convinced that the miller of Léguer is here, and that he is trying to free the Princess from the enchantment which we have placed upon her."

A hurried search at once took place, the demons scrambling from one part of the room to the other, tearing down the curtains and making every effort to discover the hiding-place of the intruder. At last Boiteux, peering under the bed, saw the miller crouching there, and cried out: "Here is the rogue beneath the bed."

The unlucky miller was then seized by the foot and dragged into the shrieking and leaping circle. With a gesture of command the chief demon subdued the antics of his followers.

"So, my jolly miller," said he, "our friend the Princess has found a champion in you, has she? Well, we are going to have some sport with you, which I fear will not be quite to your taste, but I can assure you that you will not again have the opportunity of assisting a princess in distress."

With this he seized the miller and thrust him from him with great force. As he flew like a stone from a sling, another of the fiends seized him, and the unhappy man was thrown violently about from one to the other. At last they threw him out of the window into the court-yard, and as he did not move they thought that he was dead. But in the midst of their laughter and rejoicing at the easy manner in which they had got rid of him, cockcrow sounded, and the diabolic company swiftly disappeared. They had scarcely taken their departure when the Princess arrived. She tenderly anointed the miller's hurts from the little pot of magic ointment she had brought with her, and, nothing daunted, now that he was thoroughly revived, the bold fellow announced his intention of seeing the matter through and remaining in the manor for the two following nights.

He had scarcely ensconced himself in his seat by the chimney-side on the second night when the twelve fiends came tumbling down the chimney as before. At one end of the room was a large heap of wood, behind which the miller quickly took refuge.

"I smell the smell of a Christian!" cried Boiteux. A search followed, and once more the adventurous miller was dragged forth.

"Oho!" cried the leader, "so you are not dead after all! Well, I can assure you that we shall not botch our work on this occasion."

One of the grisly company placed a large cauldron of oil upon the fire, and when this was boiling they seized their victim and thrust him into it. The most dreadful agony seized the miller as the liquid seethed around his body, and he was just about to faint under the intensity of the torture when once again the cock crew and the fiendish band took themselves off. The Princess quickly appeared, and, drawing the miller from the cauldron, smeared him from head to foot with the ointment.

On the third night the devils once more found the miller in the apartment. In dismay Boiteux suggested that he should be roasted on a spit and eaten, but unluckily for them they took a long time to come to this conclusion, and when they were about to impale their victim on the spit, the cock crew and they were forced to withdraw, howling in baffled rage. The Princess arrived as before, and was delighted to see that this time her champion did not require any assistance.

"All is well now," she said. "You have freed me from my enchantment and the treasure is ours."

They raised the hearthstone from its place, and, as she had said, the three casks of gold and the three casks of silver were found resting beneath it.

"Take what you wish for yourself," said the Princess. "As for me, I cannot stay here; I must at once make a journey which will last a year and a day, after which we shall never part again."

With these words she disappeared. The miller was grieved at her departure, but, consoling himself with the treasure, made over his mill to his apprentice and, apprising one of his companions of his good luck, resolved to go upon a journey with him, until such time as the Princess should return. He visited the neighbouring countries, and, with plenty of money at his disposal, found existence very pleasant indeed. After some eight months of this kind of life, he and his friend resolved to return to Brittany, and set out on their journey. One day they encountered on the road an old woman selling apples. She asked them to buy, but the miller was advised by his friend not to pay any heed to her. Ignoring the well-meant advice, the miller laughed and bought three apples. He had scarcely eaten one when he became unwell. Recalling how the fruit had disagreed with him, he did not touch the other apples until the day on which the Princess had declared she would return. When on the way to the manor to meet her, he ate the second apple. He began to feel sleepy, and, lying down at the foot of a tree, fell into a deep slumber.

Soon after the Princess arrived in a beautiful star-coloured chariot drawn by ten horses. When she saw the miller lying sleeping she inquired of his friend what had chanced to him. The man acquainted her with the adventure of the apples, and the Princess told him that the old woman from whom he had purchased them was a sorceress.

"Alas!" she said, "I am unable to take him with me in this condition, but I will come to this place to-morrow and again on the following day, and if he be awake I will transport him hence in my chariot. Here are a golden pear and a handkerchief; give him these and tell him that I will come again."

She disappeared in her star-coloured equipage. Shortly afterward the miller wakened, and his friend told him what had occurred and gave him the pear and the kerchief. The next day the friends once more repaired to the spot where the Princess had vanished, but in thoughtlessness the miller had eaten of the third apple, and once more the Princess found him asleep. In sorrow she promised to return next day for the last time, once more leaving a golden pear and a handkerchief with his friend, to whom she said:

"If he is not awake when I come to-morrow he will have to cross three powers and three seas in order to find me."

Unluckily, however, the miller was still asleep when the Princess appeared on the following day. She repeated what she had said to his friend concerning the ordeal that the unfortunate miller would have to face before he might see her again, and ere she took her departure left a third pear and a third handkerchief behind her. When the miller awoke and found that she had gone he went nearly crazy with grief, but nevertheless he declared his unalterable intention of regaining the Princess, even if he should have to travel to the ends of the earth in search of her. Accordingly he set out to find her abode. He walked and walked innumerable miles, until at last he came to a great forest. As he arrived at its gloomy borders night fell, and he considered it safest to climb a tree, from which, to his great satisfaction, he beheld a light shining in the distance. Descending, he walked in the direction of the light, and found a tiny hut made of the branches of trees, in which sat a little old man with a long white beard.

"Good evening, grandfather," said the miller.

"Good evening, my child," replied the old man. "I behold you with pleasure, for it is eighty years since I have seen any human being."

The miller entered the hut and sat down beside the old man, and after some conversation told him the object of his journey.

"I will help you, my son," said the ancient. "Do you see these enchanted gaiters? Well, I wore them at your age. When you buckle them over your legs you will be able to travel seven leagues at a single step, and you will arrive without any difficulty at the castle of the Princess you desire so much to see again."

The miller passed the night in the hut with the old hermit, and on the following morning, with the rising of the sun, buckled on the magic gaiters and stepped out briskly. All went well to begin with, nothing arrested his progress, and he sped over rivers, forests, and mountains. As the sun was setting he came to the borders of a second forest, where he observed a second hut, precisely similar to that in which he had passed the previous night. Going toward it, he found it occupied by an aged woman, of whom he demanded supper and lodging.

"Alas! my son," said the old woman, "you do ill to come here, for I have three sons, terrible fellows, who will be here presently, and I am certain that if you remain they will devour you."

The miller asked the names of the sons, and was informed by the old woman that they were January, February, and March. From this he concluded that the crone he was addressing was none other than the mother of the winds, and on asking her if this was so she admitted that he had judged correctly. While they were talking there was a terrible commotion in the chimney, from which descended an enormous giant with white hair and beard, breathing out clouds of frost.

"Aha!" he cried, "I see, mother, that you have not neglected to provide for my supper!"

"Softly, softly, good son," said the old dame; "this is

little Yves, my nephew and your cousin ; you must not eat him." The giant, who seemed greatly annoyed, retired into a corner, growling. Shortly afterward his brothers, February and March, arrived, and were told the same tale regarding the miller's relationship to them.

Our hero, resolved to profit by the acquaintanceship, asked the gigantic February if he would carry him to the palace of the Princess, whom he described.

" Ah," said February, " without doubt you speak of the Princess Starbright. If you wish I will give you a lift on my back part of the way."

The miller gratefully accepted the offer, and in the morning mounted on the back of the mighty wind-giant, who carried him over a great sea. Then, after traversing much land and a second ocean, and while crossing a third spacious water, February expressed himself as quite fatigued and said that he could not carry his new cousin any farther. The miller glanced beneath him at the great waste of waters and begged him to make an effort to reach the land on the other side. Giving vent to a deep-throated grumble, February obeyed, and at last set him down outside the walls of the town where the castle of the Princess Starbright was situated. The miller entered the town and came to an inn, and, having dined, entered into conversation with the hostess, asking her the news of the place.

" Why," said the woman, amazed, " where do you come from that you don't know that the Princess Starbright is to be married to-day, and to a husband that she does not love ? The wedding procession will pass the door in a few moments on its way to the church."

The miller was greatly downcast at these words, but

plucking up courage he placed on a little table before the inn the first of the pears and handkerchiefs that the Princess had left with his friend. Shortly afterward the wedding procession passed, and the Princess immediately remarked the pear and the kerchief, and also recognized the miller standing close by. She halted, and, feigning illness, begged that the ceremony might be postponed until the morrow. Having returned to the palace, she sent one of her women to purchase the fruit and the handkerchief, and these the miller gave the maiden without question. On the following day the same thing happened, and on the third occasion of the Princess's passing the same series of events occurred. This time the Princess sent for the miller, and the pair embraced tenderly and wept with joy at having recovered each other.

Now the Princess was as clever as she was beautiful, and she had a stratagem by which she hoped to marry the miller without undue opposition on the part of her friends. So she procured the marriage garments of the prince, her *fiancé*, and attiring the miller in them, took him to the marriage feast, which had been prepared for the fourth time at a late hour; but she hid her lover in a secluded corner from the public gaze. After a while she pretended to be looking for something, and upon being asked what she had lost, replied:

"I have a beautiful coffer, but, alas! I have lost the key of it. I have found a new key, but it does not fit the casket; should I not search until I have recovered the old one?"

"Without doubt!" cried every one. Then the Princess, going to the place where the miller was concealed, led him forth by the hand.

"My lords and gentles," she said, "the coffer I spoke of is my heart; here is the one key that can fit it, the key that I had lost and have found again."

The Princess and the miller were married amid universal rejoicings; and some time after the ceremony they did not fail to revisit the Lake of Léguer, the scene of their first meeting, the legend of which still clings like the mists of evening to its shores.

This quaint and curious tale, in which the native folklore and French elements are so strangely mingled, deals, like its predecessor, with the theme of the search for the fairy princess. We turn now to another tale of quest with somewhat similar incidents, where the solar nature of one of the characters is perhaps more obvious—the quest for the mortal maiden who has been carried off by the sun-hero. We refrain in this place from indicating the mythological basis which underlies such a tale as this, as such a phenomenon is already amply illustrated in other works in this series.

The Castle of the Sun

There once lived a peasant who had seven children, six of them boys and the seventh a girl. They were very poor and all had to work hard for a living, but the drudges of the family were the youngest son, Yvon, and his sister, Yvonne. Because they were gentler and more delicate than the others, they were looked upon as poor, witless creatures, and all the hardest work was given them to do. But the children comforted each other, and became but the better favoured as they grew up.

One day when Yvonne was taking the cattle to pasture she encountered a handsome youth, so splendidly garbed that her simple heart was filled with awe and admiration. To her astonishment he addressed her and courteously begged her hand in marriage. "To-morrow," he said, "I shall meet you here at this hour, and you shall give me an answer."

Troubled, yet secretly happy, Yvonne made her way home, and told her parents all that had chanced. At first they laughed her to scorn, and refused to believe her story of the handsome prince, but when at length they were convinced they told her she was free to marry whom she would.

On the following day Yvonne betook herself to the trysting-place, where her lover awaited her, even more gloriously resplendent than on the occasion of his first coming. The very trappings of his horse were of gleaming gold. At Yvonne's request he accompanied her to her home, and made arrangements with her kindred for the marriage. To all inquiries regarding his name and place of abode he returned that these should be made known on the wedding morning.

Time passed, and on the day appointed the glittering stranger came to claim his wife. The ceremony over, he swept her into a carriage and was about to drive away, when her brothers reminded him of his promise to reveal his identity.

"Where must we go to visit our sister?" they asked.

"Eastward," he replied, "to a palace built of crystal, beyond the Sea of Darkness."

And with that the pair were gone.

A year elapsed, and the brothers neither saw nor heard anything of their sister, so that at length they decided to go in search of her. Yvon would have accompanied them, but they bade him stay at home.

"You are so stupid," they said, "you would be of no use to us."

Eastward they rode, and ever eastward, till at length they found themselves in the heart of a great forest. Then night came on and they lost the path. Twice a great noise, like the riot of a tempest, swept over their heads, leaving them trembling and stricken with panic.

By and by they came upon an old woman tending a great fire, and of her they inquired how they might reach the abode of their brother-in-law.

"I cannot tell," said the old woman, "but my son may be able to direct you."

For the third time they heard the noise as of a great wind racing over the tree-tops.

"Hush!" said the old woman, "it is my son approaching."

He was a huge giant, this son of hers, and when he drew near the fire he said loudly:

"Oh ho! I smell the blood of a Christian!"

"What!" cried his mother sharply. "Would you eat your pretty cousins, who have come so far to visit us?"

At that the giant became quite friendly toward his 'cousins,' and when he learned of their mission even offered to conduct them part of the way.

Notwithstanding his amiability, however, the brothers spent an anxious night, and were up betimes on the following morning.

The giant made ready for departure. First of all he bade the old woman pile fresh fuel on the fire. Then he spread a great black cloth, on which he made the brothers stand. Finally he strode into the fire, and when his clothes were consumed the black cloth rose into the air, bearing the brothers with it. Its going was marked by the sound of rushing wind which had terrified them on the preceding day. At length they alighted on a vast plain, half of which was rich and fertile, while the other half was bleak and arid as a desert. The plain was dotted with horses, and, curiously enough, those on the arid side were in splendid condition, whereas those on the fertile part were thin and miserable.

The brothers had not the faintest idea of which direction they ought to take, and after a vain attempt to mount the horses on the plain they decided to return home. After many wanderings they arrived at their native place once more.

When Yvon learned of the ill-success which had attended their mission he decided to go himself in search of his sister, and though his brothers laughed at him they gave him an old horse and bade him go.

Eastward and eastward he rode, till at length he reached the forest where the old woman still tended the fire. Seeing that he was strong and fearless, she directed him by a difficult and dangerous road, which, however, he must pursue if he wished to see his sister.

It was indeed a place of terrors. Poisonous serpents lay across his track; ugly thorns and briers sprang underfoot; at one point a lake barred his way.

Finally a subterranean passage led him into his sister's country, where everything was of crystal, shining with the splendour of the sun itself. At the end of a gleaming pathway rose a castle built entirely of crystal, its innumerable domes and turrets reflecting the light in a thousand prismatic hues.

Having gained access to the castle through a cave, Yvon wandered through its many beautiful chambers, till in one of these he came upon his sister asleep on a silken couch.

Entranced with her beauty, and not daring to wake her, he slipped behind a curtain and watched her in silence; but as time went on he marvelled that she did not wake.

At eventide a handsome youth—Yvon's brother-in-law—entered the chamber, struck Yvonne sharply three times, then flung himself down by her side and went to sleep. All night Yvon waited in his place of concealment. In the morning the young man rose from his couch, gave his wife three resounding blows, and went away. Only then did Yvon emerge and wake his sister.

Brother and sister exchanged a tender greeting, and found much to talk of after their long separation. Yvon learned that the country to which he had come was a peculiar place, where meat and drink could be entirely dispensed with, while even sleep was not a necessity.

"Tell me, Yvonne," he said, remembering what he had seen of his brother-in-law, "does your husband treat you well?"

Yvonne assured him that her husband was all she could wish—that she was perfectly happy.

"Is he always absent during the day?" he asked anxiously.

"Always."

"Do you know where he goes?"

"I do not, my brother."

"I have a mind," said Yvon, "to ask him to let me accompany him on his journey. What say you, sister?"

"It is a very good plan," said Yvonne.

At sundown her husband returned home. He and Yvon became very good friends, and the latter begged to be allowed to accompany him on his journey the following day.

"You may do so," was the response, "but only on one condition: if you touch or address anyone save me you must return home."

Yvon readily agreed to accept the condition, and early next morning the two set off. Ere long they came to a wide plain, one half of which was green and fruitful, while the other half was barren and dry. On this plain cattle were feeding, and those on the arid part were fat and well-conditioned, while the others were mean and shrivelled to a degree. Yvon learned from his companion that the fat cattle represented those who were contented with their meagre lot, while the lean animals were those who, with a plentiful supply of worldly goods, were yet miserable and discontented.

Many other strange things they saw as they went, but that which seemed strangest of all to Yvon was the sight of two trees lashing each other angrily with their branches, as though each would beat the other to the ground.

Laying his hands on them, he forbade them to fight, and lo! in a moment they became two human beings, a man and wife, who thanked Yvon for releasing them from an enchantment under which they had been laid as a punishment for their perpetual bickering.

Anon they reached a great cavern from which weird noises proceeded, and Yvon would fain have advanced farther; but his companion forbade him, reminding him that in disenchanting the trees he had failed to observe the one essential condition, and must return to the palace where his sister dwelt.

There Yvon remained for a few days longer, after which

his brother-in-law directed him by a speedy route to his home.

"Go," said the prince, "but ere long you will return, and then it will be to remain with us for ever."

On reaching his native village Yvon found all trace of his dwelling gone. Greatly bewildered, he inquired for his father by name. An old greybeard replied.

"I have heard of him," he said. "He lived in the days when my grandfather's grandfather was but a boy, and now he sleeps in the churchyard yonder."

Only then did Yvon realize that his visit to his sister had been one, not of days, but of generations!

The Seigneur with the Horse's Head

Famous among all peoples is the tale of the husband surrounded by mystery—bespelled in animal form, like the Prince in the story of Beauty and the Beast, nameless, as in that of Lohengrin, or unbeheld of his spouse, as in the myth of Cupid and Psyche. Among uncivilized peoples it is frequently forbidden to the wife to see her husband's face until some time after marriage, and the belief that ill-luck will befall one or both should this law be disregarded runs through primitive story, being perhaps reminiscent of a time when the man of an alien or unfriendly tribe crept to his wife's lodge or hut under cover of darkness and returned ere yet the first glimmer of dawn might betray him to the men of her people. The story which follows, however, deals with the theme of the enchanted husband whose wife must not speak to anyone until her first child receives the sacrament of baptism, and is, perhaps, unique of its kind.

There lived at one time in the old château of Kerouez, in the commune of Loguivy-Plougras, a rich and powerful seigneur, whose only sorrow was the dreadful deformity of his son, who had come into the world with a horse's head. He was naturally kept out of sight as much as possible, but when he had attained the age of eighteen years he told his mother one day that he desired to marry, and requested her to interview a farmer in the vicinity who had three pretty young daughters, in order that she might arrange a match with one of them.

The good lady did as she was requested, not without much embarrassment and many qualms of conscience, and after conversing upon every imaginable subject, at length gently broke the object of her visit to the astonished farmer. The poor man was at first horrified, but little by little the lady worked him into a good humour, so that at last he consented to ask his daughters if any one of them would agree to marry the afflicted young lord. The two elder girls indignantly refused the offer, but when it was made plain to them that she who espoused the seigneur would one day be châtelaine of the castle and become a fine lady, the eldest daughter somewhat reluctantly consented and the match was agreed upon.

Some days afterward the bride-to-be happened to pass the castle and saw the servants washing the linen, when one cried to her:

"How in the world can a fine girl like you be such a fool as to throw herself away on a man with a horse's head?"

"Bah!" she replied, "he is rich, and, let me tell you, we won't be married for long, for on the bridal night I shall cut his throat."

Just at that moment a gay cavalier passed and smiled at the farmer's daughter.

"You are having a strange conversation, mademoiselle," he said. She coloured and looked somewhat confused. "Well, sir," she replied, "it is hateful to be mocked by these wenches because I have the bad luck to be espoused to a seigneur with a horse's head, and I assure you I feel so angry that I shall certainly carry out my threat."

The unknown laughed shortly and went his way. In time the night of the nuptials arrived. A grand *fête* was held at the château, and, the ceremony over, the bridesmaids conducted the young wife to her chamber. The bridegroom shortly followed, and to the surprise of his wife, no sooner had the hour of sunset come than his horse's head disappeared and he became exactly as other men. Approaching the bed where his bride lay, he suddenly seized her, and before she could cry out or make the least clamour he killed her in the manner in which she had threatened to kill him.

In the morning his mother came to the chamber, and was horrified at the spectacle she saw.

"Gracious heavens! my son, what have you done?" she cried.

"I have done that, my mother," replied her son, "which was about to be done to me."

Three months afterward the young seigneur asked his mother to repair once more to the farmer with the request that another of his daughters might be given him in marriage. The second daughter, ignorant of the manner of her sister's death, and mindful of the splendid wedding festivities, embraced the proposal with alacrity. Like her sister, she chanced to be passing the washing-green of the castle one day, and the laundresses, knowing of her espousal, taunted her upon it, so that at last she grew very angry and cried:

"I won't be troubled long with the animal, I can assure you, for on the very night that I wed him I shall kill him like a pig!"

At that very moment the same unknown gentleman who had overheard the fatal words of her sister passed, and said:

"How now, young women, that's very strange talk of yours!"

"Well, monseigneur," stammered the betrothed girl, "they are twitting me upon marrying a man with a horse's head; but I will cut his throat on the night of our wedding with as little conscience as I would cut the throat of a pig." The unknown gentleman laughed as he had done before and passed upon his way.

As on the previous occasion, the wedding was celebrated with all the pomp and circumstance which usually attends a Breton ceremony of the kind, and in due time the bride was conducted to her chamber, only to be found in the morning weltering in her blood.

At the end of another three months the seigneur dispatched his mother for the third time to the farmer, with the request that his younger daughter might be given him in marriage, but on this occasion her parents were by no means enraptured with the proposal. When the great lady, however, promised them that if they consented to the match they would be given the farm to have and to hold as their own property, they found the argument irresistible and reluctantly agreed. Strange to say, the girl herself was perfectly composed about the matter, and gave it as her opinion that if her sisters had met with a violent death they were entirely to blame themselves, for some reason which she could not explain, and she added that she thought that their loose and undisciplined way of talking had had much to do with their untimely fate. Just as her sisters had been, she too was taunted by the laundresses regarding her choice of a husband, but her answer to them was very different.

"If they met with their deaths," she said, "it was because of their wicked utterances. I do not in the least fear that I shall have the same fate."

As before the unknown seigneur passed, but this time, without saying anything, he hurried on his way and was soon lost to view.

The wedding of the youngest sister was even more splendid than that of the two previous brides. On the following morning the young seigneur's mother hastened with fear and trembling to the marriage chamber, and to her intense relief found that her daughter-in-law was alive. For some months the bride lived happily with her husband, who every night at set of sun regained his natural appearance as a young and handsome man. In due time a son was born to them, who had not the least sign of his semi-equine parentage, and when they were about to have the infant baptized the father said to the young mother:

"Hearken to what I have to say. I was condemned to suffer the horrible enchantment you know of until such time as a child should be born to me, and I shall be immediately delivered from the curse whenever this infant is baptized. But take care that you do not speak a word until the baptismal bells cease to sound, for if you utter a syllable, even to your mother, I shall disappear on the instant and you will never see me more."

Full of the resolve not to utter a single sound, the young mother, who lay in bed, kept silent, until at last she heard the sound of bells, when, in her joy, forgetting the warning, she turned to her mother, who sat near, with words of congratulation on her lips. A few moments afterward her husband rushed into the room, the horse's head still upon his shoulders. He was covered with sweat, and panted fiercely.

"Ah, miserable woman," he cried, "what have you done? I must leave you, and you shall never see me more!" and he made as if to quit the room. His wife rose from her bed, and strove to detain him, but he struck at her with his fist. The blood trickled out and made three spots on his shirt.

"Behold these spots," cried the young wife; "they shall never disappear until I find you."

"And I swear to you," cried her husband, "that you will never find me until you have worn out three pairs of iron shoes in doing so."

With these words he ran off at such speed that the poor wife could not follow him, and, fainting, she sank to the ground.

Some time after her husband had left her the young wife had three pairs of iron shoes made and went in search of him. After she had travelled about the world for nearly ten years the last pair of shoes began to show signs of wear, when she found herself one day at a castle where the servants were hanging out the clothes to dry, and she heard one of the laundresses say:

"Do you see this shirt? I declare it is enchanted, for although I have washed it again and again I cannot rub out these three spots of blood which you see upon it."

When the wanderer heard this she approached the

laundress and said to her: "Let me try, I pray you. I think I can wash the shirt clean."

They gave her the shirt, she washed it, and the spots disappeared. So grateful was the laundress that she bade the stranger go to the castle and ask for a meal and a bed. These were willingly granted her, and at night she was placed in a small apartment next to that occupied by the lord of the castle. From what she had seen she was sure that her husband was the lord himself, so when she heard the master of the house enter the room next door she knocked upon the boards which separated it from her own. Her husband, for he it was, replied from the other side; then, entering her room, he recognized his wife, and they were happily united after the years of painful separation. To the wife's great joy her husband was now completely restored to his proper form, and nothing occurred to mar their happiness for the rest of their lives.

The Bride of Satan

Weird and terrible as are many of the darksome legends of Brittany, it may be doubted if any are more awe-inspiring than that which we are now about to relate. "Those who are affianced three times without marrying shall burn in hell," says an old Breton proverb, and it is probably this aphorism which has given the Bretons such a strong belief in the sacred nature of a betrothal. The fantastic ballad from which this story is taken is written in the dialect of Léon, and the words are put into the mouth of a maiden of that country. Twice had she been betrothed. On the last occasion she had worn a robe of the finest stuff, embroidered with twelve brilliant stars and having the figures of the sun and moon painted upon it, like the lady in Madame d'Aulnoy's story of *Finette Cendron* (*Cinderella*). On the occasion when she went to meet her third *fiancé* in church she almost fainted as she turned with her maidens into the little road leading up to the building, for there before her was a great lord clad in steel *cap-à-pie*, wearing on his head a casque of gold, his shoulders covered by a blood-coloured mantle. Strange lights flashed from his eyes, which glittered under his casque like meteors. By his side stood a huge black steed, which ever and again struck the ground impatiently with his hoofs, throwing up sparks of fire.

The priest was waiting in the church, the bridegroom arrived, but the bride did not come. Where had she gone? She had stepped on board a barque with the dark steel-clad lord, and the ship passed silently over the waters until it vanished among the shadows of night. Then the lady turned to her husband.

"What gloomy waters are these through which we sail, my lord?" she asked.

"This is the Lake of Anguish," he replied in hollow tones. "We sail to the Place of Skulls, at the mouth of Hell."

At this the wretched bride wept bitterly. "Take back your wedding-ring!" she cried. "Take back your dowry and your bridal gifts!"

But he answered not. Down they descended into horrid darkness, and as the unhappy maiden fell there rang in her ears the cries of the damned.

This tale is common to many countries. The fickle maiden is everywhere regarded among primitive peoples with dislike and distrust. But perhaps the folk-ballad which most nearly resembles that just related is the Scottish ballad of *The Demon Lover*, which inspired

THE BRIDE OF SATAN

GWENNOLAÏK AND NOLA

the late Hamish MacCunn, the gifted Scottish composer, in the composition of his weird and striking orchestral piece, *The Ship o' the Fiend.*

The Baron of Jauioz

Another tradition which tells of the fate of an unhappy maiden is enshrined in the ballad of *The Baron of Jauioz.* Louis, Baron of Jauioz, in Languedoc, was a French warrior of considerable renown who flourished in the fourteenth century, and who took part in many of the principal events of that stirring epoch, fighting against the English in France and Flanders under the Duke of Berry, his overlord. Some years later he embarked for the Holy Land, but, if we may believe Breton tradition, he returned, and while passing through the duchy fell in love with and actually bought for a sum of money a young Breton girl, whom he carried away with him to France. The unfortunate maiden, so far from being attracted by the more splendid environment of his castle, languished and died.

"I hear the note of the death-bird," the ballad begins sadly; "is it true, my mother, that I am sold to the Baron of Jauioz?"

"Ask your father, little Tina, ask your father," is the callous reply, and the question is then put to her father, who requests the unfortunate damsel to ask her brother, a harsh rustic who does not scruple to tell her the brutal truth, and adds that she must depart immediately. The girl asks what dress she must wear, her red gown, or her gown of white delaine.

"It matters little, my daughter," says the heartless mother. "Your lover waits at the door mounted on a great black horse. Go to him on the instant."

As she leaves her native village the clocks are striking, and she weeps bitterly.

"Adieu, Saint Anne!" she says. "Adieu, bells of my native land!"

Passing the Lake of Anguish she sees a band of the dead, white and shadowy, crossing the watery expanse in their little boats. As she passes them she can hear their teeth chatter. At the Valley of Blood she espies other unfortunates. Their hearts are sunken in them and all memory has left them.

After this terrible ride the Baron and Tina reach the castle of Jauioz. The old man seats himself near the fire. He is black and ill-favoured as a carrion crow. His beard and his hair are white, and his eyes are like firebrands.

"Come hither to me, my child," says he, "come with me from chamber to chamber that I may show you my treasures."

"Ah, seigneur," she replies, the tears falling fast, "I had rather be at home with my mother counting the chips which fall from the fire."

"Let us descend, then, to the cellar, where I will show you the rich wines in the great bins."

"Ah, sir, I would rather quaff the water of the fields that my father's horses drink."

"Come with me, then, to the shops, and I will buy you a sumptuous gown."

"Better that I were wearing the working dress that my mother made me."

The seigneur turns from her in anger. She lingers at the window and watches the birds, begging them to take a message from her to her friends.

At night a gentle voice whispers: "My father, my

mother, for the love of God, pray for me!" Then all is silence.

In this striking ballad we find strong traces of the Breton love of country and other national traits. The death-bird alluded to is a grey bird which sings during the winter in the Landes country in a voice soft and sad. It is probably a bird of the osprey species. It is thought that the girl who hears it sing is doomed to misfortune. The strange and ghostly journey of the unhappy Tina recalls the *mise en scène* of such ballads as *The Bride of Satan*, and it would seem that she passes through the Celtic Tartarus. It is plain that the Seigneur of Jauioz by his purchase of their country-woman became so unpopular among the freedom-loving Bretons that at length they magnified him into a species of demon—a traditionary fate which he thoroughly deserved, if the heartrending tale concerning his victim has any foundation in fact.

The Man of Honour

The tale of the man who is helped by the grateful dead is by no means confined to Brittany. Indeed, in folk-tale the dead are often jealous of the living and act toward them with fiendish malice. But in the following we have a story in which a dead man shows his gratitude to the living for receiving the boon of Christian burial at his hands.

There was once a merchant-prince who had gained a great fortune by trading on land and sea. Many ships were his, and with these he traded to far countries, reaping a rich harvest. He had a son named Iouenn, and he was desirous that he too should embrace the career of a merchant and become rich. When, therefore, Iouenn declared his willingness to trade in distant lands his father was delighted and gave him a ship full of Breton merchandise, with instructions to sell it to the best advantage in a foreign country and return home with the gold thus gained.

After a successful voyage the vessel arrived at a foreign port, and Iouenn presented his father's letters to the merchants there, and disposed of his cargo so well that he found himself in possession of a large sum of money. One day as he was walking on the outskirts of the city he saw a large number of dogs gathered round some object, barking at it and worrying it. Approaching them, he discovered that that which they were worrying was nothing less than the corpse of a man. Making inquiries, he found that the unfortunate wretch had died deeply in debt, and that his body had been thrown into the roadway to be eaten by the dogs. Iouenn was shocked to see such an indignity offered to the dead, and out of the kindness of his heart chased the dogs away, paid the debts of the deceased, and granted his body the last rites of sepulture.

A few days afterward he left the port where these things had happened and set out on his homeward voyage. He had not sailed far when one of the mariners drew his attention to a strange ship a little distance away, which appeared to be draped entirely in black.

"That is indeed a curious vessel," said Iouenn. "Wherefore is it draped in black? and for what reason do those on board bewail so loudly?"

While he spoke the ship drew nearer, and Iouenn called to the people who thronged its decks, asking why they made such loud laments.

"Alas! good sir," replied the captain of the strange ship, "not far from here is an island inhabited by an enormous serpent, which for seven years has demanded an annual tribute of a royal princess, and we are now bearing another victim to her doom."

Iouenn laughed. "Where is the Princess?" he asked. At that moment the Princess came on deck, weeping and wringing her hands. Iouenn was so struck by her beauty that he there and then declared in the most emphatic manner that she should never become the prey of the serpent. On learning from the captain that he would hand over the maiden if a sufficient bribe were forthcoming, he paid over to him the last of the money he had gained from his trading, and taking the Princess on his own vessel sailed homeward.

In due time Iouenn arrived home and was welcomed with delight by his father; but when the old man learned the story of what had been done with his money he was furious; nor would he believe for a moment that the lady his son had rescued was a veritable princess, but chased Iouenn from his presence with hard and bitter words. Nevertheless Iouenn married the royal lady he had rescued, and they started housekeeping in a tiny dwelling. Time went on, and the Princess presented her husband with a little son, but by this time fortune had smiled upon Iouenn, for an uncle of his, who was also a merchant, had entrusted him with a fine vessel to trade in Eastern lands; so, taking with him the portraits of his wife and child, he set out on his voyage. With a fresh wind and favourable conditions generally he was not long in coming to the city where his wife's father reigned. Now, some mariners of the port, having entered the ship out of curiosity, observed the portrait of the Princess, and informed the King of the circumstance. The King himself came to the ship and demanded to know what had become of his daughter. Iouenn did not, of course, realize that the monarch was his father-in-law, and assured him that he knew nothing of his daughter, whereupon the King, growing very angry, had him cast into prison and ordered his ship to be broken to pieces and burned. In prison Iouenn made friends with his gaoler, to whom he related his history, which the gaoler in turn told the King, with the result that the prisoner was brought before the monarch, who desired him to set out at once to bring his daughter back, and for this purpose fitted him out with a new vessel. But the old monarch took the precaution of sending two of his ministers along with the Breton sailor in case he should not return. The party soon came to Brittany, and found the Princess and her infant safe.

Now one of the King's ministers had loved the Princess for a long time, and consequently did not regard her husband with any great degree of favour; so when they re-embarked on the return journey to her father's kingdom her suspicions were aroused, and, fully aware of the minister's crafty nature, she begged her husband to remain with her as much as possible. But Iouenn liked to be on the bridge, whence he could direct the operations of his mariners, and laughed at his wife's fears. One night as he leaned over the side of the vessel, gazing upon the calm of the star-strewn sea, his enemy approached very stealthily and, seizing him by the legs, cast him headlong into the waters. After this he waited for a few moments, and, hearing no sound, cried out that the captain had fallen overboard. A search was made, but with no avail. The Princess was distraught, and in the belief that her husband had perished remained in her cabin lamenting. But Iouenn was a capital swimmer and struck out lustily. He swam around for a long time, without, however, encountering any object upon which he could lay hold to support himself. Meanwhile the ship sailed on her course, and in due time arrived at the kingdom of the Princess's father, by whom she was received with every demonstration of joy. Great festivities were announced, and so pleased was the old King at his daughter's return that he willingly consented to her marriage with the treacherous minister, whom he regarded as the instrument of her deliverance. But the Princess put off the wedding-day by every possible artifice, for she felt in her heart that her husband was not really lost to her.

Let us return now to Iouenn. After swimming for some time he came upon a barren rock in the middle of the ocean, and here, though beaten upon by tempests and without any manner of shelter save that afforded by a cleft in the rock, he succeeded in living for three years upon the shell-fish which he gathered on the shores of his little domain. In that time he had grown almost like a savage. His clothes had fallen off him and he was thickly covered with matted hair. The only mark of civilization he bore was a chain of gold encircling his neck, the gift of his wife. One night he was sitting in his small dwelling munching his wretched supper of shell-fish when an eerie sound broke the stillness. He started violently. Surely these were human accents that he heard—yet not altogether human, for their weird cadence held something of the supernatural, and cold as he was he felt himself grow still more chilly.

"Cold, cold," cried the voice, and a dreadful chattering of teeth ended in a long-drawn wail of "Hou, hou, hou!" The sound died away and once more he was left amid the great silence of the sea.

The next evening brought the same experience, but although Iouenn was brave he dared not question his midnight visitor. On the third occasion, however, he demanded: "Who is there?"

Out of the darkness there crawled a man completely naked, his body covered with blood and horrible wounds, the eyes fixed and glassy.

Iouenn trembled with horror. "In the name of God, who are you?" he cried.

"Ha, so you do not remember me, Iouenn?" asked the phantom. "I am that unfortunate man whose body you gave decent burial, and now I have come to help you in turn. Without doubt you wish to leave this desert rock on which you have suffered so long."

"I do, most devoutly," replied Iouenn.

"Well, you will have to make haste," said the dead man, "for to-morrow your wife is going to be married to the minister of your father-in-law, the wretch who cast you into the sea. Now if you will promise to give me a share of all that belongs to yourself and your wife within a year and a day, I will carry you at once to the palace of your father-in-law."

Iouenn promised to do as the phantom requested, and the dread being then asked him to mount upon his back. Iouenn did so, and the corpse then plunged into the sea, and, swimming swiftly, soon brought him to the port where his father-in-law reigned. When it had set him safely on shore it turned and with a wave of its gaunt white arm cried, "In a year and a day," then plunged back into the sea.

When the door-keeper of the palace opened the gate in the morning he was astounded to see what appeared to be an animal crouching on the ground outside and crying for help. It was Iouenn. The palace lackeys crowded round him and threw him morsels of bread, which he devoured with avidity. One of the waiting-women told the Princess of the strange being who crouched outside. She descended in order to view him, and at once observed the golden chain she had given to her husband round his neck. Iouenn immediately rushed to embrace her. She took him to her chamber and clothed him suitably. By this time the bridal preparations had been completed, and, like the Princess in the story of the Miller of Léguer, the bride asked the advice of the company as to whether it were better to search for an old key that fitted a coffer in her possession or make use of a new key which did not fit; the coffer, of course, being her heart and the respective keys her husband and the minister. All the company advised searching for the old key, when she produced Iouenn and explained what she had meant. The crafty minister grew pale as death at sight of Iouenn, and the King stormed furiously.

"Ho, there!" he cried, "build a great fire, varlets, and cast this slave into it." All the company thought at first that his words were intended to apply to Iouenn, but when they saw him point at the minister whose guilt the Princess had made plain, they applauded and the wretch was hurried away to his doom.

Iouenn and the Princess lived happily at the Court, and

in time a second little son was born to them. Their first child had died, and they were much rejoiced at its place being filled. Iouenn had entirely forgotten his indebtedness to the dead man, but one day in the month of November, when his wife was sitting quietly by the fire nursing her infant, with her husband opposite her, three loud knocks resounded upon the door, which flew open and revealed the horrible form of the corpse to which Iouenn owed his freedom. The Princess shrieked at sight of the phantom, which said in deep tones: "Iouenn, remember thy bargain."

Trembling, Iouenn turned to his wife and asked her for the keys of their treasure-house, that he might give their terrible visitor a portion of their wealth, but with a disdainful wave of its arm the apparition bade him cease.

"It is not your wealth I require, Iouenn," it said in hollow tones. "Behold that which I desire," and it pointed to the infant slumbering in its mother's arms.

Once more the Princess cried aloud, and clasped her little one to her bosom.

"My infant!" cried Iouenn in despair. "Never!"

"If you are a man of honour," said the corpse, "think of your promise made on the barren rock."

"It is true," said Iouenn, wringing his hands, "but oh, remember how I saved your body from the dogs."

"I only ask what is my due," said the ghost. "Besides, I do not desire all your infant, but a share of it only."

"Wretch!" cried Iouenn, "are you without a heart? Have then your wish, for honour with me is above all."

The infant was then undressed and laid between the two upon a table.

"Take your sword," said the phantom, "and cut off a portion for me."

"Ah, I would that I were on that desert rock in the middle of the ocean!" cried the unhappy father. He raised his weapon and was about to strike, when the phantom called upon him to hold.

"Harm not your infant, Iouenn," it cried. "I see clearly that you are a man of honour and that you have not forgotten the service I rendered you; nor do I fail to remember what you did for me, and how it is through you that I am able to dwell in Paradise, which I would not have been permitted to enter had my debts not been paid and my body given burial. Farewell, until we meet above." And with these words the apparition vanished.

Iouenn and the Princess lived long, respected by all, and when the old King died Iouenn, the man of his word, was made King in his place.

CHAPTER VI: BRETON FOLK-TALES

THE stories told here under the title of 'folk-tales' are such as do not partake so much of the universal element which enters so largely into Breton romance, but those which have a more national or even local tinge and are yet not legendary. The homely flavour attached to many stories of this kind is very apparent, and it is evident that they have been put together in oral form by unknown 'makers,' some of whom had either a natural or artistic aptitude for story-telling. In the first of the following tales it is curious to note how the ancient Breton theme has been put by its peasant narrator into almost a modern dress.

The Magic Rose

An aged Breton couple had two sons, the elder of whom went to Paris to seek his fortune, while the younger one was timid by nature and would not leave the paternal roof. His mother, who felt the burden of her age, wished the stay-at-home to marry. At first he would not hear of the idea, but at last, persuaded by her, he took a wife. He had only been married a few weeks, however, when his young bride sickened and died. La Rose, for such was his name, was inconsolable. Every evening he went to the cemetery where his wife was buried, and wept over her tomb.

One night he was about to enter the graveyard on his sad errand when he beheld a terrible phantom standing before him, which asked him in awful tones what he did there.

"I am going to pray at the tomb of my wife," replied the terrified La Rose.

"Do you wish that she were alive again?" asked the spirit.

"Ah, yes!" cried the sorrowing husband. "There is nothing that I would not do in order that she might be restored to me."

"Hearken, then," said the phantom. "Return to this place to-morrow night at the same hour. Provide yourself with a pick and you will see what comes to pass."

On the following night the young widower was punctually at the rendezvous. The phantom presented itself before him and said:

"Go to the tomb of your wife and strike it with your pick; the earth will turn aside and you will behold her lying in her shroud. Take this little silver box, which contains a rose; open it and pass it before her nostrils three times, when she will awake as if from a deep sleep."

La Rose hastened to the tomb of his wife, and everything happened as the phantom had predicted. He placed the box containing the rose to his wife's nostrils and she awoke with a sigh, saying: "Ah, I have been asleep for a long time." Her husband provided her with clothes which he had brought with him, and they returned to their house, much to the joy of his parents.

Some time afterward La Rose's father died at a great age, and the grief-stricken mother was not long in following him to the grave. La Rose wrote to his brother in Paris to return to Brittany in order to receive his portion of the paternal inheritance, but he was unable to leave the capital, so La Rose had perforce to journey to Paris. He promised his wife before leaving that he would write to her every day, but on his arrival in the city he found his brother very ill, and in the anxiety of nursing him back to health he quite forgot to send his wife news of how he fared.

The weeks passed and La Rose's wife, without word of her husband, began to dread that something untoward had happened to him. Day by day she sat at her window weeping and watching for the courier who brought letters from Paris. A regiment of dragoons chanced to be billeted in the town, and the captain, who lodged at the inn directly opposite La Rose's house, was greatly attracted by the young wife. He inquired of the landlady who was the beautiful dame who sat constantly weeping at her window, and learned the details of her history. He wrote a letter to her purporting to come from La Rose's brother in Paris, telling her that her husband had died in the capital, and some time after paid his addresses to the supposed widow, who accepted him. They were married, and when the regiment left the town the newly wedded pair accompanied it.

Meanwhile La Rose's brother recovered from his illness, and the eager husband hastened back to Brittany. But when he arrived at his home he was surprised to find the doors closed, and was speedily informed of what had occurred during his absence. For a while he was too grief-stricken to act, but, recovering himself somewhat, he resolved to enlist in the regiment of dragoons in which the false captain held his commission. The beauty of his handwriting procured him the post of secretary to one of the lieutenants, but although he frequently attempted to gain sight of his wife he never succeeded in doing so. One day the captain entered the lieutenant's office, observed the writing of La Rose, and asked his brother officer if he would kindly lend him his secretary for a few days to assist him with some correspondence. While helping the captain La Rose beheld his wife, who did not, however, recognize him. Greatly pleased with his work, the captain invited him to dinner. During the repast a servant, who had stolen a silver dish, fearing that it was about to be missed, slid it into La Rose's pocket, and when it could not be found, accused the secretary of the theft. La Rose was brought before a court-martial, which condemned him to be shot.

While in prison awaiting his execution La Rose struck up an acquaintance with an old veteran named Père La Chique, who brought him his meals and seemed kindly disposed to him.

"Père La Chique," said La Rose one day, "I have two thousand francs; if you will do as I ask you they shall be yours."

The veteran promised instantly, and La Rose requested that after he was shot La Chique should go to the cemetery where he was buried and resuscitate him with the magic rose, which he had carefully preserved. On the appointed day La Rose was duly executed, but Père La Chique, with his pockets full of money, went from inn to inn, drinking and making merry. Whenever the thought of La Rose crossed his mind, he muttered to himself in bibulous accents: "Poor fellow, poor fellow, he is better dead. This is a weary world; why should I bring him back to it?"

When Père La Chique had caroused with his comrades for some days the two thousand francs had almost disappeared. Then remorse assailed him and he made up his mind to do as La Rose had wished. Taking a pick and an axe he went to the graveyard, but when he struck the grave with his tools and the earth rolled back, disclosing the body of La Rose, the old fellow was so terrified that he ran helter-skelter from the spot. A draught of good wine brought back his failing courage, however, and he returned and passed the rose three times under the nostrils of his late acquaintance. Instantly La Rose sat up.

"By my faith, I've had a good sleep!" he said, rubbing his eyes. "Where are my clothes?"

Père La Chique handed him his garments, and after he had donned them they quitted the graveyard with all haste.

La Rose now found it necessary to cast about for a living. One day he heard the sound of a drum in the street, and, following it, found that it was beaten by a crier who promised in the King's name a large reward to those who would enlist as sentinels to guard a chapel where the King's daughter, who had been changed into a monster, was imprisoned. La Rose accepted the offer, and then learned to his dismay that the sentinel who guarded the place between the hours of eleven and midnight was never seen again. On the very first night that he took up his duties this perilous watch fell to his lot. He felt his courage deserting him, and he was about to fly when he heard a voice say: "La Rose, where are you?"

La Rose trembled. "What do you wish with me?" he asked.

"Hearken to me, and no evil will befall you," replied the voice. "Soon a great and grisly beast will appear. Leave your musket by the side of the sentry-box, climb on the top, and the beast will not touch you."

As eleven o'clock struck La Rose heard a noise and hastened to climb on the top of the sentry-box. Soon a hideous monster came out of the chapel, breathing flames and crying: "Sentinel of my father, where art thou, that I may devour thee?" As it uttered these words, it fell against the musket, which it seized between its teeth. Then the creature disappeared into the chapel and La Rose descended from his perch. He found the musket broken into a thousand pieces.

The old King was delighted to learn that his sentinel had not been devoured, for in order that his daughter should be delivered from her enchantment as a beast it was necessary that the same sentinel should mount guard for three consecutive nights between the hours of eleven and midnight.

On the following night La Rose was pacing up and down on guard, when the same voice addressed him, telling him on this occasion to place his musket before the door of the chapel. The beast issued as before, seized the musket, broke it into small pieces, and returned to the chapel. On the third night the voice advised him to throw open the door of the chapel, and when the beast came out to run into the building himself, where he would see a leaden shrine, behind which he could take refuge, and where he would find a small bottle, with the contents of which he was to sprinkle the beast's head. With its usual dreadful roar the monster issued from the chapel. La Rose leapt past it and ran for the leaden shrine. It followed him with hideous howls, and he only reached the protective sanctuary in time. Seizing the little bottle which lay there, he fearlessly fronted the beast and sprinkled its contents over its head. Instantly it changed into a beautiful princess, whom La Rose escorted to her delighted parents. La Rose and the princess were betrothed and duly married, and shortly afterward the King gave up his throne to his son-in-law.

One day the new King was inspecting the regiment of dragoons to which he had once belonged.

"Colonel," he said, "I miss a man from your regiment."

"It is true, sire," replied the Colonel. "It is an old fellow called Père La Chique, whom we have left at the barracks playing his violin, the old good-for-nothing!"

"I wish to see him," said the King.

Père La Chique was brought forward trembling, and the King, tearing the epaulettes from the shoulders of the captain who had stolen his wife, placed them on those of Père La Chique. He then gave orders for a great fire to be lit, in which were burned the wicked captain and the wife who had so soon forgotten her husband.

La Rose and his Queen lived happily ever afterward—which is rather odd, is it not, when one thinks of the treatment meted out to his resuscitated spouse? But if the lights in folk-tale are bright, the shadows are correspondingly heavy, and rarely does justice go hand in hand with mercy in legend!

Norouas, the North-west Wind

Brittany has an entire cycle of folk-tales dealing with the subject of the winds—which, indeed, play an extraordinary part in Breton folk-lore. The fishermen of the north coast frequently address the winds as if they were living beings, hurling opprobrious epithets at them if the direction in which they blow does not suit their purpose, shaking their fists at them in a most menacing manner the while. The following story, the only wind-tale it is possible to give here, well illustrates this personalization of the winds by the Breton folk.

There was once a goodman and his wife who had a little field on which they grew flax. One season their patch yielded a particularly fine crop, and after it had been cut they laid it out to dry. But Norouas, the North-west Wind, came along and with one sweep of his mighty wings tossed it as high as the tree-tops, so that it fell into the sea and was lost.

When the goodman saw what had happened he began to swear at the Wind, and, taking his stick, he set out to follow and slay Norouas, who had spoiled his flax. So hasty had he been in setting forth that he had taken no food or money with him, and when evening came he arrived at an inn hungry and penniless. He explained his plight to the hostess, who gave him a morsel of bread and permitted him to sleep in a corner of the stable. In the morning he asked the dame the way to the abode of Norouas, and she conducted him to the foot of a mountain, where she said the Winds dwelt.

The goodman climbed the mountain, and at the top met with Surouas, the South-west Wind.

"Are you he whom they call Norouas?" he asked.

"No, I am Surouas," said the South-west Wind.

"Where then is that villain Norouas?" cried the goodman.

"Hush!" said Surouas, "do not speak so loud, goodman, for if he hears you he will toss you into the air like a straw."

At that moment Norouas arrived, whistling wildly and vigorously.

"Ah, thief of a Norouas," cried the goodman, "it was you who stole my beautiful crop of flax!" But the Wind took no notice of him. Nevertheless he did not cease to cry: "Norouas, Norouas, give me back my flax!"

"Hush, hush!" cried Norouas. "Here is a napkin that will perhaps make you keep quiet."

"With my crop of flax," howled the goodman, "I could have made a hundred napkins such as this. Norouas, give me back my flax!"

"Be silent, fellow," said Norouas. "This is no common napkin which I give you. You have only to say, 'Napkin, unfold thyself,' to have the best spread table in the world standing before you."

The goodman took the napkin with a grumble, descended the mountain, and there, only half believing what Norouas had said, placed the napkin before him, saying, "Napkin, unfold thyself." Immediately a table appeared spread with a princely repast. The odour of cunningly cooked dishes arose, and rare wines sparkled in glittering vessels. After he had feasted the table vanished, and the goodman folded up his napkin and went back to the inn where he had slept the night before.

"Well, did you get any satisfaction out of Norouas?" asked the hostess.

"Indeed I did," replied the goodman, producing the napkin. "Behold this: Napkin, unfold thyself!" and as he spoke the magic table appeared before their eyes. The hostess, struck dumb with astonishment, at once became covetous and resolved to have the napkin for herself. So that night she placed the goodman in a handsome apartment where there was a beautiful bed with a soft feather mattress, on which he slept more soundly than ever he had done in his life. When he was fast asleep the cunning hostess entered the room and stole the napkin, leaving one of similar appearance in its place.

In the morning the goodman set his face homeward, and duly arrived at his little farm. His wife eagerly asked him if Norouas had made good the damage done to the flax, to which her husband replied affirmatively and drew the substituted napkin from his pocket.

"Why," quoth the dame, "we could have made two hundred napkins like this out of the flax that was destroyed."

"Ah, but," said the goodman, "this napkin is not the same as others. I have only to say, 'Napkin, unfold thyself,' and a table covered with a most splendid feast appears. Napkin, unfold thyself—unfold thyself, dost thou hear?"

"You are an old fool, goodman," said his wife when nothing happened. Her husband's jaw dropped and he seized his stick.

"I have been sold by that rascal Norouas," he cried. "Well, I shall not spare him this time," and without more ado he rushed out of the house and took the road to the home of the Winds.

He slept as before at the inn, and next morning climbed the mountain. He began at once to call loudly upon Norouas, who was whistling up aloft, demanding that he should return him his crop of flax.

"Be quiet, down there!" cried Norouas.

"I shall not be quiet!" screamed the goodman, brandishing his bludgeon. "You have made matters worse by cheating me with that napkin of yours!"

"Well, well, then," replied Norouas, "here is an ass; you have only to say 'Ass, make me some gold,' and it will fall from his tail."

The goodman, eager to test the value of the new gift, at once led the ass to the foot of the mountain and said: "Ass, make me some gold." The ass shook his tail, and a *rouleau* of gold pieces fell to the ground. The goodman hastened to the inn, where, as before, he displayed the phenomenon to the hostess, who that night went into the stable and exchanged for the magical animal another similar in appearance to it. On the evening of the following day the goodman returned home and acquainted his wife with his good luck, but when he charged the ass to make gold and nothing happened, she railed at him once more for a fool, and in a towering passion he again set out to slay Norouas. Arrived at the mountain for the third time, he called loudly on the North-west Wind, and when he came heaped insults and reproaches upon him.

"Softly," replied Norouas; "I am not to blame for your misfortune. You must know that it is the hostess at the inn where you slept who is the guilty party, for she stole your napkin and your ass. Take this cudgel. When you say to it, 'Strike, cudgel,' it will at once attack your enemies, and when you want it to stop you have only to cry, '*Ora pro nobis.*'"

The goodman, eager to test the efficacy of the cudgel, at once said to it, "Strike, cudgel," whereupon it commenced to belabour him so soundly that he yelled, "*Ora pro nobis!*" when it ceased.

Returning to the inn in a very stormy mood, he loudly demanded the return of his napkin and his ass, whereupon the hostess threatened to fetch the gendarmes.

"Strike, cudgel!" cried the goodman, and the stick immediately set about the hostess in such vigorous style that she cried to the goodman to call it off and she would at once return his ass and his napkin.

When his property had been returned to him the goodman lost no time in making his way homeward, where he rejoiced his wife by the sight of the treasures he brought with him. He rapidly grew rich, and his neighbours, becoming suspicious at the sight of so much wealth, had him arrested and brought before a magistrate on a charge of wholesale murder and robbery. He was sentenced to death, and on the day of his execution he was about to mount the scaffold, when he begged as a last request that his old cudgel might be brought him. The boon was granted, and no sooner had the stick been given into his hands than he cried, "Strike, cudgel!"

And the cudgel *did* strike. It belaboured judge, gendarmes, and spectators in such a manner that they fled howling from the scene. It demolished the scaffold and cracked the hangman's crown. A great cry for mercy arose. The goodman was instantly pardoned, and was never further molested in the enjoyment of the treasures the North-west Wind had given him as compensation for his crop of flax.

The Foster-Brother

The weird tale which follows has many parallels in world folk-lore, but is localized at Tréguier, an old cathedral town in the Côtes-du-Nord at the junction of the Jaudy and the Guindy, famous for the beautiful windows of its celebrated church, founded by St Tugdual.

Gwennolaïk was the most noble and beautiful maiden in

Tréguier, but, alas! she was almost friendless, for at an early age she had lost her father, her mother, and her two sisters, and her sole remaining relative was her stepmother. Pitiful it was to see her standing at the door of her manor, weeping as if her heart would break. But although she had none of her own blood to cherish she still nursed the hope that her foster-brother, who had journeyed abroad for some years, might one day return, and often would she stand gazing fixedly over the sea as if in search of the vessel that would bring him home. They had been playmates, and although six years had passed since he had left the country, the time had gone quickly, and when Gwennolaïk thought of the young man it was as the boy who had shared the games and little amusements of her childhood. From these day-dreams she would be rudely awakened by the harsh voice of her stepmother calling to her: "Come here, my girl, and attend to the animals. I don't feed you for loafing and doing nothing."

Poor Gwennolaïk had a sad life with her stepmother. Noble as she was she was yet forced by the vindictive old woman to rise in the early hours of the morning, even two or three hours before daylight in winter, to light the fire and sweep the house and perform other menial work. One evening as she was breaking the ice in the well in order to draw water for the household she was interrupted by a cavalier returning to Nantes.

"Good e'en to you, maiden. Are you affianced to anyone?"

The girl did not reply, but hung her head.

"Come, don't be afraid," said the handsome horseman, "but answer my question."

She looked at him almost fearfully. "Saving your grace, I have never been affianced to anyone."

"Good," replied the cavalier. "Take this gold ring and say to your stepmother that you are now affianced to a cavalier of Nantes who has been in a great battle and who has lost his squire in the combat; and you may also add that he has been wounded in the side by a sword-stroke. In three weeks and three days, when my wound is healed, I will return and will take you to my manor with joy and festival."

The maiden returned to the house and looked at the ring. It was the same as her foster-brother used to wear on his left hand!

Three weeks ran by, but the cavalier did not return. Then the stepmother said one morning: "It is time, daughter, that you should marry, and I may tell you that I have found you a husband after my own heart."

"Saving your grace, good stepmother, I do not wish to marry anyone except my foster-brother, who has returned. He has given me a golden wedding-ring, and has promised to come for me within a few days."

"A fig for your gold ring," cried the malignant hag. "*Bon gré, mal gré*, you shall marry Job the Witless, the stable boy."

"Marry Job! Oh, horror! I should die of grief! Alas, my mother, were you but here now to protect me!"

"If you must howl, pray do so in the courtyard. You may make as many grimaces as you please, but in three days you shall be married for all that."

. . . . .

The old grave-digger slowly patrolled the road, his bell in his hand, carrying the news of those who had died from village to village. In his doleful whine he cried : "Pray for the soul of a noble cavalier, a worthy gentleman of a good heart, who was mortally wounded in the side by the stroke of a sword in the battle near Nantes. He is to be buried to-day in the White Church."

At the marriage feast the bride was all in tears. All the guests, young and old, wept with her, all except her stepmother. She was conducted to the place of honour at supper-time, but she only drank a sip of water and ate a morsel of bread. By and by the dancing commenced, but when it was proposed that the bride should join in the revels she was not to be found ; she had, indeed, escaped from the house, her hair flying in disorder, and where she had gone no one knew.

All the lights were out at the manor, every one slept profoundly. The poor young woman alone lay concealed in the garden in the throes of a fever. She heard a footstep close by. "Who is there?" she asked fearfully.

"It is I, Nola, your foster-brother."

"Ah, is it you? You are truly welcome, my dear brother," cried Gwennolaïk, rising in rapture.

"Come with me," he whispered, and swinging her on to the crupper of his white horse he plunged madly into the night.

"We fly fast," she cried. "We must have ridden a hundred leagues, I think. Ah, but I am happy with thee! I will never leave thee more."

The owl hooted and night noises came to her ears.

"Ah, but thy horse is swift," said she, "and thine armour, how brilliant it is! How happy I am to have found thee, my foster-brother! But are we near thy manor?"

"We shall arrive there in good time, my sister," he replied.

"Thy heart is cold, thy hair is wet! Ah, how chill are thy hands!"

"Listen, my sister; do you not hear the noise of the gay musicians who shall play at our wedding?" He had not finished speaking when his horse threw itself back on its haunches all at once, trembling and whinnying loudly.

Gwennolaïk looked around, and found herself on an island where a crowd of people were dancing. Lads and lasses, they danced most bravely beneath the green trees heavy with apples, and the music to which they tripped was as that of heaven.

Suddenly the sun rose above the eastern mountains and flooded this strange new world with rich light, and there Gwennolaïk found her mother and her two sisters, and there was nothing in her heart but beauty and joy.

On the following morning, as the sun rose, the young women carried the body of Gwennolaïk and laid it in the tomb of her foster-brother in the White Church.

In this ballad—for the original from which we take the tale is cast in ballad form—we are once more in touch with the Celtic Otherworld. It is a thousand pities that this interesting piece breaks off where it does, thus failing to provide us with a fuller account of that most elusive realm. The short glimpse we do get of it, however, reminds us very much of the descriptions of it we possess in Irish lore. We have also once more the phenomenon of the dead lover who comes to claim the living bride, the midnight gallop, and other circumstances characteristic of ballad literature. There was a tradition in Lower Brittany, however, that no soul might be admitted to the other world which had not first received burial, but here, of course, we must look for Christian influence.

CHAPTER VII: POPULAR LEGENDS OF BRITTANY

"THE legend," says Gomme, in a passage most memorable for students of folk-lore as containing his acute and precise definition of the several classes of tradition, "belongs to an historical personage, locality, or event,"[1] and it is in this general sense that the term is employed in regard to the contents of this chapter, unless where mythic or folklore matter is introduced for the sake of analogy or illustration. There is, however, a broad, popular reading of the term as indicating the fanciful-historical. When we read of the King of Ys, or Arthur, for example, we are not aware whether they ever existed or not, but they are alluded to by tradition as ancient rulers of Brittany and Britain, just as Cymbeline and Cole are spoken of as British monarchs of the distant past. They linger as personal figures in the folk-memory, but they scarcely seem as the personages of folk-tale. Let us say, then, for the purposes of our classification of Breton tradition, that we include in the term 'legend' all tales of great personal figures who are historical or over whom folk-tale has cast an historical *vraisemblance*, remembering at the same time that in the case of personages whose existence is doubtful we may be dealing with a folk-tale disguised or even a distorted myth.

The Dark Story of Gilles de Retz

Of the dark and terrible legends to which Brittany has given birth, one of the most gloomy and romantic is the story of Gilles de Retz, alchemist, magician, and arch-

[1] *Folk-lore as an Historical Science*, p. 129.

criminal. But the story is not altogether legendary, although it has undoubtedly been added to from the great stores of tradition. Gilles is none other than the Bluebeard of the nursery tale, for he appears to have actually worn a beard bluish-black in hue, and it is probable that his personality became mingled with that of the hero of the old Oriental story.

Gilles de Laval, Lord of Retz and Marshal of France, was connected with some of the noblest families in Brittany, those of Montmorency, Rocey, and Craon, and at his father's death, about 1424, he found himself lord of many princely domains, and what, for those times, was almost unlimited power and wealth. He was a handsome youth, lithe and of fascinating address, courageous, and learned as any clerk. A splendid career lay before him, but from the first that distorted idea of the romantic which is typical of certain minds had seized upon him, and despite his rank and position he much preferred the dark courses which finally ended in his disgrace and ruin to the dignities of his seigneury. Gilles took his principal title from the barony of Retz or Rais, south of the Loire, on the marches of Brittany. As a youth he did nothing to justify an evil augury of his future, for he served with zeal and gallantry in the wars of Charles VI against the English and fought under Jeanne Darc at the siege of Orléans. In virtue of these services, and because of his shrewdness and skill in affairs, the King created him Marshal of France. But from that time onward the man who had been the able lieutenant of Jeanne Darc and had fought by her side at Jargeau and Patay began to deteriorate. Some years before he had married Catherine de Thouars, and with her had received a large dowry; but he had expended immense sums in the national cause, and his private life was as extravagant as that of a prince in a fairy tale. At his castle of Champtocé he dwelt in almost royal state; indeed, his train when he went hawking or hunting exceeded in magnificence that of the King himself. His retainers were tricked out in the most gorgeous liveries, and his table was spread with ruinous abundance. Oxen, sheep, and pigs were roasted whole, and viands were provided daily for five hundred persons. He had an insane love of pomp and display, and his private devotions were ministered to by a large body of ecclesiastics. His chapel was a marvel of splendour, and was furnished with gold and silver plate in the most lavish manner. His love of colour and movement made him fond of theatrical displays, and it is even said that the play or mystery of Orléans, dealing with the story of Jeanne Darc, was written with his own hand. He was munificent in his patronage of the arts, and was himself a skilled illuminator and bookbinder. In short, he was obviously one of those persons of abnormal character in whom genius is allied to madness and who can attempt and execute nothing except in a spirit of the wildest excess.

The reduction of his fortune merely served his peculiar and abnormal personality with a new excuse for extravagance. At this time the art of alchemy flourished exceedingly and the works of Nicolas Flamel, the Arabian Geber, and Pierre d'Estaing enjoyed a great vogue. On an evil day it occurred to Gilles to turn alchemist, and thus repair his broken fortunes. In the first quarter of the fifteenth century alchemy stood for scientific achievement, and many persons in our own enlightened age still study its maxims. A society exists to-day the object of which is to further the knowledge of alchemical science. A common misapprehension is current to the effect that the object of the alchemists was the transmutation of the baser metals into gold, but in reality they were divided into two groups, those who sought eagerly the secret of manufacturing the precious metals, and those who dreamed of a higher aim, the transmutation of the gross, terrestrial nature of man into the pure gold of the spirit.

The latter of these aims was beyond the fevered imagination of such a wild and disorderly mind as that of Gilles de Retz. He sent emissaries into Italy, Spain, and Germany to invite adepts in the science to his castle at Champtocé. From among these he selected two men to assist him in his plan—Prelati, an alchemist of Padua, and a certain physician of Poitou, whose name is not recorded. At their instigation he built a magnificent laboratory, and when it was completed commenced to experiment. A year passed, during which the necessities of the 'science' gradually emptied many bags of gold, but none returned to the Marshal's coffers. The alchemists slept soft and fed sumptuously, and were quite content to pursue their labours so long as the Seigneur of Retz had occasion for their services. But as the time passed that august person became greatly impatient, and so irritable did he grow because of the lack of results that at length his assistants, in imminent fear of dismissal, communicated to him a dark and dreadful secret of their art, which, they assured him, would assist them at arriving speedily at the desired end. The nature of the experiment they proposed was so grotesque that its acceptance by Gilles proves that he was either insane or a victim of the superstition of his time. His wretched accomplices told him that the Evil One alone was capable of revealing the secret of the transmutation of the baser metals into gold, and they offered to summon him to their master's aid. They assured Gilles that Satan would require a recompense for his services, and the Marshal retorted that so long as he saved his soul intact he was quite willing to conclude any bargain that the Father of Evil might propose.

It was arranged that the ceremony should take place within a gloomy wood in the neighbourhood. The nameless physician conducted the Lord of Retz to a small clearing in this plantation, where the magic circle was drawn and the usual conjurations made. For half an hour they waited in silence, and then a great trembling fell upon the physician. A deadly pallor overspread his countenance. His knees shook, he muttered wildly, and at last he sank to the ground. Gilles stood by unmoved. The insanity of egotism is of course productive of great if not lofty courage, and he feared neither man nor fiend. Suddenly the alchemist regained consciousness and told his master that the Devil had appeared to him in the shape of a leopard and had growled at him horribly. He ascribed Gilles' lack of supernatural vision to want of faith. He then declared that the Evil One had told him where certain herbs grew in Spain and Africa, the juices of which possessed the power to effect the transmutation, and these he obligingly offered to search for, provided the Lord of Retz furnished the means for his travels. This Gilles gladly did, and of course never beheld the Poitevin knave again.

Days and months passed and the physician did not

return. Gilles grew uneasy. It was imperative that gold should be forthcoming immediately, for not only was he being pressed on every side, but he was unable to support his usual magnificence. In this dilemma he turned to Prelati, his remaining alchemical assistant. This man appears to have believed in his art or he would not have made the terrible suggestion he did, which was that the Lord of Retz should sign with his own blood a compact with the Devil, and should offer up a young child in sacrifice to him. To this proposal the unhappy Gilles consented. On the following night Prelati quitted the castle, and returned shortly afterward with the story that the fiend had appeared to him in the likeness of a young man who desired to be called Barron, and had pointed out to him the resting-place of a hoard of ingots of pure gold, buried under an oak in the neighbouring wood. Certain conditions, however, must be observed before the treasure was dug up, the chief of which was that it must not be searched for until a period of seven times seven weeks had elapsed, or it would turn into slates. With these conditions de Retz would not comply, and, alarmed at his annoyance, the obliging Prelati curtailed the time of waiting to seven times seven days. At the end of that period the alchemist and his dupe repaired to the wood to dig up the treasure. They worked hard for some time, and at length came upon a load of slates, inscribed with magical characters. Prelati pretended great wrath, and upbraided the Evil One for his deceit, in which denunciation he was heartily joined by de Retz. But so credulous was the Seigneur that he allowed himself to be persuaded to afford Satan another trial, which meant, of course, that Prelati led him on from day to day with

THE DEVIL IN THE FORM OF A LEOPARD APPEARS BEFORE THE ALCHEMIST

THE ESCAPE OF KING GRADLON FROM THE FLOODED CITY OF YS

specious promises and ambiguous hints, until he had drained him of nearly all his remaining substance. He was then preparing to decamp with his plunder when a dramatic incident detained him.

For some time a rumour had been circulating in the country-side that numerous children were missing and that they had been spirited away. Popular clamour ran high, and suspicion was directed toward the castle of Champtocé. So circumstantial was the evidence against de Retz that at length the Duke of Brittany ordered both the Seigneur and his accomplice to be arrested. Their trial took place before a commission which de Retz denounced, declaring that he would rather be hanged like a dog, without trial, than plead before its members. But the evidence against him was overwhelming. It was told how the wretched madman, in his insane quest for gold, had sacrificed his innocent victims on the altar of Satan, and how he had gloated over their sufferings. Finally he confessed his enormities and told how nearly a hundred children had been cruelly murdered by him and his relentless accomplice. Both he and Prelati were doomed to be burned alive, but in consideration of his rank he was strangled before being cast into the flames. Before the execution he expressed to Prelati a hope that they would meet in Paradise, and, it is said, met his end very devoutly.

The castle of Champtocé still stands in its beautiful valley, and many romantic legends cluster about its grey old walls. "The hideous, half-burnt body of the monster himself," says Trollope, "circled with flames—pale, indeed, and faint in colour, but more lasting than those the hangman kindled around his mortal form in the meadow under the walls of Nantes—is seen, on bright moonlight nights, standing now on one topmost point of craggy wall, and now on another, and is heard mingling his moan with the sough of the night-wind. Pale, bloodless forms, too, of youthful growth and mien, the restless, unsepulchred ghosts of the unfortunates who perished in these dungeons unassoiled . . . may at similar times be seen flitting backward and forward, in numerous groups, across the space enclosed by the ruined wall, with more than mortal speed, or glancing hurriedly from window to window of the fabric, as still seeking to escape from its hateful confinement."[1]

Comorre the Cursed

As has been said, the story of Gilles de Retz is connected by tradition with that of Bluebeard, but it is probable that this traditional connexion arises simply from the association of two famous tales. The other legend in question is that of Comorre the Cursed, whose story is told in the frescoes which cover the wall of the church of St Nicolas de Bieuzy, dedicated to St Triphyne, in which the tale of Bluebeard is depicted as the story of the saint, who in history was the wife of Comorre. Comorre was a chief who ruled at Carhaix, in Finistère, and his tale, which owes its modern dress to Émile Souvestre, himself a Breton, and author of *Derniers Bretons* and the brilliant sketch *Un Philosophe sous les Toits*. The tale, translated, runs as follows:

Guerech, Count of Vannes, 'the Country of White Corn,' had a daughter, Triphyna, whom he tenderly loved. One day ambassadors arrived from Comorre, a prince of Cornouaille, 'the Country of Black Corn,' demanding

[1] *Western France*, vol. ii.

her in marriage. Now this caused great distress, for Comorre was a giant, and one of the wickedest of men, held in awe by every one for his cruelty. As a boy, when he went out, his mother used to ring a bell to warn people of his approach; and when unsuccessful in the chase he would set his dogs on the peasants to tear them to pieces. But most horrible of all, he had had four wives, who had all died one after the other, it was suspected either by the knife, fire, water, or poison. The Count of Vannes, therefore, dismissed the ambassadors, and advanced to meet Comorre, who was approaching with a powerful army; but St Gildas went into Triphyna's oratory and begged her to save bloodshed and consent to the marriage. He gave her a silver ring, which would warn her of any intended evil by turning as black as a crow's wing at the approach of danger.

The marriage took place with great rejoicings. The first day six thousand guests were invited; on the next day as many poor were fed, the bride and the bridegroom themselves serving at the tables. For some time all went well. Comorre's nature seemed altered; his prisons were empty, his gibbets untenanted. But Triphyna felt no confidence, and every day went to pray at the tombs of his four wives. At this time there was an assembly of the Breton princes at Rennes, which Comorre was obliged to attend. Before his departure he gave Triphyna his keys, desiring her to amuse herself in his absence. After five months he unexpectedly returned, and found her occupied trimming an infant's cap with gold lace. On seeing the cap Comorre turned pale; and when Triphyna joyfully announced to him that soon he would be a father he drew back in a rage and rushed out of the apartment. Triphyna saw that her ring had turned black, which betokened danger, she knew not why. She descended into the chapel to pray. When she rose to depart the hour of midnight struck, and suddenly a sound of movement in the silent chapel chilled her at the heart; shrinking into a recess, she saw the four tombs of Comorre's wives open slowly, and the women all issued forth in their winding-sheets.

Faint with terror, Triphyna tried to escape; but the spectres cried: "Take care, poor lost one! Comorre seeks to kill you."

"Me," said the Countess. "What evil have I done?"

"You have told him that you will soon become a mother; and, through the Spirit of Evil, he knows that his child will slay him. He murdered us when we told him what he has just learned from you."

"What hope, then, of refuge remains for me?" cried Triphyna.

"Go back to your father," answered the phantoms.

"But how escape when Comorre's dog guards the court?"

"Give him this poison which killed me," said the first wife.

"But how can I descend yon high wall?"

"By means of this cord which strangled me," answered the second wife.

"But who will guide me through the dark?"

"The fire that burnt me," replied the third wife.

"And how can I make so long a journey?" returned Triphyna.

"Take this stick which broke my skull," rejoined the fourth spectre.

Armed with the poison, the rope, and the stick, Triphyna set out, silenced the dog, scaled the wall, and, miraculously guided on her way through the darkness by a glowing light, proceeded on her road to Vannes. On awaking next morning Comorre found that his wife had fled, and pursued her on horseback. The poor fugitive, seeing her ring turn black, turned off the road and hid herself till night in the cabin of a shepherd, where there was only an old magpie in a cage at the door, and here her baby was born. Comorre, who had given up the pursuit, was returning home by that road, when he heard the magpie trying to imitate her complaints and calling out "Poor Triphyna!" Guessing that his wife had passed that way, he set his dog on the track. Meanwhile Triphyna felt she could proceed no farther, and lay down on the ground with her baby boy. As she clasped the child in her arms she saw over her head a falcon with a golden collar, which she recognized as her father's. The bird came at her call, and giving it the warning ring of St Gildas she told it to fly with it to her father. The bird obeyed, and flew like lightning to Vannes; but almost at the same instant Comorre arrived. Having parted with her warning ring, Triphyna, who had no notice of his approach, had only time to conceal her babe in the cavity of a tree when Comorre threw himself upon her, and with one blow from his sword severed her head from her body.

When the falcon arrived at Vannes he found the Count at dinner with St Gildas. He let the ring fall into the silver cup of his master, who, recognizing it, exclaimed: "My daughter is in danger! Saddle the horses, and let Saint Gildas accompany us." Following the falcon, they soon reached the spot where Triphyna lay dead. After they had all knelt in prayer, St Gildas said to the corpse: "Arise, take thy head and thy child, and follow us." The dead body obeyed, the bewildered troop followed; but, gallop as fast as they could, the headless body was always in front, carrying the babe in her left hand, and her pale head in the right. In this manner they reached the castle of Comorre.

"Count," called St Gildas before the gates, "I bring back thy wife such as thy wickedness has made her, and thy child such as heaven has given it thee. Wilt thou receive them under thy roof?"

Comorre was silent. The Saint three times repeated the question, but no voice returned an answer. Then St Gildas took the new-born infant from its mother and placed it on the ground. The child marched alone to the edge of the moat, picked up a handful of earth, and, throwing it against the castle, exclaimed: "Let the Trinity execute judgment." At the same instant the towers shook and fell with a crash, the walls yawned open, and the castle sunk, burying Comorre and all his partners in crime. St Gildas then replaced Triphyna's head upon her shoulders, laid his hands upon her, and restored her to life, to the great joy of her father. Such is the history of Triphyna and Comorre.

The Legend of Ys

The legend of the submerged city of Ys, or Is, is perhaps the most romantic and imaginative effort of Breton popular legend. Who has not heard of the submerged bells of Ys, and who has not heard them ring in the echoes of his own imagination?

This picturesque legend[1] tells us that in the early days

[1] See Le Braz, *La Légende de la Mort*, t. i, p. 39, t. ii, pp. 37 ff.; Albert Le Grand, *Vies des Saints de la Bretagne*, p. 63; Villemarqué, *Chants populaires*, pp. 38 ff.

of the Christian epoch the city of Ys, or Ker-is, was ruled by a prince called Gradlon, surnamed Meur, which in Celtic means 'the Great.' Gradlon was a saintly and pious man, and acted as patron to Gwénnolé, founder and first abbé of the first monastery built in Armorica. But, besides being a religious man, Gradlon was a prudent prince, and defended his capital of Ys from the invasions of the sea by constructing an immense basin to receive the overflow of the water at high tide. This basin had a secret gate, of which the King alone possessed the key, and which he opened and closed at the necessary times.

Gradlon, as is so often the case with pious men, had a wayward child, the princess Dahut, who on one occasion while her father was sleeping gave a secret banquet to her lover, in which the pair, excited with wine, committed folly after folly, until at last it occurred to the frivolous girl to open the sluice-gate. Stealing noiselessly into her sleeping father's chamber she detached from his girdle the key he guarded so jealously and opened the gate. The water immediately rushed in and submerged the entire city.

But, as usual, there is more than one version of this interesting legend. The city of Ys, says another account, was a place rich in commerce and the arts, but so given over to luxury as to arouse the ire of St Gwénnolé, who, in the manner of Jeremiah, foretold its ruin. It was situated where now a piece of water, the Étang de Laval, washes the desolate shores of the Bay of Trépassés—though another version of the tale has it that it stood in the vast basin which now forms the Bay of Douarnenez. A strong dike protected it from the ocean, the sluices only admitting sufficient water for the needs of the town. Gradlon constantly bore round his neck a silver key which opened at the same time the vast sluices and the city gates. He lived in great state in a palace of marble, cedar, and gold, and his only grief was the conduct of his daughter Dahut, who, it is said, "had made a crown of her vices and taken for her pages the seven capital sins." But retribution was at hand, and the wicked city met with sudden destruction, for one night Dahut stole the silver key for the purpose of opening the city gates to admit her lover, and in the darkness by mistake opened the sluices. King Gradlon was awakened by St Gwénnolé, who commanded him to flee, as the torrent was reaching the palace. He mounted his horse, and, taking his worthless daughter behind him, set off at a gallop, the incoming flood seething and boiling at his steed's fetlocks. The torrent was about to overtake and submerge him when a voice from behind called out : "Throw the demon thou carriest into the sea, if thou dost not desire to perish." Dahut at that moment fell from the horse's back into the water, and the torrent immediately stopped its course. Gradlon reached Quimper safe and sound, but nothing is said as to his subsequent career.

An ancient ballad on the subject, which, however, bears marks of having been tampered with, states, on the other hand, that Gradlon led his people into extravagances of every kind, and that Dahut received the key from him, the misuse of which precipitated the catastrophe. Dahut, the ballad continues, became a mermaid and haunted the waters which roll over the site of the city where she loved and feasted. "Fisherman," ends the ballad, "have you seen the daughter of the sea combing her golden hair in the midday sun at the fringes of the beach?" "Yes," replies the fisherman, "I have seen the white daughter of the sea, and I have heard her sing, and her songs were plaintive as the sound of the waves."

The legend of Ys, of the town swallowed up by the sea, is common to the several branches of the Celtic race. In Wales the site of the submerged city is in Cardigan Bay, and in Ireland it is Lough Neagh, as Tom Moore says:

> On Lough Neagh's bank as the fisherman strays,
> When the clear, cold eve's declining,
> He sees the round towers of other days
> In the wave beneath him shining.

This legend had its rise in an extraordinary story which was given currency to by Giraldus Cambrensis in his *Topography of Ireland*, to the effect that a certain extremely wicked tribe were punished for their sins by the inundation of their territory.

"Now there was a common proverb," says Gerald, "in the mouths of the tribe, that whenever the well-spring of that country was left uncovered (for out of reverence shown to it, from a barbarous superstition, the spring was kept covered and sealed), it would immediately overflow and inundate the whole province, drowning and destroying the whole population. It happened, however, on some occasion that a young woman, who had come to the spring to draw water, after filling her pitcher, but before she had closed the well, ran in great haste to her little boy, whom she had heard crying at a spot not far from the spring where she had left him. But the voice of the people is the voice of God; and on her way back she met such a flood of water from the spring that it swept off her and the boy, and the inundation was so violent that they both, and the whole tribe, with their cattle, were drowned in an hour in this partial and local deluge. The waters, having covered the whole surface of that fertile district, were converted into a permanent lake. A not improbable confirmation of this occurrence is found in the fact that the fishermen in that lake see distinctly under the water, in calm weather, ecclesiastical towers, which, according to the custom of the country, are slender and lofty, and moreover round; and they frequently point them out to strangers travelling through these parts, who wonder what could have caused such a catastrophe."

In the Welsh version of this fascinating legend it is the bard Gwyddno, of the twelfth century, who tells of the downfall of the submerged city, and two of the strophes which occur in his poem are also found in the Breton poem. The Welsh bard may have received the story from Breton sources, or the converse may be the case.

The legend that Cardigan Bay contains a submerged territory is widely known, and strangely enough seems to be corroborated by the shape of the coast-line, the contour of which suggests the subsidence of a large body of land. Like their brothers of Ireland, the fishermen of Wales assert that at low tide they can see the ruins of ancient edifices far down beneath the clear waters of the bay.[1]

Before the days of the French Revolution there was still to be seen at Quimper, between the two towers of the cathedral, a figure of King Gradlon mounted on his faithful courser, but in the stormy year of 1793 the name of king was in bad odour and the ignorant populace deprived the statue of its head. However, in 1859 it

[1] See MacCulloch, *Religion of the Ancient Celts*, p. 372 and notes.

was restored. Legend attributes the introduction of the vine into Brittany to King Gradlon, and on St Cecilia's Day a regular ritual was gone through in Quimper in connexion with his counterfeit presentment. A company of singers mounted on a platform. While they sang a hymn in praise of King Gradlon, one of the choristers, provided with a flagon of wine, a napkin, and a golden hanap (or cup), mounted on the crupper of the King's horse, poured out a cup of wine, which he offered ceremoniously to the lips of the statue and then drank himself, carefully wiped with his napkin the moustache of the King, placed a branch of laurel in his hand, and then threw down the hanap in the midst of the crowd below, in honour of the first planter of the grape in Brittany. To whoever caught the cup before it fell, and presented it uninjured to the Chapter, was adjudged a prize of two hundred crowns.

There is a distinct savour of myth about all this. Can it be that Gradlon was a Breton Bacchus? There are notices of Celtic goddesses in whose honour Bacchic rites were held, and the place of these was sometimes taken by a corn god. Later the festival in its memorial aspect appears to have been associated with different kings[1] in the various parts of the Celtic world, and it seems likely that Gradlon was such a monarch who had taken the place of a vanished deity. It must be left to Celtic scholars to determine whether the name Gradlon possesses any deific significance hidden in its etymology.

The Clerk of Rohan

Jeanne de Rohan, daughter of Alain, fifth of the name, Viscount of Rohan, married in the year 1236 Matthew,

[1] MacCulloch, *op. cit.*, p. 274.

Seigneur of Beauvau, son of René, Constable of Naples. Breton popular poetry has in many ballads recounted the adventures of Jeanne and her husband, one of which is as follows[1]:

At the age of thirteen Jeanne consented to be married, but she desired that she herself should be allowed to choose her husband. Accordingly the cavaliers and barons of the district were invited to pay their court to her, and she fixed her affections upon the Seigneur of Beauvau, a valiant noble with large possessions in Italy. He was loyal and courteous, and when the pair were wedded their happiness seemed perfect.

At this period the war in Palestine against the infidels was agitating the whole of Europe. The Seigneur of Beauvau desired to join the Crusaders, but his wife was by no means anxious that he should leave his home. But his principle was *noblesse oblige*. "I am of the most noble blood," he said; "therefore it behoves me to be the first to lead the way."

He confided the care of his estates and his affairs in general to his wife's cousin, who was known as the Clerk of Rohan, and begged him to look well after Jeanne and his little son. Then, having bid farewell to them all, he mounted his horse and rode away to the wars.

Jeanne was inconsolable. For days she wandered about the château carrying her baby boy in her arms and sobbing. All the domestic circle seemed disturbed at the Seigneur's departure except the Clerk of Rohan,

[1] Villemarqué avouches that this version was taken down by his mother from the lips of an old peasant woman of the parish of Névez. It bears the stamp of ballad poetry, and as it has parallels in the folk-verse of other countries I see no reason to question its genuineness.

to whom Count Matthew had so trustingly confided the charge of his affairs.

The Seigneur had declared that he would return within a year's time. A year passed, however, and no news of him had been received. Now the Clerk was a perfidious and wicked schemer, and one morning as he and Jeanne were in conversation he hinted that the year within which the Seigneur had promised to return was now gone by and that the war in which he had been engaged had come to an end. He made no secret of his passion for the lady, but she on her part turned upon him angrily, saying: "Is it the fashion nowadays for women to consider themselves widows, knowing well that their husbands are alive? Go to, miserable Clerk, thy heart is full of wickedness. If my husband were here he would break thee in little pieces!"

When the Clerk heard this he went secretly to the kennels, and there he slew the Seigneur's favourite greyhound. Taking some of its blood, he wrote with it a letter to Count Matthew telling him that his wife was most unhappy because of an accident which had occurred; that she had been hunting the deer, and that in the chase his favourite greyhound had died from over-exertion. The Seigneur duly received the letter, and in his reply told the Clerk to comfort the lady, as he was quite able to replace the hound. At the same time he desired that hunting should cease for the present, as the huntsmen seemed unskilful in their conduct of the chase.

The wicked Clerk once more sought the lady.

"Alas!" said he, "you are losing your beauty by weeping night and day."

"I will know how to recover my beauty when my husband returns," she replied coldly.

"Do not cheat yourself," he said. "Surely you can see by this time that he is either dead or has taken another wife. In the East there are many beautiful girls who are far wealthier than you."

"If he has taken another wife," said the lady, "I shall die; and if he be dead I ask for naught but death. Leave me, miserable wretch. Thy tongue is poisoned with deceit."

When the Clerk had sufficiently recovered from this second rebuff, he betook himself to the stables, where the Seigneur's horse, the most beautiful in the country, stood champing in its stall. The wretch, drawing his poignard, thrust it into the noble steed's entrails, and, as he had done in the case of the greyhound, took some of the blood and wrote once more to the Count.

"Another accident has occurred at the château," he said, "but, my dear Seigneur, pray do not trouble yourself on account of it. When your wife was returning from a feast in the night your favourite horse fell and broke two of his legs, and had to be destroyed."

The Seigneur replied that he was grieved to hear of the circumstance, and that in order to avoid further mischances of the sort it would be better that his wife should frequent no more feasts.

A third time the perfidious Clerk sought the lady. On this occasion he threatened her with death if she would not be his, but she replied in the most spirited manner that she loved death a thousand times better than him. At these words he could not contain his rage, and, drawing his dagger, thrust fiercely at her head. But the lady's guardian angel turned the stroke and the weapon struck harmlessly against the wall. She fled from the room, closing the door behind her as she went; whereupon the Clerk rushed downstairs to the nursery where her child was quietly sleeping in its cradle, and, seeing no one beside it, stabbed the slumbering infant to the heart.

Then he wrote to the Seigneur: "Hasten your return, I beg of you, for it is necessary that you should be here to establish order. Your dog and your white courser have perished, but that is not the worst. Your little son, alas! is also dead. The great sow devoured him when your wife was at a ball with the miller for a gallant."

When the Seigneur received this letter he returned at once from the wars, his anger rising higher and higher with every homeward league. When he arrived at the château he struck three times upon the door with his hand, and his summons was answered by the Clerk.

"How now, evil Clerk," shouted the infuriated Count, "did I not leave my wife in your care?" and with these words he thrust his lance into the Clerk's open mouth, so that the point stood out at the nape of his neck. Then, mounting the stairs, he entered his wife's chamber, and without speaking a word stabbed her with his sword.

The ballad then goes on to speak of the burial of the victims of the wicked Clerk. The lady, dressed all in white, was laid in her tomb by the light of the moon and the stars. On her breast lay her little son, on her right the favourite greyhound, and on her left the white courser, and it is said that in her grave she first caresses one and then the other, and the infant, as if jealous, nestles closer to his mother's heart.

The Lady of La Garaye

The château of La Garaye, near Dinan, is rendered famous by the virtues and boundless charity of its Count, Claude Toussaint Marot de La Garaye, and his wife. Their interesting story is told in the charming poem of Mrs Norton, *The Lady of La Garaye*:

> Listen to the tale I tell,
> Grave the story is—not sad;
> And the peasant plodding by
> Greets the place with kindly eye,
> For the inmates that it had.

Count Claude de La Garaye and his wife were young, beautiful, and endowed with friends, riches, and all that could make life bright and happy. They entertained generously and enjoyed the pleasures and amusements of the world. But one day misfortune overtook them, for the Countess was thrown from her horse, and she was left a cripple for life, while all expectations of an heir vanished. Both were inconsolable at their disappointment. One day a monk came to visit them, and tried to comfort them, seeking by his conversation to turn their thoughts from earthly afflictions to heavenly consolation.

"Ah, my father," said the lady, "how happy are you, to love nothing on earth!"

"You are mistaken," answered the monk; "I love all those who are in sorrow or suffering. But I submit myself to the will of the Almighty, and bend myself with resignation to every blow He strikes."

He proceeded to show them that there was still a great deal of happiness in store for them in ministering to the needs of others. Following his counsel, they went to

Paris, where for three years the Count studied medicine and surgery, and his wife became a skilful oculist. On their return to La Garaye they gave up all the amusements of society and devoted themselves to relieving the sufferings of their fellow-creatures. Their house was converted into a hospital for the sick and afflicted, under the ministering care of the Count and his benevolent wife:

> Her home is made their home; her wealth their dole;
> Her busy courtyard hears no more the roll
> Of gilded vehicles, or pawing steeds,
> But feeble steps of those whose bitter needs
> Are their sole passport. Through that gateway press
> All varying forms of sickness and distress,
> And many a poor, worn face that hath not smiled
> For years, and many a feeble crippled child,
> Blesses the tall white portal where they stand,
> And the dear Lady of the liberal hand.

Nor was their philanthropy confined to their own province. In 1729 they offered themselves to M. de Belsunce—"Marseilles' good bishop"—to assist him during the visitation of the plague. The fame of their virtues reached even the French Court, and Louis XV sent Count de La Garaye the Order of St Lazarus, with a donation of 50,000 livres and a promise of 25,000 more. They both died at an advanced age, within two years of each other, and were buried among their poor at Taden. Their marble mausoleum in the church was destroyed during the French Revolution. The Count left a large sum to be distributed among the prisoners, principally English, pent up in the crowded gaols of Rennes and Dinan. He had attended the English prisoners at Dinan during a contagious fever called the 'peste blanche,' and in acknowledgment of his humanity Queen Caroline sent him two dogs with silver collars round their necks, and an English nobleman made him a present of six more.

The ruined château is approached by an ivy-covered gateway, through an avenue of beeches. As Mrs Norton renders it:

> And like a mourner's mantle, with sad grace,
> Waves the dark ivy, hiding half the door
> And threshold, where the weary traveller's foot
> Shall never find a courteous welcome more.

The ruin is fast falling to pieces. The principal part remaining is an octagonal turret of three stories, with elegant Renaissance decoration round the windows.

The Falcon

An interesting and picturesque ballad sung in the Black Mountains is that of *The Falcon.* Geoffrey, first Duke of Brittany, was departing for Rome in the year 1008, leaving the government of the country in the hands of his wife Ethwije, sister of Richard of Normandy. As he was about to set out on his pilgrimage the falcon which he carried on his wrist after the manner of the nobles of the period, swooped down on and killed the hen of a poor peasant woman. The woman in a rage seized a large stone and cast it at the bird with such violence that it slew not only the falcon but the Duke himself. The death of the Duke was followed by a most desperate insurrection among the people. History does not enlighten us as to the cause of this rising, but tradition attributes it to the invasion of Brittany by the Normans (whom the widow of Geoffrey at once brought into the country on the demise of her husband) and the

A PEASANT INSURRECTION

MORVAN RETURNS TO HIS RUINED HOME

exactions which were wrung from the peasants by these haughty aliens.

The ballad, which was used as a war-song by the Bretons at a later day, begins in true ballad style: "The falcon has strangled the fowl, the peasant woman has slain the Count who oppressed the people, the poor people, like a brute-beast."

The hate of the stranger so characteristic of the old Bretons then flashes forth. "The country has been polluted by the foreigner, by the men of the Gallic land, and because of the death of a hen and a falcon Brittany is on fire, blood flows, and there is great dole among the people."

On the summit of the Black Mountain thirty stout peasants had gathered to celebrate the ancient feast of the good St John. Among them was Kado the Striver, who stood there gravely leaning on his iron pitchfork. For a while he looked upon his comrades; then he opened his lips:

"What say you, fellow-peasants? Do you intend to pay this tax? As for me, I shall certainly not pay it. I had much rather be hanged. Nevermore shall I pay this unjust tax. My sons go naked because of it, my flocks grow less and less. No more shall I pay. I swear it by the red brands of this fire, by Saint Kado my patron, and by Saint John."

"My fortunes are broken, I am completely ruined," growled one of his companions. "Before the year is out I shall be compelled to beg my bread."

Then all rose at once as if by a common impulse.

"None of us will pay this tax! We swear it by the Sun and by the Moon, and by the great sea which encircles this land of Brittany!"

Kado, stepping out from the circle, seized a firebrand, and holding it aloft cried: "Let us march, comrades, and strike a blow for freedom!"

The enthusiasm of his companions burst out afresh. Falling into loose ranks they followed him. His wife marched by his side in the first rank, carrying a reaping-hook on her shoulder and singing as she marched.

"Quickly, quickly, my children! We go to strike a blow for liberty! Have I brought thirty sons into the world to beg their bread, to carry firewood or to break stones, or bear burdens like beasts? Are they to till the green land and the grey land with bare feet while the rich feed their horses, their hunting-dogs, and their falcons better than they are fed? No! It is to slay the oppressors that I have borne so many sons!"

Quickly they descended the mountains, gathering numbers as they went. Now they were three thousand strong, five thousand strong, and when they arrived at Langoad nine thousand strong. When they came to Guérande they were thirty thousand strong. The houses of those who had ground them down were wrapped in flames, fiercely ends the old ballad, "and the bones of those who had oppressed them cracked, like those of the damned in Tartarus."

History tells us nothing concerning Kado the Striver, but it is most unlikely that he is a mere figment of popular imagination. What history does record, however, is that the wicked Duchess and her host of mercenary Normans were forced to flee, and that her place was taken by a more just and righteous ruler.

The Marquis of Guérande

Breton tradition speaks of a wild young nobleman, Louis-François de Guérande, Seigneur of Locmaria, who flourished in the early part of the seventeenth century. He was wealthy, and lived a life of reckless abandon; indeed, he was the terror of the parish and the despair of his pious mother, who, whenever he sallied forth upon adventure bent, rang the bell of the château, to give the alarm to the surrounding peasantry. The ballad which tells of the infamous deeds of this titled ruffian, and which was composed by one Tugdual Salaün, a peasant of Plouber,[1] opens upon a scene of touching domestic happiness. The Clerk of Garlon was on a visit to the family of his betrothed.

"Tell me, good mother," he asked, "where is Annaïk? I am anxious that she should come with me to dance on the green."

"She is upstairs asleep, my son. Take care," added the old woman roguishly, "that you do not waken her."

The Clerk of Garlon ran lightly up the staircase and knocked at Annaïk's door.

"Come, Annaïk," he cried; "why are you asleep when all the others go to dance upon the village green?"

"I do not wish to go to the dance, for I fear the Marquis of Guérande," replied the girl.

The Clerk of Garlon laughed. "The Marquis of Guérande cannot harm you so long as I am with you," he said lightly. "Come, Annaïk; were there a hundred such as he I should protect you from them."

[1] See "Maro Markiz Gwerrand," in the *Bulletin de la Société Académique de Brest*, 1865.

Reassured by her lover's brave words, the girl rose and put on her dress of white delaine. They were a joyous and beautiful pair. The Clerk was gaily dressed, with a peacock's feather in his hat and a chain on his breast, while his betrothed wore a velvet corsage embroidered with silver.

On that evening the Marquis of Guérande leaped on his great red steed and sallied forth from his château. Galloping along the road, he overtook the Clerk of Garlon and his betrothed on their way to the dance.

"Ha!" he cried, "you go to the dance, I see. It is customary to wrestle there, is it not?"

"It is, Seigneur," replied the Clerk, doffing his hat.

"Then throw off your doublet and let us try a fall or two," said Guérande, with a wicked look at Annaïk which was not lost upon her lover.

"Saving your grace, I may not wrestle with you," said the Clerk, "for you are a gentleman and I am nobody. You are the son of a lord and I am the son of a peasant."

"Ha! what! The son of a peasant, say you, and you take your choice of the pretty girls of the village?"

"Seigneur, pardon me. I did not choose this maiden; God gave her to me."

During this parley Annaïk stood by, trembling violently. She had heard of the Marquis of Guérande, and was only too well aware of the evil and reckless character he bore. The Clerk tried to calm her fears by whispered words and pressures of the hand, but the wicked Marquis, observing the state of terror she was in, exulted in the alarm he was causing her.

"Well, fellow," said he, "since you cannot wrestle with me perhaps you will try a bout of sword-play."

At these words Annaïk's rosy cheeks became deathly white; but the Clerk of Garlon spoke up like a man.

"My lord," he said, "I do not wear a sword. The club is my only weapon. Should you use your sword against me it would but stain it."

The wicked Marquis uttered a fiendish laugh. "If I stain my sword, by the Saints, I shall wash it in your blood," he cried, and as he spoke he passed his rapier through the defenceless Clerk's body.

At the sight of her slain lover the gentle heart of Annaïk broke, and a great madness came upon her. Like a tigress she leapt upon the Marquis and tore his sword from his hand. Without his rapier he was as a child in the grasp of the powerful Breton peasant woman. Exerting all her strength, in a frenzy of grief she dragged the wretch to the green where the dance was in progress, haling him round and round it until exhausted. At last she dropped his senseless body on the green turf and hastened homeward.

And once again we encounter the haunting refrain: "My good mother, if you love me make my bed, for I am sick unto death."

"Why, daughter, you have danced too much; it is that which has made you sick."

"I have not danced at all, mother; but the wicked Marquis has slain my poor Clerk. Say to the sexton who buries him: 'Do not throw in much earth, for in a little while you will have to place my daughter beside him in this grave.' Since we may not share the same marriage-bed we shall at least sleep in the same tomb, and if we have not been married in this world we shall at least be joined in heaven."

The reader will be relieved to learn that the hero of

this ballad, the Clerk of Garlon, was not killed after all, and that for once fact is enabled to step in to correct the sadness of fiction ; for, when one comes to think of it, there are few sadder things in the world than the genuine folk-ballad, which, although at the time it may arouse æsthetic emotions, may yet afterward give rise to haunting pain. We are glad to be able to chronicle, then, that the worthy Clerk did not die of his wound as stated by Tugdual Salaün of the parish of Plouber, author of the ballad, and that the wicked Marquis escaped the halter, which, according to Breton custom, he would not otherwise have done had the Clerk died. His good mother took upon herself the burden of an annual pension to the Clerk's aged parents, and adopted the second child of Annaïk, who had duly married her sweetheart, and this little one she educated, furthering its interests in every possible manner. As for the Marquis, he actually settled down, and one cannot help feeling chagrined that such a promising rogue should have turned talents so eminently suitable for the manufacture of legendary material into more humdrum courses. Conscious of the gravity of his early misdemeanours, he founded a hospital for the poor of the parish, and each evening in one of the windows of this place the peasants could see a light which burned steadily far into the night. If any asked the reason for this illumination he was told : "It is the Marquis of Guérande, who lies awake praying God to pardon his youth."

The Châteaux of Brittany

The châteaux of Brittany may truly be called the historical and legendary shrines of the province, for within their halls, keeps, and donjons Breton tradition and history were made. It is doubtful, indeed, if the castellated mansions of any other country, save, perhaps, those of the Rhine, harbour so many legends, arising either from the actual historical happenings connected with them or from those more picturesque yet terrible associations which they are popularly supposed to have with the powers of evil. The general appearance of such a building as the Breton château admirably lends itself to sombre tradition. The massy walls seem thick enough to retain all secrets, and the cry for vengeance for blood spilt within them cannot pass to the outer world through the narrow *meurtrières* or arrow-slits of the *avant-corps.* The broad yet lofty towers which flank the front rise into a *toiture* or *coiffe* like an enchanter's conical cap. The *lucarnes*, or attic casements, are guarded on either side by gargoyles grim of aspect, or perhaps by griffins holding the shield-borne arms of dead and gone seigneurs. Seek where you will, among the wizard-houses of old Prague, the witch-dens of ancient Edinburgh, the bat-haunted castles of Drachenfels or Rheinstein, you will come at nothing built of man more informed with the soul of the Middle Ages, more drenched with their peculiar savour of mystery, than these stark keeps whose crests and *girouettes* rise above encircling woods or frown upon mirroring rivers over the length and breadth of the Breton land.

La Roche-Jagu

One of the most typical of the châteaux of Brittany is that of La Roche-Jagu, at one time the guardian of the mouth of the river Trieux. It is built on the top of a hill which overhangs the Trieux, and from one of its battlemented galleries a splendid view of the windings of the river can be obtained. The wall on this side of the fortress is so thick as to allow of a chapel being hewn out of its solidity. A most distinctive architectural note is struck by the fourteen wonderful chimney-shafts of cut stone ornamented with iron spikes.

Tonquédec

Some miles farther down the river, but on its opposite side, is the imposing castle of Tonquédec, perhaps the finest remnant of the medieval military architecture of Brittany. It has always remained in the family of the Viscounts of Coêtman, who ranked among the foremost of the Breton nobility, though one of them espoused the cause of the Constable Clisson against Duke John IV, and had the anguish of seeing his ancestral fortress razed to the ground. Under Henry IV, however, the castle was restored, only to be again demolished by order of Cardinal Richelieu, who strongly and forcibly disapproved of such powerful fortalices.

It had an outer enclosure, and had to be entered by a drawbridge, and it was strengthened in every way conceivable to the military art of the times. It was surrounded by dwellings for the convenience of the seigneur's retainers, a fine *salle d'armes* still remaining. To the keep, four stories high, a flying bridge led, in order to facilitate the withdrawal of the garrison in case of siege. Behind walls ten feet thick, so long as food and ammunition lasted, the inmates could hold the enemy in scorn.

Clisson

The château of Clisson, once the property of the great Constable Oliver de Clisson, whom the Viscount of

Coëtman and the Bretons of Penthièvre had championed, is now only a grand old ruin, a touching monument of the architectural splendours of former days. By moonlight it makes a scene not easily forgotten, gaunt and still and ruggedly imposing, the silent reminder of events and people tales of whom will not readily die, the treasurer of secrets it will probably never yield. Its antithesis is the castle of Nantes, with the stamp of the Renaissance upon its delicately sculptured balconies and window-frames. It is now an arsenal, a fact which robs it of some of the romantic interest of Clisson, or, indeed, of ruins in general, yet within its walls are the prison chambers in which Gilles de Laval, the ambitious Finance Minister Fouquet, the Cardinal de Retz, and the Duchess of Berry once languished. For many years it served as one of the political prisons of France, though it is also associated with brighter and happier times; for here, on pleasure bent, lingered many of the Kings of France from Louis XI onward, and here in 1675 Madame de Sévigné sojourned, a circumstance which casts about it a literary as well as a romantic glamour. The great well in the courtyard, with its ornamental railing of wrought iron, is quite equal to the famous well of Quentin Matsys at Antwerp.

Josselin

The castle of Josselin, also associated with the history of the great Constable Clisson and his allies, as well as with the notorious League whose followers wrought such intolerable misery in Brittany, is built on a rocky foundation near the river Oust. With its imposing front and conically roofed towers it is one of the best examples of a twelfth-century fortress-château. Very different in tone is the architecture of the interior court, being that of the period when the lighter traceries and more imaginative lines of the Renaissance were in favour. The window-openings of the two first stories are beautiful enough to rival those of Chambord and equal those of Blois. Above the windows an open gallery runs, and in the space between each the device of the Rohans is carved, with their motto, *A Plus*, this celebrated family having built this part of the château. About the year 1400 Clisson added a keep, walls, and parapets, but in 1629, when the fortress was no longer a stronghold of the League, these were permitted to fall into ruin. Through the courtesy of the family now in residence this wonderfully preserved castle may be visited, a circumstance for which the tourist in Brittany should indeed be grateful. Interest within these massy walls clings around the well, with its ornamental railings, the noble and lofty hall, the library, with its magnificent chimney-piece, repeating again, in stone, the Rohan motto, *A Plus*, and the equestrian statue of Clisson, by Frémiet, in the dining-room.

Hennebont and Largoet

Of the old château of Hennebont, where John of Montfort breathed his last after escaping from the Louvre of his day, only a heap of stones remains. The old fortress of Largoet is in much the same condition, nothing of the ancient structure having been conserved save the famous Tour d'Elven, considered to be the most beautiful castle keep in all Brittany, which has also a literary distinction as being the scene of some of the most touching episodes in Octave Feuillet's *Roman d'un jeune Homme pauvre*.

Châteaubriant

At Châteaubriant, which owes its name to the compounding of the word 'château' with that of 'Briant,' the family style of its original lord, the old feudal fortress is now a ruin, but the castle, built by Jean de Laval, Governor of Brittany under Francis I, is in good repair. An inscription giving the date of the completion of the new château as 1538 is above the portal of the colonnade. There is a gruesome legend associated with the old château, in which for some time dwelt the unfortunate Françoise de Foix, Countess of Châteaubriant and beloved of Francis I. Tiring or becoming suspicious of her royal lover, she decided to return to her husband, the old Count of Laval. The reunion, however, was not productive of happiness, owing to the fever of jealousy in which her elderly husband lived because of the love affair with the King. This jealousy eventually flared into mania when he heard that she had actually visited her former lover in prison after he had been captured at Pavia. Instantly he "shut his young wife up in a darkened and padded cell, and finally had her cut into pieces by two surgeons," so the story goes. Terrified at what he had done and of the consequences which were sure to follow when the King heard of his savagery, the Count fled the country immediately afterward.

The château of Brodineuf (dating from the twelfth century) and that of Caradeuc are in good repair, but the latter is ancient only in parts. It shelters two Murillos within its walls. The picturesque château of Combourg was in early times a feudal fortress, and in it René Châteaubriand's infancy was passed. This place may be visited by interested sightseers, and there they may view the writing-table of the author of *Le Génie du Christianisme*, and, in the bedroom he occupied at Combourg, the bed on which he died in Paris. The château of Vitré is also in a state of preservation, and is considered one of the best specimens of military architecture in the province. Comparatively near is the château of Rochers, once the home of Mme de Sévigné, and in consequence one of the famous sights of the country. The many letters she dated from this castle paint a vivid and detailed picture of social life in the seventeenth century, and fortunately the atmosphere of the time has been happily retained in the building itself.

Another twelfth-century structure is that of the château of Rustefan, near Quimperlé. It was built by Stephen, Count of Penthièvre, and belonged in the next century to Blanche of Castile, the mother of St Louis. The ruins now in existence are those of the château built in the fifteenth century, and its cylindrical tower, pinnacled doorway, and the stone mullions of the windows still remain fairly intact. The château of Kerjolet, in Concarneau, is one which has been saved from decay, restored as it was by Countess Chaveau-Narishkine and presented by her to the department. It contains a museum in which are specimens of all the costumes and *coiffes* of Lower Brittany, and antiquities of prehistoric and medieval times, which all students of Breton and Celtic lore should see.

Palaces of the Past

The château of Tourlaville is situated among very beautiful surroundings, and is built in the classic style of the Renaissance, with an angular tower. On chimney-piece and fireplace throughout the castle there are numerous sentimental devices in which Cupids and flaming hearts and torches figure largely, with the occasional accompaniment of verses and mottoes of an equally amatory nature. These are all seventeenth-century examples and may be taken as expressions of the time. In a boudoir called the Blue Chamber, because of the colour of its draperies and decorations, many coats-of-arms are emblazoned; but all the greatness to which these testify has become a thing of the past, for the château has now been turned into a farmhouse.

The château of Dinan may also be classed among the palaces of the past, for now, despite the fact that it was built by the Dukes of Brittany, it has become a prison. From the tourist as well as the romantic point of view this is somewhat of a tragedy. The Tower of Coëtquen, one of the ancient towers of the city wall, is practically part of the castle, and the keep, or Queen Anne's Tower, is the most distinctive feature remaining. This keep is of four stories, and is over a hundred feet high, the last story being reached by a spiral staircase. What was once the oratory of the Duchess Anne is now the guard-room. There are still several dungeons whose original gruesomeness has been left untouched, and whose use in bygone days can well be imagined.

Suscino

The château of Suscino is one of the chief sights of the neighbourhood of Vannes, because it is the ruin of what was once a marvellous structure of the thirteenth century, and follows the finest Gothic traditions of the time. All the roofing of the building has quite disappeared, but its battlemented towers and walls remain to give a good idea of the architectural perfection that must have belonged to it. At one time it fell into the hands of Charles of Blois, only to be retaken by his rival, Montfort, in 1364, and in 1373 it was occupied by an English garrison. Eventually it was bestowed upon John of Châlons, Prince of Orange, by Anne of Brittany, but in time Francis I relieved him of it in order to present it to Françoise de Foix, the celebrated Lady of Châteaubriant. The irregular pentagon formed by the château is possibly somewhat modified from the original plan of 1320, and of the seven towers which flanked its gates and walls in the beginning six have weathered the storms of the times through which they have passed. Its orchid-shaped machicolations have also survived, and even to-day they are noticeably beautiful. The new tower is a fine cylindrical keep, dating from the fourteenth century, and over the entrance this legend still remains:

Ici Est Né
Le Duc Arthur III
le 24 Août, 1393.

We have already dealt with many of the stories connected with the ancient castles of Brittany, and these will be found in nearly every chapter of this book, so varied are they. But no tale, however vivid, can hope to capture and retain all the wonder and mystery of these grand old strongholds, which must be seen in order to leave upon the imagination and memory the full impress of their weird and extraordinary fascination.

CHAPTER VIII: HERO-TALES OF BRITTANY

SOON after the Vicomte Hersart de la Villemarqué published his *Barzaz-Breiz*, a collection of popular ballads from the Breton, critics who possessed a knowledge of the language and were acquainted with its literature exposed the true nature of the work, acting, indeed, as did British critics when Macpherson published his fragments of Ossian. Villemarqué was, in fact, a Breton Macpherson. He would hear a Breton ballad sung or recited, and would then either enlarge upon it and torture it out of all resemblance to its original shape, or he would instigate a literary friend to do so. We must remember that such a proceeding was fashionable at the time, as no less a personage than Sir Walter Scott had led the way, and he had been preceded by Burns in the practice. But whereas Burns made no secret of what he did and greatly enhanced the poetical value of the songs and ballads he altered, Scott and his friends, Kirkpatrick Sharpe, Leyden, and others, indulged in what they described as the "mystification" of their acquaintances by these semi-forgeries. Like theirs, Villemarqué's work had usually an historical or legendary basis, but it is impossible to say how much of it is original matter of folk-song and how much his own invention, unless we compare his versions with those furnished by M. Luzel in his *Guerziou Breiz-Izel* (1868), which, however, only contains a few of the originals of the tales given in the *Barzaz-Breiz*, and those not the most interesting.

I have cast the following tales into narrative form from the ballads published in the *Barzaz-Breiz*, where they obviously appear as traditional tales in a polished, modern dress.[1] They may be regarded, largely, as efforts of the modern imagination regarding the Breton past. In any case the author of a book on Breton romances would not be justified in omitting all mention of Villemarqué and refraining from affording the reader a specimen of his work, any more than he would be in founding solely upon the labours of the Vicomte.

Lez-Breiz, the Prop of Brittany

Morvan, chief of Léon, so celebrated in the history of the ninth century as one of the upholders of Breton independence, and known to tradition as 'the Prop of Brittany,' is the subject of a remarkable series of ballads or hero-tales in the *Barzaz-Breiz* which together constitute what is almost an epic. These tell of his life, death, adventures, travels, and the marvellous feats of derring-do he accomplished. In some measure he is to Breton legend what Arthur is to British or Holger to that of Denmark. That he is familiar to Breton tradition there can be no question, and whether Villemarqué himself wove the following adventures around him or not they are certainly typical of the age in which the hero flourished.

Morvan's First Adventure

One day the child Morvan was sitting at the edge of the forest when a cavalier issued from its depths

[1] For the criticism on Villemarqué's work see H. Gaidoz and P. Sébillot, "Bibliographie des Traditions et de la Littérature populaire de la Bretagne" (in the *Revue Celtique*, t. v, pp. 277 ff.). The title *Barzaz-Breiz* means "The Breton Bards," the author being under the delusion that the early forms of the ballads he collected and altered had been composed by the ancient bards of Brittany.

armed at all points and riding a great charger. The boy, excited by his martial appearance, ran from him in terror, calling out that here indeed was St Michael; but the cavalier rode so swiftly that he soon came up with the lad, who devoutly threw himself on his knees and made the sign of the Cross, calling out:

"Seigneur Saint Michael, in the name of God I pray thee do me no harm!"

The knight laughed loudly. "Why, lad," he said, "I am no more Saint Michael than I am a thief, but merely a belted knight, such as one may meet with by the score in this land of chivalry."

"I have never seen a knight," replied Morvan; "and what may that be which you carry?"

"That is called a lance, my boy."

"And what are these that you wear on your head and breast?"

"The one is a casque and the other a breast-plate. They are intended to protect me from the stroke of sword and spear. But tell me, lad, have you seen any one pass this way?"

"Yes, Seigneur, a man went by this very road not half an hour agone."

"Thank you, boy," replied the knight. "If you are asked who spoke to you, say the Count of Quimper," and with these words he spurred his horse and set off down the road in the direction which the little Morvan had indicated.

Morvan returned to his mother, who had been sitting some distance away, and began to tell her of his meeting. He was so full of the gallantry of the knight he had met, his grace and martial bearing, that the good dame could not stem the torrent of words which flowed from him.

"Oh, mother," he babbled on, "you never saw anyone so splendid as him whom I have seen to-day, a man more beautiful than the Lord Michael the Archangel, whose image is in our church."

His mother smiled and patted him fondly on the cheek.

"Come, my son," she said, "there is no man so beautiful as the Archangel Michael."

But little Morvan shook his head.

"Saving your grace, there are, my mother," he said gravely. "There are many men more splendid than Saint Michael, and they are called knights. How I wish that I might grow up and become a knight too!"

At these words the poor lady, who had lost her husband in battle and who dreaded that her only son might be taken from her, was seized with such dismay that she sank to the ground unconscious. The little Morvan, without turning his head, entered the stables and led out a fresh horse. Jumping lightly on the steed's back, he turned its head in the direction in which the splendid cavalier had gone and rode hastily after him.

The Return of Morvan

Ten years passed—years full of martial achievement and adventure for young Morvan. Then a desire to return to the ancestral mansion seized upon the youth, and he made his way homeward. But great was his dismay when he entered the courtyard of the manor and looked about him, for the blackberry bushes and the nettles were growing round the threshold of the house and the walls were half ruined and covered with ivy. As he was about to enter he observed a poor old blind woman standing in the entrance.

"Pardon me, dame, but perhaps you can give me hospitality for the night," he said.

"Alas! sir, we have but little," she replied. "This house has been allowed to go to ruin since its son and heir quitted it."

As she ceased speaking a young damsel descended the broken stone steps, and after regarding Morvan for a moment burst into tears.

"How now, maiden," said Morvan, "wherefore do you weep?"

"Alas, Seigneur," replied the maiden, "I have a brother who left us ten years ago to lead the life of a warrior, and every time that I see a youth about his age I feel myself compelled to weep."

"Tell me, my child," said Morvan, "have you no other brother?"

"None in the world, Sir Knight."

"And your mother, what of her?"

"Alas! sir, she too is gone. There is no one but myself and my old nurse in the house. My poor mother died of grief when my brother rode off to become a knight."

On hearing these words Morvan was deeply affected.

"Alas!" he cried, "wretch that I am, I have slain her who gave me birth!"

When he spoke thus the damsel turned deadly pale.

"In the name of heaven, sir, who are you?" she cried. "How are you named?"

"I am Morvan, son of Conan, and Lez-Breiz is my surname, my sister."

The young girl stared for a moment, sighed, and then

fell into his arms; but soon she opened her eyes and praised God that she had found her long-lost brother.

The King's Cavalier

But Lez-Breiz could not remain long at home. The tented field was his fireside, the battle his sport. Adventure followed adventure in his full and stirring life. One day he said to his young squire:

"Arouse you, my squire, and furnish my sword, my casque, and my shield, that I may redden them in the blood of the Franks, for with the help of God and this right arm I shall carry slaughter into their ranks this day."

"Tell me, my lord," asked the squire, "shall I not fight along with you to-day?"

Morvan smiled at the lad's eagerness, perhaps because he remembered his own on the day he met the Count of Quimper, then a grave shadow crossed his face.

"Think of your mother, lad," said he. "What if you never return to her? Think of her grief should you die this day."

"Ah, Seigneur," entreated the stripling, "if you love me, grant my prayer; let me fight along with you."

When Morvan rode out to battle an hour later his squire rode beside him, knee to knee. Passing near the church of St Anne of Armor they entered.

"O Saint Anne, most holy dame," prayed Morvan, "I am not yet twenty years old and I have been in twenty battles. All those I have gained by your aid, and if I return again to this land I shall make you a rich gift. I shall give you enough candles to go three times round the walls of your church, and thrice round your churchyard—

aye, thrice round your lands, when I come home again; and further I shall give you a banner of white satin with an ivory staff. Also shall I give you seven silver bells which will ring gaily night and day above your head. And three times on my knees will I draw water for your use."

The enemy saw Morvan coming from afar. He was mounted on a small white ass with a halter of hemp, to signify his contempt for them. Lorgnez, his chief foe, came against him with a troop of warriors, while Morvan had only his little squire behind him. The foemen came on, ten by ten, until they reached the Wood of Chestnuts. For a moment the little squire was dismayed, but a word from his master rallied him, and, drawing his sword, he spurred forward. Soon they came front to front with Lorgnez and hailed him in knightly fashion.

"Ho! Seigneur Lorgnez, good day to you."

"Good morrow, Seigneur Morvan. Will you engage in single combat?"

"No; I despise your offer. Go back to your King and tell him that I mock him; and as for yourself, I laugh at you and those with you. Return to Paris, stay among your women, take off your mail and put on the silken armour of fops."

Lorgnez's face flamed with anger.

"By heaven!" he cried, "the lowest varlet in my company shall hew your casque from your head for this!"

At these words Morvan drew his great sword.

. . . . .

The old hermit of the wood heard some one knocking on the door of his cell. He opened it quickly and saw the young squire standing before him. He started back at the sight of the youth's blood-stained armour and death-pale countenance.

"Ha, my son," he cried, "you are sorely hurt. Come and wash your wounds at the fountain and repose for a little."

"I may not rest here, good father," replied the squire, shaking his head. "I have come to find water to take to my young master, who has fallen in the fight. Thirty warriors lie slain by his hand. Of these the Chevalier Lorgnez was the first."

"Brave youth!" said the hermit. "Alas that he has fallen!"

"Do not grieve, father. It is true that he has fallen, but it is only from fatigue. He is unwounded and will soon recover himself."

When he was recovered Morvan betook him to the chapel of St Anne and rendered the gifts he had promised her.

"Praise be to Saint Anne," cried he, "for she it is who has gained this victory."

The King's Blackamoor

One day the King of the Franks was sitting among his courtiers.

"Would that some one would rid me of this pestilent Morvan, who constantly afflicts the Frankish land and slays my doughtiest warriors," he said, on hearing of a fresh exploit on the part of the Breton chief.

Then the King's blackamoor, who heard these words, arose and stood before his master. He was tall and great of thew and sinew—a giant among men, towering head and shoulders even above the tall Frankish warriors.

"Allow me to fulfil your wishes, sire," he said. "Sir Morvan has sent me his glove, and if to-morrow I do not bring you his head I will willingly part with my own."

On the next morning Morvan's squire came to his master trembling violently.

"Seigneur," he said, with ashy countenance, "the King's Moor is here and bids you defiance."

Morvan rose and took his sword.

"Alas! my dear master," said the squire, "take heed what you do, I pray you, for I assure you that this Moor is nothing but a demon who practises the most horrible enchantments."

Morvan laughed. "Well, we shall see whether this demon can withstand cold steel or not," he said. "Go and saddle my black horse."

"Saving your grace," said the page, "if you will hearken to my words you will not fight on the black charger. He has been bewitched. Moreover, you will notice that when you enter the lists to fight the Moor he will cast his mantle to the ground. But do not follow his example, for should your mantle fall beneath his the strength of the black giant will be doubled. When the Moor advances to the attack make the sign of the Cross with the shaft of your lance, and when he rushes upon you in his battle-fury receive him with the steel. If you do this you may be sure that your lance will not break."

The heroes met within the lists. The King of France and his nobles had followed the giant Moor in order to witness the combat, and when all had been seated the trumpets sounded and the two champions rushed together with the utmost fury. They circled round one another like eagles seeking an opening to strike. Now one struck, then the other, and the blood flowed down their bright armour. The Frankish King in high excitement called out:

'Ho! black crow of the sea, pierce me now this merle." At these words the giant assailed Morvan most furiously, as a great tempest assails a ship. The lances crossed, but that of the Moor broke like matchwood. Both leaped to earth, sword in hand, and rushed at each other like lions. Many lusty strokes were given and taken, and from their armour flew sparks like those from a smith's anvil. Then the Moor, grasping his sword with both hands, made ready to strike a mighty blow, when swift and trenchantly Morvan thrust his blade far into the arm-pit and the heart and the giant tumbled to the earth like a falling tree. Morvan placed his foot on the dead man's breast, withdrew his sword, and cut off the Moor's head. Then, attaching the bleeding trophy to the pommel of his saddle, he rode home with it and affixed it to the gate of his castle. All men praised him for his doughty deed, but he gave the grace of his victory entirely to St Anne, and declared that he would build a house of prayer in her honour on the heights between Léguer and the Guindy.

Morvan Fights the King

One day Morvan sallied forth to encounter the King of the Franks himself. The King brought no fewer than five thousand mounted men-at-arms. As this host was about to set out, a great clap of thunder resounded in the vault of heaven, and the King's nobles perforce regarded it as a bad omen.

"For heaven's sake, sire, go not hence," said one of them, "since the day has begun with such an evil token."

"Impossible," was the royal reply. "I have given the order ; we must march."

That morning, on the other hand, the sister of Morvan said to her brother: "My dear brother, if you love me seek not this combat, for if you do you will certainly go to your death, and what will become of me afterward? I see on the shore the white sea-horse, the symbol of Brittany. A monstrous serpent entwines him, seizing him round the hind legs and the body with his enormous coils. The sea-steed turns his head to seize the reptile. The combat is unequal. You are alone; the Franks are legion!"

But Morvan was already beyond ear-shot.

. . . . .

As the hermit of the wood of Helléan[1] slept three knocks sounded on his door.

"Good hermit," said some one, "open the door. I seek an asylum and help from you."

The wind blew coldly from the country of the Franks. It was the hour when savage beasts wander here and there in search of their prey. The hermit did not rise with alacrity.

"Who are you who knock at my door at this hour of night demanding an entrance?" he asked sulkily; "and by what sign shall I know whether you are a true man or otherwise?"

"Priest, I am well known in this land. I am Morvan Lez-Breiz, the Hatchet of Brittany."

"I will not open my door to you," said the hermit hastily.

[1] Once a part of the forest of Broceliande. It has now disappeared.

"You are a rebel; you are the enemy of the good King of the Franks."

"How, priest!" cried Morvan angrily, "I am a Breton and no traitor or rebel. It is the King of the Franks who has been a traitor to this land."

"Silence, recreant!" replied the hermit. "Rail not against the King of the Franks, for he is a man of God."

"Of God, say you? Nay, rather of the devil! Has he not ravaged and wasted the Breton land? The gold that he wrings from the Breton folk is expended for the good of Satan. Open, hermit, open!"

"Not so, my son, for should I do so the Franks would surely fix a quarrel upon me."

"You refuse?" shouted Morvan in a voice of thunder. "Good; then I shall burst into your cell," and with these words he threw himself against the door, which creaked ominously.

"Hold, my son, hold!" cried the old hermit in tremulous tones. "Forbear and I will open to you"; and seizing a torch he lit it at the remains of his fire and went to open the door.

The Severed Head

He unlocked it and drew it back, but as he did so he recoiled violently, for he saw advancing upon him a terrible spectre, holding its head in its two hands. Its eyes seemed full of blood and fire, and rolled round and round in a most horrible manner. The hermit was about to shriek in terror when the head of the apparition, after laughing grimly, addressed him:

"Come now, old Christian, do not be afraid. God permits this thing to be. He has allowed the Franks to decapitate me, but for a time only, and as you see me now I am only a phantom. But He will permit you yourself to replace my head on my shoulders if you will."

The hermit stammered and drew back. This was not his first encounter with the supernatural, which he had good reason to dread, but like all Bretons he had come under the magnetism of Morvan, even although he believed that the King of the Franks was his rightful overlord; so, steeling himself against his natural timidity, he said:

"If God permits this thing I shall be very willing to replace your head on your shoulders."

"Take it, then," said the decapitated Morvan, and with trembling hands the priest took the gory trophy and replaced it on the Breton chief's shoulders, saying at the same time: "I replace your head, my son, in the name of God the Father, the Son, and the Spirit."

And by virtue of this benediction the phantom once more became a man.

"Morvan," said the hermit, "you must do penance, heavy penance, with me. You must carry about with you for seven years a robe of lead, padlocked to your neck, and each day at the hour of twelve you must go to fetch water from the well at the summit of the mountain yonder."

"I will do as you desire," said Morvan; "I will follow your saintly wish."

When the seven years of the penance had passed the robe had flayed Morvan's skin severely, and his beard, which had become grey, and the hair of his head, fell almost to his waist. Those who saw him did not recognize him; but a lady dressed in white, who passed through the greenwood, stopped and gazed earnestly at him and her eyes filled with tears.

"Morvan, my dear son, it is indeed you," she said. "Come here, my beloved child, that I may free you of your burden," and she cut the chain which bound the shirt of lead to the shoulders of the penitent with a pair of golden scissors, saying:

"I am your patron, Saint Anne of Armor."

Now for seven years had the squire of Morvan sought his master, and one day he was riding through the greenwood of Helléan.

"Alas!" he said, "what profits it that I have slain his murderer when I have lost my dear lord?"

Then he heard at the other end of the wood the plaintive whinnying of a horse. His own steed sniffed the air and replied, and then he saw between the parted branches a great black charger, which he recognized as that of Lez-Breiz. Once more the beast whinnied mournfully. It almost seemed as if he wept. He was standing upon his master's grave!

But, like Arthur and Barbarossa, Morvan Lez-Breiz will yet return. Yes, one day he will return to fight the Franks and drive them from the Breton land!

We have sundry intimations here of the sources from which Villemarqué drew a part at least of his matter. There are resemblances to Arthurian and kindred romances. For example, the incident which describes the flight of young Morvan is identical with that in the Arthurian saga of *Percival le Gallois*, where the child Percival quits his mother's care in precisely the same fashion. The Frankish monarch and his Court, too, are distinctly drawn in the style of the *chansons de gestes*, which celebrated the deeds of Charlemagne and his peers. There are also hints that the paganism against which Charlemagne fought, that of the Moors of Spain, had attracted the attention of the author, and this is especially seen in his introduction of the Moorish giant, so common a figure in the Carlovingian stories.

The Ballad of Bran

A sorrowful and touching ballad, claimed by Villemarqué as being sung in the Breton dialect of Léon, tells of the warrior Bran, who was wounded in the great fight of Kerlouan, a village situated on the coast of Léon, in the tenth century. The coast was raided by the Norsemen, and the Bretons, led by their chief, Even the Great, marched against them and succeeded in repelling them. The Norsemen, however, carried off several prisoners, among them a warrior called Bran. Indeed, a village called Kervran, or 'the village of Bran,' still exists near the seashore, and here it was, tradition relates, that the warrior was wounded and taken by the Scandinavian pirates. In the church of Goulven is to be seen an ancient tablet representing the Norse vessels which raided the coast.

The ballad recounts how Bran, on finding himself on the enemy's ship, wept bitterly. On arriving in the land of the Norsemen he was imprisoned in a tower, where he begged his gaolers to allow him to send a letter to his mother. Permission to do so was granted, and a messenger was found. The prisoner advised this man, for his better safety, to disguise himself in the habit of a beggar, and gave him his gold ring in order that his mother might know that the message came from her son in very truth. He added: "When you arrive in my country proceed at once to my mother, and if she is willing to ransom me show a white sail on your return, but if she refuses, hoist a black sail."

When the messenger arrived at the warrior's home in the country of Léon the lady was at supper with her family and the bards were present playing on their harps.

"Greeting, lady," said the messenger. "Behold the ring of your son, Bran, and here is news from him contained in this letter, which I pray you read quickly."

The lady took the missive, and, turning to the harpers, told them to cease playing. Having perused the letter she became extremely agitated, and, rising with tears in her eyes, gave orders that a vessel should be equipped immediately so that she might sail to seek her son on the morrow.

One morning Bran, the prisoner, called from his tower: "Sentinel, Sentinel, tell me, do you see a sail on the sea?"

"No," replied the sentinel, "I see nothing but the sea and the sky."

At midday Bran repeated the question, but was told that nothing but the birds and the billows were in sight. When the shadows of evening gathered he asked once more, and the perfidious sentinel replied with a lie:

"Yes, lord, there is a ship close at hand, beaten by wind and sea."

"And what colour of a sail does she show?" asked Bran. "Is it black or white?"

"It is black, lord," replied the sentinel, in a spirit of petty spite.

When the unhappy warrior heard these words he never spoke more.

That night his mother arrived at the town where he

had been imprisoned. She asked of the people: "Why do the bells sound?"

"Alas! lady," said an ancient man, "a noble prisoner who lay in yonder tower died this night."

With bent head the lady walked to the tower, her white hair falling upon her folded arms. When she arrived at its foot she said to the guard: "Open the door quickly; I have come to see my son."

And when the great door was opened she threw herself upon the corpse of Bran and breathed her last.

. . . . .

On the battlefield of Kerlouan there is an oak which overshadows the shore and which marks the place where the Norsemen fled before the face of Even the Great. On this oak, whose leaves shine in the moon, the birds gather each night, the birds of the sea and the land, both of white and black feather. Among them is an old grey rook and a young crow. The birds sing such a beautiful song that the great sea keeps silence to hear it. All of them sing except the rook and the crow. Now the crow says: "Sing, little birds, sing; sing, little birds of the land, for when you die you will at least end your days in Brittany.

The crow is of course Bran in disguise, for the name Bran means 'crow' in the Breton tongue, and the rook is possibly his mother. In the most ancient Breton traditions the dead are represented as returning to earth in the form of birds. A number of the incidents in this piece are paralleled in the poem of *Sir Tristrem*, which also introduces a messenger who disguises himself for the purpose of travelling more safely in a foreign country, a ring of gold, which is used to show the messenger's *bona-fides*, a perfidious gaoler, and the idea of the black or white sail. The original poem of *Sir Tristrem* was probably composed about the twelfth or thirteenth century, and it would seem that the above incidents at least have a Breton source behind them. A mother, however, has been substituted for a lover, and the ancient Breton dame takes the place of Ysonde. There is, indeed, little difference between the passage which relates the arrival of the mother in the Norsemen's country and that of Ysonde in Brittany when she sails on her last voyage with the intention of succouring Tristrem. Ysonde also asks the people of the place why the bells are ringing, one of the ancient inhabitants tells her of the death of her lover, and, like the Breton mother, she casts herself on the body of him she has lost.

"This passage," says Villemarqué, with wonderful *sang-froid*, "duly attests the prior claim of the Armorican piece"! But even if he had been serious, he wrote without the possession of data for the precise fixing of the period in which the Breton ballad was composed; and in any case his contention cannot assist the Breton argument for Armorican priority in Arthurian literature, as borrowing in ballad and folk-tale is much more flagrant than he, writing as he did in 1867, could ever have guessed—more flagrant even than any adaptation he himself ever perpetrated!

He adds, however, an antiquarian note to the poem which is of far greater interest and probably of more value than his supposition. He alludes to the passage contained in the ballad regarding the harpers who are represented as playing in the hall of Bran's mother while she sits at supper. The harp, he states, is no longer popular in Brittany, and he asks if this was always the case. There can be very little doubt that in Brittany, as in other Celtic countries—for example, Wales, Ireland and Scotland—the harp was in ancient times one of the national instruments. It is strange that it should have been replaced in that country by the *biniou*, or bagpipe, just as the *clairschach*, or Highland harp, was replaced by the same instrument in the Highlands of Scotland.

Fontenelle

Guy Eder de Fontenelle, a son of the house of Beaumanoir, was one of the most famous partisans of the Catholic League, and, according to one who saw him in 1587, had then begun to show tendencies to the wild life he was afterward to lead. He was sent as a scholar to Paris to the College of Boncotest, but in 1589, when about sixteen years of age, he became impatient of scholastic confinement, sold his books and his robe, and bought a sword and poignard. Leaving the college, he took the road to Orléans, with the object of attaching himself to the army of the Duke of Mayenne, chief of the Catholic party in France, but, returning to his native Brittany, he placed himself at the head of the populace, which had risen in arms on behalf of the Leaguers. As he was of good family and a Breton and displayed an active spirit, they obeyed him very willingly. Soon he translated his intentions into action, and commenced to pillage the smaller towns and to make captive those who differed from him politically. He threatened Guingamp, which was held for the King, and made a sally into Léon, carrying away the daughter of the Lady of Coadelan, a wealthy heiress, who was only about eight or nine years of age. This occurrence Villemarqué has related for us in Breton verse, assuring us that it was 'recovered' by the Comte de Kergariou, a friend of his. Fontenelle is supposed to have encountered the little heiress plucking flowers in a wayside ditch.

"Tell me, little one," said he, "for whom do you pluck these flowers?"

"For my foster-brother, whom I love. But I am afraid, for I know that Fontenelle is near."

"Ha, then, so you know this terrible Fontenelle, my child?"

"No, sir, I do not know him, but I have heard tell of him. I have heard folk say that he is a very wicked man and that he carries away young ladies."

"Yes," replied Fontenelle, with a laugh, "and, above all, heiresses."

He took the child in his arms and swung her on to the crupper of his saddle. Then, dashing the spurs into his charger's flanks, he set off at a gallop for Saint-Malo, where he placed the little heiress in a convent, with the object of marrying her when she had arrived at the age of fourteen.

Years afterward Fontenelle and the heiress, who was now his wife, went to live at their manor of Coadelan. They had a little child beautiful as the day, who greatly resembled his father. One day a letter arrived for the Seigneur, calling upon him to betake himself to Paris at once. His wife was inconsolable.

"Do not set forth alone for Paris, I pray you," she said, "for if you do I shall instantly follow you. Remain at home, I beg of you, and I will send a messenger in your stead. In the name of God, do not go, husband, for if you do you will never return."

But Fontenelle disregarded his wife's entreaties, and, begging her to take good care of their son during his absence, set forth on his journey to the capital. In due time he arrived in Paris and stood before the King and Queen. He greeted them courteously, but they looked coldly on him, and the King told him bluntly that he should not return to Coadelan, adding: "There are sufficient chains in my palace to restrain you."

On hearing this Fontenelle called his little page and begged him to return at once to his mistress and tell her to discard her finery, because she would soon be a widow, and to bring him back a coarse shirt and a white sheet, and, moreover, to bring a gold plate on which his enemies might expose his head after his death.

"And, little page," he added, "take a lock of my hair and place it on the door of Coadelan, so that all men as they go to Mass may say, 'God have mercy on the soul of Fontenelle.'"

The page did as he was bidden, but as for the plate of gold it was useless, for Fontenelle's head was thrown on the pavement to serve as a ball for the children of the gutter.

All Paris was surprised when one day a lady from a distant country arrived and made great stir in its narrow streets. Every one asked his neighbour who this dame might be. It was the heiress of Coadelan, dressed in a flowing robe of green. "Alas!" said the pitiful burgesses, "if she knew what we know she would be dressed in black." Shortly she stood before the King.

"Sire," said she, "give me back my husband, I beg of you."

"Alas! madam," replied the King, with feigned sorrow, "what you ask is impossible, for but three days ago he was broken on the wheel."

"Whoso goes to Coadelan to-day will turn away from it with grief, for the ashes are black upon the hearth and the nettles crowd around the doorway—and still," the ballad ends naïvely, "still the wicked world goes round and the poor folk weep with anguish, and say, 'Alas that she is dead, the mother of the poor.'"

The Return from England

There is a good deal of evidence to show that a considerable body of Bretons accompanied the invading army of William the Conqueror when he set forth with the idea of gaining the English crown. They were attached to his second battle corps, and many of them received land in England. A ballad which, says Villemarqué, bears every sign of antiquity deals with the fortunes of a young Breton, Silvestik, who followed in the train of the Conqueror. The piece is put into the mouth of the mother of Silvestik, who mourns her son's absence, and its tone is a tender and touching one.

"One night as I lay on my bed," says the anxious mother, "I could not sleep. I heard the girls at Kerlaz singing the song of my son. O God, Silvestik, where are you now? Perhaps you are more than three hundred leagues from here, cast on the great sea, and the fishes feed upon your fair body. Perhaps you may be married now to some Saxon damsel. You were to have been wed to a lovely daughter of this land, Mannaïk de Pouldergat, and you might have been among us surrounded by beautiful children, dwelling happily in your own home.

THE FINDING OF SILVESTIK

HÉLOÏSE AS SORCERESS

"I have taken to my door a little white dove which sits in a small hollow of the stone. I have tied to his neck a letter with the ribbon of my wedding-dress and have sent it to my son. Arise, my little dove, arise on your two wings, fly far, very far across the great sea, and discover if my son is still alive and well."

Silvestik rested in the shade of an English wood, and as he did so a familiar note fell upon his ear.

"That sound resembles the voice of my mother's little white dove," he said. The sound grew louder; it seemed to say, "Good luck to you, Silvestik, good luck to you. I have here a letter for you."

Silvestik in high happiness read the letter, and resolved to return home to his sorrowing parent.

Two years passed, three years passed, and the dove did not return to delight the heart of the longing mother, who day by day walked the dismal seashore waiting for the vessel that never came. One day of storm she was wandering on the beach as usual when she saw a vessel being driven with great force upon the iron coast. Even as she watched it it dashed upon the rocks. Soon there were cast upon the shore the forms of many dead, and when the gale abated and the heart-sick mother was able to search among them she found Silvestik!

Several competent judges are of opinion that this ballad is contemporary with the events which it relates. Many of the Breton lords who sailed with William the Conqueror did not return for several years after the expedition had accomplished its object, and some not at all. Nothing is known regarding the hero. The bird is frequently the messenger between lovers in ballad literature, but it is seldom that it is found carrying letters between a mother and her son—indeed, this is perhaps the only instance known.

The Marriage-Girdle

This ballad has reference to the Breton expedition which sailed for Wales in 1405 to assist the Welsh under Owen Glendower to free their principality from the English yoke. The Bretons rendered material assistance to their Welsh brothers, and had the satisfaction on their return of knowing that they had accomplished that which no French king had ever been able to achieve—the invasion of English territory. The expedition was commanded by Jean de Rieux, Marshal of France, and numbered ten thousand men.

The ballad tells how a young man on the morning after his betrothal received orders to join the standard of de Rieux "to help the Bretons oversea." It was with bitterness in his heart, says the lover, that he entered the house of his betrothed with the object of bidding her farewell. He told her that duty called him, and that he must go to serve in England. At this her tears gushed forth, and she begged him not to go, reminding him how changeful was the wind and how perfidious the sea.

"Alas!" said she, "if you die what shall I do? In my impatience to have news of you my heart will break. I shall wander by the seashore, from one cottage to another, asking the sailors if they have heard tell of you."

"Be comforted, Aloïda," said her lover, "and do not weep on my account. I will send you a girdle from over the sea, a girdle of purple set with rubies."

They parted at daybreak, he to embark on the sea, she

to weep, and as he sought his ship he could hear the magpies cackle: "If the sea is changeable women are even more so."

When the autumn had arrived the young girl said: "I have looked far over the sea from the heights of the mountains of Arez. I have seen upon the waters a ship in danger, and I feel that upon it was him whom I love. He held a sword in his hand, he was engaged in a terrible combat, he was wounded to death and his garments were covered with blood. I am certain that he is dead."

And before many weeks had passed she was affianced to another.

Then good news arrived in the land. The war was finished and the cavalier returned to his home with a gay heart. No sooner had he refreshed himself than he went to seek his beloved. As he approached her dwelling he heard the sound of music, and observed that every window in the house was illuminated as if for a festival. He asked some revellers whom he met outside the cause of this merrymaking, and was told that a wedding was proceeding.

It is the custom in Brittany to invite beggars to a wedding, and when these were now admitted one of them asked hospitality for the night. This was at once granted him, but he sat apart, sad and silent. The bride, observing this, approached him and asked him why he did not join in the feasting. He replied that he was weary with travel and that his heart was heavy with sorrow. Desirous that the marriage festivities should not flag, the bride asked him to join her in the dance, and he accepted the invitation, saying, however, that it was an honour he did not merit.

Now while they danced he came close to her and murmured in her ear:

"What have you done with the golden ring that you received from me at the door of this very house?"

The bride stared at him in wild dismay. "Oh, heaven," she cried, "behold, I have now two husbands! I who thought I was a widow!"

"You think wrongly, *ma belle*," hissed the beggar; "you will have no husband this side of the grave," and drawing a dagger from under his cloak he struck the lady to the heart.

In the abbey of Daoulas there is a statue of the Virgin decorated with a splendid girdle of purple sparkling with rubies, which came from across the sea. If you desire to know who gave it to her, ask of a repentant monk who lies prostrate on the grass before the figure of the Mother of God.

It is strange that the faithless damsel should have alleged that she saw her lover perish in a naval combat when in the very year to which the circumstances of the ballad refer (1405) a Breton fleet encountered and defeated an English flotilla several leagues from Brest. "The combat was terrible," says a historian of the Dukes of Burgundy, "and was animated by the ancient hate between the English and the Bretons." Perhaps it was in this sea-fight that the lady beheld her lover; and if, as she thought, he was slain, she scarcely deserves the odium which the balladeer has cast upon her memory.

The Combat of Saint-Cast

This ballad somewhat belies its name, for it has some relation to an extraordinary incident which was the means rather of preventing than precipitating a battle. In 1758 a British army was landed upon the shores of Brittany with the object of securing for British merchant ships safety in the navigation of the Channel and of creating a diversion in favour of the German forces, then our allies. A company of men from Lower Brittany, from the towns of Tréguier and Saint-Pol-de Léon, says Villemarqué, were marching against a detachment of Scottish Highlanders. When at a distance of about a mile the Bretons could hear their enemies singing a national song. At once they halted stupefied, for the air was one well known to them, which they were accustomed to hear almost every day of their lives. Electrified by the music, which spoke to their hearts, they arose in their enthusiasm and themselves sang the patriotic refrain. It was the Highlanders' turn to be silent. All this time the two companies were nearing one another, and when at a suitable distance their respective officers commanded them to fire; but the orders were given, says the tradition, "in the same language," and the soldiers on both sides stood stock-still. Their inaction, however, lasted but a moment, for emotion carried away all discipline, the arms fell from their hands, and the descendants of the ancient Celts renewed on the field of battle those ties of brotherhood which had once united their fathers.

However unlikely this incident may seem, it appears to be confirmed by tradition, if not by history. The air which the rival Celts sang is, says Villemarqué,[1] common

[1] *Barzaz-Breiz*, p. 335. Sébillot (*Traditions de la Haute-Bretagne*, t. i, p. 346) says that he could gain nothing regarding this incident at the village of Saint-Cast but "vague details."

to both Brittany and "the Highlands of Scotland." With the music before me, it seems to bear a marked resemblance to *The Garb of Old Gaul*, composed by General Reid (1721–1807). Perhaps Reid, who was a Highlander, based his stirring march on an older Celtic theme common to both lands.

The Song of the Pilot

One of the most famous of Breton nautical traditions tells of the chivalry displayed by a Breton crew toward the men of a British warship. During the American War of Independence much enthusiasm was excited in France in connexion with the valiant struggle for liberty in which the American colonies were engaged. A number of Breton ships received letters of marque enabling them to fight on the American side against Great Britain, and these attempted to blockade British commerce. The *Surveillante*, a Breton vessel commanded by Couëdic de Kergoaler, encountered the British ship *Quebec*, commanded by Captain Farmer. In the course of the action the *Surveillante* was nearly sunk by the British cannonade and the *Quebec* went on fire. But Breton and Briton, laying aside their swords, worked together with such goodwill that most of the British crew were rescued and the *Surveillante* was saved, although the *Quebec* was lost, and this notwithstanding that nearly every man of both crews had been wounded in the fighting.

I have here attempted a very free translation of the stirring ballad which relates this noteworthy incident, which cannot but be of interest at such a time as the present.

The Song of the Pilot

THE SONG OF THE PILOT

Yo ho, ye men of Sulniac!
We ship to-day at Vannes,
We sail upon a glorious track
To seek an Englishman.
Our saucy sloop the *Surveillante*
Must keep the seaways clear
From Ushant in the north to Nantes:
Aboard her, timoneer!

See, yonder is the British craft
That seeks to break blockade;
St George's banner floats abaft
Her lowering carronade.
A flash! and lo, her thunder speaks,
Her iron tempest flies
Beneath her bows, and seaward breaks,
And hissing sinks and dies.

Thunder replied to thunder; then
The ships rasped side by side,
The battle-hungry Breton men
A boarding sally tried,
But the stern steel of Britain flashed,
And spite of Breton vaunt
The lads of Morbihan were dashed
Back on the *Surveillante.*

Then was a grim encounter seen
Upon the seas that day.
Who yields when there is strife between
Britain and Brittany?
Shall Lesser Britain rule the waves
And check Britannia's pride?
Not while her frigate's oaken staves
Still cleave unto her side!

But hold! hold! see, devouring fire
Has seized the stout *Quebec.*
The seething sea runs high and higher,
The *Surveillante's* a wreck.

Their cannon-shot has breached our side,
Our bolts have fired the foe.
Quick, to the pumps! No longer bide!
Below, my lads! below!

The yawning leak is filled, the sea
Is cheated of its prey.
Now Bretons, let the Britons see
The heart of Brittany!
Brothers, we come to save, our swords
Are sheathed, our hands are free.
There is a fiercer fight toward,
A fiercer foe than we!

A long sea-day, till sank the sun,
Briton and Breton wrought,
And Great and Little Britain won
The noblest fight ere fought.
It was a sailors' victory
O'er pride and sordid gain.
God grant for ever peace at sea
Between the Britains twain!

CHAPTER IX: THE BLACK ART AND ITS MINISTERS

SORCERY is a very present power in most isolated communities, and in the civilized portions of Brittany it is but a thing of yesterday, while in the more secluded departments it is very much a thing of to-day. The old folk can recall the time when the farm, the dairy, and the field were ever in peril of the spell, the enchantment, the noxious beam of the evil eye, and tales of many a "devilish cantrip sleight," as Burns happily characterized the activity of the witch and the wizard, were told in hushed voices at the Breton fireside when the winter wind blew cold from the cruel sea and the heaped faggots sent the red glow of fire-warmth athwart the thick shadows of the great farm kitchen, and old and young from grandsire to herd-boy made a great circle to hearken to the creepy tales so dear to the Breton heart.

As in the East, where to refuse baksheesh is to lay oneself open to the curse of the evil eye, the beggar was regarded as the chief possessor of this bespelling member. The guild of tattered wanderers naturally nourished this superstition, and to permit one of its members to hobble off muttering threats or curses was looked upon as suicidal. Indeed, the mendicants were wont to boast of their feats of sorcery to the terrified peasants, who hastened to placate them by all the means in their power.

Certain villages, too, appear to have possessed an evil reputation among the country-folk as the dwelling-places of magicians, centres of sorcery, which it was advisable to shun. Thus we read in Breton proverb of the sorcerers of Fougères, of Trèves, of Concoret, of Lézat.

The strangest circumstances were connected with the phenomena of sorcery by the credulous Bretons. Thus, did a peasant join a dance of witches, the sabots he had on would be worn out in the course of the merrymaking. A churn of turned butter, a sour pail of milk, were certain to be accounted for by sorcery. In a certain village of Moncontour the cows, the dog, even the harmless, necessary cat, died off, and the farmer hastened to consult a diviner, who advised him to throw milk in the fire and recite certain prayers. The farmer obeyed and the spell was broken!

In the town of Rennes about fifty years ago dwelt a knowing fellow called Robert, a very 'witch-doctor,' who investigated cases of sorcery and undertook the dissipation of enchantments. On a certain large farm the milk would yield no butter. An agricultural expert might have hinted at poor pasturage, but the farmer and his wife had other views as to the cause of the 'insufficiency of fats,' as an analyst would say, in the lacteal output of the establishment. Straightway they betook themselves to the mysterious Robert, who on arriving to investigate the affair was attired in a skin dyed in two colours. He held in leash a large black dog, evidently his familiar. He exorcized the dairy, and went through a number of strange ceremonies. Then, turning to the awestruck farm hands, he said:

"You may now proceed with your work. The spell is raised. It has been a slow business. I must go now, but don't be afraid if you see anything odd."

With these words he whistled, and a great black horse

at once appeared as if from nowhere. Placing his hand on its crupper, he vaulted into the saddle, bade good-bye to the astonished rustics, and while they gazed at him open-mouthed, vanished 'like a flash.'

Many kinds of amulets or talismans were used by the Breton peasantry to neutralize the power of sorcerers. Thus, if a person carried a snake with him the enchanters would be unable to harm his sight, and all objects would appear to him under their natural forms. Salt placed in various parts of a house guarded it against the entrance of wizards and rendered their spells void.

But many consulted the witch and the sorcerer for their personal advantage, in affairs of the heart, to obtain a number in the casting of lots for conscription which would free them from military service, and so forth; and, as in other countries, there grew up a class of middlemen between the human and the supernatural who posed as fortune-tellers, astrologers, and quack mediciners.

It was said that sorcerers were wont to meet at the many Roches aux Fées in Brittany at fixed periods in order to deliberate as to their actions and settle their affairs. If anyone, it was declared, wandered into their circle or was caught by them listening to their secret conclave he seldom lived long. Others, terrified at the sight presented by the gleaming eyes of the cat-sorcerers, blazing like live coals, fled incontinently from their presence, and found that in the morning the hair of their heads had turned white with the dread experience. Long afterward they would sit by the fireside trembling visibly at nothing, and when interrogated regarding their very evident fears would only groan and bury their faces in their hands.

A story is told of one, Jean Foucault, who one moonlight night had, like Tam o' Shanter, sat overlong

> Fast by an ingle bleezin' finely,
> Wi' reaming swats that drank divinely,

where the cider was as good as the company, and, issuing at midnight's weary hour from his favourite inn, was not in a mood to run away from anything, however fearsome. Walking, or rather rolling, across the moor singing the burden of the last catch he had trolled with his fellows at the ale-house, all on a sudden he stumbled into a circle of sorcerer-cats squatting around a cross of stone. They were of immense size and of all colours, black, grey, white, tortoise-shell, and when he beheld them seated round the crucifix, their eyes darting fire and the hair bristling on their backs, his song died upon his lips and all his bellicose feelings, like those of Bob Acres, leaked out at his finger-tips. On catching sight of him the animals set up a horrible caterwauling that made the blood freeze in his veins. For an awful moment the angry cats glared at him with death in their looks, and seemed as if about to spring upon him. Giving himself up for lost, he closed his eyes. But about his feet he could hear a strange purring, and, glancing downward, he beheld his own domestic puss fawning upon him with every sign of affection.

"Pass my master, Jean Foucault," said the animal.

"It is well," replied a great grey tom, whom Jean took to be the leader; "pass on, Jean Foucault."

And Jean, the cider fumes in his head quite dissipated, staggered away, more dead than alive.

Druidic Magic

Druidic Magic

The more ancient sorcerers of Brittany deserve a word of notice. Magic among the Celtic peoples in olden times was so clearly identified with Druidism that its origin may be said to have been Druidic. Whether Druidism was of Celtic origin, however, is a question upon which much discussion has taken place, some authorities, among them Rhys, believing it to have been of non-Celtic and even non-Aryan origin, and holding that the earliest non-Aryan or so-called Iberian people of Britain introduced the Druidic religion to the immigrant Celts. An argument advanced in favour of this theory is that the Continental Celts sent their neophyte Druid priests to Britain to undergo a special training at the hands of the British Druids, and that this island seems to have been regarded as the headquarters of the cult. The people of Cisalpine Gaul, for instance, had no Druidic priesthood. Cæsar has told us that in Gaul Druidic seminaries were very numerous, and that within their walls severe study and discipline were entailed upon the neophytes, whose principal business was to commit to memory countless verses enshrining Druidic knowledge and tradition. That this instruction was astrological and magical we have the fullest proof.[1]

The Druids were magi as they were priests in the same sense that the American Indian shaman is both magus and priest. That is, they were medicine-men on a higher scale, and had reached a loftier stage of transcendental knowledge than the priest-magicians of more barbarous races. Thus they may be said to be a

[1] Rice Holmes, *Cæsar's Conquest*, pp. 532–536.

link between the barbarian shaman and the magus of medieval times. Many of their practices were purely shamanistic, while others more closely resembled medieval magical rite. But they were not the only magicians of the Celts, for frequently among that people we find magic power the possession of women and of the poetic craft. The magic of Druidism had many points of comparison with most magical systems, and perhaps approximated more to that black magic which desires power for the sake of power alone than to any transcendental type. Thus it included the power to render the magician invisible, to change his bodily shape, to produce an enchanted sleep, to induce lunacy, and to inflict death from afar.

The arts of rain-making, bringing down fire from heaven, and causing mists, snow-storms, and floods were also claimed for the Druids. Many of the spells probably in use among them survived until a comparatively late period, and are still employed in some remote Celtic localities, the names of saints being substituted for those of Celtic deities. Certain primitive ritual, too, is still carried out in the vicinity of some megalithic structures in Celtic areas, as at Dungiven, in Ireland, where pilgrims wash before a great stone in the river Roe and then walk round it, and in many parts of Brittany.[1]

In pronouncing incantations the usual method employed was to stand upon one leg and to point with the forefinger to the person or object on which the spell was to be laid, at the same time closing one eye, as if to concentrate the force of the entire personality upon that which was to be placed under ban. A manuscript

[1] See Rolleston, *Myths and Legends of the Celtic Race*, p. 66.

possessed by the monastery of St Gall, and dating from the eighth or ninth century, includes magical formulæ for the preservation of butter and the healing of certain diseases in the name of the Irish god Diancecht. These and others bear a close resemblance to Babylonian and Etruscan spells, and thus go to strengthen the hypothesis often put forward with more or less plausibility that Druidism had an Eastern origin. At all magical rites spells were uttered. Druids often accompanied an army, to assist by their magical arts in confounding the enemy.[1]

There is some proof that in Celtic areas survivals of a Druidic priesthood have descended to our own time in a more or less debased condition. Thus the existence of guardians and keepers of wells said to possess magical properties, and the fact that in certain families magical spells and formulæ are handed down from one generation to another, are so many proofs of the survival of Druidic tradition, however feeble. Females are generally the conservators of these mysteries, and that there were Druid priestesses is fairly certain.

The sea-snake's egg, or adder's stone, which is so frequently alluded to in Druidic magical tales, otherwise called *Glain Neidr*, was said to have been formed, about midsummer, by an assemblage of snakes. A bubble formed on the head of one of them was blown by others down the whole length of its back, and then, hardening, became a crystal ring. It was used as one of the insignia of the Archdruid, and was supposed to assist in augury.

The *herbe d'or*, or 'golden herb,' was a medicinal plant much in favour among the Breton peasantry. It is the

[1] See Gomme, *Ethnology in Folk-lore*, p. 94.

selago of Pliny, which in Druidical times was gathered with the utmost veneration by a hand enveloped with a garment once worn by a sacred person. The owner of the hand was arrayed in white, with bare feet, washed in pure water. In after times the plant was thought to shine from a distance like gold, and to give to those who trod on it the power of understanding the language of dogs, wolves, and birds.

These, with the mistletoe, the favourite Druidical plant, the sorcerer is entreated, in an old balled, to lay aside, to seek no more for vain enchantments, but to remember that he is a Christian.

Abélard and Héloïse

The touching story of the love of Abélard and Héloïse has found its way into Breton legend as a tale of sorcery. Abélard was a Breton. The Duke of Brittany, whose subject he was born, jealous of the glory of France, which then engrossed all the most famous scholars of Europe, and being, besides, acquainted with the persecution Abélard had suffered from his enemies, had nominated him to the Abbey of St Gildas, and, by this benefaction and mark of his esteem, engaged him to pass the rest of his days in his dominions. Abélard received this favour with great joy, imagining that by leaving France he would quench his passion for Héloïse and gain a new peace of mind upon entering into his new dignity.

The Abbey of St Gildas de Rhuys was founded on the inaccessible coast near Vannes by St Gildas, a British saint, the schoolfellow and friend of St Samson of Dol and St Pol of Léon, and counted among its monks the Saxon St Dunstan, who, carried by pirates from his native isle, settled on the desolate shores of Brittany and became, under the name of St Goustan, the patron of mariners.

St Gildas built his abbey on the edge of a high, rocky promontory, the site of an ancient Roman encampment, called Grand Mont, facing the shore, where the sea has formed numerous caverns in the rocks. The rocks are composed chiefly of quartz, and are covered to a considerable height with small mussels. Abélard, on his appointment to the Abbey of St Gildas, made over to Héloïse the celebrated abbey he had founded at Nogent, near Troyes, which he called the Paraclete, or Comforter, because he there found comfort and refreshment after his troubles. With Nogent he was to leave his peace. His gentle nature was unable to contend against the coarse and unruly Breton monks. As he writes in his well-known letter to Héloïse, setting forth his griefs: "I inhabit a barbarous country where the language is unknown to me. I have no dealings with the ferocious inhabitants. I walk the inaccessible borders of the stormy sea, and my monks have no other rule than their own. I wish that you could see my dwelling. You would not believe it an abbey. The doors are ornamented only with the feet of deer, of wolves and bears, boars, and the hideous skins of owls. I find each day new perils. I expect at every moment to see a sword suspended over my head."

It is scarcely necessary to outline the history of Abélard. Suffice it to say that he was one of the most brilliant scholars and dialecticians of all time, possessing a European reputation in his day. Falling in love with Héloïse, niece of Fulbert, a canon of Paris, he awoke in her a similar absorbing passion, which resulted in their mutual disgrace and Abélard's mutilation by the incensed uncle. He and his Héloïse were buried in one tomb at the Paraclete. The story of their love has been immortalized by the world's great poets and painters. An ancient Breton ballad on the subject has been spoken of as a "naïf and horrible" production, in which one will find "a bizarre mixture of Druidic practice and Christian superstition." It describes Héloïse as a sorceress of ferocious and sanguinary temper. Thus can legend magnify and distort human failing! As its presentation is important in the study of Breton folk-lore, I give a very free translation of this ballad, in which, at the same time, I have endeavoured to preserve the atmosphere of the original.

THE HYMN OF HÉLOÏSE

O Abélard, my Abélard,
Twelve summers have passed since first we kissed.
There is no love like that of a bard:
Who loves him lives in a golden mist!

Nor word of French nor Roman tongue,
But only Brezonek could I speak,
When round my lover's neck I hung
And heard the harmony of the Greek,

The march of Latin, the joy of French,
The valiance of the Hebrew speech,
The while its thirst my soul did quench
In the love-lore that he did teach.

The bossed and bound Evangel's tome
Is open to me as mine own soul,
But all the watered wine of Rome
Is weak beside the magic bowl.

The Hymn of Héloïse

The Mass I chant like any priest,
Can shrive the dying or bury the dead,
But dearer to me to raise the Beast
Or watch the gold in the furnace red.

The wolf, the serpent, the crow, the owl,
The demons of sea, of field, of flood,
I can run or fly in their forms so foul,
They come at my call from wave or wood.

I know a song that can raise the sea,
Can rouse the winds or shudder the earth,
Can darken the heavens terribly,
Can wake portents at a prince's birth.

The first dark drug that ever we sipped
Was brewed from toad and the eye of crow,
Slain in a mead when the moon had slipped
From heav'n to the fetid fogs below.

I know a well as deep as death,
A gloom where I cull the frondent fern,
Whose seed with that of the golden heath
I mingle when mystic lore I'd learn.

I gathered in dusk nine measures of rye,
Nine measures again, and brewed the twain
In a silver pot, while fitfully
The starlight struggled through the rain.

I sought the serpent's egg of power
In a dell hid low from the night and day:
It was shown to me in an awful hour
When the children of hell came out to play.

I have three spirits—seeming snakes;
The youngest is six score years young,
The second rose from the nether lakes,
And the third was once Duke Satan's tongue.

The wild bird's flesh is not their food,
No common umbles are their dole;
I nourish them well with infants' blood,
Those precious vipers of my soul.

O Satan ! grant me three years still,
But three short years, my love and I,
To work thy fierce, mysterious will,
Then gladly shall we yield and die.

Héloïse, wicked heart, beware !
Think on the dreadful day of wrath,
Think on thy soul ; forbear, forbear !
The way thou tak'st is that of death !

Thou craven priest, go, get thee hence !
No fear have I of fate so fell.
Go, suck the milk of innocence,
Leave me to quaff the wine of hell !

It is difficult to over-estimate the folk-lore value of such a ballad as this. Its historical value is clearly *nil.* We have no proof that Héloïse was a Breton ; but fantastic errors of this description are so well known to the student of ballad literature that he is able to discount them easily in gauging the value of a piece.

In this weird composition the wretched abbess is described as an alchemist as well as a sorceress, and she descends to the depths of the lowest and most revolting witchcraft. She practises shape-shifting and similar arts. She has power over natural forces, and knows the past, the present, and the things to be. She possesses sufficient Druidic knowledge to permit her to gather the greatly prized serpent's egg, to acquire which was the grand aim of the Celtic magician. The circumstances of the ballad strongly recall those of the poem in which the Welsh bard Taliesin recounts his magical experiences, his metamorphoses, his knowledge of the darker mysteries of nature.

Nantes of the Magicians

The poet is in accord with probability in making the magical exploits of Abélard and Héloïse take place at Nantes—a circumstance not indicated in the translation owing to metrical exigencies. Nantes was, indeed, a classic neighbourhood of sorcery. An ancient college of Druidic priestesses was situated on one of the islands at the mouth of the Loire, and the traditions of its denizens had evidently been cherished by the inhabitants of the city even as late as the middle of the fourteenth century, for we find a bishop of the diocese at that period obtaining a bull of excommunication against the local sorcerers, and condemning them to the eternal fires with bell, book, and candle.[1]

The poet, it is plain, has confounded poor Héloïse with the dark sisterhood of the island of the Loire. The learning she received from her gifted lover had been her undoing in Breton eyes, for the simple folk of the duchy at the period the ballad gained currency could scarcely be expected to discriminate between a training in rhetoric and philosophy and a schooling in the *grimoires* and other accomplishments of the pit.

[1] It is of interest to recall the fact that Abélard was born near Nantes, in 1079.

CHAPTER X: ARTHURIAN ROMANCE IN BRITTANY

FIERCE and prolonged has been the debate as to the original birthplace of Arthurian legend, authorities of the first rank, the 'Senior Wranglers' of the study, as Nutt has called them, hotly advancing the several claims of Wales, England, Scotland, and Brittany. In this place it would be neither fitting nor necessary to traverse the whole ground of argument, and we must content ourselves with the examination of Brittany's claim to the invention of Arthurian story—and this we will do briefly, passing on to some of the tales which relate the deeds of the King or his knights on Breton soil.

Confining ourselves, then, to the proof of the existence of a body of Arthurian legend in Brittany, we are, perhaps, a little alarmed at the outset to find that our manuscript sources are scanty. "It had to be acknowledged," says Professor Saintsbury, "that Brittany could supply *no ancient texts whatever*, and hardly any ancient traditions."[1] But are either of these conditions essential to a belief in the Breton origin of Arthurian romance? The two great hypotheses regarding Arthurian origins have been dubbed the 'Continental' and the 'Insular' theories. The first has as its leading protagonist Professor Wendelin Förster of Bonn, who believes that the immigrant Britons brought the Arthur legend with them to Brittany and that the Normans of Normandy received it from their descendants and gave it wider territorial scope. The second school, headed by the brilliant M. Gaston Paris, believes that it originated in Wales.

[1] *The Flourishing of Romance and the Rise of Allegory*, p. 135.

If we consider the first theory, then, we can readily see that ancient *texts* are not essential to its acceptance. In any case the entire body of Arthurian texts prior to the twelfth century is so small as to be almost negligible. The statement that "hardly any ancient traditions" of the Arthurian legend exist in Brittany is an extraordinary one. In view of the circumstances that in extended passages of Arthurian story the scene is laid in Brittany (as in the Merlin and Vivien incident and the episode of Yseult of the White Hand in the story of Tristrem), that Geoffrey of Monmouth speaks of "the Breton book" from which he took his matter, and that Marie de France states that her tales are drawn from old Breton sources, not to admit the possible existence of a body of Arthurian tradition in Brittany appears capricious. Thomas's *Sir Tristrem* is professedly based on the poem of the Breton Bréri, and there is no reason why Brittany, drawing sap and fibre as it did from Britain, should not have produced Arthurian stories of its own.

On the whole, however, that seems to represent the sum of its pretensions as a main source of Arthurian romance. The Arthurian story seems to be indigenous to British soil, and if we trace the origin of certain episodes to Brittany we may safely connect these with the early British immigrants to the peninsula. This is not to say, however, that Brittany did not influence Norman appreciation of the Arthurian saga. But that it did so more than did Wales is unlikely, in view of documentary evidence. Both Wales and Brittany, then, supplied matter which the Norman and French poets shaped into verse, and if Brittany was not the birthplace of the legend it was, in truth, one of its cradle-domains.

The Sword of Arthur

Let us collect, then, Arthurian incidents which take place in Brittany. First, Arthur's finding of the marvellous sword Excalibur would seem to happen there, as Vivien, or Nimue, the Lady of the Lake, was undoubtedly a fairy of Breton origin who does not appear in British myth.

For the manner in which Arthur acquired the renowned Excalibur, or Caliburn, the *Morte d'Arthur* is the authority. The King had broken his sword in two pieces in a combat with Sir Pellinore of Wales, and had been saved by Merlin, who threw Sir Pellinore into an enchanted sleep.

"And so Merlin and Arthur departed, and as they rode along King Arthur said, 'I have no sword.' 'No force,'[1] said Merlin; 'here is a sword that shall be yours, an I may.' So they rode till they came to a lake, which was a fair water and a broad; and in the midst of the lake King Arthur was aware of an arm clothed in white samite, that held a fair sword in the hand. 'Lo,' said Merlin unto the King, 'yonder is the sword that I spoke of.' With that they saw a damsel going upon the lake. 'What damsel is that?' said the King. 'That is the Lady of the Lake,' said Merlin; 'and within that lake is a rock, and therein is as fair a place as any on earth, and richly beseen; and this damsel will come to you anon, and then speak fair to her that she will give you that sword.' Therewith came the damsel to King Arthur and saluted him, and he her again. 'Damsel,' said the King, 'what sword is that which the arm holdeth yonder above the water? I would it were

[1] No matter.

KING ARTHUR AND MERLIN AT THE LAKE

TRISTREM AND YSONDE

mine, for I have no sword.' 'Sir King,' said the damsel of the lake, 'that sword is mine, and if ye will give me a gift when I ask it you, ye shall have it.' 'By my faith,' said King Arthur, 'I will give you any gift that you will ask or desire.' 'Well,' said the damsel, 'go into yonder barge, and row yourself unto the sword, and take it and the scabbard with you; and I will ask my gift when I see my time.' So King Arthur and Merlin alighted, tied their horses to two trees, and so they went into the barge. And when they came to the sword that the hand held, King Arthur took it up by the handles, and took it with him, and the arm and the hand went under the water; and so came to the land and rode forth. King Arthur looked upon the sword, and liked it passing well. 'Whether liketh you better,' said Merlin, 'the sword or the scabbard?' 'Me liketh better the sword,' said King Arthur. 'Ye are more unwise,' said Merlin, 'for the scabbard is worth ten of the sword; for while ye have the scabbard upon you, ye shall lose no blood, be ye never so sore wounded; therefore keep well the scabbard alway with you.'"

Sir Lancelot du Lac, son of King Ban of Benwik, was stolen and brought up by the Lady of the Lake, from whose enchanted realm he took his name. But he does not appear at all in true Celtic legend, and is a mere Norman new-comer.

Tristrem and Ysonde

Following the Arthurian 'chronology' as set forth in the *Morte d'Arthur*, we reach the great episode of Sir Tristrem of Lyonesse, a legendary country off the coast of Cornwall. This most romantic yet most human tale must be accounted one of the world's supreme love stories. It has inspired some of our greatest poets, and moved Richard Wagner to the composition of a splendid opera.

One of the first to bring this literary treasure to public notice was Sir Walter Scott, who felt a strong chord vibrate in his romantic soul when perusing that version of the tale of which Thomas of Ercildoune is the reputed author. Taking this as the best and most ancient version of *Tristrem*, we may detail its circumstances as follows:

The Duke Morgan and Roland Rise, Lord of Ermonie, two Cymric chieftains, had long been at feud, and at length the smouldering embers of enmity burst into open flame. In the contest that ensued the doughty Roland prevailed, but he was a generous foe, and granted a seven years' truce to his defeated adversary. Some time after this event Roland journeyed into Cornwall to the Court of Mark, where he carried off the honours in a tourney. But he was to win a more precious prize in the love of the fair Princess Blancheflour, sister of King Mark, who grew to adore him passionately.

Meanwhile Duke Morgan took foul advantage of the absence of Roland, and invaded his land. Rohand, a trusty vassal of Roland, repaired to Cornwall, where he sought out his master and told him of Morgan's broken faith. Then Roland told Blancheflour of his plight, how that he must return to his own realm, and she, fearing her brother Mark, because she had given her love to Roland without the King's knowledge, resolved to fly with her lover. The pair left Cornwall hurriedly, and, reaching one of Roland's castles, were wed there. Roland, however, had soon to don his armour, for news was brought to him that Duke Morgan was coming against him with a great army. A fierce battle ensued, in which Roland at first had the advantage, but the Duke, being reinforced, pressed him hotly, and in the end Roland was defeated and slain. Blancheflour received news of her lord's death immediately before the birth of her son, and, sore stricken by the woeful news, she named him Tristrem, or 'Child of Sorrow.' Then, recommending him to the care of Rohand, to whom she gave a ring which had belonged to King Mark, her brother, to prove Tristrem's relationship to that prince, she expired, to the intense grief of all her attendants. To secure the safety of his ward, Rohand passed him off as his own child, inverting the form of his name to 'Tremtris.' Duke Morgan now ruled over the land of Ermonie, and Rohand had perforce to pay him a constrained homage.

When he arrived at a fitting age Tristrem was duly instructed in all knightly games and exercises by his foster-father, and grew apace in strength and skill. Once a Norwegian vessel arrived upon the coast of Ermonie laden with a freight of hawks and treasure (hawks at that period were often worth their weight in gold). The captain challenged anyone to a game of chess with him for a stake of twenty shillings, and Rohand and his sons, with Tristrem, went on board to play with him. Tristrem moved so skilfully that he overcame the captain, and won from him, in many games, six hawks and the sum of a hundred pounds. While the games were proceeding Rohand went on shore, leaving Tristrem in the care of his preceptor, and the false captain, to avoid paying what he had lost, forced the preceptor to go on shore alone and put to sea with the young noble.

The ship had no sooner sailed away than a furious gale arose, and as it continued for some days the mariners became convinced that the tempest was due to the injustice of their captain, and being in sore dread, they paid Tristrem his winnings and set him ashore. Dressed in a robe of 'blihand brown' (blue-brown), Tristrem found himself alone on a rocky beach. First he knelt and requested Divine protection, after which he ate some food which had been left him by the Norwegians, and started to journey through a forest, in which he encountered two palmers, who told him that he was in Cornwall. He offered these men gold to guide him to the Court of the king of the country, which they willingly undertook to do. On their way the travellers fell in with a hunting party of nobles, and Tristrem was shocked to see the awkward manner in which the huntsmen cut up some stags they had slain. He could not restrain his feeling, and disputed with the nobles upon the laws of venerie. Then he proceeded to skin a buck for their instruction, like a right good forester, and ended by blowing the *mort* or death-token on a horn.

Tristrem as Forester

The nobles who beheld his skill were amazed, and speedily carried the news to King Mark, who was highly interested. Tristrem was brought to his presence and told his story, but Mark did not recognize that he was speaking to his own nephew. The King's favourable impression was confirmed by Tristrem's skill in playing the harp, and soon the youth had endeared himself to the heart of the King, and was firmly settled at the Court. Meanwhile Rohand, distracted by the loss of his foster-son, searched for him from one land to another without even renewing his tattered garments. At last he encountered one of the palmers who had guided Tristrem to the Court of King Mark, and learned of the great honour accorded to his ward. At Rohand's request the palmer took him to Mark's hall; but when Rohand arrived thither his tattered and forlorn appearance aroused the contempt of the porter and usher and they refused him entrance. Upon bestowing liberal largess, however, he was at length brought to Tristrem, who presented him to King Mark as his father, acquainting him at the same time with the cause of their separation. When Rohand had been refreshed by a bath, and richly attired by order of King Mark, the whole Court marvelled at his majestic appearance.

Rohand, seated by King Mark's side at the banquet, imparted to him the secret of Tristrem's birth, and in proof showed him the ring given him by Blancheflour, whereupon Mark at once joyfully recognized Tristrem as his nephew. Rohand further told of the tragic fate of Tristrem's parents through the treachery of Duke Morgan, and Tristrem, fired by the tale of wrong, vowed to return at once to Ermonie to avenge his father's death.

Tristrem Returns to Ermonie

Although applauding his pious intention, Mark attempted to dissuade his nephew from such an enterprise of peril, until, seeing that Tristrem would not be gainsaid, the King conferred upon him the honour of knighthood, and furnished him with a thousand men-at-arms. Thus equipped, Tristrem set sail for Ermonie, and, safely arrived in that kingdom, he garrisoned Rohand's castle with his Cornish forces.

He had no intention of remaining inactive, however, and once his men were cared for, he repaired to the Court of the usurper, Duke Morgan, accompanied by fifteen knights, each bearing a boar's head as a gift. But Rohand, apprehending rashness on the part of his foster-son, took the precaution of following with the Cornish men-at-arms and his own vassals.

When Tristrem arrived the Duke was at the feast-board, and he demanded Tristrem's name and business. Tristrem boldly declared himself, and at the end of an angry parley the Duke struck him a sore blow. A moment later swords were flashing, and it might have gone ill with Tristrem had not Rohand with his men come up in the nick of time. In the end Duke Morgan was slain and his followers routed. Having now recovered his paternal domains Sir Tristrem conferred them upon Rohand, to be held of himself as liege lord, and having done so he took leave of his foster-father and returned to Cornwall.

The Combat with Moraunt

On arriving at the palace of Mark, Tristrem found the Court in dismay, because of a demand for tribute made by the King of England. Moraunt, the Irish ambassador to England, was charged with the duty of claiming the tribute, which was no less than three hundred pounds of gold, as many of coined silver, as many of tin, and a levy every fourth year of three hundred Cornish children. Mark protested bitterly, and Tristrem urged him to bid defiance to the English, swearing that he would himself defend the freedom of Cornwall. His aid was reluctantly accepted by the Grand Council, and he delivered to Moraunt a declaration that no tribute was due. Moraunt retorted by giving Tristrem the lie, and the champions exchanged defiance. They sailed in separate boats to a small island to decide the issue in single combat, and when they had landed Tristrem turned his boat adrift, saying sternly that one vessel would suffice to take back the victor. The champions mounted their steeds at the outset, but after the first encounter Tristrem, leaping lightly from the saddle, engaged his adversary on foot. The Knight of Ermonie was desperately wounded in the thigh, but, rallying all his strength, he cleft Moraunt to the chine, and, his sword splintering, a piece of the blade remained in the wound.

Tristrem now returned to the mainland, where so great was the joy over his return that he was appointed heir to Cornwall and successor to Mark the Good. But his wound, having been inflicted by a poisoned blade, grew more grievous day by day. No leech might cure it, and the evil odour arising from the gangrene drove every one from his presence save his faithful servitor Gouvernayl.

Fytte the Second

Fytte (or Part) the Second commences by telling how Tristrem, forsaken by all, begged King Mark for a ship that he might leave the land of Cornwall. Mark reluctantly granted his request, and the luckless Tristrem embarked with Gouvernayl, his one attendant, and his harp as his only solace. He steered for Caerleon, and remained nine weeks at sea, but meeting contrary winds he was driven out of his course, and at length came to the Irish coast, where he sought the haven of Dublin.

On arriving there he feigned that he had been wounded by pirates, and learning that he was in Ireland, and recollecting that Moraunt, whom he had slain, was the brother to the Queen of that land, he thought it wise to assume once more the name of Tremtris.

Soon his fame as a minstrel reached the ears of the Queen of Ireland, a lady deeply versed in the art of healing. She was, indeed, "the best Couthe of Medicine"[1] Tristrem had seen, and in order to heal his wound she applied to it "a plaster kene." Later she invited him to the Court, where his skill in chess and games astonished every one. So interested in him did the royal lady become at last that she undertook to cure him, and effected her object by means of a medicated bath and other medieval remedies. Then, on account of his fame as a minstrel, he was given the task of instructing the Princess Ysonde—as the name 'Yseult' is written in this particular version.

This princess was much attached to minstrelsy and poetry, and under the tuition of Tristrem she rapidly advanced in these arts, until at length she had no equal in Ireland save her preceptor. And now Tristrem, his health restored, and having completed Ysonde's instruction, felt a strong desire to return to the Court of King Mark. His request to be allowed to depart was most unwillingly granted by the Queen, who at the leave-taking loaded him with gifts. With the faithful Gouvernayl he arrived safely in Cornwall, where Mark received him joyfully. When the King inquired curiously how his wound had been cured, Tristrem told him of the great kindness of the Irish Queen, and praised Ysonde so

[1] *I.e.* had the best knowledge of medicine. *Couthe*, from A.S. *cunnan* to know.

highly that the ardour of his uncle was aroused and he requested Tristrem to procure him the hand of the damsel in marriage. He assured Tristrem that no marriage he, the King, might contract would annul the arrangement whereby Tristrem was to succeed to the throne of Cornwall. The nobles were opposed to the King's desires, which but strengthened Tristrem in his resolve to undertake the embassage, for he thought that otherwise it might appear that he desired the King to remain unmarried.

The Marriage Embassy

With a retinue of fifteen knights Tristrem sailed to Dublin in a ship richly laden with gifts. Arrived at the Irish capital, he sent magnificent presents to the King, Queen, and Princess, but did not announce the nature of his errand. Hardly had his messengers departed than he was informed that the people of Dublin were panic-stricken at the approach of a terrible dragon. This monster had so affrighted the neighbourhood that the hand of the Princess had been offered to anyone who would slay it. Tristrem dared his knights to attack the dragon, but one and all declined, so he himself rode out to give it battle. At the first shock his lance broke on the monster's impenetrable hide, his horse was slain, and he was forced to continue the fight on foot. At length, despite its fiery breath, he succeeded in slaying the dragon, and cut out its tongue as a trophy. But this exuded a subtle poison which deprived him of his senses.

Thus overcome, Tristrem was discovered by the King's steward, who cut off the dragon's head and returned with it to Court to demand the hand of Ysonde. But the Queen and her daughter were dubious of the man's story, and upon visiting the place where the dragon had been slain, they came upon Tristrem himself. Their ministrations revived him, and he showed them the dragon's tongue as proof that he had slain the dread beast. He described himself as a merchant, and Ysonde, who did not at first recognize him, expressed her regret that he was not a knight. The Queen now caused him to be conveyed to the palace, where he was refreshed by a bath, and the false steward was cast into prison. Meanwhile the suspicions of the Princess had been aroused, and the belief grew that this 'merchant' who had slain the dragon was none other than Tremtris, her old instructor. In searching for evidence to confirm this conjecture she examined his sword, from which, she found, a piece had been broken. Now, she possessed a fragment of a sword-blade which had been taken out of the skull of Moraunt, her uncle, and she discovered that this fragment fitted into the broken place in Tristrem's sword, wherefore she concluded that the weapon must have been that which slew the Irish ambassador. She reproached Tristrem, and in her passion rushed upon him with his own sword. At this instant her mother returned, and upon learning the identity of Tristrem she was about to assist Ysonde to slay him in his bath when the King arrived and saved him from the infuriated women. Tristrem defended himself as having killed Moraunt in fair fight, and, smiling upon Ysonde, he told her that she had had many opportunities of slaying him while he was her preceptor Tremtris. He then proceeded to make known the object of his embassy. He engaged that his uncle, King Mark, should marry Ysonde, and it was agreed that she should be sent under his escort to Cornwall.

It is clear that the Queen's knowledge of medicine was accompanied by an acquaintance with the black art, for on the eve of her daughter's departure she entrusted to Brengwain, a lady of Ysonde's suite, a powerful philtre or love potion, with directions that Mark and his bride should partake of it on the night of their marriage. While at sea the party met with contrary winds, and the mariners were forced to take to their oars. Tristrem exerted himself in rowing, and Ysonde, remarking that he seemed much fatigued, called for drink to refresh him. Brengwain, by a fateful error, presented the cup which held the love potion. Both Tristrem and Ysonde unwittingly partook of this, and a favourite dog, Hodain,

> That many a forest day of fiery mirth
> Had plied his craft before them,[1]

licked the cup. The consequence of this mistake was, of course, the awakening of a consuming passion each for the other in Tristrem and Ysonde. A fortnight later the ship arrived at Cornwall. Ysonde was duly wed to King Mark, but her passion for Tristrem moved her to induce her attendent Brengwain to take her place on the first night of her nuptials.

Afterward, terrified lest Brengwain should disclose the secret in her possession, Ysonde hired two ruffians to dispatch her. But the damsel's entreaties softened the hearts of the assassins and they spared her life. Subsequently Ysonde repented of her action and Brengwain was reinstated in full favour.

[1] Swinburne, *Tristram of Lyonesse.*

The Minstrel's Boon

An Irish earl, a former admirer of Ysonde, arrived one day at the Court of Cornwall disguised as a minstrel and bearing a harp of curious workmanship, the appearance of which excited the curiosity of King Mark, who requested him to perform upon it. The visitor demanded that the King should first promise to grant him a boon, and the King having pledged his royal word, the minstrel sang to the harp a lay in which he claimed Ysonde as the promised gift.[1] Mark, having pledged his honour, had no alternative but to become forsworn or to deliver his wife to the harper, and he reluctantly complied with the minstrel's demand. Tristrem, who had been away hunting, returned immediately after the adventurous earl had departed with his fair prize. He upbraided the King for his extravagant sense of honour, and, snatching up his rote, or harp, hastened to the seashore, where Ysonde had already embarked. There he sat down and played, and the sound so deeply affected Ysonde that she became seriously ill, so that the earl was induced to return with her to land. Ysonde pretended that Tristrem's music was necessary to her recovery, and the earl, to whom Tristrem was unknown, offered to take him in his train to Ireland. The earl had dismounted from the horse he was riding and was preparing to return on board, when Tristrem sprang into the saddle, and, seizing Ysonde's horse by the bridle, plunged into the forest. Here the lovers remained for a week, after which Tristrem restored Ysonde to her husband.

[1] This incident is common in Celtic romance, and seems to have been widely used in nearly all medieval literatures.

Meriadok's Suspicions

Not unnaturally suspicion was aroused regarding the relations between Tristrem and Ysonde. Meriadok, a knight of Cornwall, and an intimate friend of Tristrem, was perhaps the most suspicious of all, and one snowy evening he traced his friend to Ysonde's bower, to which Tristrem gained entrance by a sliding panel. In this a piece of Tristrem's green kirtle was left, and Meriadok bore the fragment to the King, to whom he unfolded his suspicions. To test the truth of these Mark pretended that he was going on a pilgrimage to the Holy Land, and asked his wife to whose care she would wish to be committed. Ysonde at first named Tristrem, but on the advice of Brengwain resumed the subject later and feigned a mortal hatred for her lover, which she ascribed to the scandal she had suffered on his account. The fears of the simple Mark were thus lulled to sleep; but those of Meriadok were by no means laid at rest. On his advice Mark definitely separated the lovers, confining Ysonde to a bower and sending Tristrem to a neighbouring city. But Tristrem succeeded in communicating with Ysonde by means of leafy twigs thrown into the river which ran through her garden, and they continued to meet. Their interviews were, however, discovered by the aid of a dwarf who concealed himself in a tree. One night Mark took the dwarf's place, but the lovers were made aware of his presence by his shadow and pretended to be quarrelling, Tristrem saying that Ysonde had supplanted him in the King's affections. Mark's suspicions were thus soothed for the time being. On another occasion Tristrem was not so fortunate, and, being discovered, was forced to flee the country.

The Ordeal by Fire

Mark now resolved to test his wife's innocence by the dread ordeal by fire, and he journeyed with his Court to Westminster, where the trial was to take place. Tristrem, disguised as a peasant, joined the retinue, and when the party arrived in the Thames he carried Ysonde from the ship to the shore. When the moment for the ordeal came the Queen protested her innocence, saying that no man had ever laid hands upon her save the King and the peasant who had carried her from the ship. Mark, satisfied by her evident sincerity, refused to proceed further with the trial, and Ysonde thus escaped the awful test.

Tristrem then betook him to Wales, and the fame of his prowess in that land came at length to Cornwall, so that at last his uncle grew heavy at heart for his absence and desired sight of him. Once more he returned, but his fatal passion for Ysonde was not abated, and became at length so grievous to the good King that he banished both of the lovers from his sight. The two fled to a forest, and there dwelt in a cavern, subsisting upon venison, the spoil of Tristrem's bow. One day, weary with the chase, Tristrem lay down to rest by the side of the sleeping Ysonde, placing his drawn sword between them. Mark, passing that way, espied them, and from the naked sword inferring their innocence, became reconciled to them once more. But again suspicion fell upon them, and again Tristrem was forced to flee.

Tristrem in Brittany

After many adventures in Spain Tristrem arrived in Brittany, where he aided the Duke of that country with his sword. The Duke's daughter, known as Ysonde of the White Hand, hearing him sing one night a song of the beauty of Ysonde, thought that Tristrem was in love with her. The Duke therefore offered Tristrem his daughter's hand, and, in despair of seeing Ysonde of Ireland again, he accepted the honour. But on the wedding-day the first Ysonde's ring dropped from his finger as if reproaching him with infidelity, and in deep remorse he vowed that Ysonde of Brittany should be his wife in name only.

Now the Duke of Brittany bestowed on Tristrem a fair demesne divided by an arm of the sea from the land of a powerful and savage giant named Beliagog, and he warned his son-in-law not to incur the resentment of this dangerous neighbour. But one day Tristrem's hounds strayed into the forest land of Beliagog, and their master, following them, was confronted by the wrathful owner. A long and cruel combat ensued, and at last Tristrem lopped off one of the giant's feet. Thereupon the monster craved mercy, which was granted on the condition that he should build a hall in honour of Ysonde of Ireland and her maiden, Brengwain. This hall was duly raised, and upon its walls was portrayed to the life the whole history of Tristrem, with pictures of Ysonde of Ireland, Brengwain, Mark, and other characters in the tale. Tristrem, the Duke, Ysonde of Brittany, and Ganhardin, her brother, were riding to see this marvel when Ysonde confessed to Ganhardin that Tristrem did not regard her as his wife. Ganhardin, angered, questioned Tristrem, who concealed nothing from him and recounted to him the story of his love for the Queen of Cornwall. Ganhardin was deeply interested, and on beholding the picture of Brengwain in the newly erected hall he fell violently in love with her.

The Forest Lovers

Tristrem now returned to Cornwall with Ganhardin, and encountered Ysonde the Queen and the fair Brengwain. But one Canados, the King's Constable, discovered them and carried the ladies back to Court. Ganhardin made the best of his way home to Brittany, but Tristrem remained in Cornwall, disguised as a beggar.

Our story now tells of a great tournament at the Cornish Court, and how Ganhardin hied him from Brittany and rejoined Tristrem. The two entered the lists and took up the challenge of Meriadok and Canados. Tristrem, tilting at his old enemy, wounded him desperately. The issue of the combat between Canados and Ganhardin hung in the balance when Tristrem, charging at the Constable, overthrew and slew him. Then, fired with the lust of conquest, Tristrem bore down upon his foes and exacted a heavy toll of lives. So great was the scathe done that day that Tristrem and Ganhardin were forced once more to fly to Brittany, where in an adventure Tristrem received an arrow in his old wound.

The French Manuscript

At this point the Auchinleck MS., from which this account is taken, breaks off, and the story is concluded, in language similar to that of the original, by Sir Walter Scott, who got his materials from an old French version of the tale.

We read that Tristrem suffered sorely from his wound, in which, as before, gangrene set in. Aware that none but Ysonde of Ireland could cure him, the stricken knight called Ganhardin to his side and urged him to go with all speed to Cornwall and tell the Queen of his mortal extremity. He entrusted him with his ring, and finally requested the Breton knight to take with him two sails, one white and the other black, the first to be hoisted upon his return should Ysonde accompany him back to Brittany, the sable sail to be raised should his embassy fail of success. Now Ysonde of Brittany overheard all that was said, her jealous fears were confirmed, and she resolved to be revenged upon her husband.

Ganhardin voyaged quickly to Cornwall, and arrived at the Court of King Mark disguised as a merchant. In order to speed his mission he presented rich gifts to the King, and also a cup to Ysonde, into which he dropped Tristrem's ring. This token procured him a private audience with the Queen, and when she learned the deadly peril of her lover, Ysonde hastily disguised herself and fled to the ship with Ganhardin. In due course the vessel arrived off the coast of Brittany, carrying the white sail which was to signify to Tristrem that Ysonde was hastening to his aid. But Ysonde of Brittany was watching, and perceiving from the signal that her rival was on board she hurried to her husband's couch. Tristrem begged her to tell him the colour of the sail, and in the madness of jealousy Ysonde said that it was black, upon which, believing himself forsaken by his old love, the knight sank back and expired.

Tristrem had scarce breathed his last when Ysonde entered the castle. At the gate an old man was mourning Tristrem's death, and hearing the ominous words which he uttered she hastened to the chamber where the corpse of him she had loved so well was lying. With a moan she cast herself upon the body, covering the dead face with kisses and pleading upon the silent lips to speak. Realizing at last that the spirit had indeed quitted its mortal tenement, she raised herself to her feet and stood for a moment gazing wildly into the fixed and glassy eyes; then with a great cry she fell forward upon the breast of her lover and was united with him in death.

Other versions of the story, with all the wealth of circumstance dear to the writer of romance, tell of the grievous mourning made at the death of the lovers, whom no fault of their own had doomed to the tyranny of a mutual passion, and it is recounted that even King Mark, wronged and shamed as he was, was unable to repress his grief at their pitiful end.

Despite the clumsiness of much of its machinery, despite its tiresome repetitions and its minor blemishes, this tale of a grand passion must ever remain one of the world's priceless literary possessions. "Dull must he be of soul" who, even in these days when folk no longer expire from an excess of the tender passion, can fail to be moved by the sad fate of the fair Queen and of her gallant minstrel-knight.

> Swiche lovers als thei
> Never schal be moe.

And so they take their place with Hero and Leander, with Abélard and Héloïse, with Romeo and Juliet.

It would be unfitting here to tell how mythology has claimed the story of Tristrem and Ysonde and has attempted to show in what manner the circumstances of their lives and adventures have been adapted to the old world-wide myth of the progress of the sun from dawn to darkness.[1] The evidence seems very complete, and the theory is probably well founded. The circumstances of the great epic of the sun-god fits most hero-tales. And it is well to recollect that even if romance-makers seized upon the plot of the old myth they did so unconscious of its mythic significance, and probably because it may have been employed in the heroic literature of "Rome la grant."

The Giant of Mont-Saint-Michel

It was when he arrived in Brittany to ward off the projected invasion of England by the Roman Emperor Lucius that King Arthur encountered and slew a giant of "marvellous bigness" at St Michael's Mount, near Pontorson. This monster, who had come from Spain, had made his lair on the summit of the rocky island, whither he had carried off the Lady Helena, niece of Duke Hoel of Brittany. Many were the knights who surrounded the giant's fastness, but none might come at him, for when they attacked him he would sink their ships by hurling mighty boulders upon them, while those who succeeded in swimming to the island were slain by him ere they could get a proper footing. But Arthur, undismayed by what he had heard, waited until nightfall; then, when all were asleep, with Kay the seneschal and Bedivere the butler, he started on his way to the Mount.

As the three approached the rugged height they beheld a fire blazing brightly on its summit, and saw also that upon a lesser eminence in the sea some distance away a smaller fire was burning. Bedivere was dispatched

[1] See Rev. Sir G. W. Cox, *Introduction to Mythology*, p. 326 ff.

in a boat to discover who had lit the fire on the smaller island. Having landed there, he found an old woman lamenting loudly.

"Good mother," said he, "wherefore do you mourn? What has befallen you in this place that you weep so sorely?"

"Ah, young sir," replied the dame, drying her tears, "get thee back from this place, I beseech thee, for as thou livest the monster who inhabits yonder mount will rend thee limb from limb and sup on thy flesh. But yesterday I was the nurse of the fair Helena, niece to Duke Hoel, who lies buried here by me."

"Alas! then, the lady is no more?" cried Bedivere, in distress.

"So it is," replied the old woman, weeping more bitterly than ever, "for when that accursed giant did seize upon her terror did so overcome her that her spirit took flight. But tarry not on this dread spot, noble youth, for if her fierce slayer should encounter thee he will put thee to a shameful death, and afterward devour thee as is his wont with all those whom he kills."

Bedivere comforted the old woman as best he might, and, returning to Arthur, told him what he had heard. Now on hearing of the damsel's death great anger took hold upon the King, so that he resolved to search out the giant forthwith and slay or be slain by him. Desiring Kay and Bedivere to follow, he dismounted and commenced to climb St Michael's Mount, closely attended by his companions.

On reaching the summit a gruesome spectacle awaited them. The great fire that they had seen in the distance was blazing fiercely, and bending over it was the giant, his cruel and contorted features besmeared with the

KING ARTHUR AND THE GIANT OF MONT-SAINT-MICHEL

THE WERE-WOLF

blood of swine, portions of which he was toasting on spits. Startled at the sight of the knights, the monster rushed to where his club lay. This purpose Arthur deemed he might prevent, and, covering himself with his shield, he ran at him while yet he fumbled for the weapon. But with all his agility he was too late, for the giant seized the mighty sapling and, whirling it in the air, brought it down on the King's shield with such force that the sound of the stroke echoed afar. Nothing daunted, Arthur dealt a trenchant stroke with Excalibur, and gave the giant a cut on the forehead which made the blood gush forth over his eyes so as nearly to blind him. But shrewd as was the blow, the giant had warded his forehead with his club in such wise that he had not received a deadly wound, and, watching his chance with great cunning, he rushed in within the sweep of Arthur's sword, gripped him round the middle, and forced him to the ground.

Iron indeed would have been the grasp which could have held a knight so doughty as Arthur. Slipping from the monster's clutches, the King hacked at his adversary now in one place, now in another, till at length he smote the giant so mightily that Excalibur was buried deep in his brain-pan. The giant fell like an oak torn up by the roots in the fury of the winds. Rushing up as he crashed to the earth, Sir Bedivere struck off the hideous head, grinning in death, to be a show to those in the tents below.

"But let them behold it in silence and without laughter," the King charged Sir Bedivere, "for never since I slew the giant Ritho upon Mount Eryri have I encountered so mighty an adversary."

And so they returned to their tents with daybreak.

A Doubting Thomas

It is strange to think that Brittany, one of the cradles of Arthurian legend, could have produced a disbeliever in that legend so early as the year of grace 1113. It is on record that some monks from Brittany journeyed to England in that year, and were shown by the men of Devon "the chair and the oven of that King Arthur renowned in the stories of the Britons." They passed on to Cornwall, and when, in the church at Bodmin, one of their servants dared to question the statement of a certain Cornishman that Arthur still lived, he received such a buffet for his temerity that a small riot ensued.[1] Does not this seem to be evidence that the legend was more whole-heartedly believed in in the Celtic parts of England, and was therefore more exclusively native to those parts than to Continental Brittany? The Cornish allegiance to the memory of Arthur seems to have left little to be desired.

Arthur and the Dragon

The manner in which Arthur slew a dragon at the Lieue de Grève, and at the same time made the acquaintance of St Efflam of Ireland, is told by Albert le Grand, monk of Morlaix. Arthur had been sojourning at the Court of Hoel, Duke of Armorica, and, having freed his own land of dragons and other monsters, was engaged in hunting down the great beasts with which Armorica abounded. But the monster which infested the Lieue de Grève was no ordinary dragon. Indeed,

[1] See Zimmer, *Zeitschrift für Französische Sprache und Literatur*, xii, pp. 106 ff.

he was the most cunning saurian in Europe, and was wont to retire backward into the great cavern in which he lived so that when traced to it those who tracked him would believe that he had just quitted it.

In this manner he succeeded in deceiving Arthur and his knights, who for days lingered in the vicinity of his cave in the hope of encountering him. One day as they stood on the seashore waiting for the dragon a sail hove in sight, and soon a large coracle made of wicker-work covered with skins appeared. The vessel grounded and its occupants leapt ashore, headed by a young man of princely mien, who advanced toward Arthur and saluted him courteously.

"Fair sir," he said, "to what shore have I come? I am Efflam, the King's son, of Ireland. The winds have driven us out of our course, and full long have we laboured in the sea."

Now when Arthur heard the young man's name he embraced him heartily.

"Welcome, cousin," he said. "You are in the land of Brittany. I am Arthur of Britain, and I rejoice at this meeting, since it may chance from it that I can serve you."

Then Efflam told Arthur the reason of his voyaging. He had been wed to the Princess Enora, daughter of a petty king of Britain, but on his wedding night a strong impulse had come upon him to leave all and make his penitence within some lonely wood, where he could be at peace from the world. Rising from beside his sleeping wife, he stole away, and rousing several trusty servitors he set sail from his native shores. Soon his frail craft was caught in a tempest, and after many days driven ashore as had been seen.

Arthur marvelled at the impulse which had prompted Efflam to seek retirement, and was about to express his surprise when the youth startled him by telling him that as his vessel had approached the shore he and his men had caught sight of the dragon entering his cave. At these words Arthur armed himself without delay with his sword Excalibur and his lance Ron, and, followed by his knights and by Efflam, drew near the cavern. As he came before the entrance the dragon issued forth, roaring in so terrible a manner that all but the King were daunted and drew back. The creature's appearance was fearsome in the extreme. He had one red eye in the centre of his forehead, his shoulders were covered with green scales like plates of mail, his long, powerful tail was black and twisted, and his vast mouth was furnished with tusks like those of a wild boar.

Grim and great was the combat. For three days did it rage, man and beast struggling through the long hours for the mastery which neither seemed able to obtain. At the end of that time the dragon retired for a space into his lair, and Arthur, worn out and well-nigh broken by the long-drawn strife, threw himself down beside Efflam in a state of exhaustion.

"A draught of water, fair cousin," he cried in a choking voice. "I perish with thirst."

But no water was to be found in that place save that of the salt sea which lapped the sands of Grève. Efflam, however, was possessed of a faith that could overcome all difficulties. Kneeling, he engaged in earnest prayer, and, arising, struck the hard rock three times with his rod. "Our blessed Lord will send us water," he exclaimed, and no sooner had he spoken than from the stone a fountain of pure crystal water gushed and bubbled.

With a cry of ecstasy Arthur placed his lips to the stream and quaffed the much-needed refreshment. His vigour restored, he was about to return to the dragon's cavern to renew the combat when he was restrained by Efflam.

"Cousin," said he of Ireland, "you have tried what can be done by force; now let us see what can be achieved by prayer."

Arthur, marvelling and humbled, sat near the young man as he prayed. All night he was busied in devotions, and at sunrise he arose and walked boldly to the mouth of the cavern.

"Thou spawn of Satan," he cried, "in the name of God I charge thee to come forth!"

A noise as of a thousand serpents hissing in unison followed this challenge, and from out his lair trailed the great length of the dragon, howling and vomiting fire and blood. Mounting to the summit of a neighbouring rock, he vented a final bellow and then cast himself into the sea. The blue water was disturbed as by a maelstrom; then all was peace again.

So perished the dragon of the Lieue de Grève, and so was proved the superiority of prayer over human strength and valour. St Efflam and his men settled on the spot as hermits, and were miraculously fed by angels. Efflam's wife, Enora, was borne to him by angels in that place, only to die when she had joined him. And when they came to tell Efflam that his new-found lady was no more and was lying cold in the cell he had provided for her, their news fell on deaf ears, for he too had passed away. He is buried in Plestin Church, and his effigy, standing triumphant above an open-mouthed dragon, graces one of its many niches.

The Isle of Avalon

The Bretons believe that an island off Trégastel, on the coast of the department of Côtes-du-Nord, is the fabled Isle of Avalon to which King Arthur, sore wounded after his last battle, was borne to be healed of his hurts. With straining eyes the fisherman watches the mist-wrapped islet, and, peering through the evening haze, cheats himself into the belief that giant forms are moving upon its shores and that spectral shapes flit across its sands—that the dark hours bring back the activities of the attendant knights and enchantresses of the mighty hero of Celtdom, who, refreshed by his long repose, will one day return to the world of men and right the great wrongs which afflict humanity.

CHAPTER XI: THE BRETON LAYS OF MARIE DE FRANCE

THE wonderful *Lais* of Marie de France must ever hold a deep interest for all students of Breton lore, for though cast in the literary mould of Norman-French and breathing the spirit of Norman chivalry those of them which deal with Brittany (as do most of them) exhibit such evident marks of having been drawn from native Breton sources that we may regard them as among the most valuable documents extant for the study and consideration of Armorican story.

Of the personal history of Marie de France very little is known. The date and place of her birth are still matters for conjecture, and until comparatively recent times literary antiquaries were doubtful even as to which century she flourished in. In the epilogue to her *Fables* she states that she is a native of the Ile-de-France, but despite this she is believed to have been of Norman origin, and also to have lived the greater part of her life in England. Her work, which holds few suggestions of Anglo-Norman forms of thought or expression, was written in a literary dialect that in all likelihood was widely estranged from the common Norman tongue, and from this (though the manuscripts in which they are preserved are dated later) we may judge her poems to have been composed in the second half of the twelfth century. The prologue of her *Lais* contains a dedication to some unnamed king, and her *Fables* are inscribed to a certain Count William, circumstances which are held by some to prove that she was of noble origin and not merely a *trouvère* from necessity.

Until M. Gaston Paris decided that this mysterious king was Henry II of England, and that the 'Count William' was Longsword, Earl of Salisbury, Henry's natural son by the 'Fair Rosamond,' the mysterious monarch was believed to be Henry III. It is highly probable that the *Lais* were actually written at the Court of Henry II, though the 'King' of the flowery prologue is hardly reconcilable with the stern ruler and law-maker of history. Be that as it may, Marie's poems achieved instant success. "Her rhyme is loved everywhere," says Denis Pyramus, the author of a life of St Edmund the King; "for counts, barons, and knights greatly admire it and hold it dear. And they love her writing so much, and take such pleasure in it, that they have it read, and often copied. These Lays are wont to please ladies, who listen to them with delight, for they are after their own hearts." This fame and its attendant adulation were very sweet to Marie, and she was justly proud of her work, which, inspired, as she herself distinctly states, by the lays she had heard Breton minstrels sing, has, because of its vivid colouring and human appeal, survived the passing of seven hundred years. The scenes of the tales are laid in Brittany, and we are probably correct in regarding them as culled from original traditional material. As we proceed with the telling of these ancient stories we shall endeavour to point out the essentially Breton elements they have retained.

The Lay of the Were-Wolf

In the long ago there dwelt in Brittany a worshipful baron, for whom the king of that land had a warm affection, and who was happy in the esteem of his peers and the love of his beautiful wife.

One only grief had his wife in her married life, and that was the mysterious absence of her husband for three days in every week. Where he disappeared to neither she nor any member of her household knew. These excursions preyed upon her mind, so that at last she resolved to challenge him regarding them.

"Husband," she said to him pleadingly one day after he had just returned from one of these absences, "I have something to ask of you, but I fear that my request may vex you, and for this reason I hesitate to make it."

The baron took her in his arms and, kissing her tenderly, bade her state her request, which he assured her would by no means vex him.

"It is this," she said, "that you will trust me sufficiently to tell me where you spend those days when you are absent from me. So fearful have I become regarding these withdrawals and all the mystery that enshrouds them that I know neither rest nor comfort; indeed, so distraught am I at times that I feel I shall die for very anxiety. Oh, husband, tell me where you go and why you tarry so long!"

In great agitation the husband put his wife away from him, not daring to meet the glance of her imploring, anxious eyes.

"For the mercy of God, do not ask this of me," he besought her. "No good could come of your knowing, only great and terrible evil. Knowledge would mean the death of your love for me, and my everlasting desolation."

"You are jesting with me, husband," she replied; "but it is a cruel jest. I am all seriousness, I do assure you. Peace of mind can never be mine until my question is fully answered."

But the baron, still greatly perturbed, remained firm. He could not tell her, and she must rest content with that. The lady, however, continued to plead, sometimes with tenderness, more often with tears and heart-piercing reproaches, until at length the baron, trusting to her love, decided to tell her his secret.

"I have to leave you because periodically I become a bisclaveret," he said. ('Bisclaveret' is the Breton name for were-wolf.) "I hide myself in the depths of the forest, live on wild animals and roots, and go unclad as any beast of the field."

When the lady had recovered from the horror of this disclosure and had rallied her senses to her aid, she turned to him again, determined at any cost to learn all the circumstances connected with this terrible transformation.

"You know that I love you better than all the world, my husband," she began; "that never in our life together have I done aught to forfeit your love or your trust. So do, I beseech you, tell me all—tell me where you hide your clothing before you become a were-wolf?"

"That I dare not do, dear wife," he replied, "for if I should lose my raiment or even be seen quitting it I must remain a were-wolf so long as I live. Never again could I become a man unless my garments were restored to me."

"Then you no longer trust me, no longer love me?" she cried. "Alas, alas that I have forfeited your confidence! Oh that I should live to see such a day!"

Her weeping broke out afresh, this time more piteously than before. The baron, deeply touched, and willing by any means to alleviate her distress, at last divulged the vital secret which he had held from her so long. But from that hour his wife cast about for ways and means to rid herself of her strange husband, of whom she now went in exceeding fear. In course of time she remembered a knight of that country who had long sought her love, but whom she had repulsed. To him she appealed, and right gladly and willingly he pledged himself to aid her. She showed him where her lord concealed his clothing, and begged him to spoil the were-wolf of his vesture on the next occasion on which he set out to assume his transformation. The fatal period soon returned. The baron disappeared as usual, but this time he did not return to his home. For days friends, neighbours, and menials sought him diligently, but no trace of him was to be found, and when a year had elapsed the search was at length abandoned, and the lady was wedded to her knight.

Some months later the King was hunting in the great forest near the missing baron's castle. The hounds, unleashed, came upon the scent of a wolf, and pressed the animal hard. For many hours they pursued him, and when about to seize him, Bisclaveret—for it was he—turned with such a human gesture of despair to the King, who had ridden hard upon his track, that the royal huntsman was moved to pity. To the King's surprise the were-wolf placed its paws together as if in supplication, and its great jaws moved as if in speech.

"Call off the hounds," cried the monarch to his attendants. "This quarry we will take alive to our palace. It is too marvellous a thing to be killed."

Accordingly they returned to the Court, where the

were-wolf became an object of the greatest curiosity to all. So frolicsome yet so gentle was he that he became a universal favourite. At night he slept in the King's room, and by day he followed him with all the dumb faithfulness of a dog. The King was extremely attached to him, and never permitted his shaggy favourite to be absent from his side for a moment.

One day the monarch held a high Court, to which his great vassals and barons and all the lords of his broad demesnes were bidden. Among them came the knight who had wed the wife of Bisclaveret. Immediately upon sight of him the were-wolf flew at him with a savage joy that astonished those accustomed to his usual gentleness and docility. So fierce was the attack that the knight would have been killed had not the King intervened to save him. Later, in the royal hunting-lodge she who had been the wife of Bisclaveret came to offer the King a rich present. When he saw her the animal's rage knew no bounds, and despite all restraint he succeeded in mutilating her fair face in the most frightful manner. But for a certain wise counsellor this act would have cost Bisclaveret his life. This sagacious person, who knew of the animal's customary docility, insisted that some evil must have been done him.

"There must be some reason why this beast holds these twain in such mortal hate," he said. "Let this woman and her husband be brought hither so that they may be straitly questioned. She was once the wife of one who was near to your heart, and many marvellous happenings have ere this come out of Brittany."

The King hearkened to this sage counsel, for he loved the were-wolf, and was loath to have him slain. Under pressure of examination Bisclaveret's treacherous wife confessed all that she had done, adding that in her heart she believed the King's favourite animal to be no other than her former husband.

Instantly on learning this the King demanded the were-wolf's vesture from the treacherous knight her lover, and when this was brought to him he caused it to be spread before the wolf. But the animal behaved as though he did not see the garments.

Then the wise counsellor again came to his aid. "You must take the beast to your own secret chamber, sire," he told the King; "for not without great shame and tribulation can he become a man once more, and this he dare not suffer in the sight of all."

This advice the King promptly followed, and when after some little time he, with two lords of his fellowship in attendance, re-entered the secret chamber, he found the wolf gone, and the baron so well beloved asleep in his bed.

With great joy and affection the King aroused his friend, and when the baron's feelings permitted him he related his adventures. As soon as his master had heard him out he not only restored to him all that had been taken from him, but added gifts the number and richness of which rendered him more wealthy and important than ever, while in just anger he banished from his realm the wife who had betrayed her lord, together with her lover.

The Were-Wolf Superstition

The were-wolf superstition is, or was, as prevalent in Brittany as in other parts of France and Europe. The term 'were-wolf' literally means 'man-wolf,' and was applied to a man supposed to be temporarily or permanently transformed into a wolf. In its origins the belief may have been a phase of lycanthropy, a disease in which the sufferer imagines himself to have been transformed into an animal, and in ancient and medieval times of very frequent occurrence. It may, on the other hand, be a relic of early cannibalism. Communities of semi-civilized people would begin to shun those who devoured human flesh, and they would in time be ostracized and classed with wild beasts, the idea that they had something in common with these would grow, and the belief that they were able to transform themselves into veritable animals would be likely to arise therefrom. There were two kinds of were-wolf, voluntary and involuntary. The voluntary included those persons who because of their taste for human flesh had withdrawn from intercourse with their fellows, and who appeared to possess a certain amount of magical power, or at least sufficient to permit them to transform themselves into animal shape at will. This they effected by merely disrobing, by taking off a girdle made of human skin, or putting on a similar belt of wolf-skin (obviously a later substitute for an entire wolf-skin; in some cases we hear of their donning the skin entire). In other instances the body was rubbed with magic ointment, or rain-water was drunk out of a wolf's footprint. The brains of the animal were also eaten. Olaus Magnus says that the were-wolves of Livonia drained a cup of beer on initiation, and repeated certain magical words. In order to throw off the wolf-shape the animal girdle was removed, or else the magician merely muttered certain formulæ. In some instances the transformation was supposed to be the work of Satan.

The superstition regarding were-wolves seems to have been exceedingly prevalent in France during the sixteenth century, and there is evidence of numerous trials of persons accused of were-wolfism, in some of which it was clearly shown that murder and cannibalism had taken place. Self-hallucination was accountable for many of the cases, the supposed were-wolves declaring that they had transformed themselves and had slain many people. But about the beginning of the seventeenth century native common sense came to the rescue, and such confessions were not credited. In Teutonic and Slavonic countries it was complained by men of learning that the were-wolves did more damage than real wild animals, and the existence of a regular 'college' or institution for the practice of the art of animal transformation among were-wolves was affirmed.

Involuntary were-wolves, of which class Bisclaveret was evidently a member, were often persons transformed into animal shape because of the commission of sin, and condemned to pass a certain number of years in that form. Thus certain saints metamorphosed sinners into wolves. In Armenia it was thought that a sinful woman was condemned to pass seven years in the form of a wolf. To such a woman a demon appeared, bringing a wolf-skin. He commanded her to don it, and from that moment she became a wolf, with all the nature of the wild beast, devouring her own children and those of strangers, and wandering forth at night, undeterred by locks, bolts, or bars, returning only with the morning to resume her human form.

In was, of course, in Europe, where the wolf was one of the largest carnivorous animals, that the were-wolf superstition chiefly gained currency. In Eastern countries, where similar beliefs prevailed, bears, tigers, and other beasts of prey were substituted for the lupine form of colder climes.

The Lay of Gugemar

Oridial was one of the chief barons of King Arthur, and dwelt in Brittany, where he held lands in fief of that monarch. So deeply was he attached to his liege lord that when his son Gugemar was yet a child he sent him to Arthur's Court to be trained as a page. In due time Arthur dubbed Gugemar knight and armed him in rich harness, and the youth, hearing of war in Flanders, set out for that realm in the hope of gaining distinction and knightly honour.

After achieving many valorous deeds in Flanders Gugemar felt a strong desire to behold his parents once more, so, setting his face homeward, he journeyed back to Brittany and dwelt with them for some time, resting after his battles and telling his father, mother, and sister Nogent of the many enterprises in which he had been engaged. But he shortly grew weary of this inactive existence, and in order to break the monotony of it he planned a great hunt in the neighbouring forest.

Early one morning he set out, and soon a tall stag was roused from its bed among the ferns by the noise of the hunters' horns. The hounds were unleashed and the entire hunt followed in pursuit, Gugemar the foremost of all. But, closely as he pursued, the quarry eluded the knight, and to his chagrin he was left alone in the forest spaces with nothing to show for his long chase. He was about to ride back in search of his companions when on a sudden he noticed a doe hiding in a thicket with her fawn. She was white from ear to hoof, without a spot. Gugemar's hounds, rushing at her, held her at bay, and their master, fitting an arrow to his bow, loosed the shaft at her so that she was wounded above the hoof and brought to earth. But the treacherous arrow, glancing, returned to Gugemar and wounded him grievously in the thigh.

As he lay on the earth faint and with his senses almost deserting him, Gugemar heard the doe speak to him in human accents:

"Wretch who hast slain me," said she, "think not to escape my vengeance. Never shall leech nor herb nor balm cure the wound which fate hath so justly inflicted upon thee. Only canst thou be healed by a woman who loves thee, and who for that love shall have to suffer such woe and sorrow as never woman had to endure before. Thou too shalt suffer equally with her, and the sorrows of ye twain shall be the wonder of lovers for all time. Leave me now to die in peace."

Gugemar was in sore dismay at hearing these words, for never had he sought lady's love nor had he cared for the converse of women. Winding his horn, he succeeded in attracting one of his followers to the spot, and sent him in search of his companions. When he had gone Gugemar tore his linen shirt in pieces and bound up his wound as well as he might. Then, dragging himself most painfully into the saddle, he rode from the scene of his misadventure at as great a pace as his injury would permit of, for he had conceived a plan which he did not desire should be interfered with.

Riding at a hand-gallop, he soon came in sight of tall cliffs which overlooked the sea, and which formed a natural harbour, wherein lay a vessel richly beseen. Its sails were of spun silk, and each plank and mast was fashioned of ebony. Dismounting, Gugemar made his way to the shore, and with much labour climbed upon the ship. Neither mariner nor merchant was therein. A large pavilion of silk covered part of the deck, and within this was a rich bed, the work of the cunning artificers of the days of King Solomon. It was fashioned of cypress wood and ivory, and much gold and many gems went to the making of it. The clothes with which it was provided were fair and white as snow, and so soft the pillow that he who laid his head upon it, sad as he might be, could not resist sleep. The pavilion was lit by two large waxen candles, set in candlesticks of gold.

As the knight sat gazing at this splendid couch fit for a king he suddenly became aware that the ship was moving seaward. Already, indeed, he was far from land, and at the sight he grew more sorrowful than before, for his hurt made him helpless and he could not hope either to guide the vessel or manage her so that he might return to shore. Resigning himself to circumstances, he lay down upon the ornate bed and sank into a deep and dreamless slumber.

When he awoke he found to his intense surprise that the ship had come to the port of an ancient city. Now the king of this realm was an aged man who was wedded to a young, fair lady, of whom he was, after the manner of old men, intensely jealous. The castle of this monarch frowned upon a fair garden enclosed from the sea by a high wall of green marble, so that if one desired to come to the castle he must do so from the water. The place was straitly watched by vigilant

GUGEMAR COMES UPON THE MAGIC SHIP

GUGEMAR'S ASSAULT ON THE CASTLE OF MERIADUS

warders, and within the wall so carefully defended lay the Queen's bower, a fairer chamber than any beneath the sun, and decorated with the most marvellous paintings. Here dwelt the young Queen with one of her ladies, her own sister's child, who was devoted to her service and who never quitted her side. The key of this bower was in the hands of an aged priest, who was also the Queen's servitor.

One day on awaking from sleep the Queen walked in the garden and espied a ship drawing near the land. Suddenly, she knew not why, she grew very fearful, and would have fled at the sight, but her maiden encouraged her to remain. The vessel came to shore, and the Queen's maiden entered it. No one could she see on board except a knight sleeping soundly within the pavilion, and he was so pale that she thought he was dead. Returning to her mistress, she told her what she had seen, and together they entered the vessel.

No sooner did the Queen behold Gugemar than she was deeply smitten with love for him. In a transport of fear lest he were dead she placed her hand upon his bosom, and was overjoyed to feel the warmth of life within him and that his heart beat strongly. At her touch he awoke and courteously saluted her. She asked him whence he came and to what nation he belonged.

"Lady," he replied, "I am a knight of Brittany. But yesterday, or so it seems to me, for I may have slumbered more than a day, I wounded a deer in the forest, but the arrow with which I slew her rebounded and struck me sorely. Then the beast, being, I trow, a fairy deer, spake, saying that never would this wound be healed save by one damsel in the whole world, and her I know not where to find. Riding seaward, I came to where this ship lay moored, and, entering it, the vessel drifted oceanward. I know not to what land I have come, nor what name this city bears. I pray you, fair lady, give me your best counsel."

The Queen listened to his tale with the deepest interest, and when Gugemar made his appeal for aid and counsel she replied: "Truly, fair sir, I shall counsel you as best I may. This city to which you have come belongs to my husband, who is its King. Of much worship is he, but stricken in years, and because of the jealousy he bears me he has shut me up between these high walls. If it please you you may tarry here awhile and we will tend your wound until it be healed."

Gugemar, wearied and bewildered at the strange things which had happened to him in the space of a day, thanked the Queen, and accepted her kind offer of entertainment with alacrity. Between them the Queen and her lady assisted him to leave the ship and bore him to a chamber, where he was laid in a fair bed and had his wound carefully dressed. When the ladies had withdrawn and the knight was left to himself he knew that he loved the Queen. All memory of his home and even of his tormenting wound disappeared, and he could brood only upon the fair face of the royal lady who had so charmingly ministered to him.

Meanwhile the Queen was in little better case. All night she could not sleep for pondering upon the handsome youth who had come so mysteriously into her life, and her maiden, seeing this, and marking how she suffered, went to Gugemar's chamber and told him in a frank and almost childlike manner how deeply her mistress had been smitten with love for him.

"You are young," she said, "so is my lady. Her lord

is old and their union is unseemly. Heaven intended you for one another and has brought you together in its own good time."

Shortly, after she had heard Mass, the Queen summoned Gugemar into her presence. At first both were dumb with confusion. At last his passion urged Gugemar to speak, and his love-words came thick and fast. The Queen hearkened to them, and, feeling that they rang true, admitted that she loved him in return.

For a year and a half Gugemar dwelt in the Queen's bower. Then the lovers met with misfortune.

For some days before the blow fell the Queen had experienced a feeling of coming evil. So powerfully did this affect her that she begged Gugemar for a garment of his. The knight marvelled at the request, and asked her playfully for what reason she desired such a keepsake as a linen shift.

"Friend," she replied, "if it chance that you leave me or that we are separated I shall fear that some other damsel may win your love. In this shift which you give me I shall make a knot, and shall ask you to vow that never will you give your love to dame or damsel who cannot untie this knot."

The knight complied with her request, and she made such a cunning knot in the garment as only she could unravel. For his part Gugemar gave the Queen a wonderfully fashioned girdle which only he could unclasp, and he begged her that she would never grant her love to any man who could not free her from it. Each promised the other solemnly to respect the vows they had made.

That same day their hidden love was discovered. A chamberlain of the King's observed them through a window of the Queen's bower, and, hastening to his master, told him what he had seen. In terrible wrath the King called for his guards, and, coming upon the lovers unaware, commanded them to slay Gugemar at once. But the knight seized upon a stout rod of fir-wood on which linen was wont to be dried, and faced those who would slay him so boldly that they fell back in dismay. The King questioned him as to his name and lineage, and Gugemar fearlessly related his story. The King was incredulous at first, but said that could the ship be found in which Gugemar had arrived he would place him upon it and send him once more out to sea. After search had been made the vessel was found, and Gugemar was placed on it, the ship began to move, and soon the knight was well at sea.

Ere long the ship came to that harbour whence she had first sailed, and as Gugemar landed he saw to his surprise one of his own vassals holding a charger and accompanied by a knight. Mounting the steed, Gugemar swiftly rode home, where he was received with every demonstration of joy. But though his parents and friends did everything possible to make him happy, the memory of the fair Queen who had loved him was ever with him night and day, so that he might not be solaced by game or tilting, the chase or the dance. In vain those who wished him well urged him to take a wife. At first he roundly refused to consider such a step, but when eagerly pressed by his friends he announced that no wife should he wed who could not first unloose the knot within his shift. So sought after was Gugemar that all the damsels in Brittany essayed the feat, but none of them succeeded and each retired sorrowfully from the ordeal.

Meanwhile the aged King had set his wife in a tower of grey marble, where she suffered agonies because of the absence of her lover. Ever she wondered what had happened to him, if he had regained his native shore or whether he had been swallowed up by the angry sea. Frequently she made loud moan, but there were none to hear her cries save stony-hearted gaolers, who were as dumb as the grey walls that enclosed her. One day she chanced in her dolour to lean heavily upon the door of her prison. To her amazement it opened, and she found herself in the corridor without. Hastening on impulse, and as if by instinct, to the harbour, she found there her lover's ship. Quickly she climbed upon its deck, and scarcely had she done so than the vessel began to move seaward. In great fear she sat still, and in time was wafted to a part of Brittany governed by one named Meriadus, who was on the point of going to war with a neighbouring chieftain. From his window Meriadus had seen the approach of the strange vessel, and, making his way to the seashore, entered the ship. Struck with the beauty of the Queen, he brought her to his castle, where he placed her in his sister's chamber. He strove in every way to dispel the sadness which seemed to envelop her like a mantle, but despite his efforts to please her she remained in sorrowful and doleful mood and would not be comforted. Sorely did Meriadus press her to wed him, but she would have none of him, and for answer showed him the girdle round her waist, saying that never would she give her love to any man who could not unloose its buckle. As she said this Meriadus seemed struck by her words.

"Strange," he said, "a right worthy knight dwells in

this land who will take no woman to his wife save she who can first untie a certain crafty knot in his shift. Well would I wager that it was you who tied this knot."

When the Queen heard these words she well-nigh fainted. Meriadus rushed to succour her, and gradually she revived. Some days later Meriadus held a high tournament, at which all the knights who were to aid him in the war were to be present, among them Gugemar. A festival was held on the night preceding the tournament, at which Meriadus requested his sister and the stranger dame to be present. As the Queen entered the hall Gugemar rose from his place and stared at her as at a vision of the dead. In great doubt was he whether this lady was in truth his beloved.

"Come, Gugemar," rallied Meriadus, "let this damsel try to unravel the knot in your shift which has puzzled so many fair dames."

Gugemar called to his squire and bade him fetch the shift, and when it was brought the lady, without seeming effort, unravelled the knot. But even yet Gugemar remained uncertain.

"Lady," he said, "tell me, I pray you, whether or not you wear a girdle with which I girt you in a realm across the sea," and placing his hands around her slender waist, he found there the secret belt.

All his doubts dispelled, Gugemar asked his loved one how she had come to the tower of Meriadus. When he had heard, he then and there requested his ally to yield him the lady, but the chieftain roundly refused. Then the knight in great anger cast down his glove and took his departure, and, to the discomfiture of Meriadus, all those knights who had gathered for the tournament and had offered to assist Meriadus accompanied Gugemar.

In a body they rode to the castle of the prince who was at war with Meriadus, and next day they marched against the discourteous chieftain. Long did they besiege his castle, but at last when the defenders were weak with hunger Gugemar and his men assailed the place and took it, slaying Meriadus within the ruins of his own hall. Gugemar, rushing to that place where he knew his lady to be, called her forth, and in peace brought her back with him to his own demesne, where they were wed and dwelt long and happily.

There are several circumstances connected with this beautiful old tale which deeply impress us with a belief in its antiquity. The incident of the killing of the deer and the incurable nature of Gugemar's wound are undoubtedly legacies from very ancient times, when it was believed to be unlucky under certain circumstances to kill a beast of the chase. Some savage races, such as the North American Indians, consider it to be most unlucky to slay a deer without first propitiating the great Deer God, the chief of the Deer Folk, and in fact they attribute most of the ills to which flesh is heir to the likelihood that they have omitted some of the very involved ritual of the chase. It will be remembered that Tristrem of Lyonesse also had an incurable wound, and there are other like instances in romance and myth.

The vessel which carries Gugemar over the sea is undoubtedly of the same class as those magic self-propelled craft which we meet with very frequently in Celtic lore, and the introduction of this feature in itself is sufficient to convince us of the Celtic or Breton origin of Marie's tale. We have such a craft in the Grail legend in the *Morte d'Arthur*, in which Galahad finds precisely such a bed. The vessel in the Grail legend is described as "King Solomon's Ship," and it is obvious that Marie or her Breton original must have borrowed the idea from a Grail source.

Lastly, the means adopted by the lovers to ensure one another's constancy seem very like the methods of taboo. The knot that may not or cannot be untied has many counterparts in ancient lore, and the girdle that no man but the accepted lover may loose is reminiscent of the days when a man placed such a girdle around his wife or sweetheart to signify his sole possession of her. If a man could succeed in purloining a mermaid's girdle she was completely in his power. So is it with fairies in an Algonquin Indian tale. Even so late as Crusading times many knights departing to fight in the Holy Land bound a girdle round their ladies' waists in the hope that the gift would ensure their faithfulness.

The Lay of Laustic

The Lay of Laustic, or the Nightingale, is purely of Breton origin, and indeed is proved to be so by its title. "Laustic, I deem, men name it in that country" (Brittany), says Marie in her preface to the lay, "which being interpreted means *rossignol* in French and 'nightingale' in good plain English." She adds that the Breton harper has already made a lay concerning it—added evidence that the tale is of Celtic and not of French origin.

In the ancient town of Saint-Malo, in Brittany, dwelt two knights whose valour and prowess brought much fame to the community. Their houses were close to one another, and one of them was married to a lady of surpassing loveliness, while the other was a bachelor. By insensible degrees the bachelor knight came to love his neighbour's wife, and so handsome and gallant was he that in time she returned his passion. He made every possible excuse for seeking her society, and on one pretext or another was constantly by her side. But he was exceedingly careful of her fair fame, and acted in such a way that not the slightest breath of scandal could touch her.

Their houses were separated by an ancient stone wall of considerable height, but the lovers could speak together by leaning from their casements, and if this was impossible they could communicate by sending written messages. When the lady's husband was at home she was guarded carefully, as was the custom of the time, but nevertheless she contrived to greet her lover from the window as frequently as she desired.

In due course the wondrous time of spring came round, with white drift of blossom and stir of life newly awakened. The short night hours grew warm, and often did the lady arise from bed to have speech with her lover at the casement. Her husband grew displeased by her frequent absences, which disturbed his rest, and wrathfully inquired the reason why she quitted his side so often.

"Oh, husband," she replied, "I cannot rest because of the sweet song of the nightingale, whose music has cast a spell upon my heart. No tune of harp or viol can compare with it, and I may not close my eyes so long as his song continues in the night."

Now the lady's husband, although a bold and hardy knight, was malicious and ungenerous, and, disliking to have his rest disturbed, resolved to deal summarily with the nightingale. So he gave orders to his servants to set traps in the garden and to smear every bough and branch with birdlime in order that the bird might speedily be taken. His orders were at once carried out, and the garden was filled with nets, while the cruel lime glittered upon every tree. So complete were the preparations of the serving-men that an unfortunate nightingale which had made the garden its haunt and had filled it with music for many a night while the lovers talked was taken and brought to the knight.

Swiftly he bore the hapless bird to his wife's chamber, his eyes sparkling with malicious glee.

"Here is your precious songster," he said, with bitter irony. "You will be happy to learn that you and I may now spend our sleeping hours in peace since he is taken."

"Ah, slay him not, my lord!" she cried in anguish, for she had grown to associate the bird's sweet song with the sweeter converse of her lover—to regard it as in a measure an accompaniment to his love-words. For answer her husband seized the unhappy bird by the neck and wrung its head off. Then he cast the little body into the lap of the dame, soiling her with its blood, and departed in high anger.

The lady pitifully raised what was left of the dead songster and bitterly lamented over it.

"Woe is me!" she cried. "Never again can I meet with my lover at the casement, and he will believe that I am faithless to him. But I shall devise some means to let him know that this is not so."

Having considered as to what she should do, the lady took a fine piece of white samite, broidered with gold, and worked upon it as on a tapestry the whole story of the nightingale, so that her knight might not be ignorant of the nature of the barrier that had arisen between them.

In this silken shroud she wrapped the small, sad body of the slain bird and gave it in charge of a trusty servant to bear to her lover. The messenger told the knight what had occurred. The news was heavy to him, but now, having insight to the vengeful nature of her husband, he feared to jeopardize the lady's safety, so he remained silent. But he caused a rich coffer to be made in fine gold, set with precious stones, in which he laid the body of the nightingale, and this small funeral urn he carried about with him on all occasions, nor could any circumstance hinder him from keeping it constantly beside him.

Wrap me love's ashes in a golden cloth
To carry next my heart. Love's fire is out,
And these poor embers grey, but I am loath
To quench remembrance also: I shall put
His relics over that they did consume.
Ah, 'tis too bitter cold these cinders to relume!

Place me love's ashes in a golden cup,
To mingle with my wine. Ah, do not fear
The old flame in my soul shall flicker up
At the harsh taste of what was once so dear.
I quaff no fire: there is no fire to meet
This bitterness of death and turn it into sweet.

The Lay of Eliduc

In the tale of Eliduc we have in all probability a genuine product of native Breton romance. So at least avers Marie, who assures us that it is "a very ancient Breton lay," and we have no reason to doubt her word, seeing that, had she been prone to literary dishonesty, it would have been much easier for her to have passed off the tale as her own original conception. There is, of course, the probability that it was so widely known in its Breton version that to have done so would have been to have openly courted the charge of plagiarism—an impeachment which it is not possible to bring against this most charming and delightful poetess.

Eliduc, a knight of Brittany, was happy in the confidence of his King, who, when affairs of State caused his absence from the realm, left his trusted adherent behind him as viceroy and regent. Such a man, staunch and loyal, could scarcely be without enemies, and the harmless pleasure he took in the chase during the King's absence was construed by evil counsellors on the monarch's return as an unwarranted licence with the royal rights of venery. The enemies of Eliduc so harped upon the knight's supposed lack of reverence for the royal authority that at length the King's patience gave way and in an outburst of wrath he gave orders for Eliduc's banishment, without vouchsafing his former friend and confidant the least explanation of this petulant action.

Dismayed by the sudden change in his fortunes, Eliduc returned to his house, and there acquainted his friends and vassals with the King's unjust decree. He told them that it was his intention to cross the sea to the kingdom of Logres, to sojourn there for a space. He placed his estates in the hands of his wife and begged of his vassals that they would serve her loyally. Then, having settled his affairs, he took ten knights of his household and started upon his journey. His wife, Guildeluec, accompanied him for several miles, and on parting they pledged good faith to one another.

In due time the cavalcade came to the seashore and took ship for the realm of Logres. Near Exeter, in this land, dwelt an aged king who had for his heir a daughter called Guillardun. This damsel had been asked in marriage by a neighbouring prince, and as her father had refused to listen to his proposals the disappointed suitor made war upon him, spoiling and wasting his land. The old King, fearful for his child's safety, had shut her up in a strong castle for her better security and his own peace of mind.

Now Eliduc, coming to that land, heard the tale of the quarrel between the King and his neighbour, and considered as to which side he should take. After due deliberation he arranged to fight on the side of the King, with whom he offered to take service. His offer was gratefully accepted, and he had not been long in the royal host when he had an opportunity of distinguishing himself. The town wherein he was lodged with his knights was attacked by the enemy. He set his men in ambush in a forest track by which it was known the enemy would approach the town, and succeeded in routing them and in taking large numbers of prisoners and much booty. This feat of arms raised him high in the estimation of the King, who showed him much favour, and the Princess, hearing of his fame, became very desirous of beholding him. She sent her chamberlain to Eliduc saying that she wished to hear the story of his deeds, and he, quite as anxious to see the imprisoned Princess of whom he had heard so much, set out at once. On beholding each other they experienced deep agitation. Eliduc thought that never had he seen so beautiful and graceful a maiden, and Guillardun that this was the most handsome and comely knight she had ever met.

For a long time they spoke together, and then Eliduc

took his leave and departed. He counted all the time lost that he had remained in the kingdom without knowing this lady, but he promised himself that now he would frequently seek her society. Then, with a pang of remorse, he thought of his good and faithful wife and the sacred promise he had made her.

Guillardun, on her part, was none the less ill at ease. She passed a restless night, and in the morning confided her case to her aged chamberlain, who was almost a second father to her, and he, all unwitting that Eliduc was already bound in wedlock to another, suggested that the Princess should send the knight a love-token to discover by the manner in which he received it whether or not her love was returned. Guillardun took this advice, and sent her lover a girdle and a ring by the hands of the chamberlain. On receiving the token Eliduc showed the greatest joy, girded the belt about his middle, and placed the ring on his finger. The chamberlain returned to the Princess and told her with what evident satisfaction Eliduc had received the gifts. But the Princess in her eagerness showered questions upon him, until at last the old man grew impatient.

"Lady," he said, somewhat testily, "I have told you the knight's words; I cannot tell you his thoughts, for he is a prudent gentleman who knows well what to hide in his heart."

Although he rejoiced at the gifts Eliduc had but little peace of mind. He could think of nothing save the vow he had made to his wife before he left her. But thoughts of the Princess would intrude themselves upon him. Often he saw Guillardun, and although he saluted her with a kiss, as was the custom of the time, he never spoke a single word of love to her, being fearful on the one hand of breaking his conjugal vow and on the other of offending the King.

One evening when Eliduc was announced the King was in his daughter's chamber, playing at chess with a stranger lord. He welcomed the knight heartily, and much to the embarrassment of the lovers begged his daughter to cherish a closer friendship for Eliduc, whom he brought to her notice as a right worthy knight. The pair withdrew somewhat from the others, as if for the purpose of furthering the friendship which the old King so ardently seemed to desire, and Eliduc thanked the Princess for the gifts she had sent him by the chamberlain. Then the Princess, taking advantage of her rank, told Eliduc that she desired him for her husband, and that, did he refuse her, she would die unwed.

"Lady," replied the knight, "I have great joy in your love, but have you thought that I may not always tarry in this land? I am your father's man until this war hath an end. Then shall I return unto mine own country." But Guillardun, in a transport of love, told him she would trust him entirely with her heart, and passing great was the affection that grew between them. Eliduc, in spite of his love for the Princess, had by no means permitted his conduct of the war to flag. Indeed, if anything, he redoubled his efforts, and pressed the foe so fiercely that at length he was forced to submit. And now news came to him that his old master, the King who had banished him from Brittany, was sore bestead by an enemy and was searching for his former vice-regent on every hand, who was so mighty a knight in the field and so sage at the council-board. Turning upon the false lords who had spoken evil of his favourite, he outlawed them from the land for ever. He sent messengers east and west and across the seas in search of Eliduc, who when he heard the news was much dismayed, so greatly did he love Guillardun. These twain had loved with a pure and tender passion, and never by word or deed had they sullied the affection they bore one another. Dearly did the Princess hope that Eliduc might remain in her land and become her lord, and little did she dream that he was wedded to a wife across the seas. For his part Eliduc took close counsel with himself. He knew by reason of the fealty he owed to his King that he must return to Brittany, but he was equally aware that if he parted from Guillardun one or other of them must die.

Deep was the chagrin of the King of Logres when he learned that Eliduc must depart from his realm, but deeper far was his daughter's grief when the knight came to bid her farewell. In moving words she urged him to remain, and when she found that his loyalty was proof even against his love, she begged of him to take her with him to Brittany. But this request he turned aside, on the plea that as he had served her father he could not so offend him as by the theft of his daughter. He promised, however, by all he held most dear that he would return one day, and with much sorrow the two parted, exchanging rings for remembrance.

Eliduc took ship and swiftly crossed the sea. He met with a joyous reception from his King, and none was so glad at his return as his wife. But gradually his lady began to see that he had turned cold to her. She charged him with it, and he replied that he had pledged his faith to the foreign lord whom he had served abroad.

Very soon through his conduct the war was brought

to a victorious close, and almost immediately thereafter Eliduc repaired across the sea to Logres, taking with him two of his nephews as his squires. On reaching Logres he at once went to visit Guillardun, who received him with great gladness. She returned with him to his ship, which commenced the return voyage at once, but when they neared the dangerous coast of Brittany a sudden tempest arose, and waxed so fierce that the mariners lost all hope of safety. One of them cried out that the presence of Guillardun on board the ship endangered all their lives and that the conduct of Eliduc, who had already a faithful wife, in seeking to wed this foreign woman had brought about their present dangerous position. Eliduc grew very wroth, and when Guillardun heard that her knight was already wedded she swooned and all regarded her as dead. In despair Eliduc fell upon his betrayer, slew him, and cast his body into the sea. Then, guiding the ship with a seaman's skill, he brought her into harbour.

When they were safely anchored, Eliduc conceived the idea of taking Guillardun, whom he regarded as dead, to a certain chapel in a great forest quite near his own home. Setting her body before him on his palfrey, he soon came to the little shrine, and making a bier of the altar laid Guillardun upon it. He then betook him to his own house, but the next morning returned to the chapel in the forest. Mourning over the body of his lady-love, he was surprised to observe that the colour still remained in her cheeks and lips. Again and again he visited the chapel, and his wife, marvelling whither he went, bribed a varlet to discover the object of his repeated absences. The man watched Eliduc and saw him enter the chapel and mourn over the body of Guillardun, and, returning, acquainted his lady with what he had seen.

Guildeluec—for such, we will remember, was the name of Eliduc's wife—set out for the shrine, and with astonishment beheld the lifelike form of Guillardun laid on the altar. So pitiful was the sight that she herself could not refrain from the deepest sorrow. As she sat weeping a weasel came from under the altar and ran across Guillardun's body, and the varlet who attended Guildeluec struck at it with his staff and killed it. Another weasel issued, and, beholding its dead comrade, went forth from the chapel and hastened to the wood, whence it returned, bearing in its mouth a red flower, which it placed on the mouth of its dead companion. The weasel which Guildeluec had believed to be dead at once stood up. Beholding this, the varlet cast his staff at the animals and they sped away, leaving the red flower behind them.

Guildeluec immediately picked the flower up, and returning with it to the altar where Guillardun lay, placed it on the maiden's mouth. In a few moments she heard a sigh, and Guillardun sat up, and inquired if she had slept long. Guildeluec asked her name and degree, and Guillardun in reply acquainted her with her history and lineage, speaking very bitterly of Eliduc, who, she said, had betrayed her in a strange land. Guildeluec declared herself the wife of Eliduc, told Guillardun how deeply the knight had grieved for her, and declared her intention of taking the veil and releasing Eliduc from his marriage vow. She conducted Guillardun to her home, where they met Eliduc, who rejoiced greatly at the restoration of his lady-love. His wife founded

ELIDUC CARRIES GUILLARDUN TO THE FOREST CHAPEL

CONVOYON AND HIS MONKS CARRY OFF THE RELICS OF ST APOTHEMIUS

a convent with the rich portion he bestowed upon her, and Eliduc, in thankfulness for Guillardun's recovery, built a fair church close by his castle and endowed it bountifully, and close beside it erected a great monastery. Later Guillardun entered the convent of which Guildeluec was the abbess, and Eliduc, himself feeling the call of the holy life, devoted himself to the service of God in the monastery. Messages passed between convent and monastery in which Eliduc and the holy women encouraged each other in the pious life which they had chosen, and by degrees the three who had suffered so greatly came to regard their seclusion as far preferable to the world and all its vanities.

The Lay of Equitan

The Lay of Equitan is one of Marie's most famous tales. Equitan was King of Nantes, in Brittany, and led the life of a pleasure-seeker. To win approval from the eyes of fair ladies was more to him than knightly fame or honour.

Equitan had as seneschal a trusty and faithful knight, who was to the pleasure-loving seigneur as his right hand. This faithful servant was also captain of Equitan's army, and sat as a judge in his courts. To his undoing he had a wife, as fair a dame as any in the duchy of Brittany. "Her eyes," says the old lay, "were blue, her face was warm in colour, her mouth fragrant and her nose dainty." She was ever tastefully dressed and courtly in demeanour, and soon attracted the attention of such an admirer of the fair sex as Equitan, who desired to speak with her more intimately. He therefore, as a subterfuge, announced that a great hunt would take place in that part of his domains in which his seneschal's castle was situated, and this gave him the opportunity of sojourning at the castle and holding converse with the lady, with whom he became so charmed that in a few days he fell deeply in love with her. On the night of the day when he first became aware that he loved her Equitan lay tossing on his bed, in a torment of fiery emotion. He debated with himself in what manner he should convey to his seneschal's wife the fact that he loved her, and at length prepared a plot which he thought would be likely to succeed.

Next day he rose as usual and made all arrangements to proceed with the chase. But shortly after setting out he returned, pleading that he had fallen sick, and took to his bed. The faithful seneschal could not divine what had occurred to render his lord so seriously indisposed as he appeared to be, and requested his wife to go to him to see if she could minister to him and cheer his drooping spirits.

The lady went to Equitan, who received her dolefully enough. He told her without reserve that the malady from which he suffered was none other than love for herself, and that did she not consent to love him in return he would surely die. The dame at first dissented, but, carried away by the fiery eloquence of his words, she at last assured him of her love, and they exchanged rings as a token of troth and trust.

The love of Equitan and the seneschal's wife was discovered by none, and when they desired to meet he arranged to go hunting in the neighbourhood of the seneschal's castle. Shortly after they had plighted their troth the great barons of the realm approached the King with a proposal that he should marry, but Equitan would have none of this, nor would he listen to even his most trusted advisers with regard to such a subject. The nobles were angered at his curt and even savage refusal to hearken to them, and the commons were also greatly disturbed because of the lack of a successor. The echoes of the disagreement reached the ears of the seneschal's wife, who was much perturbed thereby, being aware that the King had come to this decision for love of her.

At their next meeting she broached the subject to her royal lover, lamenting that they had ever met.

"Now are my good days gone," she said, weeping, "for you will wed some king's daughter as all men say, and I shall certainly die if I lose you thus."

"Nay, that will not be," replied Equitan. "Never shall I wed except your husband die."

The lady felt that he spoke truly, but in an evil moment she came to attach a sinister meaning to the words Equitan had employed regarding her husband. Day and night she brooded on them, for well she knew that did her husband die Equitan would surely wed her. By insensible degrees she came to regard her husband's death as a good rather than an evil thing, and little by little Equitan, who at first looked upon the idea with horror, became converted to her opinion. Between them they hatched a plot for the undoing of the seneschal. It was arranged that the King should go hunting as usual in the neighbourhood of his faithful servant's castle. While lodging in the castle, the King and the seneschal would be bled in the old surgical manner for their health's sake, and three days after would bathe before leaving the chamber they occupied, and the heartless wife suggested that she should make her husband's bath so fiercely hot that he would not survive after entering it. One would think that the seneschal would easily have been able to escape such a simple trap, but we must remember that the baths of Norman times were not shaped like our own, but were exceedingly deep, and indeed some of them were in form almost like those immense upright jars such as the forty thieves were concealed in in the story of Ali Baba, so that in many cases it was not easy for the bather to tell whether the water into which he was stepping was hot or otherwise.

The plot was carried out as the lady had directed, but not without much misgiving on the part of Equitan. The King duly arrived at the castle, and announced his intention to be bled, requesting that the seneschal should undergo the same operation at the same time, and occupy the same chamber by way of companionship. Then after the leech had bled them the King asked that he might have a bath before leaving his apartment, and the seneschal requested that his too should be made ready. Accordingly on the third day the baths were brought to the chamber, and the lady occupied herself with filling them. While she was doing so her lord left the chamber for a space, and during his absence the King and the lady were clasped in each other's arms. So rapt were the pair in their amorous dalliance that they failed to notice the return of the seneschal, who, when he saw them thus engaged, uttered an exclamation of surprise and wrath. Equitan, turning quickly, saw him, and with a cry of despair leapt into the bath that the lady had prepared for the seneschal, and there perished miserably, while the enraged husband, seizing his faithless wife, thrust her headlong into the boiling water beside her lover, where she too was scalded to death.

The Lay of the Ash-Tree

In olden times there dwelt in Brittany two knights who were neighbours and close friends. Both were married, and one was the father of twin sons, one of whom he christened by the name of his friend. Now this friend had a wife who was envious of heart and rancorous of tongue, and on hearing that two sons had been born to her neighbour she spoke slightingly and cruelly about her, saying that to bear twins was ever a disgrace. Her evil words were spread abroad, and at last as a result of her malicious speech the good lady's husband himself began to doubt and suspect the wife who had never for a moment given him the least occasion to do so.

Strangely enough, within the year two daughters were born to the lady of the slanderous tongue, who now deeply lamented the wrong she had done, but all to no purpose. Fearful of the gossip which she thought the event would occasion, she gave one of the children to a faithful handmaiden, with directions that it should be laid on the steps of a church, where it might be picked up as a foundling and nourished by some stranger. The babe was wrapped in a linen cloth, which again was covered with a beautiful piece of red silk that the lady's husband had purchased in the East, and a handsome ring engraved with the family insignia and set with garnets was bound to the infant's arm with silken lace. When the child had thus been attired the damsel took it and carried it for many miles into the country, until at last she came to a city where there was a large and fair abbey. Breathing a prayer that the child might have proper guardianship, the girl placed it on the abbey steps as her mistress had ordered her to do, but, afraid that it might catch cold on such a chilly bed, she looked around and saw an ash-tree, thick and leafy, with four strong branches, among the foliage of which she deposited the little one, commending it to the care of God, after which she returned to her mistress and acquainted her with what had passed.

In the morning the abbey porter opened the great doors of the house of God so that the people might enter for early Mass. As he was thus engaged his eye caught the gleam of red silk among the leaves of the ash-tree, and going to it he discovered the deserted infant. Taking the babe from its resting-place, he returned with it to his house, and, awaking his daughter, who was a widow with a baby yet in the cradle, he asked her to cherish it and care for it. Both father and daughter could see from the crimson silk and the great signet ring that the child was of noble birth. The porter told the abbess of his discovery, and she requested him to bring the child to her, dressed precisely as it had been found. On beholding the infant a great compassion was aroused in the breast of the holy woman, who resolved to bring up the child herself, calling her her niece, and since she was taken from the ash giving her the name of Frêne.

Frêne grew up one of the fairest damsels in Brittany. She was frank in manner, yet modest and discreet in bearing and speech. At Dol, where, as we have read, there is a great menhir and other prehistoric monuments, there lived a lord called Buron, who, hearing reports of Frêne's beauty and sweetness, greatly desired to behold her. Riding home from a tournament, he passed near the convent, and, alighting there, paid his respects to the abbess, and begged that he might see her niece. Buron at once fell in love with the maiden, and in order to gain favour with the abbess bestowed great riches upon the establishment over which she presided, requesting in return that he might be permitted to occupy a small apartment in the abbey should he chance to be in the neighbourhood.

In this way he frequently saw and spoke with Frêne, who in turn fell in love with him. He persuaded her to fly with him to his castle, taking with her the silken cloth and ring with which she had been found.

But the lord's tenants were desirous that he should marry, and had set their hearts upon his union with a rich lady named Coudre, daughter of a neighbouring baron. The marriage was arranged, greatly to the grief of Frêne, and duly took place. Going to Buron's bridal chamber, she considered it too mean, blinded with love as she was, for such as he, and placed the wondrous piece of crimson silk in which she had been wrapped as an infant over the coverlet. Presently the bride's mother entered the bridal chamber in order to see that all was fitting for her daughter's reception there. Gazing at the crimson coverlet, she recognized it as that in which she had wrapped her infant daughter. She anxiously inquired to whom it belonged, and was told that it was Frêne's. Going to the damsel, she questioned her as to where she had obtained the silk, and was told by Frêne that the abbess had given it to her along with a ring which had been found upon her when, as an infant, she had been discovered within the branches of the ash-tree.

The mother asked anxiously to see the ring, and on

beholding it told Frêne of their relationship, which at the same time she confessed to her husband, the baron. The father was overjoyed to meet with a daughter he had never known, and hastened to the bridegroom to acquaint him with Frêne's story. Great joy had Buron, and the archbishop who had joined him to Coudre gave counsel that they should be parted according to the rites of the Church and that Buron should marry Frêne. This was accordingly done, and when Frêne's parents returned to their own domain they found another husband for Coudre.

The Lay of Graelent

Graelent was a Breton knight dwelling at the Court of the King of Brittany, a very pillar to him in war, bearing himself valiantly in tourney and joust. So handsome and brave was he that the Queen fell madly in love with him, and asked her chamberlain to bring the knight into her presence. When he came she praised him greatly to his face, not only for his gallantry in battle, but also for his comeliness; but at her honeyed words the youth, quite abashed, sat silent, saying nothing. The Queen at last questioned him if his heart was set on any maid or dame, to which he replied that it was not, that love was a serious business and not to be taken in jest.

"Many speak glibly of love,' he said, "of whom not one can spell the first letter of its name. Love should be quiet and discreet or it is nothing worth, and without accord between the lovers love is but a bond and a constraint. Love is too high a matter for me to meddle with."

The Queen listened greedily to Graelent's words, and

when he had finished speaking she discovered her love for him ; but he turned from her courteously but firmly. "Lady," he said, "I beg your forgiveness, but this may not be. I am the King's man, and to him I have pledged my faith and loyalty. Never shall he know shame through any conduct of mine."

With these words he took his leave of the Queen. But his protestations had altered her mind not at all. She sent him messages daily, and costly gifts, but these he refused and returned, till at last the royal dame, stung to anger by his repulses, conceived a violent hatred for him, and resolved to be revenged upon him for the manner in which he had scorned her love.

The King of Brittany went to war with a neighbouring monarch, and Graelent bore himself manfully in the conflict, leading his troops again and again to victory. Hearing of his repeated successes, the Queen was exceedingly mortified, and made up her mind to destroy his popularity with the troops. With this end in view she prevailed upon the King to withhold the soldiers' pay, which Graelent had to advance them out of his own means. In the end the unfortunate knight was reduced almost to beggary by this mean stratagem. One morning he was riding through the town where he was lodged, clad in garments so shabby that the wealthy burgesses in their fur-lined cloaks and rich apparel gibed and jeered at him, but Graelent, sure of his own worth, deigned not to take notice of such ill-breeding, and for his solace quitted the crowded streets of the place and took his way toward the great forest which skirted it. He rode into its gloom deep in thought, listening to the murmur of the river which flowed through the leafy ways.

He had not gone far when he espied a white hart within a thicket. She fled before him into the thickest part of the forest, but the silvern glimmer of her body showed the track she had taken. On a sudden deer and horseman dashed into a clearing among the trees where there was a grassy lawn, in the midst of which sprang a fountain of clear water. In this fountain a lady was bathing, and two attendant maidens stood near. Now Graelent believed that the lady must be a fairy, and knowing well that the only way to capture such a being was to seize her garments, he looked around for these, and seeing them lying upon a bush he laid hands upon them.

The attendant women at this set up a loud outcry, and the lady herself turned to where he sat his horse and called him by name.

"Graelent, what do you hope to gain by the theft of my raiment?" she asked. "Have you, a knight, sunk so low as to behave like a common pilferer? Take my mantle if you must, but pray spare me my gown."

Graelent laughed at the lady's angry words, and told her that he was no huckster. He then begged her to don her garments, as he desired to have speech with her. After her women had attired her, Graelent took her by the hand and, leading her a little space away from her attendants, told her that he had fallen deeply in love with her. But the lady frowned and seemed at first offended.

"You do not know to whom you proffer your love," she said. "Are you aware that my birth and lineage render it an impertinence for a mere knight to seek to ally himself with me?"

But Graelent had a most persuasive tongue, and the deep love he had conceived for the lady rendered him doubly eloquent on this occasion. At last the fairy-woman, for such she was, was quite carried away by his words, and granted him the boon he craved.

"There is, however, one promise I must exact from you," she said, "and that is that never shall you mention me to mortal man. I on my part shall assist you in every possible manner. You shall never be without gold in your purse nor costly apparel to wear. Day and night shall I remain with you, and in war and in the chase will ride by your side, visible to you alone, unseen by your companions. For a year must you remain in this country. Now noon has passed and you must go. A messenger shall shortly come to you to tell you of my wishes."

Graelent took leave of the lady and kissed her farewell. Returning to his lodgings in the town, he was leaning from the casement considering his strange adventure when he saw a varlet issuing from the forest riding upon a palfrey. The man rode up the cobbled street straight to Graelent's lodgings, where he dismounted and, entering, told the knight that his lady had sent him with the palfrey as a present, and begged that he would accept the services of her messenger to take charge of his lodgings and manage his affairs.

The serving-man quickly altered the rather poor appearance of Graelent's apartment. He spread a rich coverlet upon his couch and produced a well-filled purse and rich apparel. Graelent at once sought out all the poor knights of the town and feasted them to their hearts' content. From this moment he fared sumptuously every day. His lady appeared whenever he desired her to, and great was the love between them. Nothing more had he to wish for in this life.

A year passed in perfect happiness for the knight, and at its termination the King held a great feast on the occasion of Pentecost. To this feast Sir Graelent was bidden. All day the knights and barons and their ladies feasted, and the King, having drunk much wine, grew boastful. Requesting the Queen to stand forth on the daïs, he asked the assembled nobles if they had ever beheld so fair a dame as she. The lords were loud in their praise of the Queen, save Graelent only. He sat with bent head, smiling strangely, for he knew of a lady fairer by far than any lady in that Court. The Queen was quick to notice this seeming discourtesy, and pointed it out to the King, who summoned Graelent to the steps of the throne.

"How now, Sir Knight," said the King; "wherefore did you sneer when all other men praised the Queen's beauty?"

"Sire," replied Graelent, "you do yourself much dishonour by such a deed. You make your wife a show upon a stage and force your nobles to praise her with lies when in truth a fairer dame than she could very easily be found."

Now when she heard this the Queen was greatly angered and prayed her husband to compel Graelent to bring to the Court her of whom he boasted so proudly.

"Set us side by side," cried the infuriated Queen, "and if she be fairer than I before men's eyes, Graelent may go in peace, but if not let justice be done upon him."

The King, stirred to anger at these words, ordered his guards to seize Graelent, swearing that he should never issue from prison till the lady of whom he had boasted should come to Court and pit herself against the Queen. Graelent was then cast into a dungeon, but he thought little of this indignity, fearing much more that his rashness had broken the bond betwixt him and his fairy bride. After a while he was set at liberty, on pledging his word that he would return bringing with him the lady whom he claimed as fairer than the Queen. Leaving the Court, he betook himself to his lodging, and called upon his lady, but received no answer. Again he called, but without result, and believing that his fairy bride had utterly abandoned him he gave way to despair. In a year's time Graelent returned to the Court and admitted his failure.

" Sir Graelent," said the King, " wherefore should you not be punished? You have slandered the Queen in the most unknightly manner, and given the lie to those nobles who must now give judgment against you."

The nobles retired to consider their judgment upon Graelent. For a long time they debated, for most of them were friendly to him and he had been extremely popular at Court. In the midst of their deliberations a page entered and prayed them to postpone judgment, as two damsels had arrived at the palace and were having speech with the King concerning Graelent. The damsels told the King that their mistress was at hand, and begged him to wait for her arrival, as she had come to uphold Graelent's challenge. Hearing this, the Queen quitted the hall, and shortly after she had gone a second pair of damsels appeared bearing a similar message for the King. Lastly Graelent's young bride herself entered the hall.

At sight of her a cry of admiration arose from the assembled nobles, and all admitted that their eyes had never beheld a fairer lady. When she reached the King's side she dismounted from her palfrey.

"Sire," she said, addressing the King, "hasty and foolish was Graelent's tongue when he spoke as he did, but at least he told the truth when he said that there is no lady so fair but a fairer may be found. Look upon me and judge in this quarrel between the Queen and me."

When she had spoken every lord and noble with one voice agreed that she was fairer than her royal rival. Even the King himself admitted that it was so, and Sir Graelent was declared a free man.

Turning round to seek his lady, the knight observed that she was already some distance away, so, mounting upon his white steed, he followed hotly after her. All day he followed, and all night, calling after her and pleading for pity and pardon, but neither she nor her attendant damsels paid the slightest attention to his cries. Day after day he followed her, but to no purpose. At last the lady and her maidens entered the forest and rode to the bank of a broad stream. They set their horses to the river, but when the lady saw that Graelent was about to follow them she turned and begged him to desist, telling him that it was death for him to cross that stream. Graelent did not heed her, but plunged into the torrent. The stream was deep and rapid, and presently he was torn from his saddle. Seeing this, the lady's attendants begged her to save him. Turning back, the lady clutched her lover by the belt and dragged him to the shore. He was well-nigh drowned, but under her care he speedily recovered, and, say the Breton folk, entered with her that realm of Fairyland into which penetrated Thomas the Rhymer, Ogier the Dane, and other heroes. His white steed when it escaped from the river grieved greatly for its master, rushing up and down the bank, neighing loudly, and pawing with its hoofs upon the ground. Many men coveted so noble a charger, and tried to capture him, but all in vain, so each year, "in its season," as the old romance says, the forest is filled with the sorrowful neighing of the good steed which may not find its master.

The story of Graelent is one of those which deal with what is known to folk-lorists as the 'fairy-wife' subject. A taboo is always placed upon the mortal bridegroom. Sometimes he must not utter the name of his wife; in other tales, as in that of Melusine, he must not seek her on a certain day of the week. The essence of the story is, of course, that the taboo is broken, and in most cases the mortal husband loses his supernatural mate. Another incident in the general *motif* is the stealing of the fairy-woman's clothes. The idea is the same as that found in stories where the fisherman steals the sea-woman's skin canoe as a prelude to making her his wife, or the feather cloak of the swan-maiden is seized by the hunter when he finds her asleep, thus placing the supernatural maiden in his power. Among savages it is quite a common and usual circumstance for the spouses not to mention each other's names for months after marriage, nor even to see one another's faces. In the story under consideration the taboo consists in the mortal bridegroom being forbidden to allude in any circumstances to his supernatural wife, who is undoubtedly the same type of being encountered by Thomas the Rhymer and Bonny Kilmeny in the ballads related of them. They are denizens of a country, a fairy realm, which figures partly as an abode of the dead, and which we are certainly justified in identifying with the Celtic Otherworld. The river which the fairy-woman crosses bears a certain resemblance to the Styx, or she tells Graelent plainly that should he reach its opposite bank he is as good as dead. Fairyland in early Celtic lore may be a place of delight, but it is none the less one of death and remoteness.

The Lay of the Dolorous Knight

Once more the scene is laid in Nantes, and "some harpers," says Marie, "call it the Lay of the Four Sorrows." In this city of Brittany dwelt a lady on whom four barons of great worship had set their love. They were not singular in this respect, as the damsel's bright eyes had set fire to the hearts of all the youths of the ancient town. She smiled upon them all, but favoured no one more than another. Out of this great company, however, the four noblemen in question had constituted themselves her particular squires. They vied with one another in the most earnest manner to gain her esteem; but she was equally gracious to all and it was impossible to say that she favoured any.

It was not surprising, then, that each one of the four nobles believed that the lady preferred him to the others. Each of them had received gifts from her, and each cried her name at tournaments. On the occasion of a great jousting, held without the walls of Nantes, the four lovers held the lists, and from all the surrounding realms and duchies came hardy knights to break a spear for the sake of chivalry.

From matins to vespers the friendly strife raged fiercely, and against the four champions of Nantes four foreign knights especially pitted themselves. Two of these were of Hainault, and the other two were Flemings. The two companies charged each other so desperately that the horses of all eight men were overthrown. The four knights of Nantes rose lightly from the ground, but the four stranger knights lay still. Their friends, however, rushed to their rescue, and soon the challengers were lost in a sea of steel.

Now the lady in whose honour the lists were defended by these four brave brethren in arms sat beholding their prowess in the keenest anxiety. Soon the knights of Nantes were reinforced by their friends, and the strife waxed furiously, sword to sword and lance to lance. First one company and then the other gained the advantage, but, urged on by rashness, the four challenging champions charged boldly in front of their comrades and became separated from them, with the dire result that three of them were killed and the fourth was so grievously wounded that he was borne from the press in a condition hovering between life and death. So furious were the stranger knights because of the resistance that had been made by the four champions that they cast their opponents' shields outside the lists. But the knights of Nantes won the day, and, raising their three slain comrades and him who was wounded, carried all four to the house of their lady-love.

When the sad procession reached her doors the lady was greatly grieved and cast down. To her three dead lovers she gave sumptuous burial in a fair abbey. As for the fourth, she tended him with such skill that ere long his wounds were healed and he was quite recovered. One summer day the knight and the lady sat together after meat, and a great sadness fell upon her because of the knights who had been slain in her cause. Her head sank upon her breast and she seemed lost in a reverie of sorrow. The knight, perceiving her distress, could not well understand what had wounded her so deeply.

"Lady," said he, "a great sorrow seems to be yours. Reveal your grief to me, and perchance I can find you comfort."

"Friend," replied the lady, "I grieve for your companions who are gone. Never was lady or damsel served by four such valiant knights, three of whom were slain in one single day. Pardon me if I call them to mind at this time, but it is my intention to make a lay in order that these champions and yourself may not be forgotten, and I will call it 'The Lay of the Four Sorrows.'"

"Nay, lady," said the knight, "call it not 'The Lay of the Four Sorrows,' but rather 'The Lay of the Dolorous Knight.' My three comrades are dead. They have gone to their place; no more hope have they of life; all their sorrows are ended and their love for you is as dead as they. I alone am here in life, but what have I to hope for? I find my life more bitter than they could find the grave. I see you in your comings and goings, I may speak with you, but I may not have your love. For this reason I am full of sorrow and cast down, and thus I beg that you give your lay my name and call it 'The Lay of the Dolorous Knight.'"

The lady looked earnestly upon him. "By my faith," she said, "you speak truly. The lay shall be known by the title you wish it to be."

So the lay was written and entitled as the knight desired it should be. "I heard no more," says Marie, "and nothing more I know. Perforce I must bring my story to a close."

The end of this lay is quite in the medieval manner, and fitly concludes this chapter. We are left absolutely in the dark as to whether the knight and the lady came together at last. I for one do not blame Marie for this, as with the subtle sense of the fitness of things that belongs to all great artists she saw how much more effective it would be to leave matters as they were between the lovers. There are those who will blame her for her inconclusiveness; but let them bear in mind that just because of what they consider her failing in this respect they will not be likely to forget her tale, whereas had it ended with wedding-bells they would probably have stored it away in some mental attic with a thousand other dusty memories.

CHAPTER XII: THE SAINTS OF BRITTANY

AN important department in Breton folk-lore is the hagiology of the province—the legendary lore of its saints. This, indeed, holds almost as much of the marvellous as its folk-tales, ballads, and historical legends, and in perusing the tales of Brittany's saintly heroes we have an opportunity of observing how the *motifs* of popular fiction and even of pagan belief reflect upon religious romance.

Just as some mythology is not in itself religious, but very often mere fiction fortuitously connected with the names of the gods, so hagiology is not of sacerdotal but popular origin. For the most part it describes the origin of its heroes and accounts for their miracles and marvellous deeds by various means, just as mythology does. It must be remembered that the primitive saint was in close touch with paganism, that, indeed, he had frequently to fight the Druid and the magician with his own weapons, and therefore we must not be surprised if in some of these tales we find him somewhat of a magician himself. But he is invariably on the side of light, and the things of darkness and evil shrink from contact with him.

St Barbe

Overlooking the valley of the Ellé, near the beautiful and historic village of Le Faouet, is a ledge of rock, approached by an almost inaccessible pathway. On this ledge stands the chapel of St Barbe, one of the strangest and most 'pagan' of the Breton saints. She protects those who seek her aid from sudden death, especially death by lightning. Of recent years popular belief has extended her sphere of influence to cover those who travel by automobile! She is also regarded as the patroness of firemen, at whose annual dinner her statue, surrounded by flowers, presides. She is extremely popular in Brittany, and once a year, on the last Sunday of June, pilgrims arrive at Le Faouet to celebrate her festival. Each, as he passes the belfry which stands beside the path, pulls the bell-rope, and the young men make the tour of a small neighbouring chapel, dedicated to St Michel, Lord of Heights. Then they drink of a little fountain near at hand and purchase amulets, which are supposed to be a preservative against sudden death and which are known as 'Couronnes de Ste Barbe.' St Barbe is said to have been the daughter of a pagan father, and to have been so beautiful that he shut her up in a tower and permitted no one to go near her. She succeeded, however, in communicating with the outer world, and sent a letter to Origen of Alexandria, entreating him to instruct her in the Christian faith, as she had ceased to believe in the gods of her fathers. Origen dispatched one of his monks to her, and under his guidance she became a Christian. She was called upon to suffer for her faith, for she was brought before the Gallo-Roman proconsul, and, since she refused to sacrifice to the pagan gods, was savagely maltreated, and sentenced to be beaten as she walked naked through the streets; but she raised her eyes to heaven and a cloud descended and hid her from the gaze of the impious mortals who would otherwise have witnessed her martyrdom. Subsequently she was spirited away to the top of a mountain, where, however, her presence was betrayed by a shepherd. Her pagan father, learning of her hiding-place, quickly ascended the height and beheaded her with his own hand. The legends of St Barbe abound in strange details, which are more intelligible if we regard the Saint as being the survival of some elemental goddess connected with fire. The vengeance of heaven descended upon her enemies, for both her father and the shepherd who betrayed her were destroyed, the former being struck by lightning on his descent from the mountain, and the latter being turned into marble.

The legend of the foundation of the chapel at Le Faouet is illustrative of the strange powers of this saint. A Lord of Toulboudou, near Guémené, was overtaken by a severe thunderstorm while hunting. No shelter was available, and as the storm increased in fury the huntsmen trembled for their lives, and doubtless repeated with much fervour the old Breton charm :

Sainte Barbe et sainte Claire,
Preservez-moi du tonnerre,
Si le tonnerre tombe
Qu'il ne tombe pas sur moi !

which may be roughly translated :

Saint Barbe the great and sainted Clair,
Preserve me from the lightning's glare.
When thunderbolts are flashing red
Let them not burst upon my head.

The Lord of Toulboudou, however, was not content with praying to the Saint. He vowed that if by her intercession he was preserved from death he would raise a chapel to her honour on the narrow ledge of rock above. No sooner had he made this vow than the storm subsided, and safety was once more assured. In the ancient archives of Le Faouet we read that on the 6th of July, 1489, John of Toulboudou bought of John of Bouteville, Lord of Faouet, a piece of ground on the flank of the Roche-Marche-Bran, twenty-five feet by sixteen feet, on which to build a chapel to the honour of St Barbe, and there the chapel stands to this day.

How St Convoyon Stole the Relics

St Convoyon, first Abbot of Redon (or Rodon) and Bishop of Quimper, was of noble birth. He was born near Saint-Malo and educated at Vannes under Bishop Reginald, who ordained him as deacon and afterward as priest. Five clerks attached themselves to him, and the company went to dwell together in a forest near the river Vilaine, finally establishing themselves at Redon. The lord of that district was very favourably inclined toward the monastery and sent his son to be educated there, and when he himself fell sick and believed his last hours to be nigh he caused himself to be carried to this religious house, where his hair was shaven to the monastic pattern. Contrary to expectation, he recovered, and after settling his affairs at his castle he returned to Redon, where he died at a later date. St Convoyon had some difficulty in obtaining confirmation of the grants given to him by this seigneur. He set out with a disciple named Gwindeluc to seek the consent of Louis the Pious, taking with him a quantity of wax from his bees at Redon, intending to present it to the King, but he was refused admission to the royal presence. But Nomenoë, Governor of Brittany, visited Redon, and encouraged the Saint to endeavour once more to obtain the King's sanction, and this time Louis confirmed the grants.

So the monastery of Redon was built and its church erected, but, as the chroniclers tell us, "there was no saintly corpse under its altar to act as palladium to the monastery and work miracles to attract pilgrims." Convoyon therefore set out for Angers, accompanied by two of his monks, and found lodging there with a pious man named Hildwall. The latter inquired as to the object of their visit to Angers, and with considerable hesitation, and only after extracting a promise of secrecy, Convoyon confessed that they had come on a body-snatching expedition. He asked his friend's advice as to what relics they should endeavour to secure. Hildwall told him that interred in the cathedral were the bones of St Apothemius, a bishop, of whom nothing was known save that he was a saint. His bones lay in a stone coffin which had a heavy lid. Hildwall added that several monks had attempted to steal the relics, but in vain. Convoyon and his monks bided their time for three days, and then on a dark night, armed with crowbars, they set out on their gruesome mission. They reached the cathedral, entered, and, after singing praises and hymns, raised the coffin lid. Securing the bones, they made off with them as quickly as possible, and in due course reached Redon with them in safety. The reception of the relics was celebrated by the monks with great pomp and ceremony. Miracles were at once performed, and the popularity of St Apothemius was firmly established.

When the Bishop of Vannes died, in 837, the see was filled by Susannus, who obtained it by bribery. Convoyon, grieved and indignant at the prevalence of corruption in the Church, urged Nomenoë to summon a council of bishops and abbots and endeavour to put a stop to these deplorable practices. At this council the canons against simony were read; but the bishops retorted that they did not sell Holy Orders, and expected no fees—though they took presents! Susannus was, naturally enough, most emphatic about this. At length it was decided that a deputation should be sent to Rome to obtain an authoritative statement on the point, and that it should consist of Susannus of Vannes, Félix of Quimper, and Convoyon, who was to carry "gold crowns inlaid with jewels" as a gift from Nomenoë to the Pope. The decision given by Pope Leo on the matter is far from clear. The Nantes chronicle asserts that Leo made Convoyon a duke, and gave him permission to wear a gold coronet. He also presented him with a valuable gift—the bones of St Marcellinus, Bishop of Rome and martyr, which Convoyon took back with him to Redon and deposited in his church there.

On a later day Nomenoë raised the standard of revolt against Charles the Bald of France—a circumstance alluded to in our historical sketch. He ravaged Poitou with sword and flame, but respected the abbey of Saint-Florent, though, to insult Charles, he forced the monks to place a statue of himself on their tower, with the face turned defiantly toward France. During Nomenoë's absence the monks sent news of his action to the hairless monarch, who tore down the statue and erected a white stone figure "of ludicrous appearance," its mocking face turned toward Brittany. In revenge Nomenoë burned Saint-Florent to the ground and carried off the spoils to enrich the abbey of Redon. The success of the Breton chief forced Charles to come to terms. Nomenoë and his son, it was agreed, should assume the insignia of royalty and hold Rennes, Nantes, and all Brittany.

Convoyon, as we have seen, benefited by the spoils won by the Breton champion. Later, as his abbey at Redon was situated by a tidal river, and was thus exposed to the ravages of the Normans, he and his monks moved farther inland to Plélan. There he died and was buried, about A.D. 868, but his body was afterward removed to Redon, where he had lived and laboured so long. His relics were dispersed during the troublous times of the Revolution.

Tivisiau, the Shepherd Saint

St Tivisiau, or, more correctly, Turiau, has a large parish, as, although he was Bishop of Dol, we find him venerated as patron saint as far west as Landivisiau. He belongs to the earlier half of the seventh century, and, unlike most other Armorican ascetics, was of Breton origin, his father, Lelian, and his mother, Mageen, being graziers on the borders of the romantic and beautiful forest of Broceliande. The young Tivisiau was set to watch the sheep, and as he did so he steeped his soul in the beauty of the wonderful forest land about him, and his thoughts formed themselves into lays, which he sang as he tended his flock, for, like that other shepherd of old, King David, his exquisite voice could clothe his beautiful thoughts. The monastery of Balon stood near the lad's home, and often he would leave his sheep in the wilderness and steal away to listen to the monks chanting. Sometimes he joined in the service, and one day the Bishop of Dol, paying a visit to this outlying portion of his diocese, heard the sweet, clear notes of the boy's voice soaring above the lower tones of the

ST TIVISIAU, THE SHEPHERD SAINT

ST YVES INSTRUCTING SHEPHERD-BOYS IN THE USE OF THE ROSARY

monks. Enthralled by its beauty, the Bishop made inquiries as to who the singer was, and Tivisiau being brought forward, the prelate asked him to sing to him. Again and again did he sing, till at last the Bishop, who had lingered as long as he might in the little out-of-the-world monastery to listen to the young songster, was obliged to take his departure. The boy's personality had, however, so won his affection that he arranged with the monks of Balon that he should take him to Dol, and so it came about that Tivisiau was educated at that ancient religious centre, where his voice was carefully trained. The Bishop made him his suffragan, and, later Abbot of Dol, and when at length he came to relinquish the burden of his office he named Tivisiau as his successor.

The story provides a noteworthy example of the power exercised in early times by a beautiful voice. But this love of music and the susceptibility to the emotion it calls forth are not peculiar to any century of Celtdom. Love of music, and the temperament that can hear the voice of the world's beauty, in music, in poetry, in the wild sea that breaks on desolate shores, or in the hushed wonder of hills and valleys, is as much a part of the Celt as are the thews and the sinews that have helped to carry him through the hard days of toil and poverty that have been the lot of so many of his race in their struggle for existence—whether in the far-off Outer Isles of the mist-wreathed and mystic west coast of Scotland, or among the Welsh mountains, or in picturesque Brittany, or in the distressful, beautiful, sorrow-haunted Green Isle.

At Landivisiau one finds much exquisite carving in the south porch, which is all that remains of the early building to show how beautiful must have been the church to which it belonged. There is also a very ancient and picturesque fountain, known to tradition as that of St Tivisiau.

St Nennocha

The legend of Nennocha is held to be pure fable, but is interesting nevertheless. It tells how a king in Wales, called Breochan, had fourteen sons, who all deserted him to preach the Gospel. Breochan then made a vow that if God would grant him another child he would give to the Church a tithe of all his gold and his lands, and later on his wife, Moneduc, bore him a daughter, whom they baptized Nennocha. Nennocha was sent away to a foster father and mother, returning home at the age of fourteen. A prince of Ireland sought her hand in marriage, but St Germain, who was then at her father's palace, persuaded her to embrace the religious life, and the disappointed King sadly gave his consent. A great multitude assembled to accompany the maiden in her renunciation of the world, "numbering in its midst four bishops and many priests and virgins." We are told how they all took ship together and sailed to Brittany. The Breton king gave the princess land at Ploermel, and there she founded a great monastery, where she lived till death claimed her.

St Enora

Several old Breton songs tell us the story of St Enora (or Honora), the wife of Efflam (already alluded to in the chapter on Arthurian legend), but these accounts vary very considerably in their details. One account giving us "stern facts" relates how St Efflam was betrothed for political reasons to Enora, a Saxon princess, and speaks of how impossible it was to expect that such a union could prove anything but disastrous when it was not a love match. So, whether partly to escape from a married life which jarred his susceptibilities, or entirely on account of his religious asceticism, Efflam left his wife and crossed to Brittany to lead the life of a religious hermit. One of the Breton songs gives the beginning of the story in a much more picturesque way. It relates how Enora, "beautiful as an angel," had many suitors, but would give her hand to none save the Prince Efflam, "son of a stranger King." But Efflam, torn by the desire to lead the religious life, far away from the world, rose "in the midst of the night, his wedding night," and crept softly away, no one seeing him save his faithful dog, which he loved. So he came to the seashore and crossed to Brittany. The story of his landing and his meeting with Arthur has already been told, and we have seen how his fate was once more, by divine agency, linked with that of Enora. The song tells us how the angels carried the princess over the sea and set her on the door-sill of her husband's cell. Presently she awoke, and, finding herself there, she knocked three times and cried out to her husband that she was "his sweetheart, his wife," whom God had sent. St Efflam, knowing her voice, came out, and "with many godly words he took her hand in his." One account says that he sent her to the south of Brittany to found a convent for nuns, as he wished to devote his life entirely to the service of God and the contemplation of nature. All versions agree on the point that he built a hut for her beside his own, and one story relates how he made her wear a veil over her face and only spoke to her through the door! But one Breton song with more of the matter of poetry in it than the rest tells how the little hut he built for her was shaded by green bushes and sheltered by a rock, and that there they lived, side by side, for a long and happy time, while the fame of the miracles they wrought spread through the land. Then one night some sailors on the sea "saw the sky open and heard a burst of heavenly music," and next day when a poor woman took her sick child to Enora to beg for her aid she could get no response, and looking in she beheld the royal lady lying dead. The humble place was alight with her radiance, and near her a little boy in white was kneeling. The woman then ran to tell St Efflam of her discovery, only to find that he too was lying dead in his cell.

Corseul the Accursed

The town of Corseul has sunk into insignificance, and its failure to achieve prosperity is said to be due to its covert hostility to St Malo—or, as he is more correctly called, Machutes. Coming to Brittany on missionary enterprise, the Saint found that Christianity had not penetrated to the district of Corseul, where the old pagan worship still obtained. He therefore decided that his work must lie chiefly among the Curiosolites of that land, and determined that his first celebration of Easter Mass there should take place in the very centre of the pagan worship, the temple of Haute-Bécherel. The people of the district received him coldly, but without open hostility, and he and his monks prepared for the Christian festival in the pagan shrine, to find to their dismay that they had omitted to bring either chalice or wine for the Eucharist. Several of the monks were sent into the town to buy these, but in all Corseul they could find no one willing to sell either cup or wine, because of the hostility of the idolatrous folk of the place. At last the Saint performed a miracle to provide these necessaries, but he never forgave the insult to his religion, and while he founded monasteries broadcast over his diocese he avoided Corseul, and as Christianity became more and more universal the pagan town gradually paid the penalty of its enmity to the cause of Christ.

St Keenan

St Keenan (sixth century) was surnamed Colodoc, or "He who loves to lose himself," a beautiful epitome of his character. As in so many instances in the chronicles of Breton hagiology, confusion regarding St Keenan has arisen among a multiplicity of chronicles. He seems to have been a native of Connaught, whence he crossed into Wales and became a disciple of Gildas. He was told to "go forward" carrying a little bell, until he reached a place called Ros-ynys, where the bell would ring of itself, and there he would find rest. He asked Gildas to provide him with a bell, but the abbot could only supply him with a small piece of metal. Keenan, however, blessed this, and it grew until it was large enough for a good bell to be cast from it. Thus equipped, the Saint set out, and journeyed until he reached an arm of the sea, where he sat down on the grass to rest. While lying at his ease he heard a herdsman call to his fellow: "Brother, have you seen my cows anywhere?" "Yes," replied the other, "I saw them at Ros-ynys." Rejoicing greatly at finding himself in the vicinity of the place he sought, Keenan descended to the shore, which has since been called by his name. Greatly athirst, he struck a rock with his staff, and water gushed forth in answer to the stroke. Taking ship, he crossed the firth and entered a little wood. All at once, to his extreme joy, the bell he carried commenced to tinkle, and he knew he had reached the end of his journey—the valley of Rosynys, afterward St David's.

Later, deciding to cross to Brittany with his disciples, Keenan dispatched some of his company to beg for corn for their journey from a merchant at Landegu. They met with a gruff refusal, but the merchant mockingly informed them they could have the corn if they carried off the whole of his barge-load. When the Saint embarked the barge broke its moorings and floated after him all the way! He landed at Cléder, where he built a monastery, which he enriched with a copy of the Gospels transcribed by his own hand.

The fatal contest between King Arthur and Modred, his nephew, caused Keenan to return to Britain, and he is said to have been present at the battle of Camelot and to have comforted Guinevere after the death of her royal husband, exhorting her to enter a convent. He afterward returned to Cléder, where he died. The monastery fell into ruin, and the place of his burial was forgotten, till one night an angel appeared in a vision to one of the inhabitants of Cléder and bade him exhume the bones of the Saint, which he would find at a certain spot. This the man did, and the relics were recovered. A fragment of them is preserved in the cathedral of Saint-Brieuc. St Keenan is popularly known in Brittany as St Ké, or St Quay.

St Nicholas

One very interesting and curious saint is St Nicholas, whose cult cannot be traced to any Christian source, and who is most probably the survival of some pagan divinity. He is specially the saint of seafaring men, and is believed to bring them good luck, asking nothing in return save that they shall visit his shrine whenever they happen to pass. This is a somewhat dilapidated chapel at Landévennec, of which the seamen seem to show their appreciation, if one may judge from the fact that the little path leading up to it is exceedingly well worn.

St Bieuzy

St Bieuzy was a friend and disciple of St Gildas. Flying from England at the coming of the Saxons, they crossed to Brittany and settled there, one of their favourite retreats being the exquisite La Roche-sur-Blavet, where they took up their abode in the shadow of the great rock and built a rough wooden shelter. The chapel there shows the 'bell' of St Gildas, and by the river is a great boulder hollowed like a chair, where Bieuzy was wont to sit and fish. St Bieuzy, however, possessed thaumaturgical resources of his own, having the gift of curing hydrophobia, and the hermitage of La Roche-sur-Blavet became so thronged by those seeking his aid that only by making a private way to the top of the great rock could he obtain respite to say his prayers. This gift of his was the cause of his tragic death. One day as he was celebrating Mass the servant of a pagan chief ran into the chapel, crying out that his master's dogs had gone mad, and demanding that Bieuzy should come immediately and cure them. Bieuzy was unwilling to interrupt the sacred service and displeased at the irreverence of the demand, and the servant returned to his master, who rushed into the chapel and in his savage frenzy struck the Saint such a blow with his sword that he cleft his head in twain. The heroic Saint completed the celebration of Mass—the sword still in the wound—and then, followed by the whole congregation, he walked to the monastery of Rhuys, where he received the blessing of his beloved St Gildas, and fell dead at his feet. He was buried in the church, and a fountain at Rhuys was dedicated to him. It is satisfactory to note that the entire establishment of the murderer of the Saint is said to have perished of hydrophobia!

St Leonorius

St Leonorius, or Léonore (sixth century), was a disciple of St Iltud, of Wales, and was ordained by St Dubricus; he crossed to Brittany in early life. The legend that most closely attaches to his name is one of the most beautiful of all the Breton beliefs, and is full of the poetry and romance that exist for the Celt in all the living things around him. The Saint and his monks had worked hard to till their ground—for the labours of holy men included many duties in addition to religious ministrations—but when they came to sow the seed they found that they had omitted to provide themselves with wheat! All their labour seemed in vain, and they were greatly distressed as to what they would do for food if they had no harvest to look forward to, when suddenly they saw, perched on a little wayside cross, a tiny robin redbreast holding in its beak an ear of wheat! The monks joyfully took the grain, and, sowing it, reaped an abundant harvest! Accounts vary somewhat in the details of this story. Some say that the bird led the monks to a store of grain, and others question the fact that the bird was a robin, but the popular idea is that the robin proffered the grain, and so universal and so strong is this belief that "Robin Redbreast's corn" is a byword in Brittany for "small beginnings that prosper."

The Saint is said to have possessed the most marvellous attainments. We are told that he learnt the alphabet in one day, the "art of spelling" the following day, and calligraphy the next! He is also said to have been a bishop at the age of fifteen. Tradition avers that he ploughed the land with stags, and that an altar was brought to him from the depth of the sea by two wild pigeons to serve for his ministrations. The circumstance that animals or birds were employed—predominantly the latter—as the divine means of rendering aid to the Saint is common to many of these legends. We thus have saintly romance linked with the 'friendly animals' formula of folk-lore.

St Patern

Many quaint and pretty stories are told of the childhood and youth of St Patern, the patron saint of Vannes. His intense religious fervour was probably inherited from his father, Petranus, who, we are told, left his wife and infant son and crossed to Ireland to embrace the life religious. One day as his mother sat by the open window making a dress for her baby she was called away, and left the little garment lying on the sill. A bird flew past, and, attracted by the soft woollen stuff, carried it off to line its nest. A year later when the nest was destroyed the dress was discovered as fresh and clean as when it was stolen—a piece of symbolism foretelling the purity and holiness of the future saint.

As soon as the child could speak his mother sent him to school. She hoped great things from the quiet, earnest boy, in whom she had observed signs of fervent piety. One day he came home and asked his mother where his father was. "All the other boys have fathers," he said; "where is mine?" His mother sadly told him that his father, wishing to serve God more perfectly than it was possible for him to do at home, had gone to Ireland to become a monk. "Thither shall I go too, when I'm a man," said Patern, and he made a resolve that when he grew up he would also enter a monastery. Accordingly, having finished his studies in the monastery of Rhuys, he set out for Britain, where he founded two religious houses, and then crossed to Ireland, where he met his father. Eventually he returned to Vannes, as one of the nine bishops of Brittany, but he did not agree with his brethren regarding certain ecclesiastical laws, and at last, not wishing to "lose his patience," he abandoned his diocese and went to France, where he ended his days as a simple monk.

There is an interesting legend to account for the foundation of the church of St Patern at Vannes. We are told how for three years after Patern left Vannes the people were afflicted by a dreadful famine. No rain fell, and the distress was great. At length it was remembered that Patern had departed without giving the people his blessing, and at once "a pilgrimage set forth to bring back his sacred body, that it might rest in his own episcopal town." But the body of the blessed Patern "refused to be removed," until one of the pilgrims, who had before denied the bishop a certain piece of ground, promised to gift it to his memory and to build a church on it to the Saint's honour, whereupon the body became light enough to be lifted from the grave and conveyed to Vannes. No sooner had the sacred corpse entered Vannes than rain fell in torrents. Hagiology abounds in instances of this description, which in many respects bring it into line with mythology.

St Samson

We have already related the story of Samson's birth. Another legend regarding him tells how one day when the youths attached to the monastery where he dwelt were out winnowing corn one of the monks was bitten by an adder and fainted with fright. Samson ran to St Iltud to tell the news, with tears in his eyes, and begged to be allowed to attempt the cure of the monk. Iltud gave him permission, and Samson, full of faith and enthusiasm, rubbed the bite with oil, and by degrees the monk recovered. After this Samson's fame grew apace. Indeed, we are told that the monks grew jealous of him and attempted to poison him. He was ordained a bishop at York, and lived a most austere life, though his humanity was very apparent in his love for animals. He was made abbot of a monastery, and endeavoured to instil temperance into the monks, but at length gave up the attempt in despair and settled in a cave at the mouth of the Severn. Then one night "a tall man" appeared to him in a vision, and bade him go to Armorica, saying to him—so the legend goes: "Thou goest by the sea, and where thou wilt disembark thou shalt find a well. Over this thou wilt build a church, and around it will group the houses forming the city of which thou wilt be a bishop." All of which came to pass, and for ages the town has been known as the episcopal city of Dol. Accompanied by forty monks, Samson crossed the Channel and landed in the Bay of Saint-Brieuc. One version of the story tells us that the Saint and numerous other monks fled from Britain to escape the Saxon tyranny, and that Samson and six of his suffragans who crossed the sea with him were known as the 'Seven Saints of Brittany.'

Brittany's Lawyer Saint

Few prosperous and wealthy countries produce saints in any great number, and in proof of the converse of this we find much hagiology in Brittany and Ireland. Let lawyers take note that while many saints spring from among the *bourgeoisie* they include few legal men. An outstanding exception to this rule is St Yves (or Yvo), probably the best known, and almost certainly the most beloved, saint in Brittany. St Yves is the only regularly canonized Breton saint. He was born at Kermartin, near Tréguier, in 1253, his father being lord of that place. The house where he first saw the light was pulled down in 1834, but the bed in which he was born is still preserved and shown. His name is borne by the majority of the inhabitants of the districts of Tréguier and Saint-Brieuc, and one authority tells us how "in the Breton tongue his praises are sung as follows:

> N'hen eus ket en Breiz, n'hen eus ket unan,
> N'hen eus ket uer Zant evel Sant Erwan.

This, in French, runs:

> Il n'y a pas en Bretagne, il n'y en a pas un,
> Il n'y a pas un saint comme saint Yves."

He began his legal education when he was fourteen, and studied law in the schools of Paris, becoming an ecclesiastical judge, and later (1285) an ordained priest and incumbent of Tredrig. Subsequently he was made incumbent of Lohanec, which post he held till his death. As a judge he possessed a quality rare in those days —he was inaccessible to bribery! That this was appreciated we find in the following *bon mot*:

> Saint Yves était Breton,
> Avocat et pas larron:
> Chose rare, se dit-on.

He invariably endeavoured to induce disputants to settle their quarrels 'out of court' if possible, and applied his talents to defending the cause of the poor and oppressed, without fee. He was known as 'the poor man's advocate,' and to-day in the department of the Côtes-du-Nord, when a debtor repudiates his debt, the creditor will pay for a Mass to St Yves, in the hope that he will cause the defaulter to die within the year! St Yves de Vérité is the special patron of lawyers, and is represented in the *mortier*, or lawyer's cap, and robe.

St Yves spent most of his income in charity, turning his house into an orphanage, and many are the stories told of his humanity and generosity. The depth of his sympathy, and its practical result, are shown in an incident told us of how one morning he found a poor, half-naked man lying on his doorstep shivering with cold, having spent the night there. Yves gave up his bed to the beggar the next night, and himself slept on the doorstep, desiring to learn by personal experience the sufferings of the poor. On another occasion, while being fitted with a new coat, he caught sight of a miserable man on the pavement outside who was clad in rags and tatters that showed his skin through many rents. Yves tore off the new coat and, rushing out, gave it to the beggar, saying to the astonished and horrified tailor: "There is plenty of wear still in my old coats. I will content myself with them." His pity and generosity led him to still further kindness when he was visiting a hospital and saw how ill-clad some of the patients were, for he actually gave them the clothes he was wearing at the time, wrapping himself in a coverlet till he had other garments sent to him from home. He was wont to walk beside the ploughmen in the fields and teach them prayers. He would sit on the moors beside the shepherd-boys and instruct them in the use of the rosary; and often he would stop little children in the street, and gain their interest and affection by his gentleness. His shrewd legal mind was of service to the poor in other ways than in the giving of advice. A story is told of how two rogues brought a heavy chest to a widow, declaring it to contain twelve hundred pieces of gold and asking her to take charge of it. Some weeks later one of them returned, claimed the box, and removed it. A few days later the second of the men arrived and asked for the box, and when the poor woman could not produce it he took her to court and sued her for the gold it had contained. Yves, on hearing that the case was going against the woman, offered to defend her, and pleaded that his client was ready to restore the gold, but only to both the men who had committed it to her charge, and that therefore both must appear to claim it. This was a blow to the rogues, who attempted to escape, and, failing to do so, at length confessed that they had plotted to extort money from the widow, the chest containing nothing but pieces of old iron.

Yves was so eloquent and earnest a preacher that he was continually receiving requests to attend other churches, which he never refused. On the Good Friday before his death he preached in seven different parishes. He died at the age of fifty, and was buried at Tréguier. Duke John V, who founded the Chapelle du Duc, had a special regard for Yves, and erected a magnificent tomb to his memory, which was for three centuries the object of veneration in Brittany.

During the French Revolution the reliquary of St Yves was destroyed, but his bones were preserved and have been re-enshrined at Tréguier. His last will and testament—leaving all his goods to the poor—is preserved, together with his breviary, in the sacristy of the church at Minihy.

The Saint is generally represented with a cat as his symbol—typifying the lawyer's watchful character—but this hardly seems a fitting emblem for such a beautiful character as St Yves.

St Budoc of Dol

The legend of St Budoc of Dol presents several peculiar features. It was first recited by professional minstrels, then "passed into the sanctuary, and was read in prose in cathedral and church choirs as a narrative of facts," although it seems curious that it could have been held to be other than fiction.

A Count of Goelc, in Brittany, sought in marriage Azénor, "tall as a palm, bright as a star," but they had not been wedded a year when Azénor's father married again, and his new wife, jealous of her stepdaughter, hated her and determined to ruin her. Accordingly she set to work to implant suspicion as to Azénor's purity in the minds of her father and husband, and the Count shut his wife up in a tower and forbade her to speak to anyone. Here all the poor Countess could do was to pray to her patron saint, the Holy Bridget of Ireland. Her stepmother, however, was not content with the evil she had already wrought, and would not rest until she had brought about Azénor's death. She continued her calumnies, and at length the Count assembled all his barons and his court to judge his wife. The unfortunate and innocent Countess was brought into the hall for trial, and, seated on a little stool in the midst of the floor, the charges were read to her and she was called upon to give her reply. With tears she protested her innocence, but in spite of the fact that no proof could be brought against her she was sent in disgrace to her father in Brest. He in turn sat in judgment upon her, and condemned her to death, the sentence being that she should be placed in a barrel and cast into the sea, "to be carried where the winds and tides listed." We are told that the barrel floated five months, "tossing up and down"—during which time Azénor was supplied with food by an angel, who passed it to her through the bung-hole.

During these five months, the legend continues, the poor Countess became a mother, the angel and St Bridget watching over her. As soon as the child was born his mother made the sign of the Cross upon him, made him kiss a crucifix, and patiently waited the coming of an opportunity to have him baptized. The child began to speak while in the cask. At last the barrel rolled ashore at Youghal Harbour, in the county of Cork. An Irish peasant, thinking he had found a barrel of wine, was proceeding to tap it with a gimlet when he heard a voice from within say: "Do not injure the cask." Greatly astonished, the man demanded who was inside, and the voice replied: "I am a child desiring baptism. Go at once to the abbot of the monastery to which this land belongs, and bid him come and baptize me." The Irishman ran to the abbot with the message, but he not unnaturally declined to believe the story, till, with a true Hibernian touch, the peasant asked him if it were likely that he would have told 'his reverence' anything about his find had there been "anything better than a baby" in the barrel! Accordingly the abbot hastened to the shore, opened the cask, and freed the long-suffering Countess of Goelc and her son, the latter of whom he christened by the name of Budoc, and took under his care.

Meantime, the "wicked stepmother," falling ill and being at the point of death, became frightened when she thought of her sin against Azénor, and confessed the lies by which she had wrought the ruin of the Countess. The Count, overcome by remorse and grief, set out in quest of his wife. Good luck led him to Ireland, where he disembarked at Youghal and found his lost ones. With great rejoicing he had a stately ship made ready, and prepared to set out for Brittany with Azénor and Budoc, but died before he could embark. Azénor remained in Ireland and devoted herself to good works and to the training of her son, who from an early age resolved to embrace the religious life, and was in due course made a monk by the Abbot of Youghal. His mother died, and on the death of the Abbot of Youghal he was elected to rule the monastery. Later, upon the death of the King of Ireland, the natives raised Budoc to the temporal and spiritual thrones, making him King of Ireland and Bishop of Armagh. After two years he wished to retire from these honours, but the people were "wild with despair" at the tidings, and surrounded the palace lest he should escape. One night, while praying in his metropolitan church, an angel appeared to him, bidding him betake himself to Brittany. Going down to the seashore, it was indicated to him that he must make the voyage in a stone trough. On entering this it began to move, and he was borne across to Brittany, landing at Porspoder, in the diocese of Léon. The people of that district drew the stone coffer out of the water, and built a hermitage and a chapel for the Saint's convenience. Budoc dwelt for one year at Porspoder, but, "disliking the roar of the waves," he had his stone trough mounted on a cart, and yoking two oxen to it he set forth, resolved to follow them wherever they might go and establish himself at whatever place they might halt. The cart broke down at Plourin, and there Budoc settled for a short time; but trouble with disorderly nobles forced him to depart, and this time he went to Dol, where he was well received by St Malglorious, then its bishop, who soon after resigned his see to Budoc. The Saint ruled at Dol for twenty years, and died early in the seventh century.

Another Celtic myth of the same type is to be found on the shores of the Firth of Forth. The story in question deals with the birth of St Mungo, or St Kentigern, the patron saint of Glasgow. His mother was Thenaw, the Christian daughter of the pagan King Lot of Lothian, brother-in-law of King Arthur, from his marriage with Arthur's sister Margawse. Thus the famous Gawaine would be Thenaw's brother. Thenaw met Ewen, the son of Eufeurien, King of Cumbria, and fell deeply in love with him, but her father discovered her disgrace and ordered her to be cast headlong from the summit of Traprain Law, once known as Dunpender, a mountain in East Lothian. A kindly fate watched over the princess, however, and she fell so softly from the eminence that she was uninjured. Such Christian subjects as Lot possessed begged her life. But if her father might have relented his Druids were inexorable. They branded her as a sorceress, and she was doomed to death by drowning. She was accordingly rowed out from Aberlady Bay to the vicinity of the Isle of May, where, seated in a skin boat, she was left to the mercy of the waves. In this terrible situation she cast herself upon the grace of Heaven, and her frail craft was wafted up the Forth, where it drifted ashore near Culross. At this spot Kentigern was born, and the mother and child were shortly afterward discovered by some shepherds, who placed them under the care of St Serf, Abbot of Culross. To these events the date A.D. 516 is assigned.

‘Fatal Children’ Legends

This legend is, of course, closely allied with those which recount the fate and adventures of the ‘fatal children.’ Like Œdipus, Romulus, Perseus, and others, Budoc and Kentigern are obviously ‘fatal children,’ as is evidenced by the circumstances of their birth. We are not told that King Lot or Azénor's father had been warned that if their daughters had a son they would be slain by that child, but it is probably only the saintly nature of the subject of the stories which caused this circumstance to be omitted. Danaë, the mother of Perseus, we remember, was, when disgraced, shut up in a chest with her child, and committed to the waves, which carried her to the island of Seriphos, where she was duly rescued. Romulus and his brother Remus were thrown into the Tiber, and escaped a similar fate. The Princess Desonelle and her twin sons, in the old English metrical romance of *Sir Torrent of Portugal*, are also cast into the sea, but succeed in making the shore of a far country. All these children grow up endowed with marvellous beauty and strength, but their doom is upon them, and after numerous adventures they slay their fathers or some other unfortunate relative. But the most characteristic part of what seems an almost universal legend is that these children are born in the most obscure circumstances, afterward rising to a height of splendour which makes up for all they previously suffered. It is not necessary to explain nowadays that this is characteristic of nearly all sun-myths. The sun is born in obscurity, and rises to a height of splendour at midday. Thus in the majority of these legends we find the sun personified. It is not sufficient to object that such an elucidation smacks too much of the tactics of Max Müller to be accepted by modern students of folk-lore. The student of comparative myth who does not make use of the best in all systems of mythological elucidation is undone, for no one system will serve for all examples. To those who may object, "Oh, but Kentigern was a *real* person," I reply that I know many myths concerning 'real' people. For the matter of that, we assist in the manufacture of these every day of our lives, and it is quite a fallacy that legends cannot spring up concerning veritable historical personages, and even around living, breathing folk. And for the rest of it mythology and hagiology are hopelessly intermingled in their *motifs*.

Miraculous Crossings

Another Celtic saint besides Budoc possessed a stone boat. He is St Baldred, who, like Kentigern, hails from the Firth of Forth, and dwelt on the Bass Rock. He is said to have chosen this drear abode as a refuge from the eternal wars between the Picts and the Scots toward the close of the seventh century. From this point of vantage, and probably during seasons of truce, he rowed to the mainland to minister to the spiritual wants of the rude natives of Lothian. Inveresk seems to have been the eastern border of his 'parish.' Tradition says that he was the second Bishop of Glasgow, and thus the successor of Kentigern, but the lack of all reliable data concerning the western see subsequent to the death of Glasgow's patron saint makes it impossible to say whether this statement is authentic or otherwise. Many miracles are attributed to Baldred, not the least striking of which is that concerning a rock to the east of Tantallon Castle, known as 'St Baldred's Boat.' At one time this rock was situated between the Bass and the adjacent mainland, and was a fruitful source of shipwreck. Baldred, pitying the mariners who had to navigate the Firth, and risk this danger, rowed out to the rock and mounted upon it; whereupon, at his simple nod, it was lifted up, and, like a ship driven by the wind, was wafted to the nearest shore, where it thenceforth remained. This rock is sometimes called 'St Baldred's Coble,' or 'Cock-boat.' This species of miracle is more commonly discovered in the annals of hagiology than in those of pure myth, although in legend we occasionally find the landscape altered by order of supernatural or semi-supernatural beings.

One rather striking instance of miraculous crossing is that of St Noyala, who is said to have crossed to Brittany on the leaf of a tree, accompanied by her nurse. She was beheaded at Beignon, but walked to Pontivy carrying her head in her hands. A chapel at Pontivy is dedicated to her, and was remarkable in the eighteenth century for several interesting paintings on a gold ground depicting this legend.

We find this incident of miraculous crossing occurring in the stories of many of the Breton saints. A noteworthy instance is that of St Tugdual, who, with his followers, crossed in a ship which vanished when they disembarked. Still another example is found in the case of St Vougas, or Vie, who is specially venerated in Tréguennec. He is thought to have been an Irish bishop, and is believed to have mounted a stone and sailed across to Brittany upon it. This particular version of the popular belief may have sprung from the fact that there is a rock off the coast of Brittany called 'the Ship,' from a fancied resemblance to one. In course of time this rock was affirmed to have been the ship of St Vougas.

Azénor the Pale

There is a story of another Azénor, who, according to local history, married Yves, heritor of Kermorvan, in the year 1400. A popular ballad of Cornouaille tells how this Azénor, who was surnamed 'the Pale,' did not love her lord, but gave her heart to another, the Clerk of Mezléan.

One day she sat musing by a forest fountain, dressed in a robe of yellow silk, wantonly plucking the flowers which grew on the mossy parapet of the spring and binding them into a bouquet for the Clerk of Mezléan. The Seigneur Yves, passing by on his white steed at a hand-gallop, observed her "with the corner of his eye," and conceived a violent love for her.

The Clerk of Mezléan had been true to Azénor for many a day, but he was poor and her parents would have none of him.

One morning as Azénor descended to the courtyard she observed great preparations on foot as if for a festival.

"For what reason," she said, "has this great fire been kindled, and why have they placed two spits in front of it? What is happening in this house, and why have these fiddlers come?"

Those whom she asked smiled meaningly.

"To-morrow is your wedding-day," said they.

At this Azénor the Pale grew still paler, and was long silent.

"If that be so," she said, "it will be well that I seek my marriage chamber early, for from my bed I shall not be raised except for burial."

That night her little page stole through the window.

"Lady," he said, "a great and brilliant company come hither. The Seigneur Yves is at their head, and behind him ride cavaliers and a long train of gentlemen. He is mounted on a white horse, with trappings of gold."

Azénor wept sorely.

"Unhappy the hour that he comes!" she cried, wringing her hands. "Unhappy be my father and mother who have done this thing!"

Sorely wept Azénor when going to the church that day. She set forth with her intended husband, riding on the crupper of his horse. Passing by Mezléan she said:

"I pray you let me enter this house, Seigneur, for I am fatigued with the journey, and would rest for a space."

"That may not be to-day," he replied; "to-morrow, if you wish it."

At this Azénor wept afresh, but was comforted by her little page. At the church door one could see that her heart was breaking.

"Approach, my daughter," said the aged priest. "Draw near, that I may place the ring upon your finger."

"Father," replied Azénor, "I beg of you not to force me to wed him whom I do not love."

"These are wicked words, my child. The Seigneur Yves is wealthy, he has gold and silver, châteaux and broad lands, but the Clerk of Mezléan is poor."

"Poor he may be, Father," murmured Azénor, "yet had I rather beg my bread with him than dwell softly with this other."

But her relentless parents would not hearken to her protestations, and she was wed to the Lord Yves. On arriving at her husband's house she was met by the Seigneur's mother, who received her graciously, but only one word did Azénor speak, that old refrain that runs through all ballad poetry.

"Tell me, O my mother," she said, "is my bed made?"

"It is, my child," replied the châtelaine. "It is next the Chamber of the Black Cavalier. Follow me and I will take you thither."

Once within the chamber, Azénor, wounded to the soul, fell upon her knees, her fair hair falling about her.

"My God," she cried, "have pity upon me!"

The Seigneur Yves sought out his mother.

"Mother of mine," said he, "where is my wife?"

"She sleeps in her high chamber," replied his mother. "Go to her and console her, for she is sadly in need of comfort."

The Seigneur entered. "Do you sleep?" he asked Azénor.

She turned in her bed and looked fixedly at him. "Good morrow to you, widower," she said.

"By the saints," cried he, "what mean you? Why do you call me widower?"

"Seigneur," she said meaningly, "it is true that you are not a widower yet, but soon you will be."

Then, her mind wandering, she continued: "Here is my wedding gown; give it, I pray you, to my little servant, who has been so good to me and who carried my letters to the Clerk of Mezléan. Here is a new cloak which my mother broidered; give it to the priests who will sing Masses for my soul. For yourself you may take my crown and chaplet. Keep them well, I pray, as a souvenir of our wedding."

Who is that who arrives at the hamlet as the clocks are striking the hour? Is it the Clerk of Mezléan? Too late! Azénor is dead.

"I have seen the fountain beside which Azénor plucked flowers to make a bouquet for her 'sweet Clerk of Mezléan,'" says the Vicomte Hersart de la Villemarqué, "when the Seigneur of Kermorvan passed and withered with his glance her happiness and these flowers of love. Mezléan is in ruins, no one remains within its gates, surmounted by a crenellated and machicolated gallery."

There is a subscription at the end of the ballad to the effect that it was written on a round table in the Manor of Hénan, near Pont-Aven, by the "bard of the old Seigneur," who dictated it to a damsel. "How comes it," asks Villemarqué, "that in the Middle Ages we still find a seigneur of Brittany maintaining a domestic bard?" There is no good reason why a domestic bard should not have been found in the Brittany of medieval times, since such singers of the household were maintained in Ireland and Scotland until a relatively late date—up to the period of the '45 in the case of the latter country.

St Pol of Léon

St Pol (or Paul) of Léon (sixth century) was the son of a Welsh prince, and, like so many of the Breton saints, he was a disciple of St Iltud, being also a fellow-student of St Samson and St Gildas. At the age of sixteen he left his home and crossed the sea to Brittany. In the course of time other young men congregated round him, and he became their superior, receiving holy orders along with twelve companions. Near these young monks dwelt Mark, the King of Vannes, who invited Pol to visit his territory and instruct his people. The Saint went to Vannes and was well received, but after dwelling for some time in that part of the country he felt the need of solitude once more, and entreated the King that he might have permission to depart and that he might be given a bell; "for," as the chronicler tells us, "at that time it was customary for kings to have seven bells rung before they sat down to meat."

The King, however, vexed that Pol should wish to leave him, refused to give him the bell, so the Saint went without it. Before leaving Vannes Pol visited his sister, who lived in solitude with other holy women on a little island, but when the time came for him to depart she wept and entreated him to stay, and the Saint remained with her for another three days. When he was finally taking leave of her, she begged him that as he was "powerful with God" he would grant her a request, and when Pol asked what it was she desired him to do, she explained that the island on which she dwelt was small "and incommodious for landing" and requested him to pray to God that it might be extended a little into the sea, with a "gentle shore." Pol said she had asked what was beyond his power, but suggested that they should pray that her desire might be granted. So they prayed, and the sea began to retreat, "leaving smooth, golden sand where before there had been only stormy waves." All the nuns came to see the miracle which had been wrought, and the sister of St Pol gathered pebbles and laid them round the land newly laid bare, and strewed them down the road that she and her brother had taken. These pebbles grew into tall pillars of rock, and the avenue thus formed is to this day called 'the Road of St Pol.' Thus do the peasants explain the Druidical circles and avenue on the islet.

After this miracle Pol departed, and rowed to the island of Ouessant, and later he travelled through Brittany, finally settling in the island of Batz, near the small town encompassed by mud walls which has since borne his name. There he founded a monastery. The island was at that time infested by a dreadful monster, sixty feet long, and we are told how the Saint subdued this dragon. Accompanied by a warrior, he entered its den, tied his stole round its neck, and, giving it to his companion to lead, he followed them, beating the animal with his stick, until they came to the extremity of the island. There he took off the stole and commanded the dragon to fling itself into the sea—an order which the monster immediately obeyed. In the church on the island a stole is preserved which is said to be that of St Pol. Another story tells us how St Jaoua, nephew of St Pol, had to call in his uncle's aid in taming a wild bull which was devastating his cell. These incidents remind us of St Efflam's taming of the dragon. St Pol is one of the saints famous for his miraculous power over wild beasts.

The Saint's renown became such that the Breton king made him Archbishop of Léon, giving him special care and control of the city bearing his name. We are told how the Saint found wild bees swarming in a hollow tree, and, gathering the swarm, set them in a hive and taught the people how to get honey. He also found a wild sow with her litter and tamed them. The descendants of this progeny remained at Léon for many generations, and were regarded as royal beasts. Both of these stories are, of course, a picturesque way of saying that St Pol taught the people to cultivate bees and to keep pigs.

St Pol's early desire to possess a bell was curiously granted later, as one day when he was in the company of a Count who ruled the land under King Childebat a fisherman brought the Count a bell which he had picked up on the seashore. The Count gave it to St Pol, who smiled and told him how he had longed and waited for years for such a bell. In the cathedral at Saint-Pol-de-Léon is a tiny bell which is said to have belonged to St Pol, and on the days of pardon "its notes still ring out over the heads of the faithful," and are supposed to be efficacious in curing headache or earache.

In the cathedral choir is the tomb of St Pol, where "his skull, an arm-bone, and a finger are encased in a little coffer, for the veneration of the devout." St Pol built the cathedral at Léon, and was its first bishop. Strategy had to be resorted to to secure the see for him. The Count gave Pol a letter to take in person to King Childebat, which stated that he had sent Pol to be ordained bishop and invested with the see of Léon. When the Saint discovered what the letter contained he wept, and implored the King to respect his great disinclination to become a bishop; but Childebat would not listen, and, calling for three bishops, he had him consecrated. The Saint was received with great joy by the people of Léon, and lived among them to a green old age.

In art St Pol is most generally represented with a dragon, and sometimes with a bell, or a cruse of water and a loaf of bread, symbolical of his frugal habits.

St Ronan

Of St Ronan there is told a tale of solemn warning to wives addicted to neglecting their children and "seeking their pleasure elsewhere," as it is succinctly expressed. St Ronan was an Irish bishop who came to Léon, where he retired into a hermitage in the forest of Névet. Grallo, the King of Brittany, was in the habit of visiting him in his cell, listening to his discourses, and putting theological questions to him. The domestic question must have been a problem even in those days, since we find Grallo's Queen, Queban, in charge of her five-year-old daughter. Family cares proving rather irksome, Queban solved the difficulty of her daughter by putting the child into a box, with bread and milk to keep her quiet, while she amused herself with frivolous matters. Unfortunately, this ingeniously improvized *crêche* proved singularly unsuccessful, for the poor little girl choked on a piece of crust, and when the Queen next visited the child she found to her horror that she was dead. Terrified at the fatal result of her neglect, and not daring to confess what had happened, the Queen, being a woman of resource, closed the box and raised a hue and cry to find the girl, who she declared must have strayed. She rushed in search of her husband to St Ronan's cell, and upbraided the hermit for being the cause of the King's absence. "But for you," she declared, "my daughter would not have been lost!" But it was a fatal mistake to accuse the Saint, or to imagine that he could be deceived. Sternly rebuking her, he challenged her with the fact that the child lay dead in a box, with milk and bread beside her! Rising, he left his cell, and, followed by the agitated royal couple, he led the way to where the proof of the Queen's neglect and deceit was found. Small mercy was shown in those days to erring womanhood, and the guilty Queen was instantly "stoned with stones till she died." The Saint completed his share in the matter by casting himself on his knees beside the child, whereupon she was restored to life.

St Goezenou

St Goezenou (*circ.* A.D. 675) was a native of Britain whose parents crossed to Brittany and settled near Brest, where

QUEEN QUEBAN STONED TO DEATH

MODERN BRITTANY

the Saint built an oratory and cabin for himself. The legend runs that the prince of the neighbourhood having offered to give him as much land as he could surround with a ditch in one day, the Saint took a fork and dragged it along the ground after him as he walked, in this way enclosing a league and a half of land, the fork as it trailed behind him making a furrow and throwing up an embankment, on a small scale. This story is quite probably a popular tradition, which grew up to explain the origin of old military earthworks in that part of the country, which were afterward utilized by the monks of St Goezenou.

It is also related of this worthy Saint that he had such a horror of women that he set up a huge menhir to mark the boundary beyond which no female was to pass under penalty of death. On one occasion a woman, either to test the extent of the Saint's power or from motives of enmity, pushed another woman who was with her past this landmark; but the innocent trespasser was unhurt and her assailant fell dead.

On one occasion, we are told, Goezenou asked a farmer's wife for some cream cheeses, but the woman, not wishing to part with them, declared that she had none. "You speak the truth," said the Saint. "You had some, but if you will now look in your cupboard you will find they have been turned into stone," and when the ungenerous housewife ran to her cupboard she found that this was so! The petrified cheeses were long preserved in the church of Goezenou—being removed during the Revolution, and afterward preserved in the manor of Kergivas.

Goezenou governed his church for twenty-four years, till he met with a violent death. Accompanied by his brother St Magan, he went to Quimperlé to see the monastery which St Corbasius was building there, but he began to praise the architecture of his own church, and this so enraged the master builder that he dropped his hammer on the critic's head. To add to the grief of St Magan, St Corbasius endeavoured to appropriate the body of the murdered Saint. He consented, however, to allow St Magan to have such bones as he was able to identify as belonging to his brother, whereupon St Magan prayed all night, and next morning spread a sheet for the bones, which miraculously arranged themselves into an entire skeleton, which the sorrowing Magan was thus enabled to remove.

St Winwaloe, or Gwenaloe

St Winwaloe, born about 455, was the son of Fragan, Governor of Léon, who had married a wealthy lady named Gwen. Their son was so beautiful that they named him Gwenaloe, or 'He that is white.' When the lad was about fifteen years old he was given to the care of a holy man, with whom he lived on the islet called Ile-Verte. One day a pirate fleet was sighted off the coast, near the harbour of Guic-sezne, and Winwaloe, who was with his father at the time, is said to have exclaimed, "I see a thousand sails," and to this day a cross which marks the spot is called 'the Cross of the Thousand Sails,' to commemorate the victory which Fragan and his son won over the pirates, who landed but were utterly defeated by the Governor and his retainers. During the fight Winwaloe, "like a second Moses," prayed for victory, and when the victory had been won he entreated his father to put the booty gained to a holy use and to build a monastery on the site of the battle. This was done, and the monastery was called Loc-Christ.

Leaving his master after some years, Winwaloe settled on the island of Sein, but finding that it was exposed to the fury of every gale that blew from the Atlantic he left it and went to Landévennec, on the opposite side of the harbour at Brest. There he established a monastery, gathered round him many disciples, and dwelt there until his death, many years later. He died during the first week of Lent, "after bestowing a kiss of peace on his brethren," and his body is preserved at Montreuil-sur-Mer, his chasuble, alb, and bell being laid in the Jesuit church of St Charles at Antwerp.

In art St Winwaloe is represented vested as an abbot, with staff in one hand and a bell in the other, standing beside the sea, from which fishes arise as if in answer to the sound of his bell.

CHAPTER XIII: COSTUMES AND CUSTOMS OF BRITTANY

DISTINCTIVE national costume has to a great extent become a thing of the past in Europe, and for this relinquishment of the picturesque we have doubtless in a measure to thank the exploitation of remote districts as tourist and sporting centres. Brittany, however, has been remarkably faithful to her sartorial traditions, and even to-day in the remoter parts of the west and in distant sea-coast places her men and women have not ceased to express outwardly the strong national and personal individuality of their race. In these districts it is still possible for the traveller to take a sudden, bewildering, and wholly entrancing step back into the past.

In Cornouaille the national costume is more jealously cherished than in any other part of the country, even to the smallest details, for here the men carry a *pen-bas*, or cudgel, which is as much a supplement to their attire and as characteristic of it as the Irish shillelagh is of the traditional Irish dress. Quimper is perhaps second to Cornouaille in fidelity to the old costume, for all the men wear the national habit. On gala days this consists of gaily embroidered and coloured waistcoats, which often bear the travelling tailor's name, and voluminous *bragou-bras*, or breeches of blue or brown, held at the waist with a broad leather belt with a metal buckle and caught in at the knee with ribbons of various hues, the whole set off with black leather leggings and shoes ornamented with silver buckles. A broad-brimmed hat, beneath which the hair falls down sometimes to below the shoulders, finishes a toilet which on weekdays or work-days has to give place to white *bragou-bras* of tough material, something more sombre in waistcoats, and the ever serviceable sabot.

Hats and Hymen

In the vast stretch of the salt-pans of Escoublac, between Batz and Le Croisic, where the entire population of the district is employed, the workers, or *paludiers*, affect a smock-frock with pockets, linen breeches, gaiters, and shoes all of white, and with this dazzling costume they wear a huge, flapping black hat turned up on one side to form a horn-shaped peak. This peak is very important, as it indicates the state of the wearer, the young bachelor adjusting it with great nicety over the ear, the widower above his forehead, and the married man at the back of his head. On Sundays or gala-days, however, this uniform is discarded in favour of a multicoloured and more distinctive attire, the breeches being of fine cloth, exceedingly full and pleated and finished with ribbons at the knees, the gaiters and white shoes of everyday giving place to white woollen stockings with clocks embroidered on them and shoes of light yellow, while the smock is supplanted by several waistcoats of varying lengths and shades, which are worn one above the other in different coloured tiers, finished at the neck with a turnover muslin collar. The holiday hat is the same, save for a roll of brightly and many tinted chenille.

Several petticoats of pleated cloth, big bibs or plastrons called *pièces*, of the same shade as their dresses, and a shawl with a fringed border, compose the costume of the women. The aprons of the girls are very plain and devoid of pockets, but the older women's are rich in texture and design, some of them being of silk and others even of costly brocade. The women's head-dress is almost grotesque in its originality, the hair being woven into two rolls, swathed round with tape, and wound into a coronet across the head. Over this is drawn tightly a kind of cap, which forms a peak behind and is crossed in front like a handkerchief. Should widowhood overtake a woman she relinquishes this *coiffe* and shrouds her head and shoulders in a rough black triangular-shaped sheepskin mantle.

The toilette of a bride is as magnificent as the widow's is depressing and dowdy. It consists of three different dresses, the first of white velvet with apron of moire-antique, the second of purple velvet, and the third of cloth of gold with embroidered sleeves, with a *pièce* of the same material. A wide sash, embroidered with gold, is used for looping up all these resplendent skirts in order to reveal the gold clocks which adorn the stockings. These, and all gala costumes, are carefully stored away at the village inn, and may be seen by the traveller sufficiently interested to pay a small fee for the privilege.

Quaint Head-dresses

Though the dress of the Granville women does not attempt to equal or rival the magnificence just described, nevertheless it is as quaint and characteristic. They favour a long black or very dark coat, with bordering frills of the same material and shade, and their cap is a sort of *bandeau*, turning up sharply at the ears, and crested by a white handkerchief folded square and laid flat on top.

In Ouessant the peasant women adopt an Italian style of costume, their head-dress, from under which their hair falls loosely, being exactly in almost every detail like that which one associates with the women of Italy. The costume of the man from St Pol is, like that of the Granville women, soberer than most others of Brittany. Save for his buttons, the buckle on his hat, and the clasps of white metal fastening his leather shoes, his dress, including spencer, waistcoat, trousers, and stockings, is of black, and his hair is worn falling on his shoulders, while he rarely carries the *pen-bas*—an indication, perhaps, of his rather meditative, pious temperament.

At Villecheret the cap of the women is bewilderingly varied and very peculiar. At first sight it appears to consist of several large sheets of stiff white paper, in some cases a sheet of the apparent paper spreading out at either side of the head and having another roll placed across it; in other cases a ridged roof seems to rest upon the hair, a roof with the sides rolling upward and fastened at the top with a frail thread; while a third type of head-dress is of the skull-cap order, from which is suspended two ties quite twenty inches long and eight inches wide, which are doubled back midway and fastened again to the top of the skull-cap. The unmarried woman who adopts this *coiffe* must wear the ties hanging over the shoulders.

Originality in head-dress the male peasant leaves almost entirely to the woman, for nearly everywhere in Brittany one meets with the long, wide-brimmed, black hat, with a black band, the dullness of which is relieved by a white or blue metal buckle, as large as those usually found on belts. To this rule the Plougastel man is one of the exceptions, wearing a red cap with his trousers and coat of white flannel.

At Muzillac, some miles distant from La Roche-Bernard, the women supplant the white *coiffe* with a huge black cap resembling the cowl of a friar, while at Pont l'Abbé and along the Bay of Audierne the cap or *bigouden* is formed of two pieces, the first a species of skull-cap fitting closely over the head and ears, the second a small circular piece of starched linen, shaped into a three-cornered peak, the centre point being embroidered and kept in position by a white tape tie which fastens under the chin. Over the skull-cap the hair is dressed *en chignon.* The dress accompanying this singular *coiffe* and *coiffure* has a large yellow *pièce*, with sleeves to match. The men wear a number of short coats, one above the other, the shortest and last being trimmed with a fringe, and occasionally ornamented with sentences embroidered in coloured wools round the border, describing the patriotic or personal sentiments of the wearer. The women of Morlaix are also partial to the tight-fitting *coiffe.* This consists of five broad folds, forming a base from which a fan-like fall of stiffened calico spreads out from ear to ear, completely shading the nape of the neck and reaching down the back below the shoulders. Many of the women wear calico tippets, while the more elderly affect a sort of mob-cap with turned-up edges, from which to the middle of the head are stretched two wide straps of calico, joined together at the ends with a pin. Most of the youths of Morlaix wear the big, flapping hat, but very often a black cloth cap is also seen. This is ridiculous rather than picturesque, for so long is it that with almost every movement it tips over the wearer's nose. The tunic accompanying either hat or cap is of blue flannel, and over it is worn a black waistcoat. The porters of the market-places wear a sort of smock. The young boys of Morlaix dress very like their elders, and nearly all of them wear the long loose cap, with the difference that a tasselled end dangles down the back.

On religious festivals the gala dress is always donned in all vicinities of Brittany, and the costume informs the initiated at once in what capacity the Breton is present. For instance, the *porteuses*, or banner-bearers, of certain saints are dressed in white; others may be more gorgeously or vividly attired in gowns of bright-coloured silk trimmed with gold lace, scarves of silver thread, aprons of gold tissue or brocade, and lace *coiffes* over caps of gold or silver tissue; while some, though in national gala dress, will have flags or crosses to distinguish them from the more commonplace worshipper.

Religious Festivals

This dressing for the part and the occasion is interwoven with the Breton's existence as unalterably as sacred and profane elements are into the occasions of his religious festivals. A feast day well and piously begun is interspersed and concluded with a gaiety and abandon which by contrast strikes a note of profanity. Yet Brittany is quite the most devotedly religious of all the French provinces, and one may see the great cathedrals filled to their uttermost with congregations including as many men as women. Nowhere else, perhaps, will one find such great masses of people so completely lost in religious fervour during the usual Church services and the grander and more impressive festivals so solemnly observed. This reverence is attributed by some to the power of superstition, by others to the Celtic temperament of the worshippers; but from whatever cause it arises no one who has lived among the Bretons can doubt the sincerity and childlike faith which lies at the base of it all, a faith of which a medieval simplicity and credence are the keynotes.

The Pardons

This pious punctiliousness is not confined to Church services and ceremonies alone, for rarely are wayside crosses or shrines unattended by some simple peasant or peasants telling beads or unfolding griefs to a God Who, they have been taught, takes the deepest interest in and compassionates all the troubles and trials which may befall them. Between May and October the religious ardour of the Breton may be witnessed at its strongest, for during these months the five great 'Pardons' or religious pilgrimage festivals are solemnized in the following sequence: the Pardon of the Poor, at Saint-Yves; the Pardon of the Singers, at Rumengol; the Pardon of the Fire, at Saint-Jean-du-Doigt; the Pardon of the Mountain, at Troménie-de-Saint-Renan; the Pardon of the Sea, at Sainte-Anne-la-Palud.

The Pardon of the Poor, the Pardon of the Singers, and the Pardon of the Sea are especially rigorous and exacting, but the less celebrated Pardon of Notre Dame de la Clarté, in Morbihan, has an earthly as much as a celestial object, for while the pilgrimage does homage to the Virgin it is at the same time believed to facilitate marriage. Here, once the sacred side of the festival has been duly observed, the young man in search of a wife circles about the church, closely scrutinizing all the eligible demoiselles who come within range of his vision. As soon as he decides which maiden most appeals to him, he asks her politely if she will accept a gift from him, and at the same time presents a large round cake, with which he has armed himself for that occasion. "Will mademoiselle break the cake with me?" is the customary form of address, and in the adoption or rejection of this suggestion lies the young peasant's yea or nay.

The Pardon of Saint-Jean-du-Doigt takes place on the 22nd of June, and is, perhaps, the most solemn of these festivals. During its celebration the relic of the Saint, the little finger of his right hand, is held before the high altar of the church by an *abbé* clad in his surplice. The finger is wrapped in the finest of linen, and one by one the congregation files past the *abbé* for the purpose of touching for one brief moment the relic he holds. At the same time another cleric stands near the choir, holding the skull of St Mériadec, and before this the pilgrims also promenade, reverently bowing their heads as they go. The devotees then repair to a side wall near which there is a fountain, the waters of which have been previously sanctified by bathing in them the finger of St Jean suspended from a gold chain, and into this the pilgrims plunge their palms and vigorously rub their eyes with them, as a protection against blindness. This concludes the religious side of the Pardon, and immediately after its less edifying ceremonies begin.

The Pardon of the Mountain is held on Trinity Sunday at Troménie. Every sixth year there is the 'Grand Troménie,' an event which draws an immense concourse of people from all parts. The principal feature of this great day from the spectator's point of view is the afternoon procession. It is of the most imposing description, and all who have come to take part in the Pardon join it, as with banners flying and much hymn-singing it takes its way out of the town to wind round a mountain in the vicinity.

Barking Women

In the old days of religious enthusiasm a remarkable phenomenon often attended these festivals, when excitement began to run high, as it was certain to do among a Celtic people. This was the barking of certain highly strung hysterical women. In time it became quite a usual feature, but now, happily, it is a part of the ceremony which has almost entirely disappeared. There is a legend in connexion with this custom that the Virgin appeared before some women disguised as a beggar, and asked for a draught of water, and, when they refused it, caused them and their posterity to be afflicted with the mania.

The Sacring Bell

Another custom of earlier times was that of ringing the sacring bell. These bells are very tiny, and are attached at regular intervals to the outer rim of a wooden wheel, wrongly styled by some 'the Wheel of Fortune,' from which dangles a long string. In most places the sacring bell is kept as a curiosity, though in the church of St Bridget at Berhet the *Sant-e-roa*, or Holy Wheel, is still rung by pilgrims during Mass. The bells are set pealing through the medium of a long string by the impatient suppliant, to remind the saint to whom the *Sant-e-roa* may be dedicated of the prayerful requests with which he or she has been assailed.

There are in many of the churches of Brittany wide, old-fashioned fireplaces, a fact which testifies to a very sensible practice which prevailed in the latter half of the sixteenth century—that of warming the baptismal water before applying it to the defenceless head of the lately born. The most famous of these old fireplaces belong to the churches of St Bridget in Perguet, Le Moustoir-le-Juch, St Non at Penmarch, and Brévélenz. In the church at the latter place one of the pinnacles of the porch forms the chimney to its historic hearth.

The Venus of Quinipily

Childless people often pay a visit to some standing stone in their neighbourhood in the hope that they may thereby be blessed with offspring. Famous in this respect is the 'Venus,' or *Groabgoard*, of Quinipily, a rough-hewn stone in the likeness of a goddess. The letters . . . LIT . . . still remain on it—part of a Latin inscription which has been thought to have originally read ILITHYIA, "a name in keeping with the rites still in use before the image," says MacCulloch.[1]

Holy Wells

The holy well is another institution dating from early days, and there is hardly a church in Brittany which does not boast one or more of these shrines, which are in most cases dedicated to the saint in whose honour the church has been raised. So numerous are these wells that to name them and dwell at any length on the curative powers claimed for their waters would fill a large volume. Worthy of mention, however, is the Holy Well of St Bieuzy, as typical of most of such sacred springs. It is close to the church of the same name in Bieuzy, and flows from a granite wall. Its waters are said to relieve and cure the mentally

[1] *Religion of the Ancient Celts*, p. 289.

deranged. Some of the wells are large enough to permit the afflicted to bathe in their waters, and of these the well near the church of Goezenou is a good example. It is situated in an enclosure surrounded by stone seats for the convenience of the devotees who may desire to immerse themselves bodily in it. Several of these shrines bear dates, but whether they are genuine is a matter for conjecture.

Reliquaries

Every Breton churchyard worthy of the name has its reliquary or bone-house. There may be seen rows of small boxes like dog-kennels with heart-shaped openings. Round these openings, names, dates, and pious ejaculations are written. Looking through the aperture, a glimpse of a skull may startle one, for it is a gruesome custom of the country to dig up the bones of the dead and preserve the skulls in this way. The name upon the box is that once borne by the deceased, the date that of his death, and the charitable prayer is for the repose of his soul. Occasionally these boxes are set in conspicuous places in the church, but generally they remain in the reliquary. In the porch of the church of St Trémeur, the son of the notorious Breton Bluebeard, Comorre, there is one of the largest collections of these receptacles in Brittany. Rich people who may have endowed or founded sacred edifices are buried in an arched recess of the abbey or church they have benefited.

Feeding the Dead

In some parts of Brittany hollows are found in tombstones above graves, and these are annually filled with holy water or libations of milk. It would seem as if this custom linked prehistoric with modern practice and that the cup-hollows frequently met with on the top of dolmens may have been intended as receptacles for the food of the dead. The basins scooped in the soil of a barrow may have served the same purpose. On the night of All Souls' Day, when this libation is made, the supper is left spread on the table of each cottage and the fire burns brightly, so that the dead may return to refresh and warm themselves after the dolours of the grave.

The Passage de l'Enfer

How hard custom dies in Brittany is illustrated by the fact that it is still usual at Tréguier to convey the dead to the churchyard in a boat over a part of the river called the 'Passage de l'Enfer,' instead of taking the shorter way by land. This custom is reminiscent of what Procopius, a historian of the sixth century, says regarding Breton Celtic custom in his *De Bello Gothico.* Speaking of the island of Brittia, by which he means Britain, he states that it is divided by a wall. Thither fishermen from the Breton coast are compelled to ferry over at darkest night the shades of the dead, unseen by them, but marshalled by a mysterious leader. The fishermen who are to row the dead across to the British coast must go to bed early, for at midnight they are aroused by a tapping at the door, and they are called in a low voice. They rise and go down to the shore, attracted by some force which they cannot explain. Here they find their boats, apparently empty, yet the water rises to the bulwarks, as if they were crowded. Once they commence the voyage their vessels cleave the water speedily, making the passage, usually a day and a half's sailing, in an hour. When the British shore is reached the souls of the dead leave the boats, which at once rise in the sea as if unloaded. Then a loud voice on shore is heard calling out the name and style of those who have disembarked.

Procopius had, of course, heard the old Celtic myth of an oversea Elysium, and had added to it some distorted reminiscence of the old Roman wall which divided Britain. The 'ship of souls' is evidently a feature of Celtic as well as of Latin and Greek belief.

Calvaries

Calvaries, or representations of the passion on the Cross, are most frequently encountered in Brittany, so much so, indeed, that it has been called 'the Land of the Calvaries.' Over the length and breadth of the country they are to be met at almost every turn, some of them no more than rude, simple crosses originating in local workshops, and others truly magnificent in carving and detail. Some of the most famous are those situated at Plougastel, Saint-Thégonnec, and Guimiliau. The Calvary of Plougastel dates from the early sixteenth century, and consists of an arcade beneath a platform filled with statues. The surrounding frieze has carvings in bas-relief representing incidents in the life of Christ. The Calvary of Saint-Thégonnec represents vividly the phases of the passion, being really a 'way of the Cross' in sculpture. It bears the unmistakable stamp of the sixteenth century. The Calvary of Guimiliau is dated 1580 and 1588. A platform supported by arches bears the three crosses, the four evangelists, and other figures connected with the principal incidents in the life and passion of our Lord. The principal

THE SOULS OF THE DEAD

figures, that of Christ and those of the attending Blessed Virgin and St John, are most beautifully and sympathetically portrayed. The figures in the representations from the life of Christ, which are from necessity much smaller than those of the Crucifixion, are dressed in the costume of the sixteenth century. The entire Calvary is sculptured in Kersanton stone.

Whether these and other similar groups are really works of art is perhaps a matter for discussion, but regarding their impressiveness there cannot be two opinions. By the bulk of the people they are held in great reverence, and rarely are they unattended by tiny congregations of two or three, while on the occasion of important religious festivals people flock to them in hundreds.

Weddings

In many of their religious observances the Bretons are prone to confuse the sacred with the profane, and chief among these is the wedding ceremony—the customs attendant on which in some ostensibly Christian countries are yet a disgrace to the intellect as well as the good feeling of man. In rural Brittany, however, the revelry which ensues as soon as the church door closes on the newly wedded pair is more like that associated with a children's party than the recreation of older people. Should the marriage be celebrated in the morning, tables laid out with cakes are ranged outside the church door, and when the bridal procession files out of the church the bride and bridegroom each take a cake from the table and leave a coin in its stead for the poor. The guests follow suit, and then the whole party repairs to the nearest meadow, where endless *ronds* are begun.

The *rond* is a sort of dance in which the whole assembly joins hands and revolves slowly with a hop-skip-and-a-jump step to the accompaniment of a most wearisome and unvarying chant, the music for which is provided by the *biniou*, or bagpipe, and the flageolet or hautboy, both being occasionally augmented by the drum. Before the ceremony begins the musicians who are responsible for this primitive harmony are dispatched to summon the guests, who, of course, arrive in the full splendour of the national gala costume. As soon as the *ronds* are completed to the satisfaction of everybody the custom common to so many countries of stealing the bride away is celebrated. At a given signal she speeds away from the party, hotly pursued by the young gallants present, and when she is overtaken she presents the successful swain with a cup of coffee at a public *café*. This interlude is followed by dinner, and after that the *ronds* are resumed. These festivities, in the case of prosperous people, sometimes last three days, during which time the guests are entertained at their host's expense. If the wedding happens to be held in the evening, dancing is about the only amusement indulged in, and this follows an elaborate wedding supper. The *biniou* and its companions are decidedly *en évidence*, while sometimes the monotony of the *ronds* is varied by the *grand rond*, a much more graceful and intricate affair, containing many elaborate and difficult steps; but the more ordinary dance is the favourite, probably because of the difficulties attending the other.

Breton Burials

An ancient Breton funeral ceremony was replete with symbolic meaning and ritual, which have been carried down through the Middle Ages to the present time. As soon as the head of the family had ceased to breathe, a great fire was lit in the courtyard, and the mattress upon which he had expired was burned. Pitchers of water and milk were emptied, for fear, perhaps, that the soul of the defunct might be athirst. The dead man was then enveloped from head to foot in a great white sheet and placed in a description of funeral pavilion, the hands joined on the breast, the body turned toward the east. At his feet a little stool was placed, and two yellow candles were lit on each side of him. Then the beadle or gravedigger, who was usually a poor man, went round the country-side to carry the news of death, which he usually called out in a high, piping voice, ringing his little bell the while. At the hour of sunset people arrived from all parts for the purpose of viewing the body. Each one carried a branch, which he placed on the feet of the defunct. The evening prayer was recited by all, then the women sang the canticles. From time to time the widow and children of the deceased raised the corner of the shroud and kissed it solemnly. A repast was served in an adjoining room, where the beggar sat side by side with the wealthy, on the principle that all were equal before death. It is strange that the poor are always associated with the griefs as with the pleasures of Breton people; we find them at the feast of death and at the baptism as at the wedding rejoicing.

In the morning the rector of the parish arrived and all retired, with the exception of the parents, if these chanced to be alive, in whose presence the beadle closed the coffin. No other member of the family was permitted to take part in this solemn farewell, which was regarded as a sacred duty. The coffin was then placed on a car drawn by oxen, and the funeral procession set out, preceded by the clergy and followed by the female relations of the deceased, wearing yellow head-dresses and black mantles. The men followed with bared heads. On arriving at the church the coffin was disposed on trestles, and the widow sat close by it throughout the ceremony. As it was lowered into the tomb the last words of the prayer for the dead were repeated by all, and as it touched the soil beneath a loud cry arose from the bereaved.

The Breton funeral ceremony, like those prevalent among other Celtic peoples, is indeed a lugubrious affair, and somewhat recalls the Irish wake in its strange mixture of mourning and feasting; but curiously enough brightness reigns afterward, for the peasant is absolutely assured that at the moment his friend is placed in the tomb he commences a life of joy without end.

Tartarus and Paradise

Two very striking old Breton ballads give us very vivid pictures of the Breton idea of Heaven and its opposite. That dealing with the infernal regions hails from the district of Léon. It is attributed to a priest named Morin, who flourished in the fifteenth century, but others have claimed it for a Jesuit father called Maunoir, who lived and preached some two hundred years later. In any case it bears the ecclesiastical stamp. "Descend, Christians," it begins, "to see what unspeakable tortures the souls of the condemned suffer through the justice of God, Who has chained them in the midst of flames for having abused their gifts in this world. Hell is a profound abyss, full of shadow, where not the least gleam of light ever comes. The gates have been closed and bolted by God, and He will never open them more. The key is lost!

"An oven heated to whiteness is this place, a fire which constantly devours the lost souls. There they will eternally burn, tormented by the intolerable heat. They gnash their teeth like mad dogs; they cannot escape the flames, which are over their heads, under their feet, and on all sides. The son rushes at his father, and the daughter at her mother. They drag them by the hair through the midst of flames, with a thousand maledictions, crying, 'Cursed be ye, lost woman, who brought us into the world! Cursed be ye, heedless man, who wert the cause of our damnation!'

"For drink they have only their tears. Their skins are scorched, and bitten by the teeth of serpents and demons, and their flesh and their bones are nothing but fuel to the great fire of Hell!

"After they have been for some time in this furnace, they are plunged by Satan into a lake of ice, and from this they are thrown once more into the flames, and from the flames into the water, like a bar of iron in a smithy. 'Have pity, my God, have pity on us!' they call; but they weep in vain, for God has closed His ears to their plaints.

"The heat is so intense that their marrow burns within their bones. The more they crave for pity, the more they are tormented.

"This fire is the anger of God which they have aroused; verily it may never be put out."

One turns with loathing, with anger, and with contempt

from this production of medieval ecclesiasticism. When one thinks of the thousands of simple and innocent people who must have been tortured and driven half wild with terror by such infamous utterances as this, one feels inclined to challenge the oft-repeated statement concerning the many virtues of the medieval Church. But Brittany is not the only place where this species of terrorism was in vogue, and that until comparatively recent times. The writer can recall such descriptions as this emanating from the pulpits of churches in Scottish villages only some thirty years ago, and the strange thing is that people of that generation were wont to look back with longing and admiration upon the old style of condemnatory sermon, and to criticize the efforts of the younger school of ministers as being wanting in force and lacking the spirit of menace so characteristic of their forerunners. There are no such sermons nowadays, they say. Let us thank God that to the credit of human intelligence and human pity there are not!

The opposite to this picture is provided by the ballad on Heaven. It is generally attributed to Michel de Kerodern, a Breton missionary of the seventeenth century, but others claim its authorship for St Hervé, to whom we have already alluded. In any case it is as replete with superstitions as its darker fellow. The soul, it says, passes the moon, sun, and stars on its Heavenward way, and from that height turns its eyes on its native land of Brittany. "Adieu to thee, my country! Adieu to thee, world of suffering and dolorous burdens! Farewell, poverty, affliction, trouble, and sin! Like a lost vessel the body lies below, but wherever I turn my eyes my heart is filled with a thousand felicities.

I behold the gates of Paradise open at my approach and the saints coming out to receive me. I am received in the Palace of the Trinity, in the midst of honours and heavenly harmonies. The Lord places on my head a beautiful crown and bids me enter into the treasures of Heaven. Legions of archangels chant the praise of God, each with a harp in his hand. I meet my father, my mother, my brothers, the men of my country. Choirs of little angels fly hither and thither over our heads like flocks of birds. Oh, happiness without equal! When I think of such bliss to be, it consoles my heart for the pains of this life."

GLOSSARY & INDEX

A

ABÉLARD. A Breton monk; the story of Héloïse and, 248–253

ABERLADY BAY. A bay in the Firth of Forth, Scotland, 357

ABERNETHY. A town in Scotland; the Round Tower at, 52

ABERYSTWYTH. A town in Wales; Taliesin buried at, 22

ADDER'S STONE. A substance supposed to have magical properties, employed in Druidic rites, 247; Héloïse, represented as a sorceress, said to have possessed, 252

ALAIN III. Count of Brittany (Count of Vannes); drives back the Northmen, 25

ALAIN IV (BARBE-TORTE). Archchief of Brittany; defeats the Northmen, 25–26

ALAIN V. Duke of Brittany, 27, 28

ALAIN FERGANT. Duke of Brittany, 30

ALAIN. Son of Eudo of Brittany, 29

ALBERT LE GRAND. Monk of Morlaix, 278

ALCHEMY. The art of; the position of, in the fifteenth century, 175; Gilles de Retz experiments in, 175–179

ALGONQUINS. A race of North American Indians; mentioned, 302

ALI BABA. The story of; mentioned, 316

ALL SOULS' DAY. The custom of leaving food for the dead on, 383

ALOÏDA. A maiden; in the ballad of the Marriage-girdle, 234–236

'ALPINE' RACE. A European ethnological division; the Bretons probably belong to, 14, 37 *n.*

AMENOPHIS III. An Egyptian king; mentioned, 43

AMERICA. *See* United States.

ANGERS. A town in France; St Convoyon goes to, to obtain holy relics from the cathedral, 336

ANIMALS. Frequently the bearers of divine aid, in legends of the saints, 347; St Pol noted for his miraculous power over wild beasts, 366

ANIMISM, 86–87

ANKOU, THE. The death-spirit of Brittany, 101–102

ANNAÏK. A maiden; in a story of the Marquis of Guérande, 199–202

ANNE. Duchess of Brittany; married to Charles VIII of France, and then to Louis XII, 36; the oratory of, in the château of Dinan, 209; gives the château of Suscino to John of Châlons, 210

ANTWERP. The city; relics of St Winwaloe preserved in the Jesuit church of St Charles at, 371; mentioned, 205

APPLE, THE. Said to have been introduced into Brittany by Telio, 18

ARDMORE. A town in Ireland; the Round Tower at, 51–52

AREZ, MOUNTAINS OF. Same as Montagnes d'Arrée, *which see*

ARGOED. A place in Wales; battle of, 22

ARMAGH. A city in Ireland; Budoc made Bishop of, 356

ARMENIA. The country; werewolf superstition in, 291

ARMOR ('On the Sea'). The ancient Celtic name for Brittany, 13

ARMORICA. The Latin name for the country of Brittany, 13, 15; Julius Cæsar in, 16; two British kingdoms in, 19; the first monastery in, founded by Gwénnolé, 185; King Arthur hunts wild beasts in, 278; St Samson bidden to go to, 349

ARTHUR, KING. British chieftain, of legendary fame; his finding of Excalibur, 256–257; his encounter with the giant of Mont-Saint-Michel, 275–277; his existence doubted by Bretons in the twelfth century, 278; his fight with the dragon at the Lieue de Grève, 278–281; carried to the Isle of Avalon after his last battle, 282; Gugemar at the Court of, 292; his contest with Modred, 344; his sister Margawse the wife of King Lot of Lothian, 357; mentioned, 64, 66, 173, 212, 224

ARTHUR. Duke of Brittany, son of Geoffrey Plantagenet; murdered by King John of England, 30

ARTHURIAN ROMANCE. Resemblances in Villemarqué's *Barzaz-Breiz* to, 224; the controversy as to the original birthplace of, 228, 254–255; indigenous to British soil, 255

ARZ. *See* Ile d'Arz

ASH-TREE, THE LAY OF THE. One of the *Lais* of Marie de France, 317–320

AUCHENTORLIE. An estate in Scotland; inscribed stones at, 46

AUCHINLECK MS. A manuscript containing a version of the story of Tristrem and Ysonde, 272

AUDIERNE, BAY OF. A bay on the Breton coast; national costume in the district of, 376

AULNOY, COMTESSE D'. Noted seventeenth-century French authoress; mentioned, 144

AURAY. A town in Brittany; battle at, 35; centre from which to visit the megaliths of Carnac, 42

AVALON, ISLE OF. A fabled island to which King Arthur was carried after his last battle, 282

AVENUE OF SPHINXES. At Karnak, Egypt, 43

AZÉNOR. Mother of St Budoc of Dol, 354–356

AZÉNOR THE PALE. A maiden; the legend of, 360–364

B

BACCHUS. The Greek god of wine; mentioned, 189

BALON. Monastery of; St Tivisiau and, 338–339

BAN. King of Benwik; father of Sir Lancelot, 257

BANGOR TEIVI. A village in Wales; Taliesin said to have died at, 22

BARANTON, THE FOUNTAIN OF. A magical fountain in Broceliande, 70–71

BARD. Singer or poet attached to noble households; late survival of the custom of maintaining, 364

BARKING WOMEN. A phenomenon connected with religious festivals, 380

BARON OF JAUIOZ, THE. A ballad, 145–147

BARRON. A fictitious youth; in a story of Gilles de Retz, 178

BARZAZ-BREIZ ("The Breton Bards"). A collection of Breton ballads made by Villemarqué; cited (under sub-title, *Chants populaires de la Bretagne*), 57 *n.*; criticism of, 211–212

BASS ROCK. An islet in the Firth of Forth, 359

BATZ. I. An island off the coast of Brittany; St Pol settles on, 365–366. II. A town in Brittany, 373

BAYARD, THE CHEVALIER DE. A famous French knight; mentioned, 31

BEAN NIGHE ('The Washing Woman'). An evil spirit of the Scottish Highlands, 100

BEAUMANOIR. A Breton noble house, 229

BEAUTY AND THE BEAST. The story of; mentioned, 137

BEAUVAU. Matthew, Seigneur of; in the story of the Clerk of Rohan, 190–193

BEDIVERE, SIR. One of King Arthur's knights; accompanies Arthur on his expedition against the giant of Mont-Saint-Michel, 275–277

BEES. Cultivated by the monks of Dol, 19; St Pol taught the people to cultivate, 366

BEIGNON. A town in Brittany, 360

BELGIUM. Mentioned, 52

BELIAGOG. A giant; in the story of Tristrem and Ysonde, 271

BELSUNCE DE CASTELMORON, HENRI-FRANÇOIS-XAVIER DE. Bishop of Marseilles; mentioned, 195

BENEDICTION OF THE BEASTS. A festival held at Carnac, 45

BERHET. A village in Brittany; the custom of ringing the sacring bell still observed in the church of St Bridget at, 380

BERRY. John, Duke of; mentioned, 145
BERRY. Caroline, Duchess of; imprisoned in the castle of Nantes, 205
BERTRAND DE DINAN. A Breton knight, 29
BIEUZY. A town in Brittany; the Holy Well of St Bieuzy at, 381
BIGOUDEN. A cap worn by the women in some parts of Brittany, 376
BINIOU. A musical instrument resembling the bagpipe; one of the national instruments of Brittany, 229; played at weddings, 386
BIRDS. In Breton tradition, the dead supposed to return to earth in the form of, 227; frequently messengers in ballad literature, 233; in the legends of the saints, commonly the bearers of divine aid, 347
BISCLAVERET. The Breton name for a were-wolf; in the Lay of the Were-wolf, 287–289, 291
BLACK MOUNTAIN. The name of one of the peaks of the Black Mountains, 197
BLACK MOUNTAINS. A mountain chain in Brittany, 196
BLANCHE OF CASTILE. Mother of Louis IX, 208
BLANCHEFLOUR. Princess, sister of King Mark, mother of Tristrem; in the story of Tristrem and Ysonde, 258–259, 261
BLOIS. A famous French château; mentioned, 206
BLOIS, CHARLES OF. Duke of Brittany; contests the succession to the duchy, 30–32; taken prisoner by Joan of Flanders, 31; the marriage of, with Joan of Penthièvre, 32; defeated at Auray, 35; the château of Suscino taken by, 210
BLUEBEARD. The villain in the nursery-tale; Gilles de Retz identified with, 174, 180; the story of, identified with the story of Comorre and Triphyna, 180
BLUE CHAMBER. A boudoir in the château of Tourlaville, 209
BODMIN. A town in Cornwall; mentioned, 278
BOITEUX. A fiend; in the story of the Princess Starbright, 123, 124, 125
BONCOTEST, COLLEGE OF. One of the colleges of the old University of Paris; Fontenelle at, 229
BONNY KILMENY. A ballad by James Hogg; mentioned, 327
BOURDAIS, MARC. A peasant, nicknamed Maraud; in the story of the Lost Daughter, 75–77
BOUTEVILLE. John of, Seigneur of Faouet; mentioned, 335
BOY WHO SERVED THE FAIRIES, THE. The story of, 88–95
BRAN ('Crow'). A Breton warrior; the story of, 225–227; analogies between the story of, and the poem of *Sir Tristrem*, 227–228
BRENGWAIN. A lady of Ysonde's suite; in the story of Tristrem and Ysonde, 267, 269, 271, 272
BRENHA, FATHER JOSÉ. A Portuguese antiquary; mentioned, 47
BREOCHAN. A legendary Welsh king, father of St Nennocha, 340
BRÉRI. A Breton poet, 255
BREST. A town in Brittany, 354, 368, 371
BRETON. The language, 15–16
BRETONS. The race; their origin and affinities, 13–15, 17, 37 *n.*; Bretons join William of Normandy in his expedition against England, 29, 232, 233; send an expedition to help Owen Glendower, 234; defeat the English in a naval battle, 236
BREVELENZ. A village in Brittany; a fireplace in the church of, 381
BREZONEK. The language spoken by the Bretons, 15–16
BRIAN. Son of Eudo of Brittany, 29
BRIDE OF SATAN, THE. The story of, 143–144; mentioned, 147
BRITAIN. Celts flee from, to Brittany, before the Saxon invaders, 15, 17; subject kingdoms of, in Brittany, 19; immigrants from, in Brittany, form a confederacy and fight against the Franks, 22–23; the headquarters of the Druidic cult, 245; Arthurian romance indigenous to, 255; St Patern founds religious houses in, 348; St Samson fled from, to

Brittany, 350; Procopius' story of the ferrying of the Breton dead over to, 383–384

BRITONS. The race; members of, emigrate to Brittany, 15, 17, 22–23; carried Arthurian romance to Brittany, 254, 255

BRITTANY. Divisions and character of the country, 13; Julius Cæsar in, 16; the Latin tongue did not spread over, 17; the origin of the name, 17; Nomenoë wins the independence of, 23; invaded by Northmen, 25; the Northmen expelled from, 26; division of, into counties and seigneuries, 27; relations with Normandy, 27–30; French influences in, 30; the War of the Two Joans, 30–31, 35–36; annexed to France by Francis I, 36; the prehistoric stone monuments of, 37–53; the fairies of, 54–95; the sprites and demons of, 96–105; 'world-tales' in, 106–155; folk-tales of, 156–172; popular legends of, 173–202; the châteaux of, 202–210; hero-tales of, 211–240; sends help to Owen Glendower in his conflict with the English, 234; a British army in, 237; the black art in, 241–253; Arthurian romance in, 254–282; Arthur found Excalibur in, 256; Tristrem in, 270–271, 272; the scene of the *Lais* of Marie de France, 284; the saints of, 332–371; many saints in, 350; costumes of, 372–377; customs of, 378–388; religious observance in, 377–378; holy wells in, 381–382; observances relating to the dead and interments, 382–384, 386–388; Calvaries in, 384–385; wedding ceremonies in, 385–386

BRITTANY, COUNTS AND DUKES OF. *See under* Alain; Arthur; Blois, Charles of; Conan; Dreux; Eudo; Francis; Geoffrey; Hoel; John; *and* Salomon

BRITTIA. Procopius' name for Britain, 383

BROCELIANDE. A forest in Brittany, 54–73; the shrine of Arthurian story, 55; the Korrigan a denizen of, 56; the scene of the adventures of Merlin and Vivien, 64; the fountain of Baranton in, 70–71; lines on, 71; in the story of Bruno of La Montagne, 72–73; the wood of Helléan a part of, 221; mentioned, 338

BRODINEUF. A Breton château, 207

BROWNIES. Elfish beings of small size; distinct from fairies, 87

BRUNHILDA. Queen of Austrasia; mentioned, 31

BRUNO OF LA MONTAGNE. The story of, 72–73

BRUYANT. A friend of Butor of La Montagne; in the story of Bruno of La Montagne, 72–73

BUGELNOZ, or TEUS. A beneficent spirit of the Vannes district, 100

BURIAL CUSTOMS. In Brittany, 382–384, 386–388

BURNS, ROBERT. The poet; his use of old songs and ballads, 211; mentioned, 241

BURON. A knight; in the Lay of the Ash-tree, 318–320

BUTOR. Baron of La Montagne; in the story of Bruno of La Montagne, 72

C

CADOUDAL, GEORGES. A Chouan leader; mentioned, 25

CAERLEON-UPON-USK. A town in Wales; Tristrem sails for, 263; mentioned, 21

CÆSAR. *See* Julius

CALENDAR, THE. Supernatural beings often associated with, 97

CALIBURN. A name for Excalibur. *See* Excalibur

CALLERNISH. A district in the island of Lewis, Outer Hebrides; mentioned, 53

CALVARIES. Representations of the passion on the Cross; common in Brittany, 384–385

CAMARET. A town in Brittany; megaliths at, 41

CAMELOT. A legendary town in England, the scene of King Arthur's Court; the battle at, in which King Arthur was killed, 344; mentioned, 64

CANADOS. King Mark's Constable, in the story of Tristrem and Ysonde, 272
CANCOET. A village in Brittany; the Maison des Follets at, 49
CARADEUC. A Breton château, 207
CARDIGAN BAY. A bay in Wales; the site of a submerged city, according to Welsh legend, 187, 188
CARDIGANSHIRE. Welsh county; mentioned, 22
CARHAIX. A town in Brittany; Comorre the ruler of, 180
CARNAC. A town in Brittany; the megaliths at, 42–45; the legend of, 44–45; the 'Benediction of the Beasts' at, 45; sometimes called 'Ty C'harriquet,' 98; its megaliths supposed to have been built by the gorics, 98; the gorics' revels around the megaliths of, 99
CAROLINE. Queen of England, wife of George II; mentioned, 196
CASTLE OF THE SUN, THE. The story of, 131–137
CATTWG. A town in Wales; Taliesin and Gildas said to have been educated at the school of, 21
CAYOT DÉLANDRE, F. M. A Breton poet, 43
'CELTIC.' The term; its disputed connotation, 37
CELTS. The race; the Bretons a division of, 14–15; Druidism may not have originated with, 245; musical and poetic elements in the temperament of, 339
CHAMBER OF THE BLACK CAVALIER. In the ballad of Azénor the Pale, 362
CHAMBORD. A famous French château; mentioned, 206
CHAMP DOLENT ('Field of Woe'). The field in which the menhir of Dol stands, 40; the battle in, 40
CHAMPTOCÉ. A Breton château; the home of Gilles de Retz, 175, 176, 179–180
CHANGELINGS. The Breton fairies and, 83
CHANSONS DE GESTES. Medieval French poems with an heroic theme; Villemarqué's work marked by the style of, 224–225
CHANTS POPULAIRES DE LA BRETAGNE. The sub-title of Villemarqué's *Barzaz-Breiz*. See *Barzaz-Breiz*
CHAPELLE DU DUC. A chapel at Tréguier, built by Duke John V, 353
CHARLEMAGNE. The Emperor; mentioned, 225
CHARLES I (THE BALD). King of France; Nomenoë rises against, 23, 337–338
CHARLES V. King of France; mentioned, 32
CHARLES VI. King of France; mentioned, 174
CHARLES VIII. King of France; Anne of Brittany married to, 36
CHARLES. A youth; in the story of the Princess of Tronkolaine, 115–121
CHASE, THE. Superstitions of, 301
CHÂTEAU DES PAULPIQUETS. A name given to a megalithic structure in Questembert, 49
CHÂTEAUX. Of Brittany; their rich legendary and historical associations, 202–203; stories of, 203–210
CHÂTEAUBRIAND. François-René-Auguste, Viscount of; famous French writer and statesman; associated with the château of Comburg, 207
CHÂTEAUBRIANT. A Breton château, 207
CHÂTEAUBRIANT. Françoise de Foix, Countess of; a story of her relations with King Francis I and her fate, 207; the château of Suscino given to, by Francis I, 210
CHAVEAU-NARISHKINE, COUNTESS. Restored the château of Kerjolet, 208
CHILDEBAT. A Breton king, 366; and St Pol, 367
CHRAMNE. Son of Clotaire I, King of the Franks, 40
CHRISTIANITY. St Samson teaches, in Brittany, 17–19; the Curiosolites refuse to receive the teachings of St Malo, 342
CHURCH. The early; hostility of, to the fairies, 56
CINDERELLA. The story of; mentioned, 144

Glossary & Index

CISALPINE GAUL. Roman province; had no Druidic priesthood, 245
CLAIRSCHACH. The Highland harp; replaced as the national instrument by the bagpipe, 229
CLAUDE. Queen of Francis I of France, 36
CLÉDER. A town in Brittany; St Keenan built a monastery at, 344
CLERK OF ROHAN, THE. The story of, 189–193
CLISSON. A Breton château, 204-205
CLISSON, OLIVER DE. A celebrated Breton soldier, Constable of France; fought in the War of the Two Joans, 35, 204; and the chateau of Clisson, 204; and the chateau of Josselin, 205, 206
CLOTAIRE I. King of the Franks, 40
COADELAN. The manor of; occupied by Fontenelle, 230, 231; has gone to decay, 232
COADELAN, THE LADY OF. Her daughter carried off by Fontenelle, 229–230
COAT-SQUIRIOU, MARQUIS OF. In the story of the Youth who did not Know, 106–109
COCKNO. A place in Scotland; inscribed stones at, 47
COESORON. A river in Brittany, 17
COÊTMAN. The house of, 204
COÊTMAN, VISCOUNT OF. A Breton nobleman; mentioned, 204–205
COËTQUEN, TOWER OF. One of the towers in the city wall of Dinan, 209
COIFFES. Of Brittany; specimens of, in the museum at Kerjolet, 208. *See* Head-dress
COLE, KING. A half-legendary British king; mentioned, 173
COLODOC. A name given to St Keenan. *See* St Keenan
COMBAT OF SAINT-CAST, THE. The ballad of, 236–238
COMBOURG. A Breton château, 207–208; Châteaubriand associated with, 208
COMORRE THE CURSED. The story of, 180–184; mentioned, 382
COMTE DE GABALIS, LE. The Abbé de Villars' work; mentioned, 64
CONAN I. Count of Brittany (Count of Rennes), 27
CONAN II. Duke of Brittany; and Duke William of Normandy, 27–29
CONAN III. Duke of Brittany, 30; patron of Abélard, 248
CONAN IV. Duke of Brittany, 30
CONAN. Father of Morvan, 215
CONCARNEAU. A town in Brittany; megaliths at, 42; the château of Kerjolet in, 208
CONCORET. A town in Brittany; had a reputation as the abode of sorcerers, 242
CONCURRUS. A village in Brittany; megaliths at, 42
CONNAUGHT. An Irish province; St Keenan a native of, 343
CONSTANCE. Daughter of Conan IV of Brittany; married to Geoffrey Plantagenet, 30
CONTES POPULAIRES DE LA HAUTE-BRETAGNE. P. Sébillot's work; cited, 83 *n.*
CORK. A county of Ireland; mentioned, 355
CORNOUAILLE. A district in Brittany; the ancient Cornubia, 19; formed by immigrants from Britain, 23; Azénor the Pale, a ballad of, 360–364; distinctive national costume in, 372; mentioned, 108
CORNUBIA. A British kingdom in Armorica, the modern Cornouaille, 19
CORNWALL. An English county, anciently a kingdom; in the story of Tristrem and Ysonde, 257–262; mentioned, 278
CORSEUL. A town in Brittany; the people of, refuse the teachings of St Malo, 342–343
CORSTORPHINE. A village near Edinburgh; the legend of the building of the church at, 51
COSTUME. Breton; specimens of, in the museum at Kerjolet, 208; the faithfulness of the Bretons to their national costume, 372; the varieties of, 372–377; the costume of Cornouaille, 372; of Quimper, 372–373; of the workers of the Escoublac district, 373–374; of the women of Granville, 374; of the women of Ouessant, 374; of the men of St Pol, 375; of Pont l'Abbé and the Bay of Audierne, 376; of

Morlaix, 376–377; gala dress in Brittany, 377
CÔTES-DU-NORD. One of the departments of Brittany, 13; part of the ancient kingdom of Domnonia, 19; mentioned, 41, 88, 167, 282, 351
COUDRE. A maiden; in the Lay of the Ash-tree, 319–320
COURILS. A race of gnomes peculiar to Brittany, 87, 98–99
COURONNES DE STE BARBE. Amulets sold at the festival of St Barbe at Le Faouet, 333
COX, REV. SIR G. W. Cited, 275 *n.*
CRAON. The house of, 174
CRIONS. A race of gnomes peculiar to the ruins of Tresmalouen, 99
CROMLECH. The term; its derivation and significance, 38
CROSS OF THE THOUSAND SAILS. A monument at Guic-sezne, 370
CRUSADES. Mentioned, 190
CULROSS. A town in Scotland; St Kentigern born at, 357
CUP-AND-RING ALTAR. A monument discovered in the Milton of Colquhoun district, Scotland, 47
CUP-AND-RING MARKINGS. Symbols inscribed on megaliths; their meaning and purpose, 46–48
CUPID AND PSYCHE. The story of; mentioned, 137
CURIOSOLITÆ. A Gallic tribe which inhabited Brittany, 16; the Curiosolites refuse to receive Christian teaching from St Malo, 342–343
CYMBELINE. A half-legendary British king; mentioned, 173

D

DAGWORTH, SIR THOMAS. An English knight; at the battle of La Roche-Derrien, 31
DAHUT. Princess, daughter of Gradlon; in the legend of Ys, 185, 186
DANAË. A maiden, in Greek mythology, mother of Perseus; mentioned, 358
DAOINE SIDHE. Irish deities, 87
DAOULAS. A village in Brittany; the statue of the Virgin in the abbey of, adorned with a girdle of rubies, 236
DEAD, THE. In Breton tradition, supposed to return to earth in the form of birds, 227; food left for, 382–383, 387; burial customs, 382–384, 386–388; the Breton dead ferried over to Britain, 383–384
DEATH-BIRD. A bird whose note is supposed to portend misfortune to the maiden who hears it, 145, 147
DEATH-SPIRIT. The Ankou, 101–102
DEER GOD. A deity of the North American Indians, 301
DÉLANDRE, CAYOT. *See* Cayot
DEMETER. Greek corn goddess; mentioned, 59
DEMON LOVER, THE. A Scottish ballad; mentioned, 144
DEMONS. Of Brittany, 96–105; the invariable accompaniment of an illiterate peasantry, 96
DENIS PYRAMUS. An Anglo-Norman chronicler; on the poems of Marie de France, 284
DESONELLE, PRINCESS. Heroine of *Sir Torrent of Portugal*; mentioned, 358
DEVIL, THE. The erection of the megalithic monuments ascribed to, 49; the Teus and, 100. *See also* Satan
DIANA. Roman moon-goddess; mentioned, 74
DIANCECHT. An Irish god; mentioned, 247
DINAN. I. A town in Brittany, 194, 195, 209. II. The château of, 209
DOL. A town in Brittany; the menhir near, 18, 39–40, 318; St Samson settled near, 18; the Northmen defeated by Alain Barbe-torte near, 26; the legend of the menhir of, 40; Buron lived at, 318; St Turiau, or Tivisiau, associated with, 338–339; the legend of the founding of, by St Samson, 350; the legend of St Budoc of, 353–358
DOL, BISHOP OF. And St Tivisiau, 338–339
DOL DES MARCHANDS. The name given to a dolmen near Dol, 48
DOLMENS. Derivation and meaning of the term, 38; purpose of the monuments, 38–39; the

dolmen-chapel at Plouaret, 41; the dolmen at Trégunc, 42; the dolmen at Rocenaud, 46; cup-and-ring markings upon, 46–48; the dolmen at Penhapp, 48; the dolmen near the wood of Rocher, 50; the dolmen at La Lande-Marie, 51; the dolmen of Essé, 53; haunted by nains, 96; cup-hollows on, may have been intended as receptacles for food for the dead, 383

DOLOROUS KNIGHT, THE LAY OF THE, or THE LAY OF THE FOUR SORROWS. One of the *Lais* of Marie de France, 328–331

DOMNONÉE. A county of Brittany, 23. *See also* Domnonia

DOMNONIA. A British kingdom in Armorica, 19, 27. *See also* Domnonée

DOTTIN, GEORGES. Cited, 37 *n.*

DOUARNENEZ, BAY OF. A bay on the Breton coast; the city of Ys said to have been situated there, 185

DRACHENFELS. A famous castle on the Rhine; mentioned, 203

DREUX, PIERRE DE. Duke of Brittany; defeats John of England at Nantes, 30

DREZ, JOB ANN. A sexton; in a story of the Yeun, 103–105

DRUIDISM. In early times, sorcery identified with, 245; the question whether Druidism was of Celtic or non-Celtic origin, 245; the nature of the practices of, 245–248; survival of Druidic spells and ritual, 246; an Eastern origin claimed for, 247; survivals of the Druidic priesthood, 247; a college of Druidic priestesses situated near Nantes, 253; mentioned, 53. *See also* Druids

DRUIDS. Origin of the cult, 245; the nature of their practices, 245–246; in the legend of Kentigern's birth, condemn Thenaw, 357. *See also* Druidism

DUBLIN. The city; Tristrem comes to, 263; Tristrem's second visit to, 265

DUBRIC. Archbishop who officiated at the marriage of King Arthur and Guinevere, 67

DU GUESCLIN, BERTRAND. A famous knight, Constable of France; helps Charles of Blois in the War of the Two Joans, 31–32; a notable figure in Breton legend, 32; buried at Saint-Denis, 32; the legend of the Ward of, 33–35; taken prisoner at the battle of Auray, 35

DUNGIVEN. A town in Ireland; Druidic ritual still observed at, 246

DUNPENDER. A mountain in East Lothian, now called Traprain Law; Thenaw cast from, 357

DUSII. Spirits inhabiting Gaul, 100

DYLAN. A British sea-god; mentioned, 69

DYONAS. A god of the Britons; Vivien sometimes represented as the daughter of, 69

E

EDINBURGH. The city; mentioned, 51, 60, 203

EDMUND. King of East Anglia; mentioned, 284

ELIDUC, THE LAY OF. One of the *Lais* of Marie de France, 305–313

ELLÉ. A river in Brittany, 19, 332

ÉLORN. A river in Brittany, 19

ELPHIN. Son of the Welsh chieftain Urien; taught by Taliesin, 21

ELVES. In Teutonic mythology, diminutive spirits; the fairy race of Celtic countries may have been confused with, 87

EMERALD COAST, THE. A district in the southern portion of Brittany, 13

ENGLAND. I. The country; loses its ancient British name, which becomes that of Brittany, 17; Bretons who accompanied William the Conqueror receive land in, 232; Bretons invade, from Wales, 234; claimed as the birthplace of Arthurian romance, 254; King Arthur moves against the Emperor Lucius' threatened invasion of, 275; the existence of King Arthur credited in, in the twelfth century, 278; Marie de France

lived in, 283. II. The State; supports John of Montfort's claim to Brittany, 31
ENORA. *See* St Enora
EQUITAN, THE LAY OF. One of the *Lais* of Marie de France, 313–317
ERDEVEN. A town in Brittany; megaliths at, 42
ERMONIE. A mythical kingdom, in the story of Tristrem and Ysonde; Roland Rise, Lord of, 258; Duke Morgan becomes Lord of, 259; Tristrem returns to, 261
ERNAULT, E. Cited, 16 *n*.
ERYRI, MOUNT. King Arthur slew the giant Ritho upon, 277
ESCOUBLAC. A town in Brittany, 373
ESSÉ. A village in Brittany; the dolmen of, 53
ESTAING, PIERRE D'. A French alchemist; mentioned, 175
ÉTANG DE LAVAL. A lake, supposed to cover the site of the submerged city of Ys, 185
ETHWIJE. Wife of Geoffrey I of Brittany, 196, 198
EUDO. Count of Brittany, son of Geoffrey I, 27, 29
EUFUERIEN. King of Cumbria, 357
EVEN THE GREAT. Breton leader; defeats the Norsemen at the battle of Kerlouan, 225, 227
EWEN. Son of Eufuerien, King of Cumbria, 357
EXCALIBUR. King Arthur's miraculous sword; given to Arthur in Brittany, 256–257; Arthur kills the giant of Mont-Saint-Michel with, 277; mentioned, 280
EXETER. The city; mentioned, 307

F

FABLES. Of Marie de France, 283
FAIRIES. Credited with the erection of the megalithic monuments, 49–52; magically imprisoned in dolmens, trees, and pillars, 52; the fairy lore of Brittany bears evidence of Celtic influence, 54; the fairies of Brittany hostile to man, 54, 55–56, 85; the Church the enemy of, 56; what derived from, in folk-lore, 73–74; the varying conceptions of, 73; the Bretons' ideas of, 74–75; the fairies of the *houles*, 75, 88; the fairies' distaste for being recognized, and stories illustrating this, 82; bestow magical sight, 82–83; and changelings, 83; prone to take animal, bird, and fish shapes, 83–84; probable reasons for the fairies' malevolence, 85–86; origin of the fairy idea, 85–87; may have originally been deities, 87; in Brittany, conceived as of average mortal height, 87; the *Margots la fée*, a variety of, 88; a story illustrating fairy malevolence, 88; the fairy-woman in the Lay of Graelent, 322–328
FAIRYLAND. Graelent enters, 326; identified with the Celtic Otherworld, 327; a place of death and remoteness, 328
FAIRY-WIFE. A folk-lore *motif*, 327
FALCON, THE. A ballad, 196–198
FARMER, CAPTAIN GEORGE. Commander of the *Quebec*; in a Breton ballad, 238
FAYS. *See* Fairies
FEBRUARY. The month; personified in the story of Princess Starbright, 128–129
FÉLIX. Bishop of Quimper, 337
FEUILLET, OCTAVE. A French novelist; mentioned, 206
FINETTE CENDRON ('Cinderella'). Mme d'Aulnoy's story of; mentioned, 144
FINISTÈRE. One of the departments of Brittany, 13; part of the ancient kingdom of Domnonia, 19; mentioned, 41, 49, 180
FIONS. A name sometimes given to the fairies in Brittany, occurring also in Scottish and Irish folk-lore, 74
FIRE-GODDESS. St Barbe probably represents the survival of a, 334
FIREPLACES in Breton churches, 380–381
FISHERMAN AND THE FAIRIES, THE. The story of, 80–83
FLAMEL, NICOLAS. A French alchemist; mentioned, 175
FLANDERS. The country; Gugemar in, 292; mentioned, 145

Glossary & Index

FOLK-TALES. Of Brittany, 156–172
FONTENELLE, GUY EDER DE. A Breton leader, associated with the Catholic League, 229–232
FÖRSTER, PROFESSOR WENDELIN. And the origin of Arthurian romance, 254
FORTH. A river in Scotland; mentioned, 357
FORTH, FIRTH OF. Mentioned, 356, 359
FOSTER-BROTHER, THE. The story of, 167–172
FOUCAULT, JEAN. A Breton peasant; a story of, 244
FOUGÈRES. A town in Brittany; had a reputation as the dwelling-place of sorcerers, 242
FOUQUET, NICOLAS. A French statesman; imprisoned in the castle of Nantes, 205
FOUR SORROWS, THE LAY OF THE, or THE LAY OF THE DOLOROUS KNIGHT. One of the *Lais* of Marie de France, 328–331
FRAGAN. Governor of Léon, father of St Winwaloe, 370
FRANCE. I. The country; manners and fashions of, spread in Brittany, 30; the were-wolf superstition prevalent in, 291. II. The State; intervenes in the conflict between Brittany and Normandy, 30; Brittany annexed by, under Francis I, 36
FRANCIS I. King of France; annexes Brittany to France, 36; and Françoise de Foix, the Countess of Châteaubriant, 207; gives the château of Suscino to Françoise de Foix, 210
FRANCIS I. Duke of Brittany, 36
FRANKS. The people; exercised a nominal suzerainty over Brittany, 23; Morvan fights with, 216–221; "Morvan will return to drive the Franks from the Breton land," 224
FRANKS, KING OF THE. In Villemarqué's *Barzaz-Breiz*; and Morvan's fight with the Moor, 218–220; Morvan fights with, 220–221; the character drawn in the style of the *chansons de gestes*, 224
FREDEGONDA. Queen of Neustria; mentioned, 31
FRÉMIET, EMMANUEL. A French sculptor; mentioned, 206
FRÊNE. A maiden; in the Lay of the Ash-tree, 318–320
FULBERT. A canon of Notre-Dame, Paris, uncle of Héloïse, 249; mutilated Abélard, 250
FUNERAL CUSTOMS AND CEREMONIES. In Brittany, 382–384, 386–388

G

GAIDOZ, H. Cited, 212 *n*.
GANHARDIN. Brother of Ysonde of the White Hand; in the story of Tristrem and Ysonde, 271–272, 273
GARB OF OLD GAUL, THE. A song; mentioned, 237
GARGANTUA. A mythical giant; the erection of the megalithic monuments ascribed to, 49
GARLON, THE CLERK OF. In a legend of the Marquis of Guérande, 199–202
GAVR'INIS ('Goat Island'). An island in the Gulf of Morbihan; the tumulus at, 48; nains' inscriptions on the megaliths of, 98
GAWAINE, SIR. One of King Arthur's knights; mentioned, 357
GEBER. An Arabian alchemist; mentioned, 175
GEOFFREY I. Duke of Brittany, 27; in the legend of the Falcon, 196
GEOFFREY II (PLANTAGENET). Duke of Brittany, 30
GEOFFREY OF MONMOUTH. An English chronicler; the presentation of Vivien in his work, 69; and the presentation of Merlin, 70; acknowledged a Breton source for his work, 255
GILDAS. A British chronicler; fellow-pupil with Taliesin at the school of Cattwg, 21; St Keenan associated with, 343; St Bieuzy a friend and disciple of, 345; the bell of, in the chapel at La Roche-sur-Blavet, 345; St Bieuzy dies in the presence of, 346; St Pol of Léon a fellow-student of, 364

GIRALDUS CAMBRENSIS. A Welsh chronicler; and the legend of the submerged city, 187
GIRDLE. Superstition of the, 302
GLAIN NEIDR. The sea-snake's egg or adder's stone, used in Druidic rites, 247; Héloïse, represented as a sorceress, said to have possessed, 252
GLASGOW. The city; mentioned, 357, 359
GOELC. A seigneury of Brittany; a Count of, the father of St Budoc of Dol, 354, 355
GOEZENOU. A village in Brittany; the cheeses petrified by St Goezenou preserved in the church of, 369; holy well at, 382
GOIDELIC DIALECT. A Celtic tongue, 15
GOLDEN BELL, CHÂTEAU OF THE. In the story of the Youth who did not Know, 111–114
GOLDEN BELL, PRINCESS. In the story of the Youth who did not Know, 110–115
GOLDEN HERB. A plant supposed in Druidical times to possess magical properties, 247–248
GOMME, SIR G. L. Cited, 173, 247 *n.*
GORICS. A race of gnomes peculiar to Brittany, 87, 98–99
GOULVEN. A village in Brittany; historical tablet in the church of, 225
GOUVERNAYL. Servitor to Tristrem; in the story of Tristrem and Ysonde, 263, 264
GRADLON MEUR. A ruler of Ys; in the legend of the city, 185–186; the statue of, at Quimper, 188–189; supposed to have introduced the vine into Brittany, 189
GRAELENT, THE LAY OF. One of the *Lais* of Marie de France, 320–328
GRAIL. Legend of the; a parallel incident in the Lay of Gugemar and, 301–302
GRALLO. King of Brittany; and St Ronan, 367
GRAND MONT. An eminence upon which St Gildas built his abbey, 249
GRAND TROMÉNIE. The special celebration of the Pardon of the Mountain held every sixth year, 379–380
GRANVILLE. A town in Brittany; women's costume in, 374
GRIFESCORNE. King of the Demons; in the story of the Youth who did not Know, 111, 114
GROABGOARD. An image at Quinipily, 381
GROTTES AUX FÉES. Name given to the megalithic monuments by the Bretons, 48, 49
GUÉMENÉ. A town in Brittany, 334
GUÉRANDE. A town in Brittany, 198
GUÉRANDE. Louis-François, Marquis of; the story of, 199–202
GUERECH. Count of Vannes; in the story of Comorre the Cursed, 180–181, 183, 184
GUGEMAR, THE LAY OF. One of the *Lais* of Marie de France, 292–302
GUIC-SEZNE. A town in Brittany, 370
GUILDELUEC. Wife of Eliduc, 306–313
GUILLARDUN. A princess; in the Lay of Eliduc, 307–313
GUILLEVIC, A. Cited, 16 *n.*
GUIMILIAU. A town in Brittany; the Calvary at, 384–385
GUINDY. A river in Brittany, 167, 220
GUINEVERE. King Arthur's Queen; mentioned, 67; comforted by St Keenan after Arthur's death, 344
GUINGAMP. A town in Brittany, 229
GWEN. Mother of St Winwaloe, 370
GWENALOE ('He that is white'). The Breton name for St Winwaloe, 370
GWENN-ESTRAD. A place in Wales; battle of, 22
GWENNOLAÏK. A maiden of Tréguier; in the story of the Foster-brother, 167–172
GWÉNNOLÉ. A holy man; in the legend of the city of Ys, 185, 186
GWEZKLEN. The Breton name for Du Guesclin, 32. *See* Du Guesclin
GWINDELUC. A monk, a disciple of St Convoyon, 335

GWYDDNO. Twelfth-century Welsh bard; relates the story of the submerged city, 188

H

HAINAULT. A Belgian province; mentioned, 328

HARP, THE. Not now popular in Brittany, but in ancient times one of the national instruments, 228–229

HATCHET OF BRITTANY, THE. An appellation of Morvan, 221

HAUTE-BÉCHEREL. A town in Brittany; pagan temple at, 342

HEAD-DRESS. Of the women of the Escoublac district, 374; of the women of Ouessant, 374; of the women of Villecheret, 375; of the men of Brittany, does not vary much, 375; headgear of the men of Plougastel, 375; of the women of Muzillac, 376; of the women of Pont l'Abbé and the Bay of Audierne, 376; of the women of Morlaix, 376. *See also* Coiffes

HEAVEN. An old Breton conception of, 388, 390–391

HELENA, LADY. Niece of Duke Hoel I of Brittany; carried off by the giant of Mont-Saint-Michel, 275, 276

HELL. In the story of the Bride of Satan, 144; an old Breton conception of, 388–389

HELLÉAN, WOOD OF. A former part of the forest of Broceliande, 221, 224

HELOÏSE. An abbess, beloved of Abélard; the story of Abélard and, 248–253; in a Breton ballad represented as a sorceress, 250–253

HÉNAN. Manor of, in Brittany, 364

HENDERSON, GEORGE. Cited, 52

HENNEBONT. A Breton château, 206

HENRY II. King of England, 30; identified as the king to whom Marie of France dedicated her *Lais*, 284

HENRY III. King of England; mentioned, 284

HENRY IV. King of France; and Fontenelle, 231–232; mentioned, 204

HENWG. A Welsh bard; said to be the father of Taliesin, 21

HERSART DE LA VILLEMARQUÉ, VICOMTE. Writer on Breton legendary lore; his poem on Nomenoë, 23; his ballad of Alain Barbe-torte, 25–27; and a story of the Clerk of Rohan, 190 *n.*; his *Barzaz-Breiz*, 211–212; stories from his *Barzaz-Breiz*, 212–237; indications of the source of his matter, 224–225; and the story of Fontenelle, 230; and the story of the Combat of Saint-Cast, 237; on the story of Azénor the Pale, 363, 364; cited, 57 *n.*, 65 *n.*, 184 *n.*, 247

HERVÉ. Son of Kyvarnion; the story of the wolf and, 22; mentioned, 390

HIGHLANDERS. Scottish; in the story of the Combat of Saint-Cast, 237

HIGHLANDS. Scottish; beliefs in, respecting stones, 52–53; the 'Washing Woman' of, 100

HILDWALL. A pious man of Angers; St Convoyon lodges with, 336

HODAIN. A dog; in the story of Tristrem and Ysonde, 267

HOEL I. Duke of Brittany, 275, 276, 278

HOEL V. Duke of Brittany, 30

HOLGER. A half-mythical Danish hero; mentioned, 212

HOLMES, T. RICE. Cited, 245 *n.*

HOLY LAND. *See* Palestine.

HOULES. Caverns; the Bretons suppose fairies to inhabit, 75

HUON DE MÉRY. A thirteenth-century writer; on the fountain of Baranton, 71

HURLERS, THE. A Cornish legend; mentioned, 44

I

IBERIANS. A non-Aryan race, supposed to have inhabited Britain; held by Rhys to be the originators of Druidism, 245

IDA. King of Bernicia; mentioned, 21, 22

ILE D'ARZ. An island off the coast of Brittany; megaliths in, 48

ILE-DE-FRANCE. A French province; Marie of France said to have been a native of, 283

ILE AUX MOINES. An island in the Gulf of Morbihan; megalithic monuments in, 48

ILE DE SEIN. An island off the Breton coast, 63; St Winwaloe settled on, 371

ILE-VERTE. An island off the Breton coast; St Winwaloe lived on, 370

ILLE-ET-VILAINE. One of the departments of Brittany, 13, 39, 50

INVERESK. A village in Scotland; mentioned, 359

IOUENN. A young man; in the story of the Man of Honour, 147–155

IRELAND. Markings on the megalithic monuments in, 46; the legend of the submerged city in, 187; the harp anciently the national instrument of, 229; Tristrem in, 264, 265–267; Petranus, father of St Patern, goes to, 347; St Patern meets his father in, 348; many saints in, 350; Azénor and Budoc in, 355–356; Budoc made King of, 356; late survival of the custom of keeping domestic bards in, 364

IRELAND, KING OF. In the story of Tristrem and Ysonde, 265, 266

IRELAND, QUEEN OF. In the story of Tristrem and Ysonde, 264–267

IRMINSUL. A Saxon idol; probable connexion between the menhir and the worship of, 18 *n.*

ISIDORE OF SEVILLE. A Spanish ecclesiastic and writer; mentioned, 100

J

JANUARY. The month; personified, in the story of the Princess Starbright, 128–129

JARGEAU. A town in France; the battle of, 174

JAUDY. A river in Brittany, 31, 167

JAUIOZ. A seigneury in Languedoc; the story of Louis, Baron of, 145–146

JEANNE DARC. The French heroine; mentioned, 174; the play or mystery of, 175

JOAN OF FLANDERS. Wife of John of Montfort; in the War of the Two Joans, 31

JOAN OF PENTHIÈVRE. *See* Penthièvre

JOB THE WITLESS. In the story of the Foster-brother, 169

JOHN (LACKLAND). King of England; mentioned, 30

JOHN III. Duke of Brittany, 30

JOHN IV. Duke of Brittany. *See* Montfort, John of

JOHN V. Duke of Brittany, son of the famous John of Montfort, 35–36; and Gilles de Retz, 179; built a magnificent tomb for St Yves, 353

JOHN. Duke of Châlons; the château of Suscino given to, 210

JOSSELIN. A Breton château, 205–206

JOYOUS GARDEN. A garden raised by enchantment by Merlin to please Vivien, 66; mentioned, 67, 69

JUD-HAEL. A Breton chieftain; the vision of, 20–21

JUDIK-HAEL. A Breton chieftain, son of Jud-Hael, 21

JULIUS CÆSAR. On the Druids of Gaul, 245

K

KADO THE STRIVER. A Breton peasant, leader of a revolt, 197–198

KARNAK. A village in Egypt; mentioned, 43

KARO. Son of a Breton chieftain; in a story of Nomenoë, 23–25

KAY, SIR. King Arthur's seneschal, 275

KENNEDY. A character in a Highland tale, 51

KERGARIOU, COMTE DE. And the story of Fontenelle, 230

KERGIVAS. A place in Brittany; the cheeses petrified by St Goezenou preserved in the manor of, 369

KERGOALER, COUÉDIC DE. Captain of the *Surveillante*; in a Breton ballad, 238

KERGONAN. A village in the Ile aux Moines; megaliths at, 48

Glossary & Index

KERIDWEN. A fertility goddess who dwelt in Lake Tegid, Wales; mentioned, 59

KER-IS. A name of the city of Ys, 185. *See* Ys

KERJOLET. A Breton château, 208

KERLAZ. A village in Brittany, 232

KERLESCANT. A village in Brittany; megaliths at, 42

KERLOUAN. A town in Brittany; battle at, between Norsemen and Bretons, 225; the oak on the battle-field at, 227

KERMARIO. A village in Brittany; megaliths at, 42

KERMARTIN. A village in Brittany; St Yves born at, 350

KERMORVAN. A place in Brittany; Yves the Seigneur of, in the ballad of Azénor the Pale, 360–363

KERODERN, MICHEL DE. A Breton missionary, 390

KEROUEZ. An old château; in the story of the Seigneur with the Horse's Head, 137

KERSANTON. A place in Brittany; stone from, forms the Calvary of Guimiliau, 385

KERVRAN. A village in Brittany; the warrior Bran taken prisoner at, 225

KING OF THE ANTS. In the story of the Princess of Tronkolaine, 118, 119, 120

KING OF THE BIRDS. In the story of the Youth who did not Know, 111, 113

KING OF THE FISHES. In a tale from Saint-Cast, 84–85; in the story of the Youth who did not Know, 110, 114

KING OF THE LIONS. In the story of the Princess of Tronkolaine, 118, 119, 120

KING OF THE SPARROW-HAWKS. In the story of the Princess of Tronkolaine, 118, 119

KIPLING, RUDYARD. Quoted, 86

KORRIGAN, THE. A forest fairy; a denizen of Broceliande, 56; in the story of the Seigneur of Nann, 57–58; associated with water, an element of fertility, 59; an enchantress, 60; in the story of the Unbroken Vow, 62–63; desired union with humanity, 64; mentioned, 69, 98

KYVARNION. A British bard, father of Hervé, 22

L

LADY OF LA GARAYE, THE. Poem by Mrs Norton; quoted, 194, 195, 196

LADY OF THE LAKE. In Arthurian legend, Vivien; foster-mother of Lancelot, 69, 257; of Breton origin, 256; gives Arthur the sword Excalibur, 256–257. *See also* Vivien

LA GARAYE. A Breton château, near Dinan; the story of the Lady of, 195

LAILOKEN. A character in early British legend; mentioned, 70

LAIS. Of Marie de France; their value in the study of Breton lore, 283; date and other circumstances of their composition, 283–284; stories from, 284–289, 292–331

LAKE OF ANGUISH, THE. A lake in Hell; in the story of the Bride of Satan, 144; in the story of the Baron of Jauioz, 146

LA LANDE MARIE. A place in Brittany; the dolmen at, 51

LANCELOT, SIR. One of the Knights of the Round Table, son of King Ban of Benwik; stolen and brought up by Vivien, 257; does not appear in Celtic legend, 257; mentioned, 64, 69

LANDÉVENNEC. A town in Brittany; a chapel of St Nicholas at, 345; a monastery built at, by St Winwaloe, 371

LANDIVISIAU. A town in Brittany, 338; fine carvings in the church of, 339–340

LANDEGU. A village in Cornwall; St Keenan at, 344

LANGOAD. A town in Brittany, 198

LANGUAGE. Brezonek, the tongue of the Bretons, 15; the old Breton tongue closely similar to Welsh, 15; the Latin tongue did not spread over Brittany, 17

LARGOET. A Breton château, 206

LA ROCHE-BERNARD. A town in Brittany, 376
LA ROCHE-SUR-BLAVET. A place in Brittany; a retreat of Gildas and St Bieuzy, 345
LA ROCHE-DERRIEN. A place in Brittany; battle at, 31
LA ROCHE-JAGU. A Breton château, 203–204
LA ROSE. A young man; in the story of the Magic Rose, 156–162
LATIN. The language; did not spread over Brittany, 17
LAUSTIC, THE LAY OF. One of the *Lais* of Marie de France, 302–305
LAVAL, GILLES DE. *See* Retz
LAVAL, JEAN DE. Governor of Brittany, 207; married to Françoise de Foix, Countess of Châteaubriant, 207
LAY OF THE WERE-WOLF, THE. One of the *Lais* of Marie de France, 284–289
LEAGUE, THE. A Catholic organization formed against the Huguenots, 205, 206; Fontenelle associated with, 229
LE BRAZ, ANATOLE. Cited, 102, 184 *n.*
LE CLERC, L. Cited, 16 *n.*
LE CROISIC. A town in Brittany, 373
LE FAOUET. A village in Brittany; the chapel of St Barbe near, 332–333, 334–335
LEGEND. The meaning of the term, 173
LE GOFF, P. Cited, 16 *n.*
LE GRAND, A. Cited, 184 *n.*
LÉGUER. A town in Brittany, 220
LÉGUER, LAKE OF. In the story of the Princess Starbright, 121, 131
LELIAN. Father of St Tivisiau, 338
LE MOUSTOIR-LE-JUCH. A village in Brittany; fireplace in the church of, 381
LEO IV. Pope; Nomenoë sends gifts to, 337; and St Convoyon, 337
LÉON. I. A county of Brittany, 23, 143, 212, 225, 226, 229, 356, 367, 388. II. The see of; given to St Pol, 367
LE ROUZIC, ZACHARIE. A Breton archæologist; mentioned, 45
LEWIS. An island in the Outer Hebrides; mentioned, 53
LEYDEN, JOHN. A Scottish poet and Orientalist; his treatment of legendary material, 211
LÉZAT. A town in Brittany; had a reputation as the abode of sorcerers, 242
LEZ-BREIZ, MORVAN. *See* Morvan
LIEUE DE GRÈVE. A place in Brittany; Arthur's fight with the dragon of, 278–281
LIVONIA. The country; were-wolf superstition in, 290
LLANVITHIN. A village in Wales; mentioned, 21
LOC-CHRIST. Monastery of, built under the persuasion of St Winwaloe, 370–371
LOCMARIA. A place in Brittany, 199
LOCMARIAQUER. A town in Brittany; megaliths at, 42
LOGRES. An ancient British kingdom; in the Lay of Eliduc, 306–311
LOGUIVY-PLOUGRAS. A town in Brittany, 137
LOHANEC. A village in Brittany; St Yves incumbent of, 351
LOHENGRIN. A knight, in German legend; mentioned, 137
LOIRE. The river; mentioned, 16, 174, 253
LOIRE-INFÉRIEURE. One of the departments of Brittany, 13
LONDON. The city; mentioned, 31, 99
LONG MEG. A Cumberland legend; mentioned, 44
LONGSWORD, WILLIAM. Earl of Salisbury; identified as the nobleman to whom Marie of France dedicated her *Fables*, 284
LORELEI. A water-spirit of the Rhine; mentioned, 64
LORGNEZ. A Frankish chieftain; Morvan fights with, and slays, 217–218
LOST DAUGHTER, THE. The story of, 75–80
LOT. King of Lothian, grandfather of St Kentigern, 357
LOTHIAN. A district in Scotland, formerly a kingdom; mentioned, 357, 359

Glossary & Index

LOTHIAN, EAST. A county of Scotland; mentioned, 357
LOUDÉAC. An *arrondissement* of Brittany, 88
LOUGH NEAGH. A lake in Ireland; according to Irish legend, the site of submerged city, 187
LOUIS I (THE PIOUS). King of France; places the native chieftain Nomenoë over Brittany, 23; St Convoyon visits, to obtain confirmation of grants, 335
LOUIS IX. King of France; mentioned, 208
LOUIS XI. King of France; mentioned, 36, 205
LOUIS XII. King of France; Anne of Brittany married to, 36
LOUIS XV. King of France; honours the Count of La Garaye, 195
LOUIS. Baron of Jauioz; the story of, 145–147
LOUVRE, THE. A palace in Paris; mentioned, 206
LUCIUS. Roman consul, sometimes referred to as Emperor; King Arthur moves against, 275
LUZEL, F. M. His *Guerziou Breiz-Izel*, mentioned, 211
LYONESSE. A legendary kingdom near Cornwall, 257

M

MACCULLOCH, J. R. Cited, 59 *n.*, 70, 102, 188 *n.*, 189 *n.*, 381
MACCUNN, HAMISH. Composer; mentioned, 145
MACHUTES. *See* St Malo
MACPHERSON, JAMES. A Scottish poet; mentioned, 23, 211
MACRITCHIE, D. Cited, 74
MAC-TIERNS ('Sons of the Chief'). A name given to Brian and Alain, sons of Count Eudo, 29
MAGEEN. Mother of St Tivisiau, 338
MAGIC. *See* Sorcery
MAGIC ROSE, THE. The story of, 156–162
MAHĀBHĀRATA. A Hindu epic; mentioned, 52
MAISON DES FOLLETS. A name given to a megalithic structure at Cancoet, 49
MAMAU, Y. Welsh deities, 87
MAN OF HONOUR, THE. The story of, 147–155
MARAUD. A peasant; in the story of the Lost Daughter, 75–77
MARCH. The month; personified in the story of Princess Starbright, 128–129
MARGAWSE. Sister of King Arthur, wife of King Lot of Lothian, 357
MARGOTS LA FÉE, LES. Fairies which inhabit large rocks and the moorlands, 88
MARGUERITE. A maiden, avenged by Du Guesclin, 33–35
MARIE DE FRANCE. A twelfth-century French poetess; acknowledged Breton sources for her work, 255, 283; the *Lais* and *Fables* of, 283–284; personal history, 283; stories from the *Lais*, 284–331; and the Lay of Laustic, 302; and the Lay of Eliduc, 305–306; and the Lay of the Dolorous Knight, 328, 330–331
MARK. King of Cornwall; in the story of Tristrem and Ysonde, 258–274
MARK. King of Vannes; and St Pol of Léon, 364
MAROT, CLAUDE TOUSSAINT. Count of La Garaye; the story of, 194–196
MARRIAGE. Costume of the bride in the Escoublac district, 374; the Pardon of Notre Dame de la Clarté made the occasion of betrothals, 378; wedding customs, 385–386
MARRIAGE-GIRDLE, THE. The ballad of, 234–236
MARSEILLES. The city; mentioned, 195
MATSYS, QUENTIN. A Flemish painter; the well of, at Antwerp, 205
MATTHEW. Seigneur of Beauvau; in the story of the Clerk of Rohan, 189–193
MAUNOIR. A Jesuit Father, 388
MAURON. A town in Brittany; battle at, 31
MAY, ISLE OF. An island in the Firth of Forth, 357
MAYENNE. Charles de Lorraine,

Duke of; one of the leaders of the Catholic League, 229
MEGALITHS. The derivation and meaning of the terms 'menhir' and 'dolmen,' 37–38; nature and purpose of the monuments, 38–39; the menhir of Dol, and its legend, 39–41; the chapel-dolmen at Plouaret, 41; the megaliths at Camaret, 41; at Penmarch, 41; at Carnac, 42–45; the tumulus at Mont-Saint-Michel, 45; the dolmen at Rocenaud, 46; 'cup-and-ring' markings, 46–48; the gallery of Gavr'inis, 48; the megaliths of the Ile aux Moines and the Ile d'Arz, 48; folk-beliefs associated with the monuments, 48–53; tales connected with them, 52; the question of the date of their erection, 53; the nains' inscriptions upon, 97–98; the megaliths of Carnac supposed to have been built by the gorics, 98. *See also* Menhir *and* Dolmen
MELUSINE. A fairy, in French folklore; mentioned, 327
MENAO. A place in Wales; battle of, 22
MÉNÉAC. A town in Brittany; megaliths at, 42
MENHIR. A megalithic monument, 18; the menhir of Dol, 18, 39–40; probably connected with pillar-worship and Irminsul-worship, 18 *n.*; derivation and meaning of the term, 38; purpose of the monuments, 38–39
MERIADOK. A Cornish knight; in the story of Tristrem and Ysonde, 269, 272
MERIADUS. A Breton chieftain; in the Lay of Gugemar, 299–301
MERLIN. An enchanter, in Arthurian legend; meets Vivien in Broceliande, and is afterward enchanted by her there, 65–69; his relationship with Vivien as presented in Arthurian legend, 69; the varying conceptions of, 70; the typical Druid or wise man of Celtic tradition, 70; protects Arthur in his combat with Sir Pellinore, 256; and Arthur's finding of Excalibur, 256–257
MEZLÉAN. A place in Brittany, 362, 363; the Clerk of, in the ballad of Azénor the Pale, 361–363
MILTON OF COLQUHOUN. A district in Scotland; inscribed stones found in, 47
MINIHY. A town in Brittany; St Yves' will and breviary preserved in the church of, 353
MODRED, SIR. Nephew of King Arthur; his contest with the King, 344
MONCONTOUR. A village in Brittany, 242
MONEDUC. Mother of St Nennocha, 340
MONTAGNES D'ARRÉE, or AREZ. A mountain chain in Brittany; the Yeun in, 102; mentioned, 235
MONTALEMBERT, COMTE DE. His *Moines d'Occident*, cited, 19
MONTFORT, JOHN OF. Duke of Brittany (John IV); disputes the succession to the Dukedom, 30–32, 35–36; captures the chateâu of Suscino, 210; mentioned, 204
MONTMORENCY. The house of; mentioned, 174
MONTREUIL-SUR-MER. A town in the Pas-de-Calais, France; St Winwaloe's body preserved at, 371
MONT-SAINT-MICHEL. I. A tumulus, 45–46. II. An island off the coast of Brittany, 45 *n.*; King Arthur's fight with the giant of, 275; mentioned, 103
MOOR, THE. In a story of Morvan; Morvan's fight with, 218–220; the character of, probably drawn from Carlovingian legend, 225
MOORS, THE. Mentioned, 225
MOORE, THOMAS. The poet; quoted, 187
MORAUNT. An Irish ambassador at the English Court; in the story of Tristrem and Ysonde, 262–263, 264, 266
MORBIHAN. I. One of the departments of Brittany, 13, 48, 49; the nains' inscriptions on the megaliths of, 98; the Pardon of Notre Dame de la Clarté held in, 378. II. An inland sea or gulf in the south of Brittany,

(Gulf of Morbihan); naval battle between the Romans and Veneti probably took place in, 16; mentioned, 48

MORGAN, DUKE. A Cymric chieftain; in the story of Tristrem and Ysonde, 258–259, 261–262

MORIN. A priest, 388

MORLAIX. A town in Brittany; the castle of, haunted by gorics, 99; the teursts of the district of, 100; in the story of the Youth who did not Know, 106, 107, 108, 109; national costume in, 376–377

MORTE D'ARTHUR. Malory's romance; the presentation of Vivien in, 69; Arthur's finding of Excalibur related in, 256; incident in, paralleled in the Lay of Gugemar, 301–302; mentioned, 257

MORVAN LEZ-BREIZ. A famous Breton hero of the ninth century, 212; stories of, 212–224; tradition that he will return to "drive the Franks from the Breton land," 224

MOURIOCHE, THE. A malicious demon, 101

MÜLLER, W. MAX. Mentioned, 358

MURILLO. A celebrated Spanish painter; paintings by, in the château of Caradeuc, 207

MUT. An Egyptian goddess; mentioned, 43

MUZILLAC. A town in Brittany; head-dress of the women of, 376

N

NAINS. A race of demons; their character, 96–98; guardians of hidden treasure, 99

NAMNETES. A Gallic tribe which inhabited Brittany, 16

NANN, THE SEIGNEUR OF. The story of, 57–59

NANTES. A city in Brittany; in a ballad, represented as the scene of magical exploits of Abélard and Héloïse, 253; traditionally associated with sorcery, 253; Equitan the King of, 313; the scene of the Lay of the Dolorous Knight, 328; Nomenoë obtains possession of, 338; mentioned, 17, 30, 168, 169, 170, 180, 337

NANTES. The castle of, 205

NEOLITHIC AGE. The race which built the stone monuments of Brittany probably belonged to, 37 *n*.

NÉVET. Forest of, in Léon, 367

NÉVEZ. A town in Brittany, 190

NEW CALEDONIA. An island in the Pacific; markings on the megalithic monuments in, 46–47

NICOLE, THE. A mischievous spirit, 100–101

NIGHTINGALE, THE LAY OF THE. One of the *Lais* of Marie de France, 302

NIGHT-WASHERS. A race of supernatural beings, 100

NIMUE. A name under which Vivien, the Lady of the Lake, appears in some romances, 69; mentioned, 256. *See* Vivien

NOGENT. Sister of Gugemar, 292

NOGENT-SUR-SEINE. A town in France; the abbey at, founded by Abélard, and made over by him to Héloïse, 249; Abélard and Héloïse buried at, 250

NOLA. A youth; in the story of the Foster-brother, 170–171

NOMENOË. A Breton chieftain, afterward King of Brittany; rises against Charles the Bald and defeats him, 23, 337–338; a story of, 23–25; and St Convoyon, 335, 336, 337; sends gifts to Pope Leo IV, 337; burns the abbey of Saint-Florent, 337

NORMANDY. The duchy; early relations of Brittany with, 27–30

NORMANS. The Bretons rise against, 196–198; spread the Arthur legend, 254, 255; mentioned, 338

NOROUAS. Personification of the north-west wind; a story of, 163–167

NORTHMEN, NORSEMEN. Invade Brittany, 25; defeated by Alain Barbe-torte and expelled from Brittany, 25–27; the battle of Kerlouan between the Bretons and, 225

NORTH-WEST WIND, THE. Personification of; a story of, 163–167

NORTON, MRS. An English poetess; her *Lady of La Garaye*, quoted, 194, 195, 196
N'OUN DOARE. A youth; in the story of the Youth who did not Know, 106–115
NUTT, A. Cited, 99 *n.*, 254

O

OBERON. King of the fairies; mentioned, 74
ŒDIPUS. King of Thebes; mentioned, 357
OGIER THE DANE. One of the paladins of Charlemagne; entered Fairyland, 326
OLAUS MAGNUS. A sixteenth-century Swedish ecclesiastic and writer; mentioned, 290
ORIDIAL. Father of Gugemar, 292
ORIGEN. One of the Fathers of the early Church; and St Barbe, 333
ORLÉANS. The city: the siege of (1428–29), 174; the play or mystery of, on Jeanne Darc, 175; mentioned, 229
OSISMII. A Gallic tribe which inhabited Brittany, 16
OSSIAN. A semi-legendary Celtic bard and warrior; mentioned, 211
OSSORY. A district in Ireland; emigration from, to Brittany, 22
OTHERWORLD. The Celtic, 171–172; Fairyland identified with, 327
OUESSANT. An island off the coast of Brittany; St Pol in, 365; the costume of the women of, 374–375
OUST. A river in Brittany, 205
OWAIN. A Welsh chieftain, son of Urien; Taliesin the bard of, 22
OWEN GLENDOWER. A Welsh chieftain; the Bretons send an expedition to help, in his conflict with the English, 234

P

PALESTINE. Mentioned, 145, 190, 269, 302
PARACLETE ('Comforter'). Name given by Abélard to his abbey at Nogent, 249; Abélard and Héloïse buried at, 250
PARDONS. Religious pilgrimage festivals of the Bretons, 378–380
PARIS. The city; mentioned, 108, 109, 112, 113, 114, 116, 117, 118, 119, 120–121, 156, 157, 158, 195, 208, 229, 230–231, 351
PARIS, GASTON. A noted French philologist; claims that Arthurian romance originated in Wales, 254; identifies the persons to whom Marie de France dedicated her *Lais* and *Fables*, 284
PASSAGE DE L'ENFER. An arm of the sea over which the Breton dead were supposed to be ferried, 383
PATAY. A village in Loiret, France; the battle of, 174
PAVIA. A city in Italy; Francis I of France taken prisoner at, 207
PELLINORE, SIR. One of the Knights of the Round Table; Arthur broke his sword in combat with, 256
PEMBROKESHIRE. Welsh county; St Samson a native of, 17
PENATES. Household gods of the Romans; mentioned, 53
PEN-BAS. A cudgel carried by the men of Cornouaille, 372; rarely carried by the men of St Pol, 375
PENHAPP. A village in the Ile aux Moines; dolmen at, 48
PENMARCH. A town in Brittany; megaliths at, 41; Ty C'harriquet near, 49; a fireplace in the church of St Non at, 381
PENRAZ. A village in the Isle of Arz; megaliths at, 48
PENTECOST. A Jewish festival; mentioned, 324
PENTHIÈVRE. A former county of Brittany, 27, 205
PENTHIÈVRE. Joan of; wife of Charles of Blois, 30; in the War of the Two Joans, 31; her marriage to Charles, 32
PENTHIÈVRE. Stephen, Count of, 208
PERCIVAL. Hero of *Percival le Gallois*; analogy between his flight and that of Morvan, 224

PERCIVAL LE GALLOIS. Arthurian saga; mentioned, 224
PÈRE LA CHIQUE. An old man; in the story of the Magic Rose, 159–160, 162
PERGUET. A village in Brittany; the fireplace in the church of St Bridget at, 381
PERSEUS. A mythical Greek hero; mentioned, 357, 358
PERTHSHIRE. Scottish county; the 'Washing Woman' in, 100
PETRANUS. Father of St Patern, 347
PHILIP VI. King of France; mentioned, 30
PICTS. The race; Celts flee from Britain to Brittany, to escape, 17; the legend that they built the original church of Corstorphine, near Edinburgh, 51; "wee fouk but unco' strang," 99
PIGS. St Pol taught the people to keep, 366
PILLAR-WORSHIP. Probable connexion of the menhir with, 18 *n*.
PILLARS. Tales of spirits enclosed in, 52
PLACE OF SKULLS, THE. In the story of the Bride of Satan, 144
PLÉLAN. A town in Brittany; St Convoyon removes to, from Redon, 338
PLESTIN-LES-GRÈVES. A town in Brittany; St Efflam buried in the church of, 281
PLOERMEL. A town in Brittany; St Nennocha founded her monastery at, 340
PLOUARET. A town in Brittany; the dolmen-chapel at, 41
PLOUBALAY. A town in Brittany; in the story of the Fisherman and the Fairies, 81
PLOUBER. A town in Brittany, 199, 202
PLOUGASTEL. A town in Brittany; the costume of the men of, 375; the Calvary of, 384
PLOUHARNEL. A village in Brittany; megaliths at, 42
PLOURIN. A village in Brittany; St Budoc lived at, 356
POITOU. A former county of France; ravaged by Nomenoë, 337; mentioned, 176
POMPONIUS MELA. A Roman geographer; quoted, 63
PONT L'ABBÉ. A town in Brittany; national costume in, 376
PONT-AVEN. A village in Brittany, 364
PONTIVY. A town in Brittany; chapel to St Noyola at, 360
PONTORSON. A town in Brittany, 275
POOR, THE. Regard paid to, at Breton festivals and ceremonies, 387
PORSPODER. A town in Brittany; St Budoc lands at, and dwells in, 356
POULDERGAT, MANNAÏK DE. The bride-to-be of Silvestik, 232
PRAGUE. Capital of Bohemia; mentioned, 203
PRELATI. An alchemist of Padua, employed by Gilles de Retz, 176, 178–179
PRINCESS STARBRIGHT, THE. The story of, 121–131; mentioned, 153
PRINCESS OF TRONKOLAINE, THE. The story of, 115–121
PROCOPIUS. A Byzantine historian; on a Breton burial custom, 383–384
PROP OF BRITTANY, THE. Name given to Morvan, chieftain of Léon, 212; stories of, 212–224

Q

QUEBAN. Wife of King Grallo; St Ronan discovers her fault, 368
QUEBEC, THE. A British vessel; her fight with the *Surveillante* 238–240
QUEEN ANNE'S TOWER. Name of the keep of the château of Dinan, 209
QUESTEMBERT. A town in Brittany; the Château des Paulpiquets at, 49
QUIBERON. A town in Brittany, 46
QUIMPER. A city in Brittany; St Convoyon Bishop of, 335; national costume in, 372–373; mentioned, 186, 1°8
QUIMPER, COUNT OF. In a story of Morvan, 213, 216

QUIMPERLÉ. A town in Brittany; the château of Rustefan near, 208; St Goezenou killed at the building of the monastery at, 370

R

RAMA. A hero in Hindu mythology; mentioned, 52
RĀMĀYANA. A Hindu epic; mentioned, 52
RAOUL LE GAEL. A Breton knight, 29
RAVELSTON QUARRY. A quarry near Edinburgh; mentioned, 51
REDON or RODON. A town in Brittany; the abbey of: founded by St Convoyon, 335–336; the bones of St Apothemius carried to, 336; the bones of St Marcellinus carried to, 337; Nomenoë takes spoil from the Abbey of Saint-Florent to, 337; St Convoyon removes from, 338; St Convoyon buried at, 338
REDONES. A Gallic tribe which inhabited Brittany, 16
REGINALD. Bishop of Vannes, 335, 336
REID, GENERAL JOHN. The composer of *The Garb of Old Gaul*, 238
REINACH, SALOMON. Cited, 53
RELIGION. Brittany the most religious of the French provinces, 377; the religious element in the Breton character, 377–378
RELIQUARIES. In Brittany, 382
REMUS. In Roman legend, brother of Romulus; mentioned, 358
RENAISSANCE ARCHITECTURE. References to, 205, 206, 209
RENÉ. Constable of Naples, 190
RENNES. A city in Brittany; the scene of Nomenoë's vengeance, 23–25; the Counts of, gain ascendancy in Brittany, 27; the marriage of Charles of Blois and Joan of Penthièvre at, 32; Robert the sorcerer dwelt in, 242; Nomenoë obtains possession of, 338; mentioned, 17, 181, 195
RESTALRIG. A village near Edinburgh; the well of St Triduana at, 59–60
RETIERS. A town in Brittany the Roches aux Fées at, 51
RETZ, or RAIS. A district in Brittany, 23, 174
RETZ, CARDINAL DE. A French politician and writer; imprisoned in the castle of Nantes, 205
RETZ, GILLES DE. A Breton nobleman; a story of, 173–180; the identification of, with Bluebeard, 174, 180
REVOLUTION, FRENCH. Of 1789; mentioned, 188, 195, 338, 353, 369
REVUE CELTIQUE. Cited, 212 *n.*
RHEINSTEIN. A famous castle on the Rhine; mentioned, 203
RHINE. The river; mentioned, 203
RHUYS. *See* St Gildas de Rhuys
RHYS, SIR JOHN. And the origin of Druidism, 245; mentioned, 70
RICHARD II. Duke of Normandy; mentioned, 196
RICHELIEU, CARDINAL. A famous French statesman; the château of Tonquédec demolished by order of, 204
RIEUX, JEAN DE. Marshal of Brittany; leader of the expedition to help Owen Glendower, 234
RITHO. A giant whom King Arthur slew, 277
ROAD OF ST POL, THE. Name given by Breton peasants to a megalithic avenue, 365
ROBERT I. Duke of Normandy, 28
ROBERT. A sorcerer who dwelt in Rennes, 242–243
ROBERT DE VITRY. A Breton knight, 29
ROCENAUD. A village in Brittany; dolmen at, 46
ROCEY. The house of, 174
ROCHE-MARCHE-BRAN. A rocky hill; the chapel of St Barbe bulit on, 335
ROCHER, THE WOOD OF. The dolmen near, 50
ROCHERS. A Breton château; Mme Sévigné associated with, 208
ROCHES AUX FÉES. Name given

to the megalithic monuments by the Bretons, 49; near Saint-Didier-et-Marpire, 50; in Rhetiers, 51; supposed to be the meeting-place of sorcerers, 243

ROCKFLOWER. A fairy maiden; in a tale from Saint-Cast, 83

RODRIGUEZ, FATHER. Mentioned, 47

ROE. A river in Ireland; Druidic ritual associated with, 246

ROGER. An English knight; in the legend of the Ward of Du Guesclin, 33–35

ROHAN. The house of, 206

ROHAN. Alain, Viscount of, 189

ROHAN. Jeanne de, daughter of Alain de Rohan; in the story of the Clerk of Rohan, 189–193

ROHAND. A vassal of Roland; in the story of Tristrem and Ysonde, 258–259, 260–261, 262

ROLAND, SIR. A knight; in the story of the Unbroken Vow, 60–63

ROLAND RISE. A Cymric chieftain, Lord of Ermonie; in the story of Tristrem and Ysonde, 258–259, 261

ROLLESTON, T. W. Cited, 246

ROLLO. A famous Norse leader, first Duke of Normandy; mentioned, 28

ROMANS, THE. In Brittany, 16

ROME. The city; mentioned, 196, 337

ROMULUS. In Roman legend, the founder of Rome; mentioned, 357, 358

RON. The name of King Arthur's lance, 280

ROND. A dance performed at weddings, 385–386

ROSAMOND. Mistress of Henry II of England (Rosamond Clifford, 'the Fair Rosamond'); mentioned, 284

ROS-YNYS. A place in Wales, afterward St David's; a story of St Keenan and, 343–344

ROUND TOWER. At Ardmore, Ireland, 51; at Abernethy, Perthshire, 52

RUMENGOL. A village in Brittany; the Pardon of the Singers held at, 378

S

SACRING BELLS. The use of, an old Breton custom, 380

ST ANNE. A Breton saint; Morvan prays to, 216-217; Morvan rewards with gifts, 218; Morvan gives praise to, for his victory over the Moor, 220; frees Morvan from his burden, 224; mentioned, 146

SAINTE-ANNE-LA-PALUD. A village in Brittany; the Pardon of the Sea held at, 378

ST APOTHEMIUS. St Convoyon steals the bones of, from Angers Cathedral, and takes them to Redon, 336

ST AUGUSTINE. Archbishop of Canterbury; mentioned, 100

ST BALDRED. A Celtic saint, 359–360

ST BALDRED'S BOAT. A rock in the Firth of Forth; the legend of, 359

ST BARBE. A Breton saint, 332–335

SAINTE-BARBE. A village in Brittany; megaliths at, 42

ST BIEUZY. A Breton saint, 345–346; the Holy Well of, at Bieuzy, 381

ST BRIDGET. An Irish saint; Azénor prays to, and is helped by, 354; church of, at Berhet, the custom of ringing the sacring bell survives in, 380; church of, at Perguet, the fireplace in, 381

SAINT-BRIEUC. I. An *arrondissement* of Brittany, 88, 350. II. A town in Brittany; a relic of St Keenan preserved in the cathedral of, 344

SAINT-BRIEUC, BAY OF. A bay on the Breton coast; the Nicole of, 100; mentioned, 18, 350

ST BUDOC. A Breton saint; the legend of, 353–356

SAINT-CAST. A village in Brittany; in the story of the Lost Daughter, 75; a story from, 84; the story of the Combat of, 236–237; mentioned, 83

ST CECILIA'S DAY. Ceremonies in honour of King Gradlon on, 189

ST CHARLES. Jesuit church of, at Antwerp; relics of St Winwaloe preserved at, 371

ST CONVOYON. A Breton saint, 335–338
ST CORBASIUS. A Breton saint; kills St Goezenou, 370
ST CORNELY. A Breton saint, the patron of cattle; in a legend of Carnac, 44–45
ST DAVID'S. A city in Wales, originally called Ros-ynys; in a story of St Keenan, 344
SAINT-DENIS. A famous abbey, in the city of Saint-Denis, in France; Du Guesclin buried in, 32
SAINT-DIDIER. A village in Brittany; the Roches aux Fées near, 50
ST DUBRICUS. A British saint; mentioned, 346
ST DUNSTAN. A British saint, called St Goustan in Brittany, 248–249
ST EFFLAM. A Breton saint; and King Arthur's encounter with the dragon of the Lieue de Grève, 278–281; the story of St Enora and, 340–342; mentioned, 366
ST ENORA, or HONORA. A Breton saint; the story of Efflam and, 279, 281, 340–342
SAINT-FLORENT. A town in France; Nomenoë and the abbey of, 337
ST GALL. A famous monastery in Switzerland; mentioned, 247
ST GERMAIN. A French saint, Bishop of Paris; the exchange of wax for wine between St Samson and, 19; persuades Nennocha to embrace the religious life, 340
ST GILDAS. A British saint; in the story of Comorre the Cursed, 181, 183–184; founded the abbey of St Gildas de Rhuys, near Vannes, 248–249
ST GILDAS DE RHUYS. An abbey near Vannes; founded by St Gildas, 248–249; Abélard appointed abbot of, 248; St Bieuzy died and was buried at, 346; St Patern educated at, 348
ST GOEZENOU. A Breton saint, 368–370
ST GOUSTAN. The Breton name of St Dunstan, 249
ST HENWG. *See* Henwg
ST HONORA, or ENORA. *See* St Enora
ST ILTUD. A Welsh saint; in a legend of St Samson, 349; St Pol a disciple of, 364; mentioned, 346
ST IVES. *See* St Yves.
SAINT-JACUT-DE-LA-MER. A village in Brittany; in the story of the Fisherman and the Fairies, 80, 84
ST JAOUA. A Breton saint, 366
SAINT-JEAN-DU-DOIGT. A village in Brittany; the Pardon of the Fire held at, 378, 379
ST JOHN. A Breton saint, 197
ST KADO. A Breton saint; mentioned, 197
ST KÉ, or ST QUAY. Popular name in Brittany for St Keenan, 344
ST KEENAN. A Breton saint, 343–344
ST KENTIGERN, or ST MUNGO. Patron saint of Glasgow; the legend of, 356–357; mentioned, 70, 359
ST LAZARUS. The Order of; Louis XV sends to the Count of La Garaye, 195
ST LEONORIUS, or LÉONORE. A Breton saint, 346–347
ST LOUIS. *See* Louis IX
ST MAGAN. A Breton saint, brother of St Goezenou, 370
ST MALGLORIOUS. A Breton saint, 356
ST MALO, or MACHUTES. A Breton saint; the people of Corseul hostile to the teachings of, 343
SAINT-MALO. A town in Brittany; the scene of the Lay of Laustic, 302; St Convoyon born near, 335; mentioned, 230
SAINT-MALO, BAY OF. The Nicole of, 100–101
ST MARCELLINUS. Bishop of Rome; the bones of, given to St Convoyon by Pope Leo IV, and taken by him to Redon, 337
ST MÉRIADEC. A Breton saint; his skull used in the ritual of the Pardon of Saint-Jean-du-Doigt, 379
ST MICHAEL. The archangel; chapel of, on the tumulus of Mont-Saint-Michel, 46; the child Morvan thinks he has seen, 213; Morvan thinks a knight more splendid than, 214

ST MICHEL. A Breton saint, 'Lord of Heights'; a chapel of, near Le Faouet, 333

ST MUNGO. *See* St Kentigern

ST NENNOCHA. A Breton saint, 340

ST NICHOLAS. A Breton saint; probably the survival of a pagan divinity, 345

ST NICOLAS DE BIEUZY. Church of, in Bieuzy, 180

ST NON. A Breton saint; a fire-place in the church of, at Penmarch, 381

ST NOYALA. A Breton saint, 360

ST PATERN. A Breton saint, 347-349

ST POL, or PAUL. Of Léon; a Breton saint, 248, 364–367

SAINT-POL-DE-LÉON. A town in Brittany; the bell of St Pol in the cathedral of, 367; St Pol buried in the cathedral of, 367; the cathedral of, built by St Pol, 367; costume of the men of, 375; mentioned, 237, 365, 366

ST ROCH. A Breton saint; shrine of, at Auray, 42; and the markings on the dolmen at Rocenaud, 46

ST RONAN. A Breton saint, 367

ST SAMSON. A British saint; settles in Brittany, 17–19; St Gildas the friend of, 248; stories of, 349–350; St Pol of Léon a fellow-student of, 364

ST SERF. A Scottish saint, abbot of Culross, 357

SAINT-THÉGONNEC. A town in Brittany; the Calvary at, 384

ST TIVISIAU, or TURIAU. A Breton saint, 338–339; the fountain of, at Landivisiau, 340

ST TREMEUR. A Breton saint, son of Comorre; the reliquary in the church of, 382

ST TRIDUANA. Guardian of a well at Restalrig, near Edinburgh, 59–60

ST TRIPHYNE. A Breton saint; wife of Comorre, 180. *See* Triphyna

ST TUGDUAL. A Breton saint; founded the church of Tréguier, 167; made a miraculous crossing to Brittany, 360

ST TURIAU. *See* St Tivisiau

ST VOUGAS, or VIE. A Breton saint, 360

ST WINWALOE. A Breton saint, 370–371

ST YVES, or YVO. Brittany's favourite saint, 350–353

SAINT-YVES. A village in Brittany; the Pardon of the Poor held at, 378

SAINTS. Stories of, an important element in Breton folk-lore, 332; the primitive saint driven to use methods similar to those of the pagan priests around him, 332; tales of the Breton saints, 332–371; the product of poor countries rather than of prosperous ones, 350

SAINTSBURY, G. E. B. Cited, 254

SALOMON III. Count of Brittany; drives back the Northmen, 25

SANT-E-ROA ('Holy Wheel'). Apparatus of the sacring bell; at the church of St Bridget, Berhet, 380

SATAN. A story of, 143–144; Gilles de Retz seeks association with, 177–179; in an old Breton conception of Hell, 389. *See also* Devil

SAXONS. The race; Celts flee from Britain to Brittany to escape, 15, 17

SCOTLAND. Markings on the megalithic monuments in, 46–47; the harp formerly the national instrument of, 229; claimed as the birthplace of Arthurian romance, 254; late survival of the custom of keeping domestic bards in, 364; mentioned, 52

SCOTS. The race; Celts flee from Britain to Brittany to escape, 17

SCOTT, SIR WALTER. The novelist; his treatment of legendary matter, 211; one of the first to bring the story of Tristrem to public notice, 258; continued the story of Tristrem beyond the point at which the Auchinleck MS. breaks off, 272

SEA OF DARKNESS, THE. In the story of the Castle of the Sun, 132

SEA-SNAKE'S EGG. *See* Adder's Stone

SÉBILLOT, PAUL. Cited, 52, 212 *n.*; mentioned, 74; and the story of the Combat of Saint-Cast, 237 *n.*

SEIGNEUR WITH THE HORSE'S HEAD, THE. The story of, 137–143

SEIGNEUR OF NANN, THE. The story of, 57–59
SEIN. *See* Ile de Sein
SERIPHOS. An island in the Ægean Sea to which Danaë was carried; mentioned, 358
SEVEN SAINTS OF BRITTANY. St Samson and six others who fled with him from Britain, 350
SEVEN SLEEPERS, THE. Seven Christian youths of Ephesus who hid to escape persecution and slept for several hundreds of years; an altar to, in the dolmen-chapel at Plouaret, 41
SEVERN. The river; mentioned, 349
SÉVIGNÉ, MME DE. A famous French epistolary writer; sojourned in the castle of Nantes, 205; wrote many of her letters from the château of Rochers, 208
SHARPE, CHARLES KIRKPATRICK. An antiquary and writer, friend of Sir Walter Scott; his treatment of legendary material, 211
SHEWALTON SANDS. A place in Scotland; inscribed stones found at, 47
SHIP, THE. A rock off the coast of Brittany, said to have been the vessel of St Vougas, 360
SHIP O' THE FIEND, THE. Orchestral work by Hamish MacCunn; mentioned, 145
SHIP OF SOULS. A feature in Breton folk-belief, 384
SIGHT, MAGICAL. Bestowed by fairies, 82–83
SILVESTIK. A young Breton who followed in the train of William the Conqueror to England; the story of, 232–233
SIMROCK, C. J. Cited, 83
SKYE. An island off the west coast of Scotland; the 'Washing Woman' in, 100
SLIEVE GRIAN. A mountain in Ireland; mentioned, 52
SMALL, A. Cited, 52
SOCIÉTÉ ACADÉMIQUE DE BREST, BULLETIN DE. Cited, 199 *n.*
SONG OF THE PILOT, THE. A Breton ballad, 238–240
SORCERY. Belief in, prevalent in Brittany, 241–243; in ancient times, identified with Druidism, 245
SOUTH-WEST WIND, THE. Personification of, in a wind-tale, 163
SOUVESTRE, ÉMILE. A French novelist and dramatist; mentioned, 180
SPAIN. Tristrem in, 270; the giant of Mont-Saint-Michel came from, 275
SPENSER, EDMUND. The poet; mentioned, 56
STONES. Folk-tales and beliefs connected with, 52–53
STYX. In Greek mythology, a river of the underworld; mentioned, 327
SUN, THE. Personified in the story of the Princess of Tronkolaine, 117–118; the story of Tristrem and Ysonde claimed as a sun-myth, 274–275; personified in the 'fatal children' stories, 358
SUN-PRINCESS. A story of the search for, 121-131
SUROUAS. Name of the south-west wind; in a wind-tale, 163
SURVEILLANTE, LE. A Breton vessel; her fight with the British ship *Quebec*, 238–240
SUSANNUS. Bishop of Vannes, 336–337
SUSCINO. A Breton château, 209–210
SWINBURNE, ALGERNON. The poet; quoted, 267

T

TADEN. A village in Brittany; the Count and Countess of La Garaye buried at, 195
TALIESIN ('Shining Forehead'). A British bard; and the vision of Jud-Hael, 20–21; early years, 21; the bard of Urien and Owain-ap-Urien, 22; death of, 22; probably sojourned in Brittany, 22; acquainted with black art, 252
TAM O' SHANTER. The character in Burns's poem; mentioned, 244

TANTALLON CASTLE. A famous ruin in Scotland; mentioned, 359
TARTARY. The country; mentioned, 115
TEGID, LLYN. A lake in Wales (Lake Bala); the dwelling-place of Keridwen, a fertility goddess, 59
TELIO. A British monk, associated with St Samson; said to have introduced the apple into Brittany, 18
TEURSTA POULICT. A variety of the teursts taking animal shape, 100
TEURSTS. A race of evil spirits, 100
TEUS, or BUGELNOZ. A beneficent spirit of the district of Vannes, 100
THENAW. Mother of St Kentigern, 357
THIERRY, J. N. A. A French historian; quoted, 17
THOMAS THE RHYMER, or THOMAS OF ERCILDOUNE. Thirteenth-century Scottish poet; his version of the story of Tristrem and Ysonde, 258 *et seq.*; visited Fairyland, 326; mentioned, 64, 255, 327
THOUARS, CATHERINE DE. Wife of Gilles de Retz, 174
THOUARS, GUY DE. A French knight; married to Constance of Brittany, 30
TIBER. The river; mentioned, 358
TINA. A maiden; in the story of the Baron of Jauioz, 145–147
TITANIA. Queen of the fairies; mentioned, 74
TONQUÉDEC. A Breton château, 204
TOPOGRAPHY OF IRELAND. A work by Giraldus Cambrensis; cited, 187
TORRENT OF PORTUGAL, SIR. A fifteenth-century English metrical romance; mentioned, 358
TOULBOUDOU. A seigneury near Guémené, 334
TOULBOUDOU. John, Lord of; builds the chapel of St Barbe at Le Faouet, 334–335
TOUR D'ELVEN. A keep of the château of Largoet, 206
TOURLAVILLE. A Breton château, 208–209
TOWER OF LONDON, THE. Charles of Blois confined in, 31; the name of, occurs frequently in Celtic and Breton romance, 99
TRAPRAIN LAW. A mountain in East Lothian, formerly called Dunpender; Thenaw cast from, 357
TREASURE, J. P. Cited, 16 *n.*
TREDRIG. A village in Brittany; St Yves the incumbent of, 351
TREES. Tales of spirits enclosed in, 52
TRÉGASTEL. A town on the Breton coast; an island near believed by the Bretons to be the fabled Isle of Avalon, 282
TRÉGUENNEC. A village in Brittany; St Vougas associated with, 360
TRÉGUIER. I. A former county of Brittany, 27, 350. II. A town in Brittany; St Yves buried at, 353; a burial custom of, 383; mentioned, 167, 168, 237, 350.
TRÉGUNC. A town in Brittany; dolmen at 42
TREMALOUEN. A hamlet in Brittany; ruins at, haunted by courils, 99
TREMTRIS. Inverted form of Tristrem's name given him by Rohand to secure his safety, 259; Tristrem assumes the name in Ireland, 264, 266
TRÉPASSÉS, BAY OF. A bay on the Breton coast, 185
TRÈVES. A village in Brittany; had a reputation as the abode of sorcerers, 242
TRIDWAN. *See* St Triduana
TRIEUX. A river in Brittany, 203, 204
TRIPHYNA (ST TRIPHYNE). A maiden, married to Comorre, 180–184
TRISTREM, SIR ('Child of Sorrow'). One of the Knights of the Round Table, son of Blancheflour; the story of, and Ysonde, 257–275; mentioned, 301

TRISTREM, SIR. An ancient metrical romance; incidents in, paralleled in the story of Bran, 227–228; date of composition of, 228; had a Breton source, 255; Sir Walter Scott one of the first to bring Thomas the Rhymer's version of, to public notice, 258; Thomas the Rhymer's version of, recounted, 258–272; Scott's continuation of the Auchinleck MS., 272–274; the story of Tristrem and Ysonde claimed as a sun-myth, 274–275

TROGOFF. The château of; in the legend of the Ward of Du Guesclin, 33–35

TROLLOPE, T. ADOLPHUS. Quoted, 179–180

TROMÉNIE-DE-SAINT-RENAN. A town in Brittany; the Pardon of the Mountain held at, 378, 379

TROYES. A city in France; Abélard's abbey of Nogent near, 249

TUGDUAL SALAÜN. A peasant of Plouber, composer of a ballad on the Marquis of Guérande, 199, 202

TY C'HARRIQUET ('The House of the Gorics'). I. A name given to a megalithic structure near Penmarch, 49. II. A name applied to Carnac, 98

TY EN CORYGANNT. A name given to a megalithic structure in Morbihan, 49

U

UNBROKEN VOW, THE. A story of Broceliande, 60–63

UNITED STATES, THE. The Bretons aid, in the War of Independence, 238

URIEN. A Welsh chieftain; Taliesin the bard of, 21, 22

V

VAL-ÈS-DUNES. A place in Brittany; Alain, Count of Brittany, defeated in battle at, 28

VALLEY OF BLOOD. A place in hell; in the story of the Baron of Jauioz, 146

VANNES. I. A former county of Brittany; mentioned, 23, 180. II. The city; the dialect of, 16 *and n.*; the ancient city of the Veneti, 17; the Teus or Bugelnoz of, 100; in the story of Comorre the Cursed, 183; the château of Suscino near, 209; the abbey of St Gildas near, 248; St Convoyon educated at, 335; St Patern the patron saint of, 347; St Patern Bishop of, 348; the legend of the founding of the church of St Patern at, 348; St Pol of Léon in, 364

VENETI. A Gallic tribe which inhabited Brittany, 16, 17

'VENUS, THE.' An image at Quinipily, 381

VILAINE. A river in Brittany, 335

VILLARS, ABBÉ DE. A French priest and writer; cited, 64

VILLECHERET. A village in Brittany; the head-dress of the women of, 375

VILLEMARQUÉ. *See* Hersart de la Villemarqué

VINE, THE. Said to have been introduced into Brittany by Gradlon, 189

VIRGIN MARY, THE. In a Breton legend, 380

VITRÉ. A Breton château, 208

VIVIEN. An enchantress, in Arthurian legend; meets Merlin in Broceliande, and afterward enchants him there, 65–69; as presented in Arthurian legend and in other romances, 69; may be classed as a water-spirit, 69; the probable purpose of the story of Merlin and, in Arthurian legend, 70; of Breton origin, and does not appear in British myth, 256; gives Arthur the sword Excalibur, 256–257; Sir Lancelot stolen and brought up by, 257

W

WACE. A twelfth-century Anglo-Norman poet; quoted, 54; and the fountain of Baranton, 71

WAGNER, RICHARD. The composer; mentioned, 258

WALES. Legend of the submerged city in, 187, 188; the harp anciently the national instrument of, 229; Bretons send an expedition to, to help Glendower, 234; claimed as the birthplace of Arthurian romance, 254; helped the development of Arthurian romance, 255; Tristrem sojourns in, and wins fame there, 270; mentioned, 59, 343

WAR OF INDEPENDENCE, AMERICAN. Bretons take part in, against England, 238

WAR OF THE TWO JOANS, THE. A war waged for the succession to the Dukedom of Brittany, 31–32, 35–36

WARD OF DU GUESCLIN, THE. A Du Guesclin legend, 33–35

WASHING WOMAN, THE. An evil spirit of the Scottish Highlands, 100

WEDDING CUSTOMS. In Brittany, 385–386. *See also* Marriage

WELLS, HOLY. In Brittany, 381–382

WELSH. The language; the Breton tongue akin to, 15

WERE-WOLF. A man transformed into a wolf; the prevalence, origin, and forms of the superstition, 289–292; a were-wolf story, 284–289

WESTMINSTER. The city; in the story of Tristrem and Ysonde, Ysonde carried to, for trial, 270

WEXFORD. A county of Ireland; emigration from, to Brittany, 22

WHEEL OF FORTUNE, THE. A name wrongly given to part of the apparatus of the sacring bell, 380

WHITE CHURCH. A church in Tréguier; in the story of the Foster-brother, 170, 171

WILLIAM II. Duke of Normandy (William the Conqueror); Conan II of Brittany and, 27, 28–29; Bretons accompany, on his expedition against England, 232, 233

WILLIAM, COUNT. The name of the nobleman to whom Marie of France dedicated her *Fables*, identified with Longsword, Earl of Salisbury, 283–284

WINDS, THE. Play a large part in Breton folk-lore, 162; a wind-tale, 163–167

WINE. St Germain exchanges for wax from the monks of Dol, 19; a wine festival in honour of King Gradlon, 189

WOMEN. In early communities, magical power often the possession of, 246; generally the conservators of surviving Druidic tradition, 247; St Goezenou's antipathy to, 369; costume of the women of Brittany — *see* Costume *and* Head-dress

WOOD OF CHESTNUTS. Mentioned in a story of Morvan, 217

Y

YEUN, THE. A morass of evil repute, 102–103; a story of, 103–105

YORK. The city, in England; St Samson ordained at, 349

YOUDIC, THE. A part of the Yeun peat-bog, 103; a story of, 103–105

YOUGHAL. A town in Ireland; Azénor and the infant Budoc washed ashore at, 355; Budoc becomes abbot of the monastery at, 356

YOUGHAL, ABBOT OF. In the legend of St Budoc, 355, 356

YOUTH WHO DID NOT KNOW. The story of, 106–115

YS, or IS. A submerged city of legend; the legend of, 184–188; such a legend common to several Celtic races, 187; Giraldus Cambrensis and the legend of, 187–188

YSEULT. *See* Ysonde

YSONDE, or YSEULT. Daughter of the King of Ireland; some incidents in her story paralleled in the ballad of Bran, 228; the story of Tristrem and, 257–274; the story of Tristrem and, claimed as a sun-myth, 274–275

YSONDE OF THE WHITE HAND, Daughter of Hoel I, Duke of Brittany; in the story of Tristrem and Ysonde, 271, 273

YVES. Husband of Azénor the Pale, 361–363

YVON. A youth; in the story of the Castle of the Sun, 131–137

YVONNE. A maiden; in the story of the Castle of the Sun, 131–137

Z

ZIMMER, H. Cited, 278